MEMORIES
OF
JAKE

Susan Moore Jordan

This is a work of fiction. All of the characters, organizations, locales and events portrayed in this novel are either products of the author's imagination or are used fictitiously. Any resemblance to similar locales, events, or persons, living or dead, is entirely coincidental.

ISBN-13: 978-1544274201
ISBN-10: 1544274203

Library of Congress Control Number: 2017904446
CreateSpace Independent Publishing Platform, North Charleston, SC

Author's photo by Tristan Flanagan
Cover by Tristan Flanagan
Sketch for cover by Theresa Lawrence
Back cover photo of Lake Wallenpaupack, PA by Michael L. Meilinger.
Used by permission

Manufactured in the United States of America.

Books by Susan Moore Jordan

The *Carousel* Trilogy:
How I Grew Up
Eli's Heart
You Are My Song

Jamie's Children

Memories of Jake

"More Fog, Please"
(non-fiction)

Table of Contents

*To all those whose souls have been bruised by war
and with admiration for those who found their way back to life
through the power of creativity.*

Susan Moore Jordan

PROLOGUE (1991)

Once again, human remains had been discovered in Swain County, North Carolina. It had been so many years since Andrew Cameron first searched for his brother there that the new sheriff called to ask permission to compare the dental records that were on file. Andrew had been waiting for several days to hear the results.

Finally the call came giving him the report. Hands shaking, he gently replaced the handset. He was having trouble catching his breath. Everything felt off, but his world only shifted; it didn't blow up as it had eighteen years earlier.

He concentrated on breathing deeply, waiting for his insides to settle and the fog in his head to clear. The late afternoon light coming through the window glowed with color; sunset came early in southeastern Pennsylvania during the dying days of autumn.

Andrew had been leaning against the kitchen counter while he listened to the sheriff's report, and now he was able to walk into the living room and to the stereo. He turned it on, selected the recording he needed, and sank into the sofa, his head against the backrest, his eyes closed.

Listening to this music always helped him reconnect with all the good in the universe, and when the second movement of Brahms' *Requiem* started, he was able to focus on the music and let it wash over him. The repeated timpani beats seemed to him the broken heartbeat of all humanity; the stately chords led into the chorus singing softly:

Behold, all flesh is as the grass,
And all the glory of man is as the flower of grass.
For lo, the grass withers,
And the flower fades away.

The orchestra returned, the chords changed and the powerful forward movement of the music culminated in the chorus now bursting forth full force with the repeat of the opening phrase and then dying away softly. But Brahms wasn't done yet. An *a cappella* section was like a light playing through the gloom:

Be patient for the coming of the Lord.
See how the farmer waits patiently
To receive the rain.

The entire first section was repeated. Then came the part Andrew found so powerful he had to remind himself to breathe. A complete change of mood, the sun bursting forth and completely destroying the darkness:

But the word of the Lord endures forever ...
And sorrow and sighing shall flee away.

Andrew had been introduced to the Brahms *Requiem* when he returned to college after his tour of duty in Vietnam. He had felt lost for a time, unable to shake the experiences of the war, no matter how hard he tried to forget them. He needed some way to reconnect with the boy he had been before he left: the boy who loved art and music and beauty and peace. Brahms' music helped bring him back; it spoke to him of hope and a great promise. Death is not the end, it proclaimed. Not even for his lost brother, no matter what may have happened to him.

Mary came in while he was listening to the last section of this movement, sat next to him and took his hand, leaning her head against his shoulder. He turned and looked at her, as always feeling he'd never really seen her before. Her blue eyes seemed to change color with her mood, and the openness of her gaze was hard to capture and put on canvas.

Andrew had painted her many times, first with watercolor and later with oil, and he had done one portrait in acrylic, her skin so luminous from the layers of glaze that one could catch a glimpse of her inner beauty. He often felt as if he were trying to paint her soul, and that seemed impossible. He hugged her with one arm, pulling her close.

Andrew felt the unspoken question and when the movement ended he stood, went to the stereo and turned off the music.

"It wasn't Jacob," he said.

CHAPTER 1 (1953)

"Wake up, Andrew." His father's voice, surprisingly gentle. He sounded happy.

Andrew opened his eyes to see his dad standing next to his bed, smiling. Jake was getting dressed.

"Good morning, Daddy." Andrew sat up, rubbing the sleep from his eyes.

Allan Martin laughed. "Good morning yourself, sleepyhead," he said, tousling his son's dark hair. "How'd you like to go on an adventure today?"

Andrew smiled a little tentatively. His father's quicksilver moods could be confusing; but Jake was excited, already dressed and jumping up and down.

"Hurry up, Andy," he said. "First we're going to the resort for breakfast, and Daddy says we can eat anything we want."

Andrew dressed quickly and joined his father and Jake as they went to his parents' bedroom. He had glanced at the clock; it was only six-thirty. He knew his mother wasn't up yet.

They tiptoed into the room, their dad shushing them but almost giggling himself. The three of them stood around the bed and stared at her. Toni woke with a start.

"Good Lord, Allan! You can scare a body half to death. What in the world is going on?" She sat up, pulling the sheet to her neck and smoothing her dark hair back from her face. Andrew thought his mother was the most beautiful woman in the whole entire world.

"Me and my boys are going on a little adventure, darlin'. Breakfast first, and then some surprises. We'll be back by suppertime." Allan was turning on the charm full blast, but Toni smiled uncertainly.

"Well … it sounds exciting. Don't you want me to come with you?"

"No, no. This is a special day for me and my boys. You just relax and read or do whatever you like to do when you have some time to not worry about being a busy mommy."

"You're sure you'll be back in time for supper?"

"Oh, thereabouts. Don't worry about cooking, though. I'll pick something up on our way home."

Toni reached for her robe and Andrew helped her with it. She stood and hugged Jake. She turned to Andrew and as she hugged him she whispered in his ear, "Take care of your little brother."

It was fun at the start. Their father took them to the resort which he managed for his family on the South Carolina coast and treated them to breakfast. "Anything you want, boys," he said grandly. "How old are you now, Andrew?"

Andrew stared at his father for a minute, thinking he must be joking. But his dad was studying the menu. "I'm eight, Daddy. Don't you remember? My birthday was last month."

"Oh, sure, sure. How could I forget that? You're quite the little man now, aren't you?"

He gave Andrew an odd smile. "So that means Jacob must be six. I sure have me two fine boys. Look just like me, too." That was true; both parents were dark haired and brown eyed, and the boys did strongly resemble each other.

After breakfast they went to the beach for a while, wading in the surf and finding shells. Allan herded them back into his car. "Let's drive for a while, why don't we? And we can stop and have burgers for lunch." They drove away from the coast for about an hour and stopped at a roadside diner. They were in the swamps now, and Andrew was uneasy. But both boys had another big meal, and they fell asleep after they got back in the car.

When Andrew woke up he could tell it was late in the afternoon, and they had just pulled up to a cabin. Allan said, almost grimly, "Out of the car, men." It frightened Andrew; when Allan spoke to them that way, sometimes bad things happened.

He almost squeaked, "Where are we, Daddy?"

"Hunting cabin. Nothing to be scared of, son. My daddy brought me and my sisters out here all the time when we were little squirts. It's fun."

He took the boys into the cabin. It was dusty, but there were cots and blankets. Allan took a pail out to a pump and filled it with water, and Andrew saw he had a bag of groceries that he'd carried in from the car. His father reached into the bag and pulled out a box of dry cereal and a box of crackers.

"I have to meet some people in a little while but I won't be gone long," Allan said.

"Why can't we go with you?" said Jake. His eyes were very large and his lip was quivering.

"Buck up, kid. Don't be a sissy. I'll be back in an hour or two. Don't go outside; if you have to pee use this other bucket." Both boys stared at him. "Just don't get this bucket mixed up with the one with water in it, or you'll be drinking your own piss." Allan laughed uproariously at this, slapped each of them on the back, and left.

***

When Andrew heard a car pull up outside the cabin the next morning, the relief that flooded through him made him dizzy. He heard his mother's voice, "Andy? Jake? Are you in there?" He took his numb arms from around his brother and ran to open the door, tears running down his face.

She hugged him to her fiercely as his daddy's sister, their Aunt Connie, went to Jake. Andrew was sobbing so hard he could hardly talk.

"It's okay, baby. We're leaving and we're never coming back."

"Mommy … something's wrong with Jacob," he choked out, and Toni went to her younger son, picked him up gently and carried him to the car. Andrew saw Jake hadn't moved from the position he seemed to be frozen in, his knees tucked up under his chin.

"Come sit up front with me, Andrew," Aunt Connie said as she got into the driver's seat. "You can be my navigator. I'll bet you're really good at that."

They stopped at the sheriff's office before they went back to the Martin home, and one of the deputies kept Andrew and Jake company while the women talked to the sheriff. Jake had barely moved and hadn't spoken a word.

"Twenty-four hours is all I can give you, Toni," Andrew heard the sheriff say as they left. The deputy followed them to their house. Toni took out every suitcase they owned, threw the boys' clothes and some of her own into them, and stuffed bags with toys and books.

Aunt Connie hugged Andrew and Jake, and he saw she was crying. "I'm so sorry, boys. I'm so sorry." She hugged her sister-in-law and said, "Go."

***

So for the second time in two years Andrew found himself living with his grandparents and his Aunt Melanie, Toni's teenage sister, in Tennessee. He started school in Pine Glen the next week.

Aunt Mellie was the most help with Jake; she held him and rocked him and sang to him. After a couple of days his rigid little body began to relax, and one night he started singing with her. Within a few days he was talking and even playing with Andrew, and he started school only two weeks after Andrew did.

Jake and Andrew figured they had probably seen the last of their father. Andrew was relieved. Jake missed his father; he seemed to like some of the crazy things their dad did, like nearly every night shooting at tin cans that he lined up along a fence in their back yard.

He hadn't even seemed to mind the time their father had put them both in a closet and locked it to punish them for being too noisy. Jake thought it was an adventure. He had a paper clip in his pocket and spent the hour trying to pick the lock. Andrew heard his mother outside the closet, trying to persuade his dad to let them out without making him mad at her.

"Allan, they weren't making that much noise. Don't you think this is harsh?"

"They have to learn, Antonia. This is nothing compared to what I got when I was a bad kid. It's good for them." Toni said nothing else and Andrew knew it was because his dad had called

16

her by her whole name. It was a warning signal for her to stop talking.

Andrew had spent the hour in the closet worrying that Jake might grow up to be like their father. But Jake seemed better now that they were in Pine Glen, almost like his old self. Andrew started to relax. They had a really nice Christmas together. But only a couple of weeks later, everything changed.

They were all together in his grandparents' home. Their Aunt Alice and Uncle Steve, Toni's sister and brother-in-law, had come for dinner and brought their baby daughters. After an early dinner, Aunt Melanie left to go to the movies. The adults were drinking coffee, talking and laughing, and eventually went into the living room to continue their conversation. Andrew and Jake joined their little cousins Gracie and Leslie on the stairs to the second floor, where they were playing with toy cars and trucks.

"Here, Leslie. Make this car drive fast and then slam on the brakes," said Jake. "Like this. *ErrrrrrKKKK!*"

Leslie giggled so hard she could hardly breathe. Andrew picked up another car and handed it to Gracie. "This one's having trouble getting started. *Rmmm ...mmm ... MMM!*"

Now Gracie was giggling as well, and the adults started laughing with the children.

It took Andrew a minute to understand what happened next. He heard heavy pounding on the front door which flew open as the result of a couple of strong kicks.

Aunt Alice screamed and immediately ran up the stairs, pushing Grace ahead of her and snatching up Leslie. "Jacob, Andrew, get upstairs." She was almost shrieking.

Andrew didn't know what was happening, but he started up the steps behind Jake.

When the first gunshot sounded Andrew knew who it was. His father. He'd heard that gun often enough. Jake turned to see what was happening and almost knocked Andrew off balance. When he turned as well, he saw the angry face of his father as he shot twice more. Uncle Steve was lying on the floor moaning. Andrew's grandfather fell as soon as he was hit, dropping to his knees and then falling forward. His grandmother, who had just started to stand up, was knocked backwards and fell against the sofa. She didn't move again.

His father had not spoken a word; he just burst into the house and started shooting.

Andrew and Jake watched in horror as their father pointed the gun directly at their mother, who never flinched but stared into his eyes. Then he turned and ran out of the house. Andrew pushed Jake the rest of the way up the stairs. He said to his aunt, "He's gone."

"Stay here with the girls," she choked out as she ran downstairs.

Andrew tried to calm the sobbing little girls. Jake had a blank look on his face that frightened him. "Help me with the girls," he said, trying to somehow reach his brother, but at the tender age of eight he didn't know what to do or how to do it.

His stomach felt funny, like something was rolling around inside it, but he sat down on the floor between the girls and put an arm around each of them, trying to rock them and soothe them. Jake still hadn't moved. "Jake! Help me with Grace," he said, trying not to yell.

Jake sat down beside Grace and put his arms around her, smoothing her taffy-colored hair and saying, "Sh. Sh. Don't cry, Gracie."

They heard police sirens come closer and closer, and when they stopped, Andrew knew they were right outside the house. Doors slammed. Heavy footsteps ran into the house. Hurried conversation. His mother's voice, shaking, shrill. More sirens, but they were different. *Maybe ambulances?* It seemed forever before the boys' mother came up the stairs, though Andrew learned later it was only about fifteen minutes. She looked scared and sad and her face seemed crumpled up, somehow.

"Some bad things just happened, and we're going next door to Mrs. Stevens' house to spend the night," she said. "Put your coats on, boys, and please help the girls get theirs on."

She was pulling blankets off the beds as she talked, pulling on her own coat. They moved down the stairs. There was a police officer standing in front of the archway to the living room and they went into the kitchen, where a second police officer spoke gently to all of them, knelt down and hugged the girls and picked them up, one in each arm. He continued to speak to them as they walked from his grandparents' house to the house next door. Andrew noticed people standing around on the sidewalk across the street. He said, "Mommy? What happened? Where's Daddy?"

"He's not here, Andrew. Don't worry about anything. You'll be safe at Mrs. Stevens' and she'll take good care of us."

"Where's Aunt Mellie? She was walking home from the movies. Did Daddy shoot her, too?" Andrew heard his voice getting higher. His stomach hurt and he kept swallowing hard.

Toni took a minute before she answered him. "She's fine, baby. She went to the hospital to be with your grandfather."

Andrew felt his heart jump. "You mean he's still alive? He might be okay?"

He saw tears in his mother's eyes when she said softly, "He was alive when the ambulance attendants took him to the hospital.

But he was very badly wounded, Andrew. I don't know what will happen."

Andrew nodded, trying to keep from crying. He understood what she was saying.

They spread blankets on the living room floor, the ones they had brought and some Mrs. Stevens provided. There were pillows for all of them and they were told to take off just their coats and shoes and get comfortable. Andrew did the best he could to help the girls, who were very quiet. They were tired from a long day, a big dinner, and frightened by what had just happened. They fell asleep quickly. Andrew saw that Jake was lying on his back, staring at the ceiling, not blinking.

His mother took Andrew aside. "I have to go and talk to the police for a while, but I'll be back as soon as I can." She pulled him into her arms and pressed her face against the top of his head. "Oh, Andrew, I am so sorry this happened. I think your Dad is really, really sick. I never dreamed ..."

"It's not your fault, Mommy." Andrew felt he had grown up almost instantly when he saw his father shoot his grandparents. He knew his grandmother was dead, and from what his mother said, he thought his grandfather would probably die, too. And maybe his uncle as well. But it wasn't his mother's fault; she had tried to keep him and Jake safe when she left their father some five months earlier.

"Thank you, my sweet Andrew," she said, tears in her voice. She hugged him, touched Jake's face, and was gone.

Andrew suddenly felt cold and shaky all over. He lay down and pulled a blanket tight around himself, shivering, determined not to cry. Sounds and images swirled in his confused mind, but gradually the physical and emotional fatigue overcame him, and he slept.

CHAPTER 2

Andrew woke once during the night when Leslie was crying. He had to think hard to remember where he was, and recalling the sights of dead people and the sounds of gunshots made him feel sick again. He opened his eyes just a slit and saw that Mrs. Stevens had picked Leslie up and was rocking her. His mother was lying on the floor between him and Jake and had an arm around each of them; she seemed to be asleep, so he didn't wake her.

Andrew wanted to go back to sleep and wake up again and his grandparents would be fixing him breakfast and then they'd go and buy him and Jake a toy. But he knew that wasn't going to happen. *Grammy and Poppy are dead.* What did that mean exactly? He knew what death was … people went away and you never saw them again. He had a difficult time realizing how that would feel; his grandparents were important to him. It was too awful to think about. He moved closer to his mother, she smelled good like she always did. She smelled like flowers, and that made him feel a little better. He squeezed his eyes shut and snuggled closer to her, and she shifted and held him tight.

The next morning they all went to Aunt Alice's little house, and Jake and Andrew were told that's where they would be living "for now."

"There's not a bedroom for me and Andy," Jake whined.

Toni said, "We'll share the sofa bed in the living room until we can figure out something better."

Jake dug his foot into the rug and made a face.

"It's okay, Jakey," said Andrew, seeing his mother's sad face. "It'll be okay."

Later that day Toni went to her parents' house and brought all the boys' clothes and toys and books to their aunt's house, and she put everything in their uncle's home office. Eventually, that room was turned into a bedroom for her sons; friends helped move the desk, chair, and filing cabinet out and set up bunkbeds for the two boys.

In the days and weeks that followed, the adults in the boys' life tried hard to help them have some understanding of what was going on without frightening and confusing them more than they already were. Years later when Andrew thought back to this time, he wondered: *How do you do that?* Nothing would ever be the same again, yet his mother and his aunts tried to give them some feeling that things would eventually be "normal."

Toni talked to her sons about their grandparents' funeral service and asked them if they wanted to go. She also explained about the viewing the night before the funeral and asked if they wanted to go to the funeral home in the afternoon, before other people came that evening, to see their grandparents one last time.

"What do they look like?" asked Jake.

"They look peaceful. They aren't really there, because their souls are in heaven. But they look like they might be resting." Andrew watched his mother closely as she said this, and he felt she wasn't really sure about what she was saying.

"Where's heaven, Mommy?" Jake was bouncing in his chair.

"No one really knows, Jacob. But I think it's a beautiful place where people are safe and happy, and see other people they love who have died. And no one is ever sick or hurt, and nobody grows old." She turned to Andrew, who was picking at his cuticles.

"What do you think, Andrew? Do you want to go and see them and tell them goodbye?"

"How can I tell them goodbye if they aren't really there? Wouldn't it be better to just say goodbye to them when I say my prayers?"

"You can do that, Andrew. I believe they will hear you because I think they're watching over us. And I think they always will."

None of the children — not Andrew, Jake, or their baby cousins — went to the funeral home or to the funeral the following day. They stayed with friends of his Aunt Alice. The boys were kept out of school for almost two weeks. They were bored and picked at each other until the adults decided school would be better. Some of the kids stared at them when they went back, but none of them said anything, and eventually things settled into a routine. Aunt Alice's house was crowded, and the boys knew their uncle was still in the hospital and wasn't doing well.

Andrew found comfort by immersing himself in a world he had discovered as a very young child. He liked the way crayons felt in his hand. Just holding one soothed him. So many colors! And he could make the colors darker or softer by the way he pressed the crayons on the paper. He liked drawing and tried to draw just about everything he saw. Toni gave him his first set of watercolor paints for Christmas the year he was seven. For the Christmas they had just celebrated she gave him a larger set with more colors, and a sketch pad so he could make his own pictures. He went into that beautiful world often and was calmed by it.

Jake spent as much time with their Aunt Melanie as he could, and one evening he cried when she had to leave for a rehearsal for the high school musical. She was playing the leading role of Julie Jordan in *Carousel*. She sat down on the sofa and cuddled him.

23

"I miss you when I'm not here, too, Jake," she told him. "I love you tons and tons, you know that."

"Why can't I go with you?" He was sniffling and rubbing his eyes.

"I won't be home until way past your bedtime."

"Why do you have to be in that stupid old play anyway?"

She pulled him close. "Let me tell you a little story, Jakey." She paused for a minute, and he settled back to listen. "Once upon a time there was a girl who loved to act and sing, and she had spent a lot of time getting ready to audition for a play with music in it. She'd been looking forward to doing that for months."

"What's a 'dyshun,' Aunt Mellie?" asked Andrew, who was sitting on the arm of the sofa.

"It's where you sing a song and read — act some scenes from the play for the people who are going to direct it, Andrew."

"Oh."

"But something really bad happened to that girl's family just a few days before the audition, and she didn't think she would be able to be in the play. Even though it really meant a lot to her. She was very sad." Both boys nodded.

"Then the directors did something really wonderful for her. They waited for an extra week just so she could try out … audition. It meant they had to change the dates the play would be performed … that people would be able to see it."

"And that girl was you," guessed Andrew.

"Yes, it was. So since they did that for me, it makes it important for me to be in the play and be the best I can, and it's fun for me but it's also a responsibility. Do you understand that?"

Jake nodded vigorously, and Melanie hugged him again. "But can we come and see you?" he asked.

"Let me talk to your mommy. We'll figure something out, I promise."

Aunt Melanie told them the story of the show, but Andrew suspected she had left some things out. She did tell them the character Billy Bigelow, who her character Julie was married to, died but came back to see her at the end of the show.

"Do you think that's real, Aunt Mellie? Can people come back from heaven to see us?"

"I believe they can, Andrew. And what happens in the play is that Julie — my character — just sees Billy for an instant. But right at the very end of the show, he talks to her, and she can hear him. It's very inspiring. It makes people hopeful."

Toni decided to take the boys to the second performance to see only the first act. She told her sons the best part is the first act because their aunt actually rode on a carousel, and Aunt Mellie would take them backstage to see it before they left. Both women assured the boys they wouldn't miss much and they might fall asleep in the second act since *Carousel* was a long show, especially for six-year-old Jake.

Jake told his brother he heard their mom talking to Aunt Alice about her real reason for not letting them see the second act.

"She said she doesn't want us to hear the gunshot that happens on stage. She said we don't need that." Jake was very matter-of-fact. "I don't think it would be so bad. We heard Daddy shooting all the time. We got used to it."

"Maybe *you* did. I never liked it."

"He was just knocking tin cans off the fence. I wish he had let me try."

"Guns are dangerous, Jakey. That's why he didn't want you to try it. You're too little."

"When I grow up I'm going to learn to shoot. I'll bet it's fun."

25

Andrew didn't answer. Jake could say things sometimes that made him uneasy. Things their father might have said.

Andrew was enchanted with the musical. He loved the music, especially the "Carousel Waltz" at the very beginning; the duet Melanie sang with Jamie Logan, who played Billy Bigelow; and the sailors' hornpipe song and dance. He and Jake met Jamie when they went backstage at intermission and he was nice to them, lifting each of them up to sit on a carousel horse. It was a good evening for them, taking their minds off the shooting completely for a while.

Two weeks later their Uncle Steve died. Andrew and Jake had never been to the hospital to see him, and they didn't go to his funeral. Neither did their mother, and Andrew asked her if she had gone to see him while he was in the hospital.

Toni seemed to struggle with finding a way to answer him. "Uncle Steve's parents were there most of the time, and they told the nurses who could come in to see him." She paused and looked away. "But I did go to see him once. He asked your Aunt Alice to tell me he wanted to see me."

"But why don't you go to the funeral, Mommy?" asked Jake. "Aunt Alice really wants you to. Why aren't you going?"

"I think it makes your Uncle Steve's mom and dad very sad to see me, Jacob. It reminds them why their son was hurt so badly, and why he's … why there has to be a funeral. I'm staying home because I think it might make it easier for them."

Andrew thought with surprise, *Uncle Steve's parents hate my mom. But why? She didn't shoot Uncle Steve.*

He put his arms around her and hugged her as tight as he could. "It wasn't your fault, Mommy," he said.

The day of the funeral she talked to them about what had happened. She told them their father had shot their grandparents and Uncle Steve because he was very sick.

"Sick how, Mommy?" Jake demanded. "He's not crippled or anything."

"No, Jacob. His sickness is in his mind."

"You mean he's crazy?" said Jake. Andrew felt sick inside. His father couldn't really be crazy. *Or maybe he could.*

"Sometimes things happen and people are made ... they just can't handle something and for a while they get very confused. And do things they wouldn't normally do. It's called 'temporary insanity,'" Toni told them. "That may be what happened to your father. I'm sure he's very sorry about what he did."

"He's going to jail, isn't he?" asked Andrew.

"He's in jail now, Andrew. He turned himself in the next day."

"He'll be there for a long time, won't he, Mommy?" Andrew didn't want his father out of jail. He was sure if he were released he'd come back and shoot all of them.

"Yes, I think he will be, Andrew."

Very little more was said about That Awful Night after that conversation. Toni filed for divorce from Allan Martin, and started using "Antonia Stewart" as her legal name. She petitioned the court to change her sons' last names as well, and informed the boys they were now Jacob and Andrew Stewart and their school records would be changed.

Allan Martin went on trial some months later. Toni had to testify since she was the only living adult eyewitness to the shooting. After the trial Toni explained to her sons that it seemed the jury might have been sympathetic to the idea that their father was "temporarily insane," but they still found him guilty. Since Uncle Steve had died from his wounds, their father had killed three people, and the law demanded he pay for the crime. He would be in jail for fourteen years.

"The best thing is to try to put it out of your mind, boys," Toni said.

Andrew figured by the time his father was released he would be a grown man and probably married with children of his own. He was relieved, and tried to put his father out of his mind.

CHAPTER 3

Andrew had nightmares. He tried not to talk about them, but one night he screamed out in his sleep and Toni came to him, took him into the living room and cuddled with him on the sofa.

"I'm sorry, Mommy. I didn't mean to wake you up," he said, clinging to her.

"Tell me what you were dreaming about, baby."

"I'm not a baby." He said it to convince himself; he liked her holding him and rocking him.

"No, I know you aren't, Andrew. But in a way, you'll always be my baby. And I need you to tell me when things are scary, or upset you. A lot happened to you this year." She was stroking his head as she talked, and he sighed and relaxed against her.

"It was just a nightmare, Mommy. I know it's not true."

"Maybe if you talk to me about it, you won't have it again," Toni said softly.

"I dreamed … I dreamed Daddy got out of jail and came back here to shoot us. You and Jake and me. But he can't get out, can he?"

"No, he can't." She hugged him closer.

He was quiet for a few minutes. "Mommy … if I'd been a better big brother and me and Jacob had been quieter, would Daddy maybe not have been so mad all the time?"

Toni pulled back and looked at her son, and he saw tears in her eyes. "Andrew, you and Jacob are the best boys in the world.

29

Don't you ever for even *one second* think any of this was your fault. Something ... *broke* in your daddy's mind. Something I guess he just couldn't help."

She hugged him tightly again. "You know what, Andrew? Let's talk about some of the good things we remember about your dad. About how he took us on that cruise ship and how much fun we had. And do you remember the trip we made to Vermont and you skied on the little hill ... what was it called?"

"The bunny hill. That was really fun." He smiled. "And you know what I liked best about the cruise ship? When Daddy took us to the ... the place where all the people were who were running the ship and we met the captain and he let us steer the ship for a couple of minutes."

Toni laughed. "Remember how much fun we had when we went to visit New York City at Christmas time one year? How Daddy took us ice skating and he kept falling on purpose so you boys wouldn't mind falling down?" Andrew laughed with her.

He grew quieter. "I guess maybe you're right, Mommy. Daddy's head got sick, and that's why he did ... what he did."

"Try to remember the good things, Andrew. That's what I do."

***

After the school year ended, Toni and Alice found a larger house where they would be more comfortable. They had managed to sell their parents' house, and Alice and Steve had been renting the house they had all been living in. Andrew understood the arrangement ... he was sure his mother wanted to be with her sisters; and since she was working, his Aunt Alice would continue to take care of him and Jake. His Aunt Melanie would be leaving for college in September and would share his mother's room when she was home during school breaks.

Andrew and Jake now had a larger bedroom, as did his little cousins Grace and Leslie. The house also had a family room which became a playroom for the four of them. It was on a dead end street, a perfect place to ride their bikes. The school they started attending in the fall stood on the other side of their street, and they had access to the playground all summer long and took advantage of it.

There were several other boys on the street and all of them enjoyed playing together, including forays into the wooded area at the end of the road. Andrew and Jake spent most of their summer outside, and the fresh air and exercise and making new friends helped take their minds off the trauma they had suffered earlier in the year.

Aunt Melanie left for college and Andrew and Jake started school. Neither of the boys was ever quizzed by their new friends about what had happened in January, and eventually it began to fade from their minds in the busy day-to-day routine.

Sometimes Jake would bring it up: "Remember That Awful Night when Daddy came to our grandparents' house and shot the place up?" Andrew usually changed the subject.

"Say, Jacob, do you remember when we went skiing in Vermont?" Andrew was determined to try not to think so much about the bad things. But occasionally he still had bad dreams, and he bit his fingernails and pulled at his cuticles, sometimes until they bled.

Both boys did well in school, especially Andrew, who loved to read. He liked music and art; painting was what he loved most, and he seemed to have a natural ability for it. Sometimes he would go outside and paint what he saw. Other times he would set up his

31

own still life subjects once his teacher had shown his class how to do that. He could lose himself in creating art. It was calming and satisfying and exciting, all at the same time. He liked listening to music as he painted.

Toni had seen the film *Song of Love* and was enchanted with the piano music. She tried to buy the soundtrack but it hadn't been released. One of the clerks at the local record store told her Arthur Rubinstein had performed for the film, though he wasn't credited, and she suggested to Toni an album of Chopin's piano music with Rubinstein playing. Toni found it beautiful and took it home, and when he heard it Andrew agreed with her. They listened to it together, and hearing it made him want to paint beautiful pictures.

Jake liked gym best. He was a natural athlete and could do it all: baseball, basketball, football. While he made good grades in everything; his strongest subjects in school were math and science. He teased his brother about his books, music, and art.

"C'mon, Andy, come outside and throw a football with me. Don't be such a sissy." And good-natured Andrew would carefully put his beloved paints away and join his little brother outside.

Before long they met a man named Ben Rogers who had started coming to the house to see Aunt Alice, and their mom told them she thought they might have a new uncle soon.

Alice remarried the following Christmas, and her new husband moved her and the girls into a different house. They were close by, and since Toni was working full-time the boys went to Aunt Alice's new house every day after school. One of the things Jake and Andrew liked best was that now they each had their own room and the family room was all theirs. Andrew began to relax and think they were going to be okay … he and Jake and their mother.

The following summer when Andrew had finished fifth grade and Jake third, the boys once again spent a lot of time playing in the woods. One day they came home for dinner to find their mom had invited a friend to join them.

"Max, meet Andrew and Jacob," she said. She looked pretty; her eyes were shining and her face was flushed. "Boys, this is Mr. Cameron. He teaches at Pine Glen High School."

Both boys shook hands with Max, and Andrew asked: "What do you teach, Mr. Cameron?"

"I teach social studies, Andrew. It's not history. It's more like what you study in current events right now." Andrew decided he liked his mom's friend. He had a firm handshake, looked each boy in the eye, and treated them like young men and not little kids.

Max was the chef that night; he made potato salad and grilled hamburgers and corn on the cob. Andrew thought he was cool for doing that. Toni had baked a cherry pie, her sons' favorite.

Max was at the house nearly every day that summer and he made a point of becoming part of Andrew's and Jake's lives. He took them seriously, listening thoughtfully to what they had to say. The three of them ... Max and the two boys ... took a day trip to the Smoky Mountains where they hiked up to Clingman's Dome. To Andrew, that seemed like something a dad might have done.

They made another trip to the Smokies, this time all four of them; first they went to Gatlinburg to see their Aunt Melanie in the outdoor drama, *Chucky Jack*. They drove to Fontana Village in North Carolina and the boys had their first experience horseback riding, which Jake loved and Andrew wasn't crazy about. After that they went to Cherokee and saw another outdoor play, *Unto These Hills*. Andrew loved seeing the shows. Jake fell asleep in the second one, which was very long.

Just before school started, Max asked the boys if he could have a talk with them. They sat together in the family room, which now had a ping-pong table that Max had bought them. Andrew thought he had an idea what Max wanted to talk about.

"You guys know I really like your mom. In fact, I love your mother. She's the woman I've been looking for all my life, and I want to take care of her and make her happy. And you know, I'm so lucky that she can bring into my life two really great boys. I love both of you; I hope you know that. I'd sure like it if you'd let me be part of your life." He stopped for a minute. "So I guess I'm asking you if it's okay if I ask your mom to marry me. Because I'm really asking all three of you."

Before he could say another word both boys started shouting and smothered him with hugs. When they let him up, he said with a grin, "So that's a 'yes,' right?" They piled on him again and they were all laughing when Toni came into the room, and it became a family group hug.

Toni pulled the boys to sit beside her, one on each side. "There's more. Max really meant it when he said he's asking all three of us to be his family." She hugged them close. "There's a way Max could be your real father, if it's okay with you."

They listened quietly. "Max wants to adopt you. He doesn't need to have anyone's permission but mine and yours. How does that sound?"

Andrew stiffened. "What about … what about …" he didn't want to say *our dad*, because he thought about Allan Martin as little as possible.

Jake finished for him. "What about Allan Martin? Won't he be mad?"

Max was kneeling in front of the three of them. "He might not like it. But because of what he did, and where he is now, he doesn't have any right to keep us apart. It's really up to you two."

Andrew was flooded with relief. He'd have a new dad, one he could talk to, who would listen to him and help him figure things out. One who loved all of them and wanted to take care of them. One he already loved with all his heart. He looked at his brother, afraid for a minute that he might object. But Jake was grinning and nodding his head; and the Camerons became a family in that moment. Andrew loved seeing the shine in his mother's eyes.

Three months later, both boys walked their mother down the aisle. Andrew thought he had never seen her look so pretty; she had on a soft wool dress that was ivory, a color he loved. He and Jake had new dark blue suits and bow ties that were the same color as Toni's dress, and Max was dressed exactly like his new sons.

After Toni and Max exchanged vows, Max and the boys did the same. Max had written his "vows" out. The formal adoption had been finalized the week before, but Max wanted his boys to understand how much they meant to him.

"Andrew and Jacob," Max said to them, "I take you as my children, to love and cherish, to help in any way I can as you grow to become the remarkable young men I know you will be. I promise to always be there for you and to have your back. To play sports with you whenever I can, to help with homework — except math — to take you camping and fishing, if that's what you want. I promise to try to be the very best dad I can, because I love you both with all my heart."

Andrew's eyes were full of tears, and Max's voice was shaking.

"If you'll have me as your dad, will you say 'I will'?"

Jake hugged Max and said, almost sobbing, "Yes, I sure will."

"I will, too," Andrew choked out, joining the hug.

All of the Stewart family members who were there were wiping their eyes, and there were audible sniffs. Their Aunt Alice made them all laugh when she said, "Back up, Max. What was that part about not helping with math homework?"

"I was a terrible math student," Max laughed. The family went into Alice's dining room, where a buffet supper had been prepared earlier. Andrew would always remember it as one of the happiest moments of his life.

Having Max as a father was a great comfort to Andrew, though he was still chewing on his nails and destroying his cuticles. Jake seemed to be fine, and Andrew was glad about that, but he had bad dreams and sometimes would think about the man in prison and become very confused. He wasn't sure how he felt about Allan Martin. He tried not to think about him but he couldn't completely forget him. He didn't want to upset his mother, so he didn't discuss this with her. But he could talk to Max, who would listen to him seriously and ask him questions that helped Andrew sort out what he was feeling.

"It has to be hard when you remember the last time you saw him," he said to Andrew.

"Well, what happened even before then. Why Mom left him, the time that Jake and I were left alone all night out in the woods. Swamps are scary, Max. We heard all kinds of noises that night and I didn't know what we'd do if an animal tried to get into the cabin."

Andrew saw a muscle work in Max's jaw as he clenched his fist. He figured Max was angry that their father had done that to them; he didn't say anything, just let Andrew continue.

"Jake doesn't talk about it. Well, Jake never talked about it. But I still think about it sometimes. Why would he do that to us? He said he loved us, but sometimes he sure didn't act like it."

"Your mom has told me that your father didn't have it easy when he was growing up. His father was hard on him and wasn't easy to live with. Sometimes that can have a really bad ... that can make people act in ways they don't really mean to, Andy. I can sure understand why you're confused. And you know what? That's okay. You have every right to be confused. But here's the most important thing for you to think about. Nothing he did was ever your fault. *Nothing he did was ever your fault.*"

Even though his mother had said that to him before, hearing it from Max made Andrew feel better. Max took him shopping the next day to a store where they bought a model airplane. Max knew that Andrew liked to paint and was very good at it, and he thought his son might enjoy putting the model together and painting it. It would also keep his hands busy and might keep him from biting his nails.

Andrew loved working on the model and he was very proud of how great it looked when he finished. He carefully put the paints away and ran into the living room where Max and Toni were watching TV.

"Can you come and look at my airplane? I don't want to pick it up because some of the paint is still drying."

"You bet," said Max, pulling Toni to her feet. They followed Andrew into the family room where he'd been hard at work for two weeks. He'd been so busy he hadn't had time to bite his nails, and it turned out model building helped Andrew break the habit. Both adults exclaimed over the careful and excellent work Andrew had done on the model, and he flushed with pleasure.

"Thanks so much for buying it for me, Dad," he said to Max. It just slipped out, but he saw his parents exchange glances, and Max had to turn his head and Andrew saw him rub his face under his eyes.

"It's beautiful, Andy. What say we get another one soon?" His voice was a little gruff. "Think I'll get some more coffee."

Andrew stayed by the table, pretending to check the paints to be sure all the caps were on securely. Toni watched Max leave the room and turned to her son.

"Did I say something wrong, Mommy?"

"No, son. You made Max very, very happy when you called him 'Dad.'"

"Well, he *is* my dad now," Andrew said. It took Jake a little longer to start referring to Max as *Dad*, but it happened eventually. The boys felt a sense of peace and security they had never really known in their lives.

Max's special times with Jake were working with him as a sports coach. Jake could throw a ball hard and fast … both a football and a baseball. Andrew enjoyed sports; Jake shone at them. Max coached their Little League baseball team, took them to the high school football and basketball games and to movies.

They took family vacations every summer, once even going to Arizona to see the Grand Canyon, and Andrew was glad to see how much happier his mother was. Max had been working toward earning his master's degree in history, and the summer before Andrew started eighth grade, Max was offered a job teaching at West Chester State College in Pennsylvania.

Toni was concerned that her sons might not want to leave Tennessee, but the two of them talked about it with each other, and agreed it was fine with them.

"I won't mind moving, not one bit. It'll be an adventure," said Jake.

"It's fine with me, too," said Andrew.

"I think you'll be as glad as I am to get out of this town. People don't say much, but everybody in town knows about That Awful Night."

Andrew just nodded, but he did feel a sense of relief. His mom had a new name now, Antonia Stewart Cameron. They were all Camerons now. Maybe when Allan Martin got out of prison he might not be able to find them. And they had a dad now who would help protect them even if he did.

They told Toni they were eager to move on, but Jake added, "Just one bad thing. I finally learned how to spell 'Tennessee' right. Now I'll have to learn to spell 'Pennsylvania'!"

Sketch #1
TONI

"I love you, Toni. I love your boys. I want us to be a family. I want to take care of all of you. Please marry me."

I couldn't believe Max had said this to me. The day I met him I learned how generous and caring he was. We were in line in the grocery store, and the woman ahead of him was having trouble. Baby food was a large part of her order, and the toddler hanging onto her skirt completed the picture.

He turned to me and shrugged his shoulders and smiled, and I returned the smile. I liked his smile, it was warm and genuine. He looked about my age, probably six feet tall, athletically built, sandy hair and hazel eyes. I noticed he was probably single ... only a few items in his basket, compared to mine which was piled high with food for two hungry boys.

The young mother at the checkout was distraught. "I don't have enough money," she said, her voice shaking a little. "I'll have to put some things back." She looked at her order and I could see the wheels turning; what could she possibly do without?

He stepped forward and asked quietly, "How much do you need?"

"Five dollars." Her voice shook; it was apparent five dollars seemed an enormous sum to her at that moment.

I saw him hand a five to the cashier, and he received a look of such gratitude I felt my eyes sting with tears. "Oh, thank you. How can I pay you back?"

He smiled and said, "Not necessary. Just do something nice for the next person you see who needs help." He checked out quickly, but before he left I touched his arm.

"What a generous thing for you to do," I said.

He looked at me for a long moment and said, "Thank you for saying that. I believe you would have done the same."

I unloaded my order and checked out, and to my surprise he was waiting just outside the door when I exited. "Please let me help you with that," he said, deftly maneuvering to take my cart. "I'm Max Cameron."

Too stunned to object to this Sir Galahad, I said, "Toni Stewart."

He helped me put the bags in my car. "I hope you don't think I'm being too forward, but it seems we both wanted to help a stranger in distress and I knew I had to meet you."

He told me later he figured I had sons, he saw the two packages of chocolate cookies. He also said he made note of the fact I wasn't wearing a wedding ring.

Max was easy to talk to. He really listened. He was thoughtful and kind. I was surprised when he told me he'd never been married. "After high school, I went into the Marines for four years, then I started college. And that turned into seven years, because I worked and went to grad school. There were just no serious romances during that time. After I taught for a few years I decided I wanted to go for my Ph.D. I'm still working on it. My dream is to teach college kids."

He smiled and kissed me. "I think I was waiting for you, Antonia Stewart."

"Then you're a gift from heaven, Maxwell Cameron. But I come with so much baggage. Why would you want me?"

"Toni, when you married Allan Martin, you were very much in love with him. No matter how he changed, he gave you two remarkable sons. You've been an incredible mother to your boys; they're the proof of that."

"I still can't believe you want me."

"What can I do or say to convince you?" He was quiet and stroked my hair back from my face. "It must be hard for you to learn to trust again."

It was. As much as I wanted to believe Max — to believe *in* Max — part of me still held back. Even though he had become not just my friend, but my protector. Pine Glen was a small town, and the gossip was hurtful; but Max put up a wall and kept

42

me and my sons safe from as much of that hurt as he could.

We hadn't become lovers yet. He was gentle and considerate and I wanted to make love with him. But a part of me was afraid. What if he wasn't the man he seemed to be?

"Do you need some time, Toni? Shall I stay away for a while? I don't want to pressure you. As much as I love you, if you don't feel the same, we'll end this. I want to marry you, but I don't want you to marry me because you think it would be a good thing for your boys. That's not good enough for me, as much as I care about them. They'll grow up – much faster than you'd like – and leave and make lives of their own. If there's not love between you and me, what would we be left with?"

"I care so much about you, Max," I said slowly. "But let's take a … a time out. I believe I need that."

I made excuses to the boys. Max had a big project; he was working on his thesis. He needed time to concentrate on that. They accepted it, though it was obvious they missed him. I missed him, too, more than I had expected I would.

I tried to imagine what our lives would be like without him. Jake and Andy adored Max. They're so different, my boys. Jakey seems more resilient, he always did. He puts on a show of being able to roll with the punches. While Andrew is sensitive, such a worrier. He worries about me; he worries about Jake. Especially about Jake. That night in the

43

swamp he was terrified because he was afraid he might not be able to take care of his little brother. And I hate to think what might have happened to Jake if Andy hadn't been there with him. Max knows all this; he's very conscious that the boys' needs are different. I think he understands my boys as well as I do.

Two weeks later Max made a date with the boys. He wanted to take them to the Smoky Mountains for a day. They would pack a picnic lunch and hike up Clingman's Dome. Just the three of them.

When I saw them off I was struck by a bitter memory: the day Allan had taken my boys for an outing that turned into a nightmare. The night he left the boys alone in the hunting cabin.

But how different this was. I had no misgivings about Max taking them; I realized I had no misgivings about Max at all. I trusted him completely. The sun rose just as they were leaving and it was more than a sunrise. It was the beginning of the rest of my life, a life with a man I knew I loved with all my heart and would trust my life and the lives of my children to with no hesitation.

When they came back that night, I asked him to stay. After the boys were asleep we easily slipped into each other's arms and I found everything I longed for. We both did.

CHAPTER 4

The Camerons made a short visit to West Chester before they moved. They explored the downtown area, walked around the college campus — where Max was shown his classroom and office — and spent time looking at several residential areas both in town and in nearby townships.

Andrew liked the town; it was so different from Pine Glen, a town which had been built hastily as part of the Manhattan Project during World War II. Where Pine Glen now stood had been farmland, fields and wooded hills before 1943. Toni pronounced West Chester "charming," and Andrew could see why. Some of the buildings were very old, most dating from the middle to late nineteenth century; a few even dating to Colonial times.

The imposing Chester County Courthouse was one building Andrew couldn't resist sketching. He sat on a bench and drew the spire and bell tower, the stately columns and heavy oak doors, while Jake hung over his shoulder and complained it was too hot for him; he wanted ice cream. Andrew was fascinated with the building exteriors in different kinds of stone. One in particular they had seen on the campus, serpentine, was a stone native to the area.

In August they moved into the spacious red brick, two-story home Max bought for them. It was roomier than they needed, but they had all fallen in love with the high ceilings, tall windows and the deep front porch that ran the entire width of the house. The kitchen had been modernized. A large room off the living room was designated as a combination office for Max and studio for Andrew. It didn't take long for them to feel at home.

The move from Tennessee had been a good decision. Andrew started eighth grade in the junior high school and Jake sixth in the elementary school. Both boys made friends easily; none of these new friends were aware of the shooting in Pine Glen.

When Andrew started tenth grade he decided to join the high school chorus. He'd always liked music; their Aunt Melanie used to sing to them when they were little and they had seen her on stage a couple of times in musicals. Jake tried to make fun of him for singing but Toni put a quick end to that. "He's not asking you to sing, Jacob."

Andrew wondered if Jake *could* sing, but he kept quiet. Jake was the athlete in the family and was on the football and baseball teams. Andrew was a sprinter on the track team and ran the last lap of the relay. He was good at that. He had no interest in contact sports.

Just before Jake entered ninth grade and Andrew eleventh, the family visited Tennessee to see their Aunt Alice and her family. Melanie was still in California; she'd made a few appearances in film and had performed on stage frequently, once in the role of "Carrie" in *Carousel*.

Alice's four daughters were all sweet girls. Leslie and Grace were now in junior high school; and after Alice married Ben Rogers, she'd had two more daughters, Louise and Stephanie, who were now in grade school. They were just as blonde and blue-eyed as their mother and sisters. All the girls were great admirers of their handsome older cousins, and those cousins were generous with them. They read, played games, watched TV, and all of them helped teach Stephanie to ride a bike.

Ben's parents had a house on Norris Lake. They had their own boat dock, and the boys had a chance to water ski, which they both enjoyed. Ben's dad liked skeet shooting and had his own skeet traps which threw the clay pigeons far above the water.

"Want to try it, boys?" he said, offering them the shotgun. Andrew hesitated, but Jake was thrilled.

"You bet! How cool is this?" He examined the gun as John Rogers explained to him how to use it; he described the correct safety precautions, and prepared to throw a pigeon above the lake for Jake to shoot at. Jake missed the first target, nicked the second, and destroyed the third. He shot too quickly the next two times, but hit the following target and yelled when it was blown to pieces in the air. He was in his element and would have continued shooting, but their host turned to Andrew.

"Try it, Andy. It's an enjoyable sport, and develops eye-hand coordination."

Andrew took the gun from Jake. He had never held a gun and had thought he never would, but the way Jake was smirking at him there was no way he wouldn't try it. John showed him how to hold the gun. "It will kick against your shoulder when you fire it. Just be prepared and stand firm. You get used to that." John showed him how to watch the trajectory and aim slightly ahead of the clay pigeon, so the bullet and the target should meet at the same instant.

Andrew wiped his sweaty palms and prepared to shoot. His heart was beating too fast, and he kept telling himself *This isn't the same. This is a sport. And I'm not Allan Martin.* He took a deep breath and focused on the target, and was successful on his first attempt. And squarely hit six pigeons in a row.

He turned to Jake with a triumphant smile and handed him the shotgun. "Here you go, little brother." He liked the disgruntled look on Jake's face.

47

"What are you doing that I didn't do? I can't believe you can shoot better than me." Jake was annoyed.

"Don't rush so much. Watch the target arc and move the barrel of the gun slightly ahead. You can get a sense of where it's going if you concentrate." Andrew was secretly delighted that he was besting Jake, the athlete. This sport required some finesse ... some art. It surprised him that he enjoyed it.

***

Andrew's passion for art had grown when he took his first high school art class as a sophomore. Working with oils made the possibilities to create seem limitless. He was fascinated by the way the paint looked when he pressed the tube and it flowed onto the palette; it glistened with invitation. He liked the smell of the paint, even the pungent odor of turpentine. There was something immensely satisfying in the way the paint felt when he swirled a brush into it, and he loved the bloom of color on the canvas that invited him to make the picture happen.

His teacher was thrilled; she told his parents she had never had a student who showed the talent Andrew did. He won every art competition for the rest of his high school career. When he was a junior, he started designing posters and every organization in school came begging him to create one for their event. His art teacher told him he had a lot of options to choose from ... teaching, commercial art, possibly even making a decent living as a painter. She took some of his landscapes, both watercolors and oil, to an auction in Philadelphia and brought Andy more than a thousand dollars. It went into his college fund, though he lent two hundred to Jake for a new racing bike.

From the time he was a sophomore, Jake was quarterback for the high school's football team and catcher for the baseball team. His fearlessness stood him in good stead, though he sometimes acted impulsively, annoying his coaches and delighting his teammates. Whatever he did may have been improvising, but it generally worked to the advantage of the team. His coaches found it tough to be hard on a player who won games for their team, even if he was unorthodox and considered a bit of a hothead.

Jake managed to keep his grades up, which surprised everyone. He wasn't the honors student Andrew was, but if he continued to do well he would likely be able to get into any college that wanted him for his athletic skills.

***

"I need to get home, Andy. Can you finish up in like ten minutes?"

Joe Davis, the stage manager, had returned to the high school after dinner to paint the eight benches for the spring musical and touch up some other set pieces. After he finished his work he watched admiringly for nearly an hour as Andrew painted the detailed decoration of a carousel horse. Only now had Joe realized how late it was getting.

"Sure, Joe. I'm sorry … I just get so engrossed in this I lose track of time." Andrew completed the delicate silver circle he was painting with a tiny brush, capped the bottle of paint and took his brushes to clean in the backstage utility sink.

He had been thrilled to learn the high school's spring musical was to be Rodgers' and Hammerstein's *Carousel*. He well remembered seeing his Aunt Melanie perform the role of Julie Jordan, and the backstage visit when he and Jake had been allowed to sit on the horses. *They were really beautiful*, he thought. *I hope mine look as good as those did.*

Joe dropped him off at his house and Andrew went inside to the kitchen. He hadn't eaten since lunch but had been painting the horses for hours, and he made himself a hearty sandwich and found coleslaw which he heaped on his plate as well. He tried to be quiet; it was nearly eleven and Toni and Max were probably asleep.

The front door opened quietly and Jake soon joined him in the kitchen. "What's up, mister scenic artist? That's the right term, right?" Jake also went to the refrigerator and took out cold cuts and cheese for a snack. "Have you finished the horses yet?"

"Nearly. I have about two hours' work left on the last one." Andrew continued eating as he watched his brother; Jake looked very pleased with himself. "So how was your date?"

Jake sat down at the kitchen table. "Do you really want to know?"

"Sure I do. Tara is a great girl." He swallowed and added, "Hey, the best man won. I don't hold any grudges."

The brothers weren't inseparable, but they had each other's backs ... for the most part. Except where girls were concerned. Any girl who seemed to take a shine to his brother was of immediate interest to Jake. Andrew liked girls, but his relationships throughout high school were generally more friendships than romances. Jake developed something of a reputation beginning in his sophomore year. Since this was Andrew's senior year, most of Jake's conquests were also seniors or juniors. Once he'd conquered a girl, he was quickly bored with her.

At the beginning of the year Andrew had a couple of dates with a junior girl, Barbara Morton, and thought this might lead to something. One day he saw Jake chatting her up in the hall, and the next thing Andrew knew Jake and Barbara were a couple. Jake dumped her after a month.

Tara Lake was another girl who had dated Andrew a couple of times. Jake moved in with his devilish charm, and Tara was his. Andrew wasn't in love with her, but still, it was annoying. He didn't date anyone for a while. Jake seemed to be more interested in Tara than the others and had hinted that she was ripe for the picking, which irked Andrew even more.

"That Tara ... she's a sweet, sweet girl, Andy." Jake swallowed half his glass of milk in one gulp. "You know, she really liked you. She thought you just weren't interested."

"I'm not looking for a commitment, Jake. I enjoyed being with her. I don't want to go steady; I've got a long way to go before I can think about a serious relationship."

Jake made himself another sandwich. "That's your problem, bro," he said. "Take what you can get when you can get it. Seems like with you it's either 'let's be friends' or 'let's get married someday.'"

"No, that's not it at all. I like girls a lot. But I don't want to move too fast. Tara ... I respected her too much for that." He poked Jake's chest with an index finger. "And you should, too. She's a nice girl, Jake. She's not a slut."

Jake refilled his glass and sat again at the table. "Here's what I don't get. You and Tara seemed to have something good going. Why didn't you tell me to butt out?"

Andrew leaned back and looked at his brother. They still could almost have been twins; both had dark hair and eyes. Jake was taller by two inches and more muscular, and Andrew knew the devilish twinkle in his eye was difficult for most girls to resist. Jake was "the handsome Cameron boy." Andrew knew he was considered "the nice Cameron boy." He was okay with that; he didn't want to compete with Jake. They moved in different circles; had different interests. Most of Jake's conquests were cheerleaders. Tara was in band and chorus, Andrew's world.

"She liked you better, I guess."

"I don't know if she did or not. Not really. She may have been trying to make you jealous. Did you ever think of that?"

"I guess not. I wasn't in love with her, Jake."

"She might have been in love with you, though. She still talks about you … a lot."

"What are you trying to say?"

Jake leaned across the table and looked into Andrew's eyes. "You never fight for anything, Andy. If you'd told me to, I would have backed off. Why do you do that, just let me take a girl away from you?"

"Why do you want to do it, Jake? You have girls tripping over themselves to get you to pay attention to them."

Both brothers sat quietly for a moment. "I don't know. I wonder …" Jake sighed and almost whispered, "Bad blood. Maybe I'm too much Allan Martin's son."

Andrew sat straight up and gripped his brother's shoulder. "Don't say that," he said sharply. "Don't you *ever* think that."

Jake gave Andrew a sad little smile. "Do you ever wonder about him?"

"No. And you shouldn't either." He took both plates and glasses and went to the sink. "It's late. We should both get to bed."

Jake stood behind him at the sink, put both hands on Andrew's shoulders, and gave them a squeeze. "I know I don't say it as much as I used to, but I'm lucky to have you as my big brother."

"Yeah, I love you, too, asshole."

Jake laughed and ruffled Andrew's hair. "Tara's okay, Andy. I'll slow down. I won't hurt her."

Andrew dried the dishes and put them away. What Jake had said was true. When they were little, Toni had often duplicated Christmas gifts, and even though they were identical, sometimes Jake wanted Andrew's. Andrew would trade with him, not thinking much about it. *What's the big deal? It's just like your fire truck, but hey, here.*

Even earlier in their lives, he recalled accepting blame for something Jake had done … a mess that hadn't been cleaned up, usually. Surprisingly, Allan had never spanked them. Sitting in a corner without moving was their punishment. *I did it, Daddy. — Go sit in the corner, Andrew.* Jake never said a word but would later offer to share a dessert or a treat with his brother. Andrew never accepted.

As they grew older, the Christmas gifts became more individualized, reflecting each boy's interests. Still, Jake helped himself to Andrew's shirts — his pants were too short for Jake — without asking. And more recently, to Andrew's girls. The one thing he never touched was his brother's art supplies; they held no interest for him.

Andrew stifled a sigh. He hadn't been entirely truthful about Tara; he had begun to take a shine to her. *Too late now*, he thought. *No way am I going to pull a Jake on Jake.* The thought made him smile, and he forgot about Jake's comment about bad blood.

Once again, Andrew tucked all thoughts of his birth father into a corner somewhere in the far recesses of his mind.

CHAPTER 5 (1964)

Andrew graduated from West Chester High School in the spring of 1964, and in August there were alarming news reports of a sea battle in the Gulf of Tonkin halfway around the world. It was described as an act of aggression committed by the North Vietnamese against a ship of the United States, and five days later Congress passed a resolution giving President Lyndon Johnson the power to assist America's allies in Southeast Asia, power that was used to deploy increasing numbers of the United States military to South Vietnam to engage the North Vietnamese in open warfare.

Max was the family member who was most concerned about these events. He had served with the Marine Corps for four years — part of that time in Okinawa and Japan, after World War II — and he used the GI bill for his educational expenses, but he had never seen combat. Still, he was aware of how quickly a war can escalate, and he kept his eyes and ears open. Andrew had registered with the selective service, but because he was a college student chances were he wouldn't be immediately affected by the draft.

***

Andrew entered West Chester State College in September as a prospective art teacher. He also signed up for and auditioned for the college chorus. Music was an important part of his life; he often painted while listening to recordings — usually classical pieces but sometimes musical theater. Mary Morrisey, another WCHS 1964 graduate, was in several of his classes and was also in choir. They had been friendly in high school; she had been an accompanist for the concert choir and also played for the musicals her last two years.

Mary was a sweet-faced girl with blue eyes, fair skin, and soft, light hair she wore to her shoulders in a kind of pageboy. She was tall; he guessed about five feet eight, because she didn't have to tip her head up too much to look into his eyes.

She had sometimes stopped by the auditorium to practice while Andrew was doing detail work on the set for *Carousel*, and he shared with her more about himself and his history than he had with anyone else.

"The horses are beautiful, Andy. Almost too pretty to ride on," she laughed.

"I hope they're okay. I really love this show."

"So do I. I love playing it. I think the audiences are going to be surprised at how good it is." She played the opening chords of the "Carousel Waltz."

"You know, my mom's sister played the role of Julie Jordan when she was in high school. She was just amazing. My grandparents were killed only a couple of weeks before auditions. I don't know how she did it."

"Oh, Andy, how sad. Did they die in an automobile accident?"

He only hesitated a moment. "Yes."

"She must have been a remarkable young woman. How brave of her."

"She said the role helped her to deal with the tragedy." He turned back to his painting, not happy that he had lied to Mary, but unwilling to tell her more. *She doesn't need to hear that.*

The summer after graduation they started seeing more of each other. For once, Jake didn't interfere; Tara had become his steady girlfriend. Once they started college Andrew and Mary began to see each other regularly, having coffee after choir rehearsal and meeting sometimes for lunch off campus. There was a sense of serenity about her which Andrew responded to; he looked for peace wherever he could find it.

"My family would like to meet you," she told him about a month into the first semester. "Can you come to dinner on Sunday?"

"I'd like that," he told her, delighted with the way she was looking at him. "Thank you for the invitation."

Mary's family consisted of parents Bill and Martha, and one sister, Leeanne, a junior high school student who looked very much like Mary and was sweet and a little shy. Andrew felt very comfortable with them; they asked questions which indicated Mary had talked about him quite a bit.

"Dinner was delicious, Mrs. Morrisey," Andrew said to his hostess as they were finishing dessert, a homemade rhubarb pie topped with ice cream. "Please let me help with the dishes."

"Thank you, Andy, that's nice of you. Mary's in charge of clean up, and I suspect she won't mind having you as assistant busboy and dishwasher." They all laughed. Mary's parents went upstairs, as did Leeanne.

"Your family is great, Mary. I figured they would be." Andrew was scraping plates into the garbage as Mary loaded the dishwasher. "Next week do you think you can come to my house? I know you've met my folks, but it would be nice for you to get to know each other better."

"Careful, Andy. People might think you're getting serious about me," she teased.

"I like you, Mary. I like being with you. People can think what they want," he said, feeling himself redden. He knew why he had never pursued her in high school. He was sure Jake would have tried to make a move on her, and he didn't want that. Mary was special.

"Why didn't we ever go out in high school, Andrew?" She looked directly at him when she asked it, and he had a feeling she knew exactly why.

"I'm not sure," he said. "I had that big art show to prepare for after *Carousel*, and it … I spent most of my time painting and getting my work ready for that."

"I would have helped you, you know," she closed the dishwasher and pushed a button. "Modern appliances. Aren't they fantastic?"

He laughed and leaned against the counter. "Want to go for a walk?"

She surprised him. She put a soft hand on his arm and said, "I'd like to play for you, if you would like that."

"I'd love it." He followed her into the living room. "A private recital. This is great." He sat near her in an easy chair. "What do you like to play most?"

"Chopin is my favorite composer of piano music," she said. "Are you familiar with his compositions?"

"We have a recording of some of the Nocturnes, and I've heard other pieces on the radio. I think a … Polonaise? And something called the 'Fantaisie Impromptu,' could that have been Chopin?"

She smiled. "If this was what you heard, that would be correct." She began the piece, and Andrew was transfixed. Mary was a different person when she shared her music. She was beautiful, and she played with confidence and passion. Andrew recognized the music immediately, but it had not moved him when he first heard it as it did now. Watching Mary's fingers fly over the keys was breathtaking; and hearing the achingly beautiful melody when the piece slowed almost brought him to tears. When she finished, she looked at him and smiled. "Was that the one?"

He nodded, having trouble making his voice work.

"Would you like to hear more? This is my favorite of Chopin's Nocturnes. You may recognize it," she told him, and took him with her again to a beautiful place where he was wrapped in sounds so lovely he wanted to paint them. He wanted to paint her, to try to capture the inner beauty he saw as she played. He went to the piano, sat next to her on the bench, and kissed her.

She returned his kiss and rested her head against his shoulder as he held her close. After a moment he said, "I think I must be in love with you. We should have done this sooner."

She pulled back and looked into his face, her eyes shining. "I've been right here, you know."

"Of course I know. I always thought you were great."

"Did you?" She put her hand on his chest. "I'm not sure you ever really saw me."

He touched her face, brushing her hair back from her forehead. "That's not true." He hesitated. "I wasn't sure … "

"You weren't sure Jake wouldn't try to take me away from you," she said. "He couldn't have, Andrew. You were the only Cameron boy I ever saw. From the moment you and I started eighth grade together."

He was quiet for a few minutes, gazing at her, again gently touching her face. "You're beautiful, Mary. I love you."

"I love you, too. I think I've loved you for a long time."

She had won his heart a little at a time with her kindness and generosity, but hearing her play had an impact on him he could hardly describe. He needed her: her passion, her peace, her music. With her in his life, he could face anything.

From that day they spent as much time together as they possibly could, Andrew sometimes coming to her house to study as she practiced, often sketching her at the piano. Mary became a frequent visitor to the Cameron household, usually helping with a family meal. Toni and Max both fell in love with her and told Andrew as much.

Tara was often there as well. She and Jake continued to be a couple; she was planning to attend West Chester State College after graduation. Through the end of the football season, Jake had his own cheering section: his parents, his girlfriend, his brother, and his brother's girlfriend. Jake was being scouted by several universities even though he had another year of school.

Andrew was happier than he had ever been in his life. He hinted to Mary that he was close to asking her to marry him. He knew they both had to complete their degrees; each of them wanted to become a teacher. For the moment, he was content to wait before moving beyond the make-out sessions they enjoyed.

He knew Jake and Tara were lovers; Jake had told him.

"Just don't go to the party without a raincoat, son," Andrew told his brother.

"Not to worry. We're careful, and Tara's going to go on the pill as soon as she finishes high school."

"Why wait? Isn't she eighteen?"

"Not until May. Trust me, bro. I have condoms stashed all over the place." He leered at Andrew. "Just say the word and I'll share."

Andrew laughed and good-naturedly slapped the back of Jake's head. "You know, you really are a piece of work."

"I try."

Susan Moore Jordan

***

As Max had feared, the war in Vietnam began to require more troops. A Marine friend he'd stayed in touch with had a position at the Pentagon, and Max called him to see what he could find out. He worried for his two sons: Andrew had turned nineteen and Jake would be eighteen in a year. What he heard made him uneasy and he spoke with Toni.

"I wish I knew what the hell this war is about," he told her. "Gene tells me LBJ is micromanaging the damn thing. He says sometimes it seems it's an open-ended commitment to the South Vietnamese government with no real war plan. That's a nightmare if it's true."

"Well, Andy's still in college, and Jake will be going to university someplace after he graduates. Penn State really has their eye on him."

More and more young men were drafted during the next months, and in the spring Max and Toni sat down with Andrew.

"I don't want to alarm you, son, but I'm not so sure you'll continue to be deferred. Last year there were about 24,000 U.S. troops deployed. At the rate it's going, by the end of this year there will be at least eight times that — close to 200,000. There's talk that student deferments might close."

Andrew felt his throat close up and the hairs on the back of his neck stand up. "I don't want to fight, Dad. You know why, Mom."

"Yes, Andrew, we both do. But your dad has explained the situation to me, and I think you need to listen to him."

Toni took her son's hand as Max said, "It concerns me that you might be getting close to graduation in a couple of years and be yanked out of school and thrown into the Army. It would mean you'd most likely be an infantryman, and in the thick of it."

"I guess I could file conscientious objector status."

"That's a real long shot." Max was quiet for a moment. "Here's what I'm thinking. You could enlist in the Marines and apply for special training. You'd be done with your obligation in two years and could come back here and finish school. It would be an interruption, but not a disruption."

"I'd still be in Vietnam."

"You might be, but if you're trained as, say, a helicopter mechanic, you'd be stationed on a base. I'm sure you'll have to fight, but you won't be in the jungle."

"What do you think, Mom?" Andrew was squeezing Toni's hand tight. He didn't like this, but he understood what his dad was saying to him.

"I'm sorry this is something you have to even think about, Andrew. But sadly, it is. This conflict isn't going away and more and more of our young men will be drafted."

"Let me think about it some more. And I need to talk to Mary. It always helps me to hear what she has to say."

Andrew put a recording of Chopin's piano music on the stereo and stood in front of his easel, staring at a blank canvas for a while. Usually, music and art would help him regain his center when he felt off balance, but this was completely different. *Enlist in the Marine Corps?* The last thing he had ever considered doing. In no way did it fit into his plans: finish college, marry his lovely girl, get a job teaching art — hopefully in the same school where Mary would teach music.

I just figured I'd be deferred because I was in college. I never thought about the war maybe going on beyond that. But even though he could see how much his mother hated the thought of his being in the military, she seemed to agree with his dad. *And Dad has always given me good advice.*

He gave up on trying to paint; his mind too much in turmoil to concentrate even on what he loved most. A long walk; looking at his town with new eyes, thinking of leaving all this for two years. His eyes misted and he felt shaky inside. *I hate this. I really hate it. But I guess it's the smart thing to do.*

***

Andrew was unusually quiet during his dinner date with Mary at Longwood Gardens. He said, "Let's take a walk, can we? I have some things I need to tell you."

It was a mild April night, and they walked to the Brandywine Creek. Sitting on a bench that was secluded from foot traffic, Andrew told Mary about the "family tragedy" he had mentioned to her the year before.

"You know I told you about my grandparents being … dying just before my mom's sister played Julie Jordan back when I was a kid." He took a deep breath, trying to relax. *This isn't going to be easy.*

"When you asked me if they died in a car wreck, I let you think that." Another deep breath; he was shaking inside. He had never told anyone about this.

"That's not what happened. A man named Allan Martin broke into their house and shot them to death." Mary took his hands to try to calm him.

"Oh, Andrew, how awful."

"That's not the worst of it, Mary." His throat closed up and he had to stop for a moment. "Allan Martin was my father."

He told her everything and she listened quietly, not commenting, continuing to hold his hands as he talked.

"Maybe I should have told you sooner. I don't like thinking about it ... about him. It's in the past."

"There must be a reason you're telling me now."

He sighed. "There is. Things in Vietnam are getting bad, you know that. Body counts on the news every night. And my dad has a friend in the Pentagon who says it's just going to get worse. There's a good chance I'll have to go."

"Not while you're in college."

"It could happen. And if I'm drafted, I'll be in the infantry. I'll be ... I'll ... I don't want to kill people, Mary." He swallowed hard.

"I can understand that, Andrew. Of course you don't." They sat quietly for a few minutes.

"Here's the thing. Dad says if I enlist in the Marine Corps, I can be part of the war without having to be directly ... without having to be on the front lines. I can request special training to maybe be a helicopter mechanic. It's not guaranteed, but if I wait to be drafted I'll be right in the middle of the war."

"Your dad's friend. Can he help with this?"

"I think he might, but Dad didn't say that." He put his arms around her and held her close. "This is an awful decision, but I think it's one I need to make."

"How long will you have to serve?"

"Right now, the Marine Corps is allowing men to enlist for two years. If I go now, I can come back and finish my degree. All my classes so far have been core classes, basic stuff. If I stay in school hoping I won't be drafted, it might be more difficult to pick up when I come back. And I'd be drafted into the Army." He looked out over the water for a moment.

"I've thought about this a lot. I feel like I ought to go, Mary. I'm proud to be an American, and I'd be proud to serve my country. I think if I don't do this I'll regret it. I don't want to shirk my duty."

Mary caressed his face. "I think you've decided, Andy. And I think it's the right decision."

He covered her hand with his, holding it tight against his cheek. "I hate leaving you."

"I hate it, too," she said, her eyes filling with tears. "But I'll write you every day. I'm not going anywhere. I'll be right here when you come home."

"Oh, Mary, I hoped you would say that." He kissed her, a long, lingering kiss, wanting it to last forever.

They held each other as they watched the moon rise and the stars appear, their reflections rippling in the water. They clung to each other, wordlessly wrapping themselves in the comfort of the peaceful night.

CHAPTER 6

"Boot camp will be rough. Like nothing you can even imagine. They'll take you apart, completely break you down, then put you back together. And it's true, Andy. Once a Marine, always a Marine. You'll be proud to wear that name for the rest of your life."

Max hadn't been kidding. He'd told Andrew exactly what to expect, but even knowing what was going to happen didn't really prepare him. He knew from the moment he got off the bus at Parris Island he would have Drill Instructors screaming in his face. He knew his head would be shaved and he'd be shamed and tormented mercilessly; in a way, taken back to infancy and childhood. The D.I. was the classroom bully and he was untouchable. Andrew soon was reeling from this treatment.

He didn't mind the physical part of training; in fact, he did well. His years on the track team stood him in good stead. It was the mental and emotional stress he struggled with, but he wasn't alone. Every recruit in his platoon went through it. Max had said, "They become your brothers. You're all in it together. And everybody is green. I mean, *green* as in the color. Marine green. No black or white."

The D.I.s were ruthless. The recruits had absolutely no privacy; they were ordered to stop thinking and only obey the orders that were screamed in their faces. They were belittled and called names that Andrew had to admit were sometimes amazingly ingenious, but there was no way he would have laughed. The D.I.s scared the wits out of him.

They marched incessantly. Close order drills. Open formation drills. And hours of standing at attention, not moving a muscle. Max had explained to him how vitally important all of this was: "Drill gives a Marine control over his body. Even learning to stand motionless is essential; if you're, say, on sentry duty, you have to keep your head and remain still as you assess a situation." Over time, Andrew actually began to enjoy it. The sense of camaraderie; the cadences the D.I. called out. There was music to it.

They were issued M-14s. "The Marines don't give a shit about you," they were told. "But we care about your rifle. Your ass is worthless, ladies. Your rifle is everything. If anything happens to your rifle, if you get one tiny scratch on it, you will wish you had never been born." They got the message. Andrew treated his rifle as if his life depended on it, convinced if he didn't the D.I.s would take him apart again and not bother putting him back together.

The lack of sleep was tough. They'd have just had lights out and their evil Drill Instructor, fire in his eye, would wake them all up and make them stand at attention while he slowly examined every foot locker, dumping their contents on the floor. He also would examine the corners of bed sheets to be sure they were properly mitered, ripping them off the beds and throwing them on the floor if they weren't.

One item out of place, one sloppily made bed, and the whole platoon had to drop and give him ten — for each offense he found. And he found an offense for each of them; he certainly didn't play favorites. Then they had to remake their beds and collect and replace the contents of their foot lockers. He would finally let them go back to bed and an hour later reveille would sound.

Brutal treatment and pain, sleeplessness and humiliation — they learned all they could count on was each other. They would be studying for a test and fight to stay awake, pounding each other on the back, splashing water in each other's faces. Andrew began to have a sense that he could trust these men with his life. Another Marine slogan: "No man left behind." He knew he would never leave any of them behind.

***

Max had warned Toni and Mary about what to write to him. "Nothing mushy. Nothing about how much you miss him and can't wait until he's home. His D.I. will have a field day with a letter like that."

Toni was shocked. "You mean he reads their mail?"

"Well, he may not *read* it, but he opens letters and packages to see if there's anything in them that shouldn't be there. And he eats the cookies moms and girlfriends send, with great relish. Takes the pictures the family sends of pets and makes fun of them."

"That's awful," said Mary.

"That's boot camp," said Max. "You'll both be so proud when you watch him graduate."

***

Andrew wasn't surprised he did well shooting; he earned his expert rifleman rating. And a bonus: because he had done well, he was allowed for the first time to call home.

"Hi, Mom."

"Andrew!" She sounded thrilled to hear him, but followed immediately with, "Is anything wrong?"

"Everything's great. I'm in the best shape I've ever been in in my entire life. I mean mentally and physically, Mom. Being here has been something else. Oh, and I earned my Expert Rifleman Badge and making this phone call is my reward."

"Congratulations, son. You sound wonderful. You sound different. Older. Stronger."

"Yes," he chuckled, "basic training will do that for a future Marine."

She laughed. "That's what your dad told me. He also told me some young men have a hard time."

"Well, it's anything but easy. But boy, do you ever learn a lot about yourself. We've had two guys in our platoon who couldn't cut it and were sent home. I felt bad for them, but our D.I. wouldn't let us get sappy about it. It happens sometimes." He didn't tell her the whole platoon made fun of the poor guys, egged on by their D.I.

"You're getting close to graduation. We can't wait to see you."

"Not much longer. I think I may even be promoted to PFC before I graduate. Ask Dad, he'll tell you that's a real accomplishment."

"That's wonderful, son. I know you probably can't talk long, so I'll let you go. We all love you so much, Andrew."

"Yeah, me too," he told her. Another member of his platoon was now standing at his elbow, eager to use the phone. "See you soon."

Two weeks before graduation Andrew underwent an ordeal he would remember all his life, one he felt prepared him for anything: Intensive Combat Training. Make or break time as nothing else had been. Almost no sleep, and that only in brief snatches. Working through fiendishly devised obstacles. Running through simulated attacks. They had to stay alert. It was as close to being in actual combat as possible. And to top it all off, a twelve mile trek in full field gear, stopping only for water and to relieve themselves.

But they did it. His entire platoon, less the two who had dropped out earlier, triumphantly returned to base, where they were treated to the "warrior's breakfast" — everything imaginable, all they could eat. *I'm a Marine now*, Andrew thought proudly.

His parents, Jake, and Mary arrived at the base the day before graduation. Andrew was in uniform, and he saw they weren't sure how to greet this assured young Marine they were meeting for the first time. He shook hands with Max and Jake, but as soon as they had some time alone he hugged each of them warmly. Toni, Max, and Jake made themselves scarce for a bit, and Andrew took Mary in his arms and kissed her hungrily.

"Oh, I've missed you," he said, kissing her again.

"Apparently," she laughed. "Though from what Max has told me, you've been kept busy constantly."

"Still dreamed about you. When I was allowed to sleep, that is," he laughed.

"You look amazing." She admiringly ran her hands over his chest and shoulders. "I think that's what's called 'ripped.' You feel so good." And she lifted her face for another kiss.

Graduation day. Emotions ran high but were kept in check. Thirteen weeks earlier, they had stepped off a bus and lined up, disoriented and scared; raw recruits. Now they were Marines. They were different; they had walked through fire and emerged victorious on the other side. Andrew proudly wore his full dress uniform as an honor graduate. He was given the privilege of carrying the banner of his platoon, the highest honor a recruit could achieve.

Mary and the Camerons told Andrew how impressive the ceremony was. The two women seemed to be in awe of him. Jake was dumbstruck by the entire experience; seeing Andrew as a warrior and being at the base. "Penny for your thoughts," Andrew said to him.

"I didn't realize how cool this was going to be. Or how amazing you are." He gazed at his brother, his eyes shining.

To Max, Andrew was now even more than his son. He was his brother in arms. Max couldn't stop smiling. He stepped back, looked at Andrew, and shook his head.

"What?"

"I'm so proud of you I can hardly stand it."

Andrew laughed. "Did you think I might not make it?"

"Of course not. Not for one second. Not for one millisecond. But you sure surprised me with how well you did, PFC Cameron. Expert Rifleman. Guidon Bearer. You're not thinking about making a career of this, are you?"

Andrew laughed. He was slightly giddy; he'd been through an ordeal and emerged out the other end in one piece. Stronger. Better. "Think they'd let me take my paints and an easel over to the Nam and paint the war?" Both men laughed so uproariously, Jake joining them, that the women stared at them in amazement.

Andrew had ten days leave before he had to report to the Naval Air Technical Training Center near Memphis, Tennessee, for his training as an Aviation Metalsmith. His responsibilities would be to keep the fuselages of the helicopters in his squadron in good repair, patching bullet holes and rips in the metal after a mission.

During his time at home he was often with Mary. They went to the Poconos for a weekend together, offering no pretense or excuse to their families. They wanted to be alone, and both sets of

70

parents respected that. They talked, they kissed, they touched each other as they never had before, content with these moments of intimacy that stopped short of the consummation they had agreed should be saved for their wedding night. They bathed together, and finally, they slept in each other's arms, blissful, for a time ignoring the world speeding past them.

***

Training at NATTC was different from boot camp. They were Marines now; no longer raw recruits, they were part of the Corps. Though all the men he was training with now would be in support positions, they were made to understand they were not exempt from being in battle. "Don't think just because you're not going to be a grunt means you won't get shot at," the Sarge told them. "You're a grunt with a tool box, and Marines *always* get shot at. Count on it."

When he returned to West Chester after his training at NATTC, Andrew's mood was sober, almost somber. When he left this time, he would be going halfway across the world to be part of a war which was becoming increasingly controversial.

There was a shadow over his time with the people he loved. Yes, he firmly believed he would come home; but he also had learned there would very likely be times he'd be fighting. A member of the support staff for the squadron often was needed to act as a door gunner, manning a machine gun to help defend an aircraft. Sometimes this would mean flying into a hot landing zone to bring back-up troops to a firefight. Sometimes they would be extracting Marines, shooting at the enemy to try to get men safely to the helicopter so they could be lifted out of the battle zone.

I'm seeing my family differently — even my dear Mary, he thought. He was memorizing their faces. He sketched all of them.

He could tell Toni and Mary both were dreading the day he would have to leave. They tried hard to make his time enjoyable, and he tried to as well.

There had been little time for Jake and Andrew to talk alone when he was on leave after his graduation from basic training, but now the two of them sat up late the night after Andrew got home. "I'm going to enlist as soon as I graduate," Jake told him.

"It's probably a good idea. You might as well get your service out of the way before you start college."

"I don't know that I'll go to college," Jake said, his eyes glittering. "I may make a career in the military. I really loved being at Parris Island. I can see myself on a military base."

"You're going to enlist in the Marine Corps, aren't you?"

"I want to fight, Andy. I'll figure out what's the best fit for me. I kind of like the idea of being a Green Beret." He took a swig of the beer he'd opened for himself. "You look different."

"Well, I feel different. I feel ready."

"Wish we were going together. We'd be a great team," Jake finished his beer in a final gulp. "Don't you die on me, bro. Whatever you do, don't you dare die."

"I have every intention of staying alive," Andrew chuckled. "And I love you, too, asshole."

He spent a lot of time at the Morriseys' listening to music; sometimes recordings Mary loved, sometimes hearing her play. She'd just heard the Rachmaninoff Second Symphony and had fallen in love with it. She wanted to share it with him.

"I don't know what Rachmaninoff was thinking when he wrote it, but it speaks to me about the time we're living in now. The first movement sounds to me like the troubled buildup to war. It starts off quietly, but then it grows and sounds ominous. It gets louder and faster; we're just being swept along with this war. It's not even a war, though, is it?"

Andrew wasn't sure how to answer her. "Well, it feels like a war to anybody who is getting ready to fight in it."

She nodded. "It feels like that to me, too. I wish ..." she paused. "I won't say that, Andrew. I'm very proud of you.

"When you listen to this incredible music, see if you agree with me. The second movement makes me think about the helicopters, and about what war in the air is like. About battles won, and the pride of the men fighting. The third movement ..." she paused again, struggling to keep her composure.

"The third movement is what's happening back here. Soldiers and Marines coming home. But not the way they should be coming home. Families who have to deal with ..." She sighed. "But the last movement gives me hope. It's strong and glorious. It's the end of the war. Or at least, of your war. It's how I'll feel when you come home to me."

They listened together, Mary resting her head on his shoulder. Andrew held her close, letting Rachmaninoff's music sweep over him. He understood why she heard the symphony as she did, but he heard more. He heard the intense beauty the universe held, a power that would never be denied. As the music ended, she pressed herself against him and kissed him.

"I want us to be together," she murmured. "Before you leave, I want to show you how much I love you. I don't want you to go off to war not knowing what's waiting for you here."

"Are you sure?" He could hardly speak. He had never wanted her as much as he did at that moment.

She pressed her forehead against his. "I'm so in love with you. I need you."

Susan Moore Jordan

The weekend before Andrew left he and Mary drove to the Pocono Mountains; she had rented a cabin on a lake so they could be alone. The fall colors flamed brilliantly in the slanting rays of the sun as it neared the western horizon. The clouds grew almost magenta and their reflection made the lake appear to be on fire. Andrew and Mary stood outside the cabin, watching in awe. *I'll have to paint this someday*, he thought. *I'll never forget it.*

Arms around each other, they went inside.

.

CHAPTER 7 (1967)

Just two years later, not the lifetime it seemed, Andrew's enlistment was up and he was with his Mary again. She leaned her head on Andrew's shoulder as they were once more driving to the lake.

"I'll never forget the first time we came up here. I was able to book the same cabin."

"You have no idea how much that helped me while I was away. Those memories and your letters saved my sanity." He smiled and kissed her forehead briefly, being careful to keep his eyes on the road.

He loved looking at her, loved seeing how she had blossomed from the pretty, sweet-faced girl he first fell in love with into the beautiful, strong woman she had become. The students on the WCSC campus now appeared so young to him; the freshmen especially, who still had the unformed, soft features of children. He knew he looked old to them. He saw it in his eyes when he looked into a mirror: he had the eyes of a man who had seen far too much, grown old before he should have. *I lost more than two years, he* thought. *I lost my youth.*

Mary kissed his cheek and snuggled against him. "I'm glad my letters helped."

They were on their way back to Lake Wallenpaupack for an October weekend. Autumn was Andrew's favorite time of year; he had missed the Pennsylvania changes of season during his tour of duty in Vietnam.

Mary grew quiet, and he knew she hoped he would say more. He didn't like to talk about Vietnam. He didn't want to think about it. When people asked him what it was like, he often replied, "I was on a base most of the time. You should ask somebody who was in the thick of it; they'll be able to tell you much more than I could. Talk to Jake when he gets home."

The day he left, she had said to him: "I'll write you every day. What should I write about?"

"Write me about beautiful things you see and hear," he told her, and she had done that. She visited the Philadelphia Art Museum. She went to Longwood Gardens. She went to concerts on campus and in Philadelphia. She wrote descriptions so vivid he could see the beauty, hear the music. Andrew could lose himself in her letters, and he read them over and over.

***

After he completed his thirteen month tour in Vietnam, Andrew had a few days of R & R in Hawaii and then spent the final months of his enlistment at the Marine Corps Air Station at Cherry Point, North Carolina. His family had twice driven down to spend weekends with him. He was glad of the time to adjust to being back stateside. In June, he was discharged and he and Mary made their first trip back to the lake to have time together.

Andrew had returned to West Chester State College in September and immersed himself in civilian life. Everything about his home state fascinated him. He saw it with new eyes; there was so much beauty. He painted constantly; watercolors, oils, sometimes acrylics. One of the reasons for this October trip was to help him recall the breathtaking beauty they had experienced on their first visit two years earlier. Andrew doubted they'd see the kind of sunset they had been treated to then, but he would never forget the color of the sky and the lake.

They arrived just after four with the rays of the sun already slanting low in the sky. The fall colors were at their height and even more brilliant than Andrew remembered. They unloaded the car and Andrew built a fire as Mary began preparations for dinner.

"I love the fragrance of burning hardwood," she said. "When we're able to buy a house, let's get one with a fireplace."

Andrew, down on one knee, looked up at her and smiled. "Is it too cool to eat on the porch?"

"I don't think it is. I'd like that." Dinner was bowls of homemade soup; they had brought it in a thermos and heated it. The evening was chilly; they kept their coats on as they snuggled together on the porch swing and watched the sun set, and Andrew had a feeling of complete happiness.

"Do you ever ..." he stopped, searching for words. "Do you ever have a moment that seems so perfect you wish you could somehow make time stop?"

"I think everyone does. I heard someone talk about 'taking a picture with your heart' when that happens; a way to perhaps hold onto a perfect memory."

"We recreated this one. This perfect memory, I mean. I thought of this when I was ... when I was away."

She kissed him. "Let's go inside. There's more to that memory we need to recreate."

***

Will he ever tell me about the months he spent in Vietnam? Andrew was sleeping; Mary touched his face softly. He seemed to have come home intact; he had picked up his life and was moving forward.

Yet there were times she would see something in his eyes; he seemed to be looking inward, or looking far beyond the horizon. Then he would turn back to her and smile, the clouds would clear and he would continue with what he had been doing: studying, or painting, or listening to music.

Give him time. In time he'll share that part of himself with me.

***

Andrew and Mary planned to be married in May, two weeks after she graduated as a Music Education Major. Max and Toni invited them to live at their house until Andrew finished his B.S. degree in Art Education while Mary completed her master's in music. They would use the room off the living room which was presently Max's study and Andrew's sometime studio; Andrew's room would become Max's study.

This arrangement would give the young couple more privacy, and they would begin to save money for a down payment on a home of their own. The plan was for them to find teaching positions the fall following graduation, hopefully at the same high school. He would then begin to work toward his graduate degree during the summers.

Andrew felt a sense of security with all these plans in place. He had written home and discussed all of this while he was in Vietnam ... another way to stay more connected to home. He'd been to war, but now that was done. He was looking ahead. He was focused on the future.

Except there were times Vietnam would interfere.

Jake had enlisted in the Army in the spring of 1966, even before he graduated from high school. Andrew had written him, *Why the Army?*

Why the Army? I'm aiming for Special Forces, bro. I told you I see myself as a career man. Don't you think I'll look great in a green beret?

Max wrote Andrew later that summer:

Jake is in his glory. Maybe he was born to serve in the armed forces; he has a special swagger when he wears his uniform. Maybe one or two people who are against the war frown when they seem him walking around town, but he ignores them. Most everybody sees him as a hero. And Jake being Jake, he basks in their attention.

Andrew had heard about the anti-war demonstrations while he was in Vietnam and Max's letters confirmed them. He knew there had been some even before he shipped out, and the demonstrations had escalated considerably. In West Chester they seemed to be non-existent, though he heard there had been a few peaceful demonstrations on campus.

Just before Andrew left Vietnam, Max wrote him:

You should know that there are stories circulating about anti-war protestors accosting returning servicemen. I felt I should tell you these seem to happen most often at airports, and I know when you get back you'll probably have to take a commercial flight out of San Francisco. That seems to be a target for some of the protestors.

Just be proud of your uniform and what you are doing and hold your head high. We'll be so relieved to have you back on U.S. soil before long.

Andrew had received some scornful looks and muttered comments in San Francisco but nobody accosted him. When he reached the base at Cherry Point he heard stories from other Marines who weren't so fortunate, but Andrew tried to put all of that out of his mind. He never talked about Vietnam at school and no one ever asked, but most people knew he had served in the Marines.

One late October day he arrived on campus to witness an anti-war demonstration. Several dozen students, some carrying signs, were listening to a student speaking through a bullhorn. This startled Andrew and made him uncomfortable. He started to walk past quickly, but instead he stopped, curious about the mindset of the listeners.

"Right on!" said one male student who was sporting longish hair and a droopy moustache. "Shit, I'm outa here. Canada, here I come. I could be drafted tomorrow. It's a bad war, and I don't want any part of it. No way, no how, and I don't see how anybody can live with himself who does."

Another guy, clean-shaven and short haired, interrupted. "Okay, protest all you want. I agree, this war is wrong. Only thing, don't give the guys who are fighting a hard time. They didn't start the damn war."

"Maybe not, but they're still fighting in it. You planning on signing up, hero?"

"I just might do it to show your sorry ass up, hippie. Coward."

Their friends separated them before it came to a showdown, and the bullhorn carrying student watched, annoyed that his impassioned speech was being totally ignored.

Shaken, Andrew continued to his class. The war showed no sign of ending. *Hell, were we fighting this war to win or not? I heard more times than I can count from the guys at Marble*

Mountain and from the grunts we picked up how frustrated they were. They felt like they were fighting the same battles in the exact same places over and over again. He took a deep breath and walked into his art class. *Don't think about it. I can't do anything about it anyway.*

He was painting a landscape … Lake Wallenpaupack with the fiery sunset he had remembered. He had sketched the cabin and trees against the background of sky and water when he and Mary were there during the summer, and added the fall colors after this most recent visit to the lake. The color of the cloudy sky and the lake weren't what he wanted yet.

Andrew had decided to give his painting a dreamy quality, not surreal but not quite realistic. He blurred the edges and softened the colors. He liked the effect, and his teacher, Isabel Jeanseau, complimented him. "Neo-impressionism, Andrew? I like where you are going with this." He smiled at her and turned back to his work.

Tucked away in his duffel bag were hundreds of sketches he had made of Vietnam. He had not taken a sketch pad with him, so these were made on envelopes he had unfolded, backs of some pages of letters he had received, scraps of paper he'd found at the base. He bought some paper at the PX, used some sheets of the stationery he had brought with him. Sketching the things he saw became important; it was a way to feel he had some control over what was happening to him. He had thought when he was home he'd turn his sketches into paintings.

But not now. Now I only want to paint the people and places I missed so much while I was away. He mixed colors, trying to recapture the exact shade of clouds and water that October evening two years earlier, and went into that inner place where he could find beauty and peace.

81

CHAPTER 8

Andrew worked on his first portrait of Mary, first sketching her indoors and out — seated in a chair, sitting on the floor with her arms wrapped around her knees, lying on the grass leaning on her elbows. But he finally decided to have her seated at the piano, turning to look at him with one arm on the music rack and the other hand resting on the keys.

"This is how I dreamed you, those few times I actually slept deeply enough to dream," he explained as he sketched.

"What do you mean?" she asked. A recording of Chopin's piano music was playing in the background. Watching Mary's face reflect her response to the sweeping phrases of the "Fantaisie Impromptu" inspired him, but also made him wonder once again if he would ever be able to truly capture everything he loved about her.

He sat back and put down his sketch pad. This was something he could share with her. "You didn't sleep in the Nam, not really. You dozed and catnapped, always on the alert, until after weeks of that exhaustion took over and you'd fall into a deep sleep."

Mary turned to listen to him, not commenting. *That's one thing I so love about her. She doesn't always feel the need to say anything, she just lets me talk.*

"When I dreamed, I always dreamed of you. And music. You playing piano. I could hear it in my head, very clearly. It was ..." he stopped, uncertain about continuing.

"I needed those dreams, but waking up afterward was kind of tough. I had to remember where I was." He picked up the sketch pad and she resumed the pose. He saw the glint of tears in her eyes.

He moved to her and kissed her. "I'm home now. I made it home."

***

Andrew felt like a person who had wandered long in the wilderness, looking for a way to quench his thirst for music. After he returned home, he listened to recordings almost non-stop when he wasn't listening to Mary play. He wasn't sure what he was seeking, but he hadn't found it yet; the long drought required something he couldn't explain.

Andrew needed art to survive. Art and music together made it possible for him to thrive. While he had been able to use his art to make sketches in Vietnam, the classical music he loved was not available to him. Even when he was in Cherry Point, he heard it rarely.

Music had brought him and Mary together. And listening to music while he painted freed Andrew; his desire for order caused him sometimes to paint too carefully, to be too aware of the technical aspects of composition and color. Music helped him find the sheer joy in painting; made it possible for him to lose himself in pursuing the beauty he knew was in the universe. With Mary, music, and painting, he could keep his memories of Vietnam and his worries about Jake at bay — most of the time.

***

He completed his sketch and began to paint; his easel was set up in the Morriseys' living room. Mary greeted him with a kiss and embrace as he arrived one morning about a week before the fall semester began.

"Before we start, there's something I want you to listen to." He could hear the excitement in her voice. "We're singing this music second semester, our choirs and the Temple University choirs, with the Philadelphia Orchestra and professional soloists."

They sat close together on the Morrisey's tapestry sofa, sharing a piano-vocal score. From the opening chords of the Brahms *Requiem*, Andrew knew he had finally found the music that would flood his soul and bring him the rest of the way back. The music affected him so powerfully that Andrew sometimes had to remind himself to breathe.

For the next weeks, when Andrew wasn't working on Mary's portrait they often sat at the piano going through the score, singing parts of the music they had found particularly beautiful. It was helpful to Andrew; he wondered what effect the two years of barely singing might have had. At first he seemed rusty but soon was able to use his voice as he had before he left.

"I guess I can still sing," he said after reading through one of the baritone solos in the piece for fun. "It feels good. Thanks for the help, sweetheart."

"Of course you can still sing. You sound great."

"Well, I don't know if I'd go that far. I'll settle for 'decent.'" he laughed.

***

Andrew's favorite art teacher, Isabel Jeanseau, was chair of the art department at West Chester State. She had grown up near Paris, studied at the famous École des Beaux-Arts and continued her study under the tutelage of several well-known European artists. She had begun to enjoy a strong reputation as an important emerging artist in Europe. In the United States she exhibited exclusively at the prestigious Wenders Gallery in Philadelphia. During a gala to celebrate her first one-woman show at the gallery, Isabel was approached by the president of West Chester State. He was enchanted by her art and her warm, accessible personality and convinced her to teach a summer oil painting workshop at the school.

For Isabel that summer was a revelation: she loved Americans, she found teaching to be immensely rewarding and decided that the experience of teaching others would only enhance her own work. She returned to France to complete her commitments there and was back as full time faculty at West Chester State for the spring semester. Petite and charming, Issy became very popular on campus with both faculty and students and was recognized as a nurturing and skillful teacher.

Andrew had been one of Issy's most promising students and she was happy to see him return after his two years in the military. He brought Mary's portrait for her to look at, and he watched closely as she examined it carefully.

"Your first attempt at a portrait, *non*?"

"Yes. I just wanted to see what I could do. I know it's far from what I'd like it to be."

"What do you see, Andrew? What do you learn about this young woman when you look at this painting?"

He took a deep breath and tried hard to be objective. Issy sometimes did this with her better students. Learn to assess your work. Try to see it as if you were looking at it for the first time.

"Well ... obviously, she's a musician. A pianist. She's very pretty." He stopped, took a harder look, and felt himself flush. "There's so much more to Mary than that, Issy."

"*Ah oui, bien sûr*. Painting someone you love is ... what is the word ... challenging, *mon ami*."

Andrew made himself look more closely. "I don't have her eyes right. And her mouth ... it's too ... prim. I wanted to paint the soft smile she always has. But instead she looks as if she has a bad taste in her mouth."

Issy's eyebrows went up. "I believe you wanted this to be perfect, *n'est-ce pas*? And so you painted very carefully. Very ... tightly. And technically, what you have done is good work."

She looked again at the painting, tipping her head first one way, then the other. "Perhaps with the next attempt to capture Mary, you will not think so much about creating the perfect likeness. What would you want us to know about Mary? What do you love most about her?"

"She's peaceful," he answered promptly.

"Andrew, study the paintings of Mary Cassatt. She captures beautifully the serenity you so love in your Mary. And when you paint your next portrait of her, perhaps use a palette knife or very large brushes held lightly in your hand; that will help you to be less rigid."

"I'll do that ... study Cassatt and use a palette knife, or maybe large brushes." He viewed his painting a little ruefully. "I guess this one goes in the trash."

Isabel's eyes widened. "*Bah non*, don't throw it away. Keep it. Then you can compare it when you paint the next portrait." She laughed, a sound that made Andrew think of tiny bells tinkling. "For a first effort there is much about it that is good. Her hands are lovely."

"Yes, well, there's a lot more to Mary than a pair of pretty hands. But okay, I'll stash it at home." He replaced the painting in the carrier bag and turned back to his lake landscape.

***

Even during his high school days Andrew had enjoyed attending the WCSC annual Christmas Carol Concert, and being part of it had been one of the best things about his freshman year. The procession into the Phillips Memorial Auditorium with the girls carrying lighted candles as they sang "O Come, All Ye Faithful" gave Andrew a feeling of warmth. He had missed this. He had missed celebrating Christmas with his family for two years. If Jake had been home, it would have been perfect.

After being away for two Christmases, Andrew enjoyed helping his parents decorate the house for the holiday. They always finished with the tree ... freshly cut at a nearby tree farm, wrestled into the house and decked with care with ornaments collected for years, some handmade by Andrew and Jake as kids.

Andrew saw tears in his mother's eyes as she took a slightly misshapen star Jake had made in second grade and found a special place for it on the tree. He put down the ornaments he was holding and wrapped his arms around her.

"He'll be okay, Mom. Jake can take care of himself. He's going to make it home."

She returned his warm hug. "I know. I keep telling myself that. And I'm so grateful you're standing right here this year. I can't tell you how wonderful it is to have you home."

Max made it a group hug as he said, "Last year was really tough, with both of you gone. At least we knew you were in

Hawaii and on your way back from Vietnam. It really helped when you called Christmas Eve."

He kissed Toni. "Andy's right, honey. Jake may be impulsive but he's not stupid, and he's had great training. Anyway, this is Andy's Christmas. Andy's and Mary's."

Toni picked up another ornament, this one a glass globe with a beautiful hand painted, almost abstract angel that Andrew had created and surprised her with that morning at breakfast. She touched it lovingly. "Next year Jake will be home to see this. And Andy and Mary will be married."

Andrew's throat constricted as he saw his mother lift her chin high. *God, think of all the mothers all over this country who don't have a son to share Christmas with ... a son who will never come home.* He put his arms around his mother again. "I love you so much, Mom."

Jake wasn't a great correspondent, but he did send brief notes home to let them know he was alive and fighting hard. Sometime in January he wrote to Andrew: *It seems as though I'll be able to be home for your wedding, so I can say pretty definitely that I'll be happy to be your best man, bro. No guarantees because of this war, but I'm sure as hell going to stay in one piece so I can do this for you and Mary.*

... stay in one piece ... With no warning, Vietnam came back to Andrew in full force. Everything. The mud, the unending rain, the heat, the searing sun that could make a man's brains boil. The sounds. Incoming and outgoing artillery. Warning sirens on the base. Screams of wounded and dying men. He shivered violently and started to hyperventilate.

He heard the whup-whup-whup of the Huey's blades above his head as he stood in the doorway supported by a harness, machine gun in hand. Bursts of flame illuminated the darkening sky. Beneath them, shapes showed briefly ... Marines, waiting at the designated pick up spot. Too close, the other forms. The enemy was too close.

They dropped low, the front of the aircraft dipping close to the ground. It rocked back on its tail, leveled, and the grunts pulled themselves on board as Andrew fired steadily at the NVA troops, keeping them at bay. Until ...

Andrew reached deep inside himself and managed to pull away from the precipice. Still shaking, he ran a hand over his face, scarcely feeling the cold sweat, and pushed himself to his feet. On leaden legs he slowly walked to the window and looked out at the peaceful night sky, the light from the house glowing softly in patches on the snow. Stars shone above the trees, winking down at him. He began to breathe more evenly and his heart stopped thudding in his chest.

He had wanted to close the door on the war, to move on, to forget it completely. But as long as Jake was there that was impossible.

Andrew went to the stereo and put on his favorite recording, moved the turntable arm to the second band:

Behold, all flesh is as the grass ...

***

Two months later, singing the Brahms *Requiem* with the Philadelphia Orchestra under the direction of Eugene Ormandy, Andrew had an experience he would never forget. In the midst of a choir of over two hundred voices, supported by one of the finest orchestras in the world and performing in Philadelphia's Academy of Music, Andrew felt his spirit soar. From beginning to end,

Brahms' music soothed his troubled spirit, calmed him, eased his pain.

When they completed the work, he felt the applause from the audience swell and fill the vast room, but in his head the strains of Brahms' majestic music resonated. When they left the stage he found Mary and saw on her face that she had shared the experience. They boarded the buses for the trip back to their campus, and surprisingly, the choir was quiet; all of them seemed awed by what they had just been part of. When they left the bus there was some quiet chatter and subdued laughter.

Andrew and Mary walked to his car with their arms around each other, still holding the moment. He turned her to face him; her lovely face glowed in the streetlight. "Stay with me tonight. We don't have to do anything, just be together. This is one of those moments … I never want this feeling to end." She nodded.

Their wedding was only two months away, and this would not be the first time she had stayed at the Camerons' overnight. She called her house and spoke briefly with her mother and joined Andy in what would be their bedroom after they were married; Mary had already brought some of her clothes to the Cameron home.

Andrew helped her remove her concert gown and she hung it up and went into the bathroom to change into a nightgown. He had his eyes closed when she joined him in bed, but he said, "I'm not asleep. Just drifting."

She snuggled up against him and he put an arm around her, but she surprised him. Mary had never initiated lovemaking, though she always responded warmly. But this night was different. This night she was his lover, touching and kissing him in ways she never had before, taking the lead, bringing them both to an ecstasy such as he had never known.

Afterward he tried to speak, but she pressed a finger to his lips and kissed his eyes, his cheek, his temple. He relaxed against her. He had never felt so cherished.

CHAPTER 9

Andrew looked at the Marine in dress blues who stared back at him from the full-length mirror in his parents' bedroom. He and Mary had discussed whether he should wear the uniform for their wedding and agreed he should, but he still felt uncomfortable. He was not a warrior.

Yet when Jake arrived two days before the wedding it convinced them both. "It's another way you're connected," Mary said. "You served honorably in the Marine Corps, Andy. And Jake is still serving. It's a way to show our support and love for him."

The soldier in question materialized beside the Marine in the mirror, proudly wearing his dress greens with corporal stripes on the sleeves and a surprising number of medals and ribbons on his chest. Jake was every inch the warrior. He had left as an eager eighteen-year-old boy seeking adventure. He was a seasoned military man now, and Andrew saw the knowledge in his eyes. *Vietnam changed you.*

"Ready, Marine?" Jake asked with a grin.

"Ready, sir." A snappy salute; Jake outranked him. Andrew had been discharged as a Lance Corporal.

The salute made Jake laugh; enlisted men didn't salute each other. But brothers could. "She's a wonderful woman, Andy. You did good."

"Do you have the ring?" The question just slipped out; of course he did.

"Right here." Jake patted his chest. "Let's do this, Lance Corporal Cameron."

Another salute. "Yes sir, Corporal Cameron."

They smiled at each other and without even thinking, did an about face and marched from the room in perfect step.

***

The First Presbyterian Church was filled with family and friends. Toni's sister Alice's entire family had made the trip from Tennessee. Max Cameron's father had traveled from Spokane for this wedding; he had come to think of Toni's sons as his grandsons. Morrisey family members from all over the state of Pennsylvania. Friends and teachers from Andrew's and Mary's high school and college days. Isabel Jeanseau was seated with Toni, Alice's family and Max's dad; she had become more than Andrew's art professor, she was also friend and mentor and a frequent dinner guest at the Camerons' table.

Andrew stood with Jake and his groomsmen, Max and his uncle Ben Rogers, both of them also in uniform — Ben had served in the Navy. Reflective organ music transitioned to the processional, and the quiet chatter stilled. Mary had selected Bach's "Jesu, Joy of Man's Desiring" for her processional music, and to Andrew it was a perfect choice — gently serene, it sounded like Mary. Two bridesmaids ... one a college friend, one a cousin of Mary's ... then her sister Leeanne, grown into a beautiful young woman of eighteen, the maid of honor. The music swelled in preparation for the bride's entrance.

Andrew had trouble breathing for a minute and a drop of sweat trickled down the back of his neck and into his uniform collar. *What am I doing here? I hardly know this person. And I'm*

93

about to join my life to hers forever? His heart was beating too fast. He felt his brother's steady hand press against his back, as if Jake sensed the moment of confusion, and it calmed him.

And then there was Mary, ethereal in a cloud of tulle, smiling at him, her eyes fixed on him with adoration and devotion, and his heart leapt for joy. Jim Morrisey kissed his daughter and placed her hand in Andrew's as he took his place next to her in front of the minister. Vows were spoken, rings exchanged, and they knelt for the blessing.

Members of the college choir sang "The Lord Bless You and Keep You" for their friends. Andrew and Mary were pronounced husband and wife and they kissed for a long moment. Leeanne handed Mary her bridal bouquet and adjusted the train on her gown, and the brilliant, vibrant strains of Widor's "Toccata" filled the church as the new Mr. and Mrs. Cameron made their way up the aisle.

***

The week-long honeymoon was a gift from the Morriseys, who offered to send them anywhere they wanted in the continental United States or Canada. Not to anyone's surprise they chose to drive to Lake Wallenpaupack. "Someday we want to buy a cabin there," Andrew explained. "It's our 'happy place.'"

For the first two days and nights they only left their bed when it was essential, immersed in their delight of each other. On the third day they finally dressed and Andrew volunteered to drive to the store to pick up a few food items. While at the store he used the pay phone to call home.

"I didn't think we'd hear from you," Toni laughed. "Aren't you still on cloud nine somewhere?"

"Just briefly zipped down to ground level to pick up milk and bread," Andrew replied, smiling. "We're great. This is perfect. My life is so good right now it's scary."

"Don't think like that. Just be grateful."

"I know. How's Jake doing? I'm glad he has a nice long leave. We really didn't have a chance to talk at all before the wedding."

She hesitated. "He's fine. He's ... been seeing a lot of Isabel."

"We must have a really bad connection, Mom. I thought I just heard you say my brother is getting it on with my art teacher."

Toni laughed. "Yes, that's exactly what I said. It's fine, Andy. Isabel seems to be everything Jake needs right now."

"Wow. Just ... wow."

"Well, when you think about it, they are really a lot alike. Isabel is an independent woman and something of a free spirit. Listening to her talk about traveling all over Europe and even to Greece and Norway when she was younger is fascinating."

"I guess ... and since he's not her student there shouldn't be any repercussions. Isabel is who she is, everybody knows that."

"They're not hiding anything. They aren't hurting anyone. They are, after all, consenting adults, and neither of them has expectations of this being some kind of commitment."

"You sound like a very modern woman, Mom. She's got to be in her thirties."

"She's thirty-three. Jake's not a child. I'm not sure he's even a young man any more. He seems incredibly mature. He says you grow up fast in Vietnam."

"He's got that right. Well, I'll tell Mary the gossip from the home front. We'll be back on Saturday."

Mary's eyes widened when Andrew told her about Jake and Issy. "Oh, my goodness."

"Yeah, that was kind of what I said. But Mom seems fine with this …uh … liaison. And she says they aren't hurting anyone. They're both single."

"Well, that's true, but I know one person who will have her nose out of joint."

"Leeanne," Andrew guessed.

"She was quite smitten with him. It was very evident at the rehearsal dinner."

"I didn't notice. I was too busy ogling the bride-to-be."

Mary laughed and kissed him. He returned the kiss, and it became apparent it was time to go back to bed. Andrew remembered to put the milk away.

***

"It just happened."

"Sure it did. C'mon, Jake, I know you better than that. Nothing ever 'just happens' with you."

"This did. I thought she was gorgeous. I knew she was your teacher."

Andrew felt a momentary flash of anger. *Jake, up to his old tricks.*

"That's it … right there. You couldn't paint with her, but you could …"

"Don't say that, Andy. Don't disrespect her that way. She thinks the world of you. I meant I figured her being your teacher made her doubly off limits. She's a colleague of Dad's." He looked into the beer he was drinking.

The brothers were relaxing at the kitchen table; Jake had commented one of the things he missed most about home was the kitchen. Airy and spacious, it was the heart of where the Cameron family lived, the place of breakfasts, lunches, late night snacks, sometimes just sitting around the table talking as they were now.

"It was an enchanted wedding, bro. Beautiful. Perfect. And the reception was great. Yeah, I probably drank too much, and maybe that's why I let my guard down. And I kid you not … *she* asked *me* to dance with her. How could I turn her down? The minute I took her in my arms … it was electric. Immediate. And the current flowed both ways. I'm not even sure … we talked, and the talk became full of double entendre. We both wanted it."

He took a sip of beer and Andrew felt his eyes widen. *Holy shit. Jake never sips a beer. He meant it; he <u>was</u> being cautious.*

"Anyway, the next morning she told me quite firmly it had been a mistake and that had to be the end of it, even though it had been a magical night for her. I told her no way in hell. She said she was sure my parents wouldn't approve." Jake tipped his chair back and ran a hand through his hair.

"So I went home and talked to them, and was completely honest, and … this just blew me away. Mom *knew*, and she thought it was great." He sat forward, the chair legs hitting the floor with a *thump*.

"She said she saw that Isabel and I … well, I'm all in this for now, but I am in no way interested in a long-term relationship. I can't be. Who knows what's going to happen to me? I'm about to join one of the most dangerous organizations on earth, the United States Army Special Forces. I'll be in training for months before I'm re-deployed. It's demanding and intense, and I have to focus on that."

Andrew nodded. He understood what his brother was saying: his life might be a very short one, and he wanted to seize the moment.

"The thing is, Isabel understands all that, and she knows what this is. It's an interlude. You know, we think of the French as a romantic people … I mean, people who tend to romanticize life. Isabel isn't like that. She's the most clear-eyed woman I've ever known. She sees life exactly the way it is. I've learned to do that as well."

"So you have Mom and Dad's blessing on this, um, interlude," Andrew surmised.

"Only after Isabel had also talked to them. In fact, …" he grinned and finished his beer. "… we had dinner with them that night. Drove to Longwood Gardens."

"Well, then, what can I say? I'm happy for you, Jake. She *is* a remarkable person."

"Oh, you have no idea, son."

Andrew held up a hand. "I don't want to hear that, and you don't want to tell me," he laughed.

"You know what she calls me? *Mon beau soldat* … 'my beautiful soldier.' She knows exactly who I am."

Jake opened another beer. "About that soldier part," he said, looking hard at Andrew.

"I don't like to talk about it," Andrew said, looking down at the table.

"I know you don't. But you need to. If you try to pretend it didn't happen, it's going to eat you up inside." He was thoughtful for a moment. "It's almost impossible to talk to somebody who wasn't there. But I've been there, and I'm going back. I'm sure that part is hard for you to understand."

"I wasn't on the ground," Andrew said, looking up at Jake. "What I saw of the war, I saw from the air. We own the air over there. For whatever good that does us."

"I know what you did. You had one of the most dangerous jobs … Andy, door gunners get killed. Too many of them. Being in the air didn't mean you weren't in combat. And you were at Marble Mountain when the base was attacked."

"Yes, I was. Two days after I arrived in country. Welcome to Vietnam," he smiled grimly. "It happened. I survived."

"You just encapsulated the whole goddam war into four words, Andy."

Andrew leaned forward. "The missions that meant something to me were when we were extracting men. Getting guys out of there, away from Charlie. I could focus on that. Taking them out of harm's way, at least for the moment." He opened a second beer as he said,

"I talked to grunts who had been on the ground. God, they were scared out of their wits, some of them. Some tried to pretend they weren't. And some really weren't. Those were the guys who scared me almost more than the Viet Cong and the NVA. They were … altered, somehow. Killing machines."

"Yes, we've all run into those guys. Who the hell knows what happened to them? I'm guessing some really bad shit." Jake looked off as if he were seeing something in the distance. "I was in command of a squad — ten men — and here's what I concentrated on. Trying to keep them alive, no matter what I had to do. And when I lost one, a little part of me died, too."

"I don't know how you did it, Jake. I could never do what you did."

"You know, when one of them went home in a box, I always wrote their family to tell them how valiantly their son had served their country. Even if it was a lie. Those families deserved to hear that. And I really knew those boys." He stopped for a minute and Andrew could see the pain in his eyes.

"Ed was from Iowa. All he wanted to do was go home and take over the family farm so his dad didn't have to work so hard. Pat was from Boston. His father was a mail carrier. Marv was from Philadelphia, he and I could talk about home."

Andrew sipped his beer, trying to frame the question he wanted to ask, finally just blurting it out: "Were you ever scared?"

"Sure I was." Jake leaned forward on one elbow, pointing at Andrew with his index finger as he held his beer bottle. "But here's something you need to know. Something I should tell you. Whenever I was scared, I remembered the worst scare of my life: the night we spent alone in that hunting cabin in a swamp in South Carolina. And you held me all night long. So when I was scared in Vietnam, I remembered the feeling of my big brother's arms around me, comforting me, keeping me safe."

Andrew couldn't hold back the tears, and Jake embraced him as they wept together.

Sketch #2
JAKE

I glanced over the list of family members we were expecting for Andy's and Mary's wedding. Aunt Alice's entire family: Alice and Ben and the four girls, Grace, Leslie, Louise and Stephanie. Grace's fiancé Sam Thomas. Grace's *fiancé*? She was barely eighteen. Mom explained Sam was a "college man" – well, okay, I guess. Max's father, Maxwell Cameron Sr.

"Where are they all staying?" I asked my mother.

"At the Holiday Inn – all except Max's dad, he's at a guest house in town."

"That took some arranging, I guess."

"Issy helped me with it."

"Issy?"

"Andy's art teacher. Well, she's more than that. She's become almost a part of the family."

I met Isabel at the rehearsal dinner at a private dining room on campus. She had made all those arrangements as well, and had planned and supervised the decorations.

I knew she was French: Isabel Jeanseau. Nobody had told me how stunning, youthful and chic she was. I couldn't keep myself from glancing at her amazing legs as she moved smoothly toward me on three-inch heels.

She smiled as she extended her hand: "And you are Jacob." Only she pronounced it *Zhah-kov*, and it made my head spin.

"Yes, I am," I said, returning her smile. "And you are my brother's art professor. What should I call you?"

She looked up at me – she was tiny, probably just over five feet – and replied, "Your family calls me Issy."

"I like Isabel," I told her. Slightly tilting her head, she looked at me again, and I nearly drowned in green eyes framed by impossibly long lashes that I thought were real.

She seemed to be sizing me up and liked what she saw. I sure knew I liked what *I* saw – those incredible eyes, fair skin, black hair that was short but stylish.

She stayed busy that whole evening, and I didn't have a chance to speak with her again; nor did I at the wedding. She sat with Mom and Aunt Alice's family, and Max's father. When the wedding party left to take pictures at Longwood Gardens ... something you just did when you were married in West Chester ... Isabel stayed behind, keeping the wedding guests watered and fed as they waited in the same dining hall room for the reception, now transformed into a fairyland, draped in strand after strand of twinkling white lights. It had an entirely different appearance from the Elizabethan decor of the night before.

I was aware of her the entire evening, and caught her glancing my way a number of times. Finally, after the bride and groom had departed and the music continued for the remaining guests, she walked up to me. Her scent reminded me of Mom's garden after a rain shower; clean and a little spicy.

"Dance with me, Jacob," she said. How could I say no?

Taking her in my arms was incredible. I heard bells, I swear to God I did. A joyful peal of bells. She fit perfectly against me, her head resting lightly on my chest when she wasn't looking up at me.

"Your uniform suits you well, Corporal Cameron," she smiled. "You wear it with just the right amount of pride. With elegance. I think you are a capable warrior, *non*?"

"I try to be," I replied, trying hard to come up with something witty and complimentary to say to her. *You're the greatest looking woman in the room*. No, not that. *Has anyone told you how beautiful your legs are? They make me want to …* nope, don't go there. Should I try my two years of high school French on her? Probably a really bad idea, even though I'd aced the classes. Maybe throw in a couple of French words?

"Your *ensemble* is lovely. You are *élégance* personified, Isabel." That wasn't awful. Not great, but not awful. I hoped I didn't sound like a real dope using the French, but her eyes sparkled when I said them.

"Ah, a lovely *compliment* from such a beautiful *jeune homme* for this older woman," Isabel laughed, and it was like tiny bells tinkling.

"I don't see you that way at all. I see before me a woman whose eyes shine with love of life, who could be any age." That was better.

She glanced at me with her head tipped to one side ... well, the word *coquette* came to mind. "Are you flirting with me, Jacob?"

"Would you mind if I were?"

"How could I object? You are very appealing. Young, yet the war has seasoned you. You've been away for many months, I believe."

And I'm lonely, and you're beautiful and I think generous, and God, I want you. "Yes. Two years. Nearly the entire time I was in country." *Stupid thing to say. I don't want pity.* "It was my choice. It made it possible for me to qualify to apply for Special Forces." *Now I sound like I'm bragging.*

"So you leave soon for more training, and then you will return to the war," she said, thinking this over. "You are an adventurer, I believe, Jacob. A man after my own heart."

"Are you? An adventurer?"

"*Mais oui.* I have not many opportunities for new adventures here in this quiet little town."

That comment was loaded. It was obvious what kind of adventure she was talking about.

"Nor do I," I said, trying hard to sound sophisticated and nonchalant.

She stretched up on tiptoe and put her mouth close to my ear. "Perhaps we could share an adventure, *mon beau soldat*."

Stupefied, all I could do was nod. She continued, speaking in a low, inviting voice. "I am walking out of here in ten minutes and will wait for you at my car for another fifteen minutes. Whether this adventure begins is up to you."

"Where are you parked? What are you driving?" I had to struggle to keep my voice from shaking.

A smile played about her lips. "A silver Porsche, first row in the parking lot." That would be impossible to miss. She said more loudly, "Thank you for dancing with me, Jacob," and turned to leave. I went to the punch bowl and drained two cups of punch, and watched as she said her goodbyes to my parents.

Seven minutes later I spoke to Max. "Dad, I think I'll wander around town for a bit. I may be late getting home; or if I run into friends I may stay out. You understand." He nodded and grinned.

I went out into the pleasant May evening, and my adventure was waiting for me.

Much, much later, her lips close to mine, Isabel breathed "*Je t'adore*, Jacob."

"*Je t'adore*, Isabel." I kissed her and said, "Should we be saying this to each other?"

"Jacob, you have been expressing love with your body. Why not speak it as well?"

My mind slipped sideways as I took her in my arms again.

CHAPTER 10

"Yes, lovely. See how much softer she is, how we don't just see her beauty, but we can feel it as you do." Issy looked closely at the portrait of Mary which Andrew was finishing.

"It's better. Her eyes still aren't right, but her mouth is softer." He wiped his hands on a paint-stained cloth. "I wonder how many times I'll have to paint Mary before I'm satisfied?"

"Andrew, you may never be completely satisfied with your portraits of Mary. But how delightful to continue to try to capture all that you love about her and share it with those who see your work." She smiled her encouragement.

Andrew had painted two more portraits of Mary, and while they were better than his first attempt, he still wasn't satisfied that her spirit shone through. He had used a palette knife as Issy suggested on the one he had just shown her. Rather than having Mary seated at the piano as he had done with the first, he painted her from the shoulders up, the edge of a page of music just visible; she had been holding it as she posed. There was a softness about her that he liked which he achieved with the palette knife.

He tried over-sized brushes for his third attempt, and while it still wasn't all that he wanted, it struck him as even more like Mary. He had removed the piano rack and she had her arms folded and was leaning forward against the piano, facing him. Both hands were visible; Andrew was good at hands. She was smiling more than in the first two, though her teeth weren't showing, but it was a happier version of Mary. In some ways, it was his favorite.

On their honeymoon, he sometimes sketched her with charcoal and used pastels to color his sketches. He liked the pastels. He liked the way they felt in his hand; it reminded him in a way of how he had liked to remove the paper from his crayons so he could feel the smooth waxy surface as he drew.

The pastels gave his work a soft, dreamy quality, and Mary was quite taken with these sketches. "I can't look like that. This woman has a … I don't know, an angelic quality about her. That is not me."

"It's how I see you. Well, it's very close to how I see you. I like trying to capture your serenity, Mary. You're my angel."

That was the beginning of Andrew's favorite nickname for his wife. "Angel, would you like me to run to the grocery store?" "Mary, angel, play this for me, will you?" Best of all, "My angel, my love, come to bed."

***

In late October of the following year Andrew received a letter:

October 28, 1969

Dear Andy,

Just wanted to let you know my good news, I'll have ten days leave right around Christmas! I do seem to be a lucky S.O.B. when it comes to my leave times. That swoop last Christmas didn't count … well, you know what that was, six of us itching to get the hell off base for a few hours. It's amazing how great the airborne guys can be ... they got us to Philly and then I grabbed a ride from there. A nice couple saw my uniform and asked where I was headed and told me to jump in. I think I told you all this last Christmas. Not everybody hates us; at least they didn't last year.

We're back at Ft. Benning, and it's unseasonably warm even for Georgia. In fact, it's downright hot, so I'll probably freeze when I get to Pennsylvania, and am I ever looking forward to that. My two years of high school French have been a plus. Since Vietnam was at one time a French colony, the Army wants me to learn to speak the language more fluently. Well, I'm not sure about how "fluent" I am, but I'm improving. It'll be fun to practice with Isabel. Yes, of course I'll spend some time with her while I'm home.

You know, Mom worried a lot about you while you were in Vietnam, more than she does about me. She knows I'm just crazy enough to take only the chances that make sense. She was concerned about her cautious son, the one who might hesitate for just a few seconds too long. She was relieved when you made it home. I can't tell you how proud I am that you served when I know how much you hated it. You're the hero, Andy. I'm just an airborne grunt who seems to always land on his feet.

I know a lot of people think Vietnam is a sorry excuse for a war and the climate and the conditions in country are beyond awful, and you'll probably think I'm crazy to say this, but I love what I'm doing. I've loved every minute of this training and have learned some pretty amazing things ... about the world, about war, and about myself. Here's the thing, bro. War is part of the history of the world. This war will eventually be over (believe it or not!), but there will be another, and then another. Mankind can't seem to help itself, as much as we say we want peace. And when there is war, there must be warriors. Some are foot soldiers, some are strong leaders. And some can handle necessary but difficult assignments that can help win a war. I'm eager to get back in country and use what I've learned.

Speaking of which, do you have any idea how much I loved those times in a high school football game when I'd see that open field that I knew I could run, mostly because I'd be doing something totally unexpected? I loved that. Faking a pass and then taking off, slipping past all those would-be tacklers. Daring to do what seemed impossible.

I guess I may be trying to find a way to recreate that thrill. I know what I don't want. I don't want to lead men again into an impossible battle and see them die on my watch. What I'll be doing is different. Each member of this force is a unit unto himself and will face situations that require an emotional and mental preparedness that's difficult to explain and more difficult to understand. It requires a commitment far beyond anything I've ever done. But I believe I am ready for this.

Man, this is the longest letter I've ever written in my life and there's some pretty deep stuff here. You may want to keep this one. I want to send Isabel a quick note before I turn in.

I'm really glad you didn't get killed in Vietnam. Yeah, I know, I'm an asshole, and you love me too.

Jake

Andrew sat with the letter in his hands, smiling as he re-read parts of it. It seemed like a lot of time had passed since Jake had begun his training for Special Forces. He'd been good about sending at least brief letters. Andrew noted the date; they hadn't heard from him for nearly two weeks.

But how great that he would be home for Christmas and would actually be with them for a while. Andrew was only a semester away from graduation, and Mary would graduate that same day, receiving her Master's in Music Education. Andrew's life was exactly on the track he had planned. It seemed that for the moment, Jake was in a good place as well. *Mom will love this. Her family together for a time, and at Christmas. Couldn't ask for much more.*

That wasn't true; they could all ask for more. They could ask for the war to end instead of intensifying; things seemed to be worse instead of better now that Nixon was President. The entire country had been shocked when LBJ opted not to run for re-election in 1968. Martin Luther King, Jr. had been assassinated in April of 1968 and Robert Kennedy was assassinated in June. There was rioting at the Democratic National Convention in Chicago that summer, and anti-war protests were appearing all over the country, not just on college campuses. The atmosphere everywhere was dark and unsettled.

Andrew's means of escape continued to be his art. He painted mostly landscapes, more impressionistic than ever, a dreaminess about them that reflected the world he wanted to see, not the one he was living in. Issy liked them; his style was very similar to hers, which showed strong influence of the early twentieth-century impressionists. He was continuing to use oils and brushes for the most part.

Issy and Andrew never discussed her relationship with Jake, even though the four of them had twice gone to Philadelphia together after Andrew and Mary had returned from their honeymoon. It was just easier for both teacher and student to keep the subject off limits when she was supervising his work. That following Christmas when Jake was able to sneak home for nearly a day, Issy had been with his family when Jake suddenly appeared, taking them all totally by surprise.

It was certainly no surprise that Jake and Isabel left the house for a time before dinner so they could be alone. Andrew wondered if he was the only family member who glanced at Isabel when Jake had burst through the door yelling "Mom! I'm home!" Issy's face was not the face of a woman in a casual relationship, though she quickly composed herself.

And now Jake's letter told him he had stayed in touch with Issy and was eager to see her again. *Maybe this is more than they'd like to think it is. If that's the case, what they are doing is really hard*, he thought. *She doesn't want him to feel any sense of commitment to her. She knows he has to focus on the task at hand. On staying alive. He doesn't want her to feel there's any future for them, because who the hell knows what could happen to him?*

Mary came in and Andrew smiled as he handed her the letter. "Jake's coming home for Christmas."

"Oh, Andy, that's wonderful. Toni will be thrilled." She sat down to read the letter, and he saw her eyes widen as she reached the part about Isabel. She didn't comment until she'd finished, folded the letter and handed it back to Andrew.

"He's still in touch with Issy," she said, frowning a little. "Do you think there's more to this relationship than we're aware of?"

"Yes, I do. Well, as we've all said, they are consenting adults. And they certainly have an … um, a strong connection."

Mary laughed. "I guess that's one way to put it. He doesn't say when he'll be home."

"He probably didn't have the exact dates. He'll let us know when he has more information."

As it happened, Jake would arrive in West Chester on December 17, and to their joy, his leave had been extended to three weeks. He would be home over Christmas and New Year's, and the Camerons wanted to make the most of it.

For Andrew, the Christmas season began with the Christmas Carol Concert at the college. Mary, who had performed this concert for six years, and Andrew, who had sung in it for four of those years with her, would be part of this beloved school tradition for the last time. It took place before Jake's return but Toni and Max were in the audience again, and Isabel was on the decorating committee as she had been since she first joined the college faculty.

The candles burned especially bright during the processional, and each of the pieces they sang seemed unusually poignant to Andrew. He attributed his emotional response to the music to the thought that these were songs he probably would never sing again, and certainly this was an experience he and Mary would never share again, at least not as performers.

Mary held tight to his arm as they walked to the dining hall for The White Supper, the traditional meal for the performers after the concert. "What a special night for us, Andy. I remember our first Christmas Carol Concert and how much we loved being part of this."

She stopped and turned to face him. "Those two years you were away ... I almost didn't come. I thought about pretending I was sick, just so I wouldn't have to be here. Maybe I shouldn't be telling you this, but thinking of you in Vietnam at Christmas was so painful. I know you missed being home, and my heart ached for you more than I can tell you."

He gently patted the tears from her cheeks. "I'm home now, Mary. I'm not going anywhere. And I'm glad you told me. I want us to always tell each other everything, even the bad things."

She looked at him expectantly and he knew exactly what she was thinking, that he had never really talked to her about his experiences in Vietnam ... and it scared her more than a little.

"Yes, the time will come when I'll talk more about Vietnam. I really don't want to think too much about it, especially since Jake is going back. And especially not now. Let's just all of us make this Christmas the best we've ever had."

Toni and Andrew met Jake's plane at the Philadelphia airport. It was the first time they had seen him in his Special Forces uniform, and his pride in being a Green Beret was evident. They talked Christmas memories and plans all the way back home. Max and Mary had finished all the dinner preparations, and they had some time to talk before dinner. Toni had invited Issy, but she said, "*Non, non*, Toni. This is family time for you with your son. There will be time for Jacob to see me if he wishes. He will be here for a while, *n'est pas?*"

After dinner Toni said to Jake, "I know Isabel is home this evening. Why don't you run over there and spend some time with her?"

"Are you sure you won't mind?"

"Well, I certainly mind," Andrew blustered, and they all looked at him in amazement.

He burst out laughing and tossed his car keys to his brother. "Get out of here. Just be sure to get home in time for breakfast Christmas morning."

Jake managed to spend more time at home than at Issy's, and she was always included in the Camerons' plans. Mary and Andrew and Isabel and Jake drove to Philadelphia a few days after his arrival to Christmas shop and to run an errand. Both Issy and Andrew had paintings on display in a private gallery, and the owner, Evelyn Wenders, had contacted Isabel and told her she had sold one of each of their works, so this was a trip to pick up checks.

"You sold the fjord? That was my favorite." Jake was frowning until Isabel showed him the check. "Holy shit, *ma belle*."

"You had a favorite painting?" Andrew was having a hard time wrapping his mind around this. Mary elbowed him in the ribs.

"What do you say ... 'not too grimy'?" Sometimes Isabel's attempt at American idioms could be vastly entertaining. The painting had sold for three thousand dollars.

"Close enough," laughed Jake.

Andrew was thrilled. He had sold a painting of the Brandywine Creek for thirteen hundred and fifty dollars. It was painted from the bench he and Mary had been seated on when they talked about him enlisting in the Marine Corps, and he had tried to recapture all the emotions of that evening. Over thirteen hundred dollars, and he hadn't yet graduated from art school. *Not bad*, he thought, and Mary gasped when she looked at the sum.

"Found money," she said. "What are you going to do with it?" She knew the answer and said with him, "Put it into the savings account."

Jake said to Isabel, "And there's the difference between the Cameron brothers in a nutshell. I'd go to the Caribbean. No, I'd take you to Scandinavia so you could paint another fjord for me."

It was a beautiful Christmas season for the Camerons, and Isabel was nearly always with them. Jake insisted, and Toni often said, "You're family, Issy. You were family even before you met Jacob, you know that."

115

They created memories throughout Jake's time at home. Andrew kept his sketch pad handy and did quick sketches of scenes he wanted always to remember: Jake in the kitchen with their mother, chopping vegetables for the stuffing; Jake and their dad side by side on the sofa, laughing at "The Carol Burnett Show"; Jake and Mary, deep in conversation about Andrew's portrait of her which hung over the piano; Jake kissing Issy under the mistletoe with a tenderness Andrew had never seen before.

After Christmas, Jake and Isabel stole away for three days to a resort in the Poconos. They said they were going skiing; the Camerons doubted they ever made it to the slopes, but they accepted the pretense. On January 6 they took two cars to the airport so they could all see him off, and they tried to match their warrior's courage when they said goodbye.

He spoke quietly to each of them as he embraced them, and when he came to his brother Jake said, "Take care of Mom and Dad for me. Just like you used to take care of me for Mom. I couldn't have a better big brother. Whatever good I may do in this life, you're a part of. I love you, Andy."

Andrew's voice shook but he managed to control himself. "I love you, Jake." He smiled and added, "Try not to do too much broken-field running over there, kid." The men embraced for a long moment.

And then Jacob was gone.

CHAPTER 11

In May, the Camerons and Morriseys sat together and watched as Mary received her Master of Science in Music Education and Andrew his Bachelor of Science in Art Education, and they celebrated with dinner at Longwood Gardens, Mary's sister Leeanne and Isabel joining them. It was a pleasant but somewhat subdued party. Jake was on all their minds; they had heard very little from him since he had returned to Vietnam.

Andrew's dream that he and Mary would teach together came true. They were both hired at Kennett High School in nearby Kennett Square. They continued to live with Toni and Max, hoping to find a house of their own in the next couple of years.

During the summer the young Camerons made a road trip to Canada; first to Niagara Falls for two days, then to Montreal for three. They went to the Cave of the Winds beneath the Falls, where they truly experienced its power as the water rushed past the awestruck onlookers. They were thankful for the slickers and rain hats that had been provided, as the spray was incessant from the vast curtain of water that roared past the opening in the cliff, almost deafening the crowd. When they returned to their hotel Andrew made sketches. He wanted to paint this remarkable natural wonder.

Andrew and Mary found Montreal a charming city that gave them a sense of being in Europe. They heard French spoken everywhere and strolled through the old part of the city, admiring the architecture from a time far in the past. Listening to the French they heard so frequently they thought of Isabel, who was spending her summer in Europe and Scandinavia.

"Wouldn't it be lovely if Issy were here to translate?" Andrew commented.

"Yes, but she told us the French spoken here can be different from what we would hear if we had gone to Paris," laughed Mary.

At times they would hear a distinctively American accent, a Southern drawl or a turn of phrase straight out of Brooklyn, and noticed the speakers were sometimes young men of their own age; and they wondered if these were American expatriates who had fled to Canada to avoid being drafted. By then, this choice had been made by tens of thousands and the exodus continued.

It was something Andrew had never considered doing, but after his experience in Vietnam he was not entirely unsympathetic. *But how can they really think it's worth it, giving up their American citizenship?*

Refreshed by their trip, they looked forward to the beginning of the school year and their new teaching positions. Andrew found he liked teaching. He liked most of the students, though he would become annoyed with those who didn't try. He especially liked being in the same building with Mary. They used the same car, and when she had after school rehearsals he would stay in his art room and paint.

He continued to work on landscapes, using some of the vistas from the drive they had taken, also doing several paintings of Niagara Falls. He especially enjoyed painting the Falls, often using a palette knife — he could lose himself in the misty, dreamy quality they had evoked in him. A world of his own, where the ugliness of what was happening in the real world — and sometimes in his dreams — couldn't interfere.

They were above the jungle; it was dusk, and they could almost see where they were headed, dropping into a landing zone to insert men. A back-up team. It seemed quiet as they dropped through the triple canopy, but as they reached the floor of the jungle, all hell broke loose. Immediately Andrew and the crew chief opened fire with their M-60s ...

"Andy, wake up, you're having a nightmare." Mary was shaking him, and he started to fight her off. Slowly the jungle and the sound of the rotors receded. She pulled him close, kissing his lips, his eyes, pressing his face to her breast. "What were you dreaming?"

He started to tell her, but the words stuck in his throat. *Why burden her with this? It wasn't her war.* "Just ... it wasn't anything. I ... I don't really remember." *Liar.*

She held him close and he relaxed. "When are you going to talk to me, my love?" she said softly.

"It's nothing, Mary. Let's get back to sleep." But they both lay awake for long minutes; he could sense her hurt. *You just don't need to hear this, Mary.*

***

Issy stopped by some of the afternoons when Andrew stayed to paint, to watch him and to chat. When Mary's rehearsal was finished the three of them would go out to dinner. None of them had heard much from Jake, but they decided that wasn't surprising. They often talked about him, and Isabel commented on something he had said to her about what his mission might include as a member of the Special Forces.

"He told me he has to be prepared to do things that he might find extremely difficult because they are not ... because they could be against his beliefs about right and wrong, but he must focus on the job at hand no matter how distasteful it might be."

Andrew commented, "Yes, I understood that when he applied for Special Forces." He said seriously, "I pray for him all the time. And I know Mary and my parents do as well."

Isabel glanced at Andrew. "You look tired, *mon ami*."

"Insomnia," Mary commented. "He has medication but he keeps refusing to take it."

"*Pourquoi*, Andrew? Staying awake won't change the events of the future. You have no control over them."

"My sweet husband has always been a worrier."

"I read someplace that one who worries doubts God, Andrew. It would surprise me to learn that of you." Isabel touched his arm lightly. "What is going to happen will happen, and all your worrying cannot change that."

Andrew didn't reply. *I wish I didn't know so much about what goes on over there*, he thought.

They spent Christmas with Mary's family. It helped not to be in their house, where Jake's presence had been so much a part of their Christmas the year before. It was cold and snowy, and Christmas night when they went home Andrew stayed outside for a few minutes.

He looked up at the stars and said a prayer for his brother. *Please, God, keep him safe*. He was suddenly overwhelmed by a crushing sadness and found himself weeping almost uncontrollably.

What the hell is the matter with me? He took a long, shuddering breath and composed himself.

He looked at the stars again, really seeing them, seeing the beauty of the starry, snowy night all around him. A sudden gust of wind touched his cheek, almost as if from the other side of the world, Jake had felt his concern and was letting him know he was okay.

Andrew took a deep breath, looked around again at the beauty of his surroundings, and went inside.

CHAPTER 12 (January 1971)

He heard the whup-whup-whup of the Huey's blades above his head as he stood in the doorway supported by a harness, machine gun in hand. Bursts of flame illuminated the darkening sky. Beneath them, shapes showed briefly ... Marines, waiting at the designated pick up spot. Too close, the other forms. The enemy was too close.

They dropped low, the front of the aircraft dipping close to the ground. It rocked back on its tail, leveled, and the grunts pulled themselves on board as Andrew fired steadily at the enemy, keeping him at bay. He and the other door gunner yelled at the pilot that they were loaded, they were clear. Andrew kept firing, waiting for the helicopter to rise. The enemy kept coming, emerging from the woods, getting closer and closer. Andrew cut one down, then another. A third was almost at the aircraft when it started to rise, and Andrew aimed directly into his face ... but it wasn't an NVA.

It was Jake.

Andrew sat up abruptly, not even aware he had cried out, shaking uncontrollably, sweat pouring from his body. He could still smell the fear coming from the men on the aircraft, taste the acrid odor of the machine gun and feel the heat from the barrel in his hands.

"Andy, darling, wake up, you're having a nightmare." Mary wrapped her arms around him and rocked him gently, using the sheet to blot the sweat.

"God, Mary, something's happened to Jake. Something ..." The muscles around his throat and midsection constricted as he struggled to breathe. Mary held him, rubbing his back, and he began to relax enough to gasp for air.

"It was a nightmare, Andy. Just a terrible nightmare." She soothed him, but he shook his head.

"Something's happened to Jake. I know it. I *saw* him."

"Andrew, are you all right?" Toni, tapping at their door.

"He had a bad dream, Toni. It's okay," Mary responded.

Andrew took deep breaths, trying to convince his racing heart to slow. Maybe Mary was right. He hadn't meant to wake up the entire house. He dropped his head in his hands, trying to wipe the sounds, smells and sights from his mind.

Mary went into the bathroom and returned with a washcloth dampened with cool water, and she gently wiped his face and neck. "Should I get you something to drink? Maybe a sleeping pill?"

"Yes, I think I will take one. I'll be groggy at school, but I have to get some sleep."

Lying in her arms, his face against her breast, her hands gently stroking his shoulders, he managed to relax enough to doze off. The alarm sounded much too quickly.

He was jumpy the rest of the day, sure he'd be called at any minute to the office to be told that he needed to go home to hear the awful news that Jake was dead. But the day ended and he and Mary went home to a pleasant dinner with Toni and Max, though Andrew remained edgy.

The evening passed without any bad news, and he began to relax. *Maybe Mary was right; just an awful nightmare. I should try to put it out of my mind.*

The ringing of the phone awakened all of them at four a.m. Andrew ran into the kitchen, picked it up and realized immediately he was speaking with a representative of the military. He was gripped with fear so powerful he could hardly breathe. *Please, no. But wait ... a phone call. That means not dead, but wounded.* He was almost dizzy with relief. The caller asked him to identify himself.

"Lance Corporal Andrew Cameron, United States Marine Corps." His was the name Jake had left to be notified in the event of death or injury while deployed. The brothers had agreed to handle it this way.

"Your brother, Sergeant Jacob Cameron, sustained serious injuries in an accident while on a mission in country. He suffered a head injury and a simple fracture of his left leg, and is being transported to Walter Reed Hospital." *That's a good sign. They're bringing him home; he's strong enough to make that long trip.*

"Can you tell me the extent of his head injury?" By now his parents and his wife were gathered around the phone, listening, scarcely breathing.

"The information I have is that he had not regained consciousness when being prepared for transport, but his vital signs were good. I have a number you can contact for additional details."

Andrew wrote down the number. "Thank you for contacting us. Do you know when this accident occurred?" He wanted to know. *It could have been when I dreamed about Jake. Maybe earlier, but I doubt it. They make these calls as quickly as they can.*

"I regret that I don't have that information. You can probably get it from the doctors when you get to the hospital."

Andrew's hand was shaking as he hung up the phone. He put his arms around his mother and looked into her fear-stricken eyes as he said gently, "He's alive, but seriously injured. He was in an accident, but he's en route to Walter Reed Hospital."

Max exploded with relief, "That's good. He's strong enough to handle that long flight. What were you told about his head injury?"

"He's unconscious. He also has a broken leg. But I was told 'simple fracture,' that's good news." Andrew felt as if he were drifting. His nightmare had come true, but it wasn't as bad as he had feared. *Jake is alive.*

Andrew called the number he had been given, and after a short wait was told Jacob's flight was expected to arrive at Andrews Air Force Base near Washington, D.C. between six and eight p.m. that evening.

He and Max both kicked into action. They could drive down. "We can leave early afternoon and get there in plenty of time to check into a hotel and be at the hospital by six."

Toni, who had remained silent and still until this moment, suddenly seemed to regain her strength as she asked, "Max, do you really want to drive? We could see if the Army would provide us transportation. I think they sometimes do that for families of wounded soldiers."

"No, I want to drive. It will give me something to concentrate on, and we'll have a car available to us."

"I'll go to the school early and let them know what's happened. I think they may need a long-term substitute for you," Mary said to Andrew.

"You're coming with us, aren't you?" Andrew put his arms around his wife. "I need you right now more than I ever have."

She gently laid a hand on his face and looked into his eyes and he grew calmer. "Of course I am. I'll only be gone long enough to notify them. Two hours at most. I'll be back by nine-thirty or ten, and I can pack then."

Toni spoke again, "Somebody should call Isabel." Mary volunteered to make the call and went upstairs to Max's study where she would have some privacy on the extension.

They now had a plan, and Max said, "We should all try to get some sleep. I think the next few days are going to be very difficult."

They agreed, and after a long hug among the three of them — Jake's brother and parents — went to bed, though no one in the house would sleep. When Mary returned to Andrew after her phone call to Isabel, she put her arms around him and he rested his head against her breast.

"You knew," she whispered in wonderment. "My dearest love. I understand more than ever the kind of bond you and Jacob have. You knew."

"He's alive, Mary. I was so afraid he was dead."

Head injury. Not conscious. What will he have left when he opens his eyes? It could be very bad.

But he's alive.

CHAPTER 13

Before they left to drive to D.C., Mary said quietly to Andrew, "You and your mother should sit together. I'll sit up front with Max and help navigate." Andrew nodded, he was sure it was the best choice. Mother and son held each other sometimes, sometimes just held hands, both focused on the boy they so loved, and they drew strength and comfort from each other.

When they arrived they were escorted to a small private waiting room, quiet and pleasant, furniture arranged in a circle. Mary sat next to Andrew and put a hand on his shoulder as he leaned forward, his fingers drumming on the arm of his chair. Max had an arm around Toni as they sat together on a loveseat. They waited anxiously for Jake's physician, Major William Forrester, hoping to be allowed to see the patient.

He entered the room and they all stood, almost as if the presence of a Major required the family of his new patient to come to attention. He motioned for them to be seated, and sat comfortably in the circle to talk to them. *He has kind eyes*, Andrew thought. Meticulously groomed, mid-forties, an athletic build and pleasant face. He shook hands with each of them and asked if they'd like coffee or a soft drink.

"Can we see Jake?" Toni asked.

"Yes, you certainly can. Right now he's sleeping. He's been sedated because of the pain from his head wound, but also from his leg and his back, which was pretty badly bruised. I know you just want to have a look at him so you know he's really here and he's safe."

There was a subtle shift in the atmosphere in the room; everyone relaxed slightly.

"So he's regained consciousness?" Andrew leaned forward again.

"He regained consciousness sometime after he was airborne. He was disoriented, though, and seemed confused. The attending physician talked with him for a while and I'm happy to report your soldier was able to converse. That's great news."

Toni was crying when she asked, "What did he say?"

Dr. Forrester opened the file he was holding. "When asked if he knew where he was, he replied 'It feels like I'm on a plane.' Then he told them his head was really hurting him and added a few expletives."

There were smiles and audible sighs of relief. Dr. Forrester raised his hand.

"He does seem to be experiencing post-traumatic amnesia, not uncommon after a severe blow to the head that resulted in loss of consciousness for a fairly long period of time."

Andrew interrupted. "How long?'

"About sixteen hours." He looked at the file again. "He knew Nixon is president but he thought it was still 1970, an understandable confusion. However, when asked to identify himself, he was unable to provide his name and was given that information by the attending physician."

"*He didn't know his own name?*" Andrew's voice rose sharply.

"Not at that moment, no. It's not unusual," Dr. Forrester repeated. "I'm going to suggest you look in on him briefly and then have dinner and get a good night's sleep, and come back in the morning when you can spend more time with him."

"You said 'head wound.' Was his skull fractured?" asked Toni.

"No, but he had a deep scalp wound on the back of his head which bled profusely, which is common with scalp wounds. At the field hospital the back of his head was shaved so the wound could be properly cleansed and closed, so his head is bandaged. Since he arrived here it has been re-dressed."

"What about his leg?" Max wanted to know.

"Simple fracture; it was set before he was boarded for transport and should heal fairly quickly. We've given him a new cast since he arrived here. He was fortunate. With any luck and no complications it should heal within six to eight weeks."

"We were told he was injured in an accident, but not exactly what happened," Andrew said.

"Yes, the helicopter he was in crashed."

"Oh, my God. Was there a fire? Where did it happen?" asked Andrew. *Please don't let him be burned. Please.* He shuddered.

"No fire, apparently. I don't know exactly; somewhere near the Vietnamese-Cambodian border, I believe. Those Special Ops guys keep a tight lid on their operations. You know that." He looked at Andrew, who nodded. "He was airlifted pretty quickly, from what I've been told. A chopper which was behind them set down and took him to the team's camp, and he was picked up there by a Dust-Off — a medical helicopter — and taken to the hospital in Saigon. His vital signs were good and his leg was put in a cast. He was unconscious, but it was apparent he was not in a deep coma."

Toni interjected. "What does that mean?"

"The corneal test performed indicated there was no damage to the brain stem, and his pupils showed some reaction to light. He

129

was breathing normally by the time he reached the field hospital, and wasn't showing any abnormal body movements. They kept thinking he'd wake up, but after twelve hours the decision was made to send him home for more sophisticated testing.

"Fortunately, there was a plane scheduled to leave and there was space for him on it. He regained consciousness before they landed in Japan, but at that point it seemed a better choice to just bring him here rather than taking him off the aircraft."

Toni smiled gratefully at the Major. "Bless whoever it was that made that decision. I just want to see Jacob."

Dr. Forrester went with them to the Intensive Care Unit and explained hospital rules: only two visitors at a time while patients were being cared for in this unit. Max and Toni went in first while Andrew and Mary waited outside. Toni was crying quietly when she and Max came back into the hall after a few moments.

"Mom?" said Andrew.

"I just wanted to hug him, but I understood I couldn't disturb him. His face is pretty banged up, Andy, be prepared. But he's in one piece. And he's here and he's safe."

Andrew and Mary went into the room. Jake looked peaceful. His face was bruised and slightly swollen, and his head was bandaged. There were wires attached to a heart monitor, more attached to a brain monitor, and an IV bag which the nurse explained was providing liquids so he wouldn't become dehydrated. He was also receiving antibiotics and pain medication. Andrew felt tears crowd his throat and understood Toni's urge to hug Jake. Mary put her arms around her husband and rested her head on his shoulder.

They stayed only briefly and then went back to the hotel and ordered room service. It was a quiet dinner; each of them lost in their own thoughts. They went to bed early, exhausted from stress and lack of sleep, and managed to get a decent night's rest.

Dr. Forrester met them the next morning outside Jake's room in the ICU. "He's still experiencing amnesia. You should identify yourselves to him when you go in, and don't be alarmed if he seems confused. He's aware his family is here to see him. And he understands that his name is Jacob Cameron, and he's a sergeant in the United States Army."

It seemed awkward to go into the room two at a time as they had the evening before, but they understood hospitals have rules for a reason. Andrew and Mary once again waited outside the room for several minutes while Toni and Max went in.

Toni was wiping her eyes when they walked into the hall. "He was sweet, but it was obvious he didn't know us," she said. "He asked what he should call us and we said whatever he was comfortable with. So he chose Toni and Max." She swallowed. "That's okay. He wanted to know if we'd flown to D.C. and Max said, 'no, we drove,' and he asked how long it took."

"He asked us if it was snowing outside. He said he'd been told it was January and he was near Washington, so he thought there might be snow." Max rubbed his face under his eyes, blinking hard. "He didn't know it was January."

Toni commented, her voice shaking, "I don't think he'll know you, so don't try to touch him. I did that and ..." she had to stop. "It upset him. He flinched."

They were all quiet for a few minutes, absorbing this information. They knew him. He did not know them. He saw them as strangers, people he'd never seen before.

"We should go in," said Mary, and holding Andrew's hand, she let him take the lead into the room.

Jake was propped up in the bed, pillows supporting his injured leg. He was pale but alert and looked hard at Andrew. "I know you," he said slowly. "You have to be my brother. Older or younger?" His speech sounded slightly slurred, and it seemed to take him a few minutes to put his thoughts together

Trying to keep it light so he wouldn't get too emotional, Andrew replied, "I'm your big brother, Jake. And don't you ever forget it." Mary squeezed his arm and Andrew almost panicked. *Why the hell did I use the word "forget"?*

Jake said softly, "I won't, I promise. We look a lot alike, don't we?"

Andrew inhaled almost audibly. "We always have. People used to ask Mom if we were twins."

Jake looked inquiringly at Mary. "I'm Andy's wife, Jake. I'm Mary."

He thought for a moment. "Where'd you guys … have to drive from … to get here?"

"West Chester, Pennsylvania. It's only about three hours away. Nice of the Army to deposit you nearby." Andrew's lame joke fell flat. *God, I am so screwing this up,* he thought.

"They said I was in Vietnam on some kind of a mission. I don't remember that," Jake mused aloud. "In fact … I don't remember … much of anything."

"Don't worry about it, Jake," said Andrew quickly. "Dr. Forrester tells us it's not unusual after a head injury."

"He's a good guy. All the people here are good." He smiled at Mary. "You remind me of one of the nurses. Her name is A …Am … Amy. She is really sweet."

Andrew saw a shadow cross Jake's face as he closed his eyes and tried to shift his position. "You're tired, I think. We should go and let you get some rest."

132

Jake opened his eyes. "Yeah, I am pretty tired, and my head … my head really hurts a lot." His eyes seemed to drift closed, and he made himself open them again. "I'm glad … you came to see me. Will you come back?" He sounded far away, almost dreamy.

Mary forgot herself and touched his hand lightly, but Jake didn't react. "Of course we will. We'll ask Dr. Forrester when he thinks would be a good time. We're not far away, Jake."

In the hall the family conferred. "What did he say to you?" Toni asked.

"Not much. I think he's in a lot of pain from his injuries," Mary replied.

"Yes, but he commented he has a pretty nurse," Andrew said. "Same old Jake. I guess that's a good sign." He sighed. "He seemed to have a little trouble talking."

"Yes, we noticed that, too. Probably from the pain, and maybe from the medication," Max said. Mary put her arms around Toni, who returned the embrace.

They stood silently for a minute, and Andrew said, "It was so great to see him. He'll get better."

Max put an arm around Toni's shoulders as they started to walk down the hall. Andrew stood where he was, staring at the door to Jake's room, reluctant to leave.

Mary took his hand. "It will be better next time we're here," she said.

CHAPTER 14

They had a chance to see Dr. Forrester later that morning and asked about coming back in the afternoon.

"I think Jake needs to rest. He's still in a considerable amount of pain, and we're going to keep him sedated so he'll be more comfortable. How was your visit this morning?"

Max answered, "It was good to see him. But you were right; he didn't recognize any of us. Well, possibly Andy. And we could tell he was in a lot of pain. Is it okay if we plan to come back next weekend?"

"Definitely. He should be better. We'll probably have him in a private room and all four of you will be able to spend time with him together."

Andrew asked, "How come he can talk pretty well but he can't even remember his own name?"

Dr. Forrester explained, "Traumatic brain injuries are all different. Different parts of the brain control different functions, even different memories. Jake's cognitive skills … his ability to speak, for example … seem to be pretty much intact. He's very lucky. Temporary memory loss isn't unusual with this type of injury. He should be better within a week or so."

Andrew had heard him say this before, but he wasn't satisfied. "What if he isn't?"

"It's hard to say how long it might take. We don't have the ability to see what's exactly happened to Jake's brain."

Dr. Forrester called their house during the week and asked if they had some photos of Jake as a little boy they could bring with them on their next visit. "I don't want to alarm you, but the amnesia may be more extensive than just post-trauma. Let's see if we can provide some 'triggers' – visual aids that might help him recall more about who he is."

Toni went to the library the day after that phone call and read everything she could find about amnesia. She came home and went into her bedroom and closed the door, and Max followed her in. It was distressing to Andrew and Mary to hear her weeping.

Andrew leaned against the wall and closed his eyes. *This is a nightmare. I just want to wake up.* Max finally opened the door for Andrew and Mary to come in.

"I keep telling your mother not to borrow trouble, but she insists she wants to prepare for the worst."

"Dr. Forrester's request scared me. I think he's hinting that Jake has retrograde amnesia, and he may need a long time to remember anything about his life before he was injured. I hope I'm wrong." Toni wiped her eyes and sighed deeply.

Andrew's knees buckled and he sat down abruptly on the bed beside his mother. "I've never even heard of that."

"Neither had I. I never knew there were different kinds of amnesia. That's why I spent the day at the library, reading."

"It could be so much worse, Mom. He could have come home in a box," Andrew was speaking as much to himself as to his mother.

"Oh, absolutely. I understand that. I'm so grateful he really wasn't severely injured physically. Men come back missing arms and legs. Confined to a wheelchair for life. Badly burned. It seems Jake was spared that kind of fate, and I am so grateful. It's just a … I guess it's something we'll have to get used to."

135

Max gently admonished her, "Toni, please don't put the cart before the horse. We don't know anything for sure yet. Let's just enjoy our time with Jake, try to let him know how much we love him, and take it a week at a time."

They were quiet, absorbing what they'd just learned. Mary said, "We need food. Andy, come help me, let's fix something for dinner." Too many scenarios were playing out in Andrew's mind, and he went gratefully, giving Toni and Max privacy.

They opened a jar of Toni's homemade vegetable soup and prepared grilled cheese sandwiches. "Comfort food," Mary commented. "I think the Camerons can do with some comforting."

She put her arms around Andrew. "Whatever happens, we can handle it," she said. "Jake's home. He's in one piece. I'm so grateful for that."

"I am, too," he said, holding her close.

***

The Camerons spent every weekend in D.C. with Jake. They barely beat a snowstorm one weekend, arriving at their hotel just as the snow began to intensify, and they had to wait the next morning for a couple of hours before they could go to the hospital. Two weeks later they had a rather harrowing trip home due to yet another storm. But they always managed to get there.

Every weekend they were aware of his physical improvement. By the second weekend he was beginning to use crutches and he said he wasn't tiring as easily.

"How's your head, Jake?" Andrew asked.

"Still hurts, but it's better. In the … on the plane somebody asked me how bad the pain was on a scale of one to ten. I told them fifteen. Now it's … it's down to about a seven."

Andrew followed up with a question. "How did you know you were on a plane?"

"I didn't, at first. But the ... the engines were so loud it hurt my ears, and the plane dropped and took my ... my stomach with it. I figured ... that's where I had to be."

So he knew what it's like to be in a plane, thought Andrew.

That was the week they brought him a small Sony portable T.V. He was like a kid with a new toy, he was so thrilled, and the nurses later told his family Jake watched it for hours.

The old Jake never watched much television. He was usually outside ... riding his bike, playing pickup basketball games, skiing in the winter, usually at that ski area near York. Andrew reminded himself Jake could hardly do any of those things in his present circumstances, but he wasn't sure how to deal with the new Jake.

Jake was always delighted to see them and always eager to hear how their week had been. By their third visit he was moving easily on crutches, and would sometimes walk up and down the hall with them.

"What's the first thing you remember?" Andrew asked him.

"Hearing the noise of the engines in the plane," Jake replied. "It was making my head hurt even more. Then somebody shone a ... um ... a light in my eyes and I thought my brain was going to explode. That hurt like a mother ... oh, sorry, ladies."

How come he knows things like not to use bad language around women, but he still doesn't know who he is? thought Andrew. *I don't understand any of this.* Andrew didn't say anything more; he didn't want to upset Jake. It was evident how difficult this was for him. *He's got to be scared.*

At each visit they spent at least a few minutes with Dr. Forrester as he discussed Jake's progress. Dr. Forrester asked Toni if Jake had ever suffered from migraines; he was experiencing severe headaches on occasion, a different kind of pain from that he felt from the wound. This new symptom was considered an after effect of his severe concussion and resulting brain trauma.

After this meeting, Andrew stayed back to talk to Major Forrester. "It's been three weeks and he hasn't remembered anything. Is that normal? Is there anything else we should be doing to help him?"

"Traumatic brain injuries are all different. People recover at different rates, so there really isn't any 'norm' for this. It can't be forced, Andy. The brain is pretty mysterious, and it's difficult to know what part or parts of Jake's brain have been injured. Obviously, those areas where his 'episodic' memory — the memories of his life — are stored were the most affected. He's very fortunate to have retained his ability to speak and reason, and he has good motor skills. He remembers quite a bit about the world we live in. General knowledge. He understands things like Washington being the capital of the country, and knows Pennsylvania isn't far from where we are. That's encouraging."

Jake surprised them on this visit when he asked if they ever listened to classical music.

Andrew replied, "Mary's a music teacher and she plays piano beautifully. I really love that music. I sang in the high school chorus and the college chorus as well."

"Yes, you did tell me that. And you're teaching art now, right? And you've even sold some of your paintings. I'd really like to see them."

"You will," said Toni. "When we take you home. Classical music, well, we have quite a nice collection of recordings, and we all love to hear Mary play. Why do you ask?"

"I've heard … one of the patients here has a portable record player and he loves classical music. It's really beautiful." He paused and asked shyly, "You've asked me if there's anything I need. Do you have an extra portable radio at home I could maybe use? There are radio stations I can pick up here that play mostly classical music." Max whispered something to Toni and left the room.

"Who's the music lover?" Andrew asked, interested.

"He's an Army lieutenant, Matthew Geiger. His favorite is opera. He's a great guy, and what's happened to him is really tough."

Andrew and Toni helped Jake get more comfortable. His head wound was still bothering him considerably, and Toni carefully put a pillow behind his head as she asked, "What happened to him, Jake?"

He smiled at her gratefully and relaxed. "He's lost his sight. He used to be a pianist ... an accompanist for the Philadelphia Opera Company."

"Oh, that is so sad," Mary said.

"It's worse than that. His right hand was really messed up. One of the nurses ... her name's Donna ... told me he's hoping it can be surgically repaired."

They were quiet for a minute, and Jake added, "But you wouldn't believe what a great attitude he has. He's learning Braille. He's brilliant, and when he talks about composers he makes them come to life. His wife Andrea told me the manager of a classical music station in Philly has spoken to her about Matt becoming one of their announcers when he's better."

"He's an inspiration," Mary said softly.

Max came back in soon afterwards with a brand new table top radio.

Jake smiled broadly, his eyes shining. "You didn't have to do that, Max. Thank you so much. This is so great."

Max plugged the radio in and they quickly found a station. Andrew enjoyed hearing the Saturday afternoon Metropolitan Opera broadcast, but Jake's response confused him. *Who is this guy listening to Puccini with tears in his eyes?* He wished Jake would tease him about enjoying "highbrow" music. He was accustomed to that.

On the drive home the next day Toni teased Max, "What a good sport you were to listen to the opera yesterday."

"What are you talking about? I love opera. At least, I do now."

"Well, Jake sure loved it," Andrew said. "I never would have dreamed he would respond like that to romantic music."

Mary laughed. "*La Bohème* is such a great opera. For your sake, Max, I'm glad the Met wasn't performing Wagner yesterday."

They laughed until they cried, and Max had to pull off the road. Then they fell silent, realizing the tension of the situation had caused them to overreact to Mary's joke. Finally, Toni wiped her eyes and said, "I think it's called 'cope and adjust.' We can do this, family."

***

The visits continued, and Dr. Forrester told them he thought it likely Jake could be released after six weeks at Walter Reed. The Camerons — even Andrew — were careful not to push Jake about remembering his past, but encouraged him to tell them about his new life and the friends he had made at the hospital, both on the staff and among the patients.

Toni told them later that was good; it meant he didn't have anterograde amnesia, and they all stared at her. "People who suffer from anterograde amnesia can't make new memories," she told them. "It seems Jake's not having any trouble doing that."

It was true; Jake was full of stories about his nurses and some of his fellow patients, Lieutenant Geiger in particular. And he definitely had something going with his pretty nurse, Amy, whom they had met on their second weekend visit. "It's okay, nothing can really happen there," Jake said. "She has a steady boyfriend."

Andrew laughed and shook his head. "I guess some things never change."

Jake joined in the laugh. "You know, bro, I can honestly say I have no idea what you're talking about."

But while Jake enjoyed looking at pictures they brought and asked questions about them, they didn't help him remember anything about his childhood. During their fifth weekend visit, Toni and Andrew went into Dr. Forrester's office to put together a list of names of people and events from Jake's past that might help him remember. It was explained these would be used later that week during testing to see how much and what kind of information Jake was able to recall.

As they began, Andrew suddenly frowned and said to his mother, "Let's not include anything about Allan Martin. How great if Jake never remembers him. I wish to God I could forget him."

Toni looked stricken. "I don't know, Andrew. It's part of his past."

"Let it stay in the past, Mom. Please." She nodded.

Jake's leg was healing well, and he asked Dr. Forrester when he could return to active duty. It was a blow for him to learn that as long as he was having serious problems with his memory, that wasn't going to happen. His distress when he reported this to his family was evident.

"I guess that makes sense. I haven't remembered anything about being in Vietnam, so I wouldn't be much use there." he said. "But I just always thought I'd go back when my leg and my head wound healed. I thought I would have remembered by then." He seemed close to tears, and they quickly changed the subject.

They asked the staff if they could take him out to dinner that night and were given permission. The idea was to cheer him up, but the outing seemed to have the opposite effect. He was confused and tired, and his head started to ache, so they cut the evening short and took him back to the hospital.

Andrew and Mary lay in each other's arms in their hotel room and he said to her, "Mary, if Jake is discharged, that might be hard for him. He wanted a career in the military. He didn't really have a 'plan B.'"

"He has a good mind, Andy. There will be something he can find to do. He's only twenty-two; he could go to college."

"I don't think that's so easy. He's been out of high school for over four years. We thought he might go to Penn State on a football scholarship, but then he decided to go into the Army. Jake was a decent student, but he never really liked to study."

He was quiet for a minute, and then he said, "He's so different."

"Yes, he is, but what do you mean specifically?"

"Jake could push my buttons like nobody else could. You know, stealing a girl I might like. Teasing me about art and music. Saying stuff just to get my knee-jerk reaction, and then ribbing me when I gave him exactly what he wanted to hear. Oh, he was never mean. Mom said he was 'high-spirited.' He sure was that; he could make me laugh harder than anybody else."

He sighed. "And there was this about him … he'd go all the way around the world to avoid helping in the kitchen, but when

Mom was sick he pitched in and did more than either Dad or I did. In fact, when anybody was sick he was a big help."

He punched the pillow behind his head to get more comfortable. "Man, did his teammates love him. Talk about loyalty. If any of those guys were hurt, Jake would go to see them every day. And he was a real leader, the way a quarterback should be. He cheered his team on harder than anybody when he was on the sidelines."

"Yes, I remember that. It's one reason everyone loved him."

Andrew leaned up on one elbow. "And then ... the times he was home on leave ... he'd grown into a man I admired and respected. We had some great talks ... about the war, about life. In some ways we were closer than we'd ever been." He sighed. "That's the Jake I remember, and I miss him. I don't know how to talk to him anymore."

He lay down again and moved closer to her. "I feel so bad for him, Mary. We walk in there every Saturday and say 'How are you?' and he knows we mean, 'Did you remember anything this week?' That's why he always says things are the same but he's feeling better. He's so eager to please us. He wants us to like him. He knows we love him, but he so much wants us to accept him the way he is now. I think he suspects he may never remember anything."

"That must be unbelievably scary. I can't even imagine what it would feel like."

Andrew nodded. "He's so unsure of himself ... not at all like Jake. But what hurts most is the look in his eyes. He looks so *lost*."

Mary put her arms around Andrew and pulled him down beside her. "I know. And you want to fix it, and you don't know how. It's going to take time, Andy. The most important thing is that Jake's alive, and he's going to be okay."

Susan Moore Jordan

"Yes, I know that." He pulled her even closer, and for a while he forgot everything except her lovely sweetness.

CHAPTER 15

"There's so much we don't know about amnesia. The human mind is still very much a mystery and we are learning all the time. You're aware that Jake's cognitive ability is quite good, and we've given him a number of tests to see what else we could find out about what he can and can't do."

The Cameron family, minus Jake, was seated in Major Forrester's office at Walter Reed Hospital. They were taking Jake home today, but Dr. Forrester had asked to speak with them before they collected their soldier.

Now he leaned forward, referring to the notes in front of him. "Here's the good news. Jake has retained the ability to make new memories, and that's important. He knows everyone on our staff and has had no problem developing relationships with some of them. He can recognize famous people and events from the past. He knows we're in a war in Vietnam, even though he doesn't remember his time in the service there. He knows Bobby Kennedy was assassinated, and he identified his picture, along with about eighty other famous people. He knows quite a bit about United States' and even world history. He has a good grasp of general knowledge — math, science, and so forth. So he's actually kept a lot."

"Well, that's good, right?" Andrew asked.

Dr. Forrester nodded. "This is the tough part. He has absolutely no episodic memory — that is, he can't recall even a single event from his past. Even with the triggers you provided, he consistently comes up blank. He knows all of you now, and he understands what you are to him — his family. But there's no recall of his history with you. That's why he seemed so distant when he first saw you — you were complete strangers to him at first."

"He recognized me," Andrew interjected. He was perched on the arm of an easy chair where Mary was sitting. Toni and Max were in side-by-side straight chairs, holding hands.

"He saw a face that was nearly identical to his own. That's what he was reacting to. You guys could be twins."

"But he'll remember. When we get him home and he's in familiar surroundings, he'll remember. Won't he?" Andrew struggled to stay calm, and Mary put her hand on his arm.

"It should help. He could begin to recall bits and pieces." Dr. Forrester paused for a moment. "Fiction writers love to use amnesia as a plot device, but they seem inevitably to get it wrong. *Bam*, some guy gets hit on the head and can't remember anything. Then *bam,* he gets another whack to the head, or some other kind of trigger, and suddenly he remembers everything."

He smiled wryly. "Well, anything is possible, but in reality, I've never heard of a case where it worked that way. Slow recall, generally of early childhood events, spotty at best. Over a period of time — months or years — the patient seems to remember more about his past life. I say 'seems,' because sometimes it's a question of whether he is actually recalling events or simply accepting that they happened because he's heard about them repeatedly.

"We've probably all experienced that. How many memories from your early childhood are actual memories, and how many are things you think you remember because someone told you about them?"

Andrew leaned forward. "But it will help him to hear about those things, won't it?"

"Of course it will. I'm cautioning you, though, to try to recognize an actual memory when he recalls one, as opposed to him repeating something you've told him about."

"So it's possible Jake may never remember his past life," said Toni, gripping Max's arm hard.

"I believe you need to accept that. Here's the tricky part. Of course he desperately wants to remember; to recall who he was. Show him pictures, take him places that might trigger something. Rejoice in every little piece he's able to recover. But please try not to pressure him. He'll put enough pressure on himself."

Andrew couldn't speak. *He will remember,* he thought. *He'll remember. I'll help him.* Mary pressed his hand gently.

"And this is vital. You have to accept him as he is now; love him as the son and brother he is *now*. Help him make new memories. It won't be easy, and he'll be different. He's already different; you told me he had never shown any interest in classical music, at least that you were aware of."

Dr. Forrester leaned back and folded his arms across his chest. "But he's still Jake. This is completely unscientific and please understand it's a personal opinion, and I'm not speaking as a doctor. I personally believe everyone has something that makes them who they are. Call it an essence, an aura … a soul. And my personal belief is that we never lose that."

He gave them a few moments to consider what he had told them, and added, "I'm not ready to make a decision yet as to whether he will need to be discharged from the Army. He's only been here for six weeks. Regardless, he'll have to have P.T. on the leg, and he'll need to see a physician and get the medication he

147

needs if the headaches continue. Let's see what happens in the next three months."

"What happens after that?" asked Mary.

"What I want to do is set up an appointment and re-evaluate him at that time. In the meantime, if you have any questions, please don't hesitate to contact me." He smiled at them. "Try to just relax and enjoy having him home for the next three months."

Toni nodded eagerly. "When can we take him home?"

"Any time you want. He's been released from the hospital. He's waiting for you in his room."

They shook hands all around, and Dr. Forrester pulled Andrew aside. "Could you stay for a minute?"

Andrew nodded, and watched as Dr. Forrester closed the door after his parents and Mary had left the room.

"I understand how important Jake is to you. From what you've told me, the two of you had a very strong emotional bond from a very young age."

"There were some things that happened when we were little. So yes, that's true."

"Because of that, what's happening with Jake may be more difficult for you to accept than even your parents."

Andrew didn't answer. *I think he can see right into my head. But that's okay. He's taking good care of Jake.*

"If you have questions about anything, I need you to promise you'll call me and talk to me about it. Your brother is very fragile emotionally, Andy." He put a hand on Andrew's shoulder. "And I believe you are as well."

"Thank you, Dr. Forrester. I won't forget it. And I will call you. I really appreciate your concern for both of us." He hesitated.

"Ask."

"What do you really think? Do you think Jake may regain his memory?"

"Honestly, Andy, it's impossible to say. It could happen, I wouldn't count on it. I gave your family a worst-case scenario because it's good to be prepared. He may remember more. He may never remember anything. Every case is different."

"When would you make a decision … I mean, about discharging him from the service?"

"Let's see where we are in three months. Just enjoy having him home. He's a pretty terrific young man."

"He sure is. Thank you again, Dr. Forrester."

"What was that about?" asked Mary when Andrew rejoined them in the hall.

"Oh, I think he's concerned I might push Jake too hard. He has me pretty well figured out."

They laughed quietly. "You mean he's aware you're Andrew the worrier," said Mary, putting her arms around his waist.

Andrew nodded. "All of you will let me know if I go too far, won't you?"

"I just want to take him home," said Toni. "Let's let Jake take the lead. Just let him look around the house and …" her voice trailed off. "Max, how do we do this?" Her voice was shaking slightly.

"The best advice Dr. Forrester gave us? Love him. Just the way he is. He's still Jake." Max put an arm around Toni's shoulders. "Let's go get our son."

***

They tried to keep the trip home light-hearted. Jake was quiet, so the talk was among the other members of his family. Mary talked about what she was teaching her students. Andrew couldn't seem to think of anything to say. Toni asked Jake if he was warm enough. Then she asked him if he was too warm. Max gave a running commentary about where they were as they traveled.

"Can you turn on the radio?" Jake said suddenly. "Is there a classical music station we can pick up?"

Max found one; orchestral music. "That's beautiful," said Jake. "Mary, do you know what it is?"

"It's Rachmaninoff's Second Symphony. One of my favorite pieces."

"Rachmaninoff. Russian composer, right? From the romantic era."

"Have you heard other of his compositions?" asked Toni.

"Yes, just a couple of days ago. The second piano concerto. I thought it was the most beautiful thing I'd ever heard."

Andrew had to bite his tongue to keep from remarking, *Where'd this new-found love of classical music come from, little brother?* He would have said that to the old Jake. He couldn't say it to the new Jake. *That's the kind of thing Dr. Forrester was talking about.*

When they reached the house, Max brought Jake's duffel bag inside and took it upstairs to his room, Jake following. Toni, Mary and Andrew waited downstairs, not sure of what to do. Jake came down and walked through the rooms, looking around.

Andrew kept himself in check, but it was difficult. *Jake, do you remember ... no, I can't say it like that. He just walked into this house for the first time in his life.*

Jake went to the piano and touched the keys. "We have a piano?"

"It's Mary's. We moved it over to our house after we were married," Andrew replied.

"That's right, you told me you're living here for now." He looked at the portrait of Mary which was on the wall near the piano, and turned to Andrew. "You painted this?"

Andrew nodded.

"You're really good. This is beautiful." Jake continued to walk around, and noticed another painting of his brother's, Lake Wallenpaupack under a fiery sky.

"This one, too?"

"Yes."

"Where is this?"

"It's a lake up in the northeastern part of Pennsylvania."

Toni said, "Let me get dinner on the table. I just have to heat up the casserole. Mary, can you give me a hand?"

Max also went into the kitchen, leaving the brothers alone.

Jake sat on the sofa. "This is a really nice house."

He was perched on the edge of his seat, his hands on his knees. Andrew sat next to him. "Yes, it is." He looked around the room; thinking how it might appear to Jake. *There are good things here. Solid, like Dad ... cherry and mahogany. Nurturing, like Mom ... comfortable chairs, sofa, colors that say "home" ... greens and yellows, a subdued floral print on the sofa. Throw pillows echoing the colors in the pattern.*

Jake settled back, crossing an ankle over the opposite knee. "How long have we lived here?"

"We moved to Pennsylvania in 1959."

"And it's ... wait ... 1971 now. So we've lived here twelve years."

"Yes, that would be right."

There was silence between them, and Jake said softly, "I'm sorry, Andy."

"For what, Jake?"

151

"That I can't remember."

"It's okay. It really is. You're my brother and I love you, and I hope you'll learn to love me, too."

"You're a really nice guy. This is a nice family. I think I'm really lucky that I'm in this family. And your wife is just great. You did good."

Andrew felt a pain stab his heart. "You said that to me the day Mary and I were married."

"I was there?"

"You were my best man." Andrew watched Jake struggling to remember and saw the brief look of pain that crossed his face. "You were a great best man. You had my back." He was rewarded with a warm smile.

Max called them in to dinner, and Jake asked them to tell him about Mary's and Andrew's wedding. It was a perfect opening, and Jake listened, smiling, as they recounted memories. As dinner was ending, there was a knock at the door.

"Oh, Jake, I forgot to tell you we have a friend stopping by. I hope it's okay," Toni said, as Andrew went to the door.

Isabel came in carrying a fruit basket. "*Salut, Jacob. Je suis contente de te voir.*"

"*Merci, m'amselle. J'suis desolé, j'suis pas sûr si je te connais.*"

Mary's and Andrew's eyes met. Jake could still speak French. They had wondered about this, and had enlisted Issy's assistance to try to find out.

"*Mais je m'oublie* ... I am forgetting myself. Your family does not speak French, while yours is quite good. I am Isabel Jeanseau, and I teach art at West Chester State College. So I am a colleague of your father's, and your brother's art teacher."

"You're Andy's art professor? You must be a great teacher. His paintings are wonderful."

Issy laughed. "*Merci*, but in truth, much of that is a tribute to Andrew. He is a gifted artist."

Andrew said, "Let me take that," and carried the fruit basket into the kitchen.

Mary followed him. "She's wonderful. She's so … easy … with him. She made him comfortable right away."

"I guess it's easier for her because she's not part of the family."

"Well, it looks as if they've made a connection already."

Andrew smiled. "Yes, it does. Wonder what will develop between them this time around?"

Mary laughed and they went back into the living room, where Isabel was saying her goodbyes. "I only stopped by to bring you a welcome home gift, Jacob. I hope you like fruit."

"I sure do. Will I see you again?"

"*Je l'aimerais bien*," Isabel said, unable to keep herself from giving Jake a sidelong glance with a flutter of eyelashes.

"She's nice," Jake said, after Isabel had gone. "Would it be okay if I go to bed? I'm really tired."

"Of course," Toni replied. "Would you like dessert before you turn in? I made a cherry pie."

Jake followed her into the kitchen. "That would be great."

Max, Andrew and Mary breathed sighs of relief. "Well," Andrew said.

"It's okay. It's going to be okay," Mary commented.

Max said what they had all been thinking. "I think he likes it here."

The three of them had a fit of silent laughter, and Toni called out, "Max, Mary, Andrew, your pie is ready."

They sat companionably at the table and enjoyed Toni's pie, complimenting her. Jake put down his napkin.

"This has to be even weirder for all of you than it is for me," he said, surprising them. "But I really feel good being here. And I liked when you talked about Andy's and Mary's wedding. I liked hearing those stories. And it seems I have a genius brother, which is very cool."

They all smiled at Jake and at each other. He was making this easier for all of them.

"Thank you, Jake. That means a lot," Toni said, carefully putting a hand on his arm.

"Dr. Forrester talked to me. He said it would help you if I just keep letting you know how I feel about stuff."

He stood and stretched and tried to stifle a yawn. "Oh, sorry. I really am tired. Thanks for everything. The pie was great, Mom."

"Thank you, son," Toni said with tears in her eyes. Jake left the room and they heard him go upstairs.

"He called me Mom. That's the first time he's done that."

"It's a good start," said Max. "But don't expect too much. Of him or of us. This is sure uncharted territory."

CHAPTER 16

Late March in the Northeast is that transition between winter and spring which seems to take a different form every year. Some years there are quick snowstorms that melt in a day or two, spreading a blanket of white briefly on forsythia and lawns with patches of green. Some years spring comes earlier and by the end of March trees are budding, lawns are green and winds are gentle and warmer. This was one of those years, and the sun shone on the Cameron family.

Jake had been home for three weeks, and they were doing as Dr. Forrester had suggested, enjoying having him there. In some ways he was like a child, delighting in the meals Toni and Mary fixed, exclaiming over dishes that were new to him all over again. He was receiving physical therapy at Chester County Hospital and had made friends with the staff, most of whom didn't live in town and didn't burden Jake with recollections of his prowess on the football field or baseball diamond.

While his headaches continued, for the most part they were managed by the medication Jake had been prescribed. When they were very bad, Toni applied cold compresses that eased the pain. She liked caring for him, and he began to have a better understanding of what having a mother meant as he felt her gentle touch and the ease of her companionship.

They settled into a comfortable routine. Jake helped Toni however he could mornings, drove himself to the hospital most afternoons, and enjoyed hearing Andrew and Mary talk about their work when they came home. Max listened to music with Jake, deciding he might as well learn something more about classical music since that had become a special love of Jake's.

Andrew was painting landscapes and had started another portrait of Mary. The landscapes were otherworldly and almost abstract — he wasn't sure where they came from. While he continued to use an area of their room as a studio, sometimes he moved his easel into the dining room, another space with good lighting. A dream: a big, spacious studio in his own home.

***

Sitting around the living room one evening after dinner, they were each busy with a task: Max, in a ladder back chair behind a card table, prepared his lesson plans; Mary, seated at the piano, studied a choral score. Toni had a book open, and Jake sprawled on the sofa beside her, flipping through a magazine.

Andrew was sitting in a chair and sketching Jake, smiling to see him so relaxed, so much part of the family. He saw Jake glance up at his painting of Lake Wallenpaupack and then stand and walk to the painting to examine it more closely.

"That color … sky and water … is just … where did you say this lake is?"

"Up north of us. Near the Pocono Mountains."

"Have I been there?"

"I don't think you've been to Lake Wallenpaupack, Jake," said Toni, "But I know you made a ski trip to the Poconos not long ago." She didn't say "with Isabel"; they had agreed to allow that relationship to either develop or not, depending on Jake and Isabel.

It could be something new for him, as a friendship or as something more.

"Are they big mountains? I can't recall."

"More like hills," said Max. "Nothing like the Smokies."

"The Smoky Mountains. In Tennessee, right?"

Max nodded and Toni said, "Yes, not far from where you boys grew up."

Jake suddenly blurted out, "Clingman's Dome."

It took a minute for it to register, but Max, Andrew and Toni stared at Jake.

Toni closed her book. "What did you say?"

"Clingman's Dome. It's a place."

"What about it?" Max asked carefully.

"I was there." He pointed at Max, then Andrew. "With ... with you ... and Andy. We climbed up it, and it was a tough climb because I was ... I was ..."

Andrew nearly stopped breathing. *Don't prompt him, let it come to him.* He stood and moved to his brother as he said softly, "What, Jakey?" The childhood nickname. That might be a trigger; the memory seemed to be unfolding for his brother.

"Little. A little kid. Maybe eight? Nine? And after we climbed that steep hill there were ..." he looked at them. "Steps? No. It was a ramp, a really long ramp. Some ... kind of building."

Max laughed. "I guess it must have seemed like a lot of climbing to you boys."

Jake was excited now. "I know what it was. It was an observation tower. I can see it in my head." He laughed aloud. "We were almost at the top when I sat down and told you I couldn't take one more step."

"You did," said Max, his eyes shining. He pushed his work aside as he stood, almost knocking the table over. "But you made it to the top."

"Yeah, but only because you carried me on your back the rest of the way, Dad."

Andrew had to turn his face away and wipe his eyes. He was laughing, but he couldn't keep from crying. He hadn't thought about this in years, and his painting had helped Jake recover a moment from his past. Andrew wanted to sink to his knees in thanksgiving.

"When we got to the top we looked out and everything was covered in fog. That was a bummer, but then Dad said, 'We're in the clouds, boys. We're so high we're up in the clouds.' And Andy and I thought that was so cool."

Jake turned to Andrew. "You climbed that sucker all by yourself, though."

"Well, I was older, remember? Actually, Jacob, I've always been older than you."

Jake grabbed his brother, put him in a head lock and rubbed his knuckles over Andrew's head; Andrew broke the hold and pinned Jake to the floor, laughing. They were all laughing by this time, and Andrew rolled away from Jake and lay on his back, staring up at the ceiling, the light from the table lamp catching the edge of his vision, broken into a thousand facets through his tears. He was eleven again, and Jake was nine. Jake struggled to his feet and extended an arm to his brother, pulling him up.

Toni, thrilled beyond words, stood and said, "Who wants ice cream?"

The family went into the kitchen and Toni and Mary pulled half gallons of ice cream from the freezer and put bowls on the table.

Jake perched on a tall stool and scooped mint chocolate chip into a bowl, drowning it with chocolate syrup. "We ate a watermelon," he said. "We put it in a creek to make it cold first. Then Dad cut it open and ... cut slices ... and we just chomped on it and spit the seeds out."

Toni said, "You three ate an entire watermelon? Nobody ever told me that."

"Well, I asked the boys to keep it quiet. I wasn't sure how you'd feel about me letting them eat a whole watermelon."

Andrew said, "It was a *small* watermelon, Mom." And he and Jake started laughing again.

"Watermelon," said Jake. And the two of them started chanting, "Watermelon, watermelon, watermelon," the words dissolving into laughter. Jake's infectious laugh finally got to all of them; Mary started to giggle and Toni and Max soon joined in, and unbridled merriment filled the Cameron kitchen.

They grew quieter, and Jake said softly, "I remembered something. I really am part of this family. I remembered." They had a group hug and let the tears flow. It was one of the happiest moments of Andrew's life.

***

While none equaled the vivid recollection of Jake's memory of Clingman's Dome, he did recall a few more bits and pieces as time went on. The family trip to Fontana Lake in North Carolina, and the horseback ride they had taken. "I don't think you liked it as much as I did, Andy. We did some other stuff on that trip ... didn't we go to see a play?"

"We saw two plays, Jake. Our Aunt Melanie was in one of them."

"Was that the one that had the merry-go-round on stage?"

A thrill. He was remembering more than he realized but had mixed up two events.

Toni said, "That was earlier, Jake. Your Aunt Melanie had the lead in the high school show when she was a senior. I took you boys to see it. And yes, there was a carousel on stage … that was the name of the show, *Carousel*."

"But she was in another play the summer we went horseback riding, wasn't she?"

"She certainly was." Toni had tears in her eyes.

"And there were Indians there. I mean, American Indians. Was she in that play?"

"That was a play called *Unto These Hills*. She was in a play called *Chucky Jack*."

Andrew interjected, "We saw them on two different nights. They were both performed outdoors, but one was in Gatlinburg, Tennessee, and *Unto These Hills* was in North Carolina. *Chucky Jack* — what I remember mostly about that is square dancing."

Jake laughed, "Lots of foot stomping and hand clapping. I do remember that. But didn't Aunt Mellie sing a solo?"

Toni said, "Yes, she did. She didn't have a big role, but she did her role well and had nice reviews from the newspapers in the area."

Jake said, "And the other one, it was very serious and there were lots of Indians in it. And it was really *long*." He grinned. "I fell asleep."

"Yes, you did. Max had to carry you to the car," Toni replied.

Another memory: Melanie singing to him. "I was sad about something. Somebody had died." Andrew stiffened, but Toni answered carefully.

"My parents. Your grandparents were … they were killed suddenly."

Surprisingly, Jake didn't pursue it. He was more interested in talking about Melanie. "She was pretty, Mom, but she wasn't … she had blonde hair. No, wait. That was another aunt."

"Your Aunt Alice."

"Oh, right. Well, I've seen pictures of Aunt Alice's family, so maybe that's not really remembering."

"You've seen pictures of Aunt Melanie, too," said Andrew.

"Yes, I know. But I remember her voice. It was so sweet. And … I remember she sang a song about … a boy."

"Yes, she did, Jake. It was from *Carousel*. She didn't sing it in the show, but she liked it and she sang to you and Andy."

Another recovered memory. At first it seemed to Andrew that Jake was talking about skeet shooting on Norris Lake, but he was mainly talking about shooting a gun. "Dad, did you have a gun?"

"No, Jake. Your Uncle Ben had a shotgun, and you and Andy tried skeet shooting one summer when were at his parents' house."

"You didn't used to line tin cans up and shoot them off a fence?"

"That was Uncle Ben," said Andrew quickly. This was getting into waters where he never wanted Jake to go.

Jake went with Max to help put air conditioners into windows, and Toni asked Andy to stay for a minute before he joined them.

"He needs to know about Allan Martin. It may help him regain more memories."

"Please don't take him there, Mom. He's doing fine."

"He can't continue to believe Max is his birth father, Andy. We're lying to him when we don't tell him the truth."

"Just wait until he starts asking. Please. I guess sooner or later he'll have to hear it, but not now. He doesn't need to have all that dumped on him now."

Toni sighed and studied her older son. "You may be right. He doesn't know anything about that awful time. It won't be easy for him to learn about it."

***

Andrew and Max were watching the evening news when Jake walked into the room. Not wanting to interrupt, he joined them to hear the announcer say: "After nearly eighty hours of deliberation, the jury has returned a guilty verdict for Lt. William Calley. Calley, who was accused of personally murdering twenty-two of the more than four hundred unarmed Vietnamese civilians massacred in the village of My Lai, could be sentenced to death for his crime."

Max turned off the TV. "Good. They did the right thing."

"I hope so," Andrew commented. "It just doesn't seem right that so far Calley is the only person who has been tried. He wasn't there by himself."

Jake looked at them both, bewildered. "What was that about?"

"There was some really bad shit that went down in Vietnam," Andrew replied. "This happened a few years ago, and some honorable men came forward with the accusations. Nothing for you to be concerned about."

"These were Army? American soldiers who did this?" His voice was shaking and rose in pitch as he spoke.

"Regrettably, yes," replied Max. "Sometimes horrific things happen in war. This was one of the worst."

Jake grabbed Andrew's arm. "When? When did this happen? Was it while I was in Vietnam?"

Andrew had never considered this. "Yes. It was March of 1968. A couple of months before you came home for my wedding."

"Good God, Andy ... could I have been part of something so ... so ..." Andrew could see the pain in his brother's face.

"Absolutely not. These men weren't from your division. You were First Infantry at that time, Jake. This was one company of the Twenty-third Infantry."

Andrew was still sorting out his feelings about My Lai, so he went on, "Things over there are really ... well, complicated. We're not just fighting the North Vietnamese Army. There's also the Viet Cong, who don't wear uniforms and use guerilla tactics. We think they're mostly North Vietnamese who've infiltrated the south, but who the hell knows? The thing is, it's hard to distinguish who's a friend and who's an enemy. There was talk at Marble Mountain after the base was attacked that some Vietnamese who were actually working for us on base were Viet Cong. They may have even helped plan the attack."

Jake sighed, and Andrew realized how much this had distressed and frightened him; his face was covered with sweat. "How the hell could I have been part of a war and not remember *one damn thing* about it?"

Andrew put a comforting hand on Jake's shoulder.

"I know how much you hate that you can't remember your time in the service, but in a way it's kind of a blessing. I wish I could forget I was ever there. A lot of people have really come to hate this war, Jake. I'm beginning to believe we should never have been there in the first place, and sometimes it feels like it's going to haunt this country forever."

163

"I heard that from some of the patients at Walter Reed. Well, not just the patients. Some of the nurses had served there as well. I don't understand why I enlisted."

"You were eager to serve your country, which was at war, trusting our leaders that it was a just war," said Max. "If you hadn't enlisted, most likely you would have been drafted. It was hard for men your age to avoid service during that time. It's become even worse. One of my colleagues just learned that his son, who's a second-year student in law school, has been drafted. I'm just thankful to have both of you home and in one piece."

Jake smiled shakily. "Thanks, Dad. Even if this piece isn't quite whole?"

Max went to Jake and embraced him. "Don't ever think of yourself like that. Ever. You're the same man you've always been, Jacob."

Andrew thought, *I am grateful he's home. I'm trying to believe that he's still Jake. I hate this. Why can't I be satisfied with him just the way he is, like Mom and Dad are?*

CHAPTER 17

Jake was reluctant to go into town. He felt safe in the house as he had felt safe in the hospital. He had been told people would recognize him and would want to talk, and he sensed that could be at least awkward.

He finally went with Andrew and Toni to a bookstore near the college hangout, "The Pig." Toni picked up her book order and as they were leaving the store, a rather portly woman, dressed as if she were attending church, stopped them to speak. "Hello, Toni. You're such a stranger these days."

Andrew tensed. Mrs. Fitzsimmons was the biggest gossip in West Chester. He was sure people were aware Jake had been home for a few weeks; no doubt there had been a lot of speculation. The Camerons had told a few people Jake had suffered a head injury and a broken leg and was recuperating for a few months. Speculation in town was rampant, and Max finally tried to end the gossip by confiding in friends that Jake had suffered some memory loss as a result of his injury.

"Hello, Andy," Mrs. Fitzsimmons said, hardly looking at him.

"How are you, Mrs. Fitzsimmons?"

"Fine, but Jake!" Her tone changed; she began to speak loudly and slowly. "How are you? We heard you were hurt. You really look fine."

Andrew watched the color begin in Jake's neck and creep up into his face, but he replied in a level voice, "Thank you, Mrs.

Fitzsimmons." He had picked up the name and used it, hoping that would satisfy her.

"Oh, but my dear boy. We heard you had a head injury." She continued in the loud slow voice. "Do you remember me?"

Jake smiled at her as he said, "Mrs. Fitzsimmons, I haven't lost my hearing. I can hear you just fine. But nope, frankly, I don't remember you at all."

Toni had to cover her mouth to keep from laughing as the woman, totally at a loss for words, said, "Well. That's good." She turned and flounced off.

"Oh, Jake, she'll have such a good time telling her friends all about this encounter," Toni laughed.

"Well, people should just try to get used to it. I don't remember anybody I've seen in this town today. And who knows if I ever will?" he tried to sound nonchalant, but Andrew thought, *This can't be easy for him. He's my hero. I need to tell him that.*

Andrew knew Jake still had occasional migraines, and even worse, that he was struggling with insomnia. Andrew often heard him come downstairs during the night and go into the kitchen. He wanted to help but wasn't sure what to do.

The night after they had gone into town he heard Jake come quietly downstairs at two a.m. Andrew carefully slid out of bed, not wanting to wake Mary, and put a sweater on over his sweat pants and tee shirt. Jake was sitting at the kitchen table with a glass of milk in front of him, elbows on the table, head in his hands. Andrew immediately felt guilty. *I should have done this sooner.*

He stood behind his brother and put his hands on Jake's shoulders, kneading them gently. "Can I help?"

"That feels good." Jake rolled his head from side to side as Andrew continued massaging his shoulders.

"Do you want to talk?"

Jake was silent for a moment. "Yes."

Andrew sat down in the chair next to him, and Jake looked at him with such sorrow and confusion in his eyes that Andrew was startled.

"I wake up sometimes … I wake up … and it takes me a while to remember where I am. And to remember that I … I'm not anybody, Andy. I know I look like Jake Cameron. I keep telling myself I'm Jake Cameron. But I'm not him. It scares the hell out of me."

"What can I do, Jake?"

Jake shook his head. "Nothing. Nobody can do anything. All of you guys are just incredible. I know you love me. Well, you love Jake Cameron. It makes me so sad that I can't be him."

"You are him. You're my brother. And you've remembered some things." Andrew didn't know what else to say. He wanted so much to reassure Jake, but he seemed unreachable.

"Really, only that one thing. That was so great. It was like I was watching a movie. But the others have just been … kind of like snapshots. I mean, I see images, but they kind of flash by. You've all tried so hard, you've told me so much about Jake. I feel like I know him. And I guess …" he stopped and swallowed hard. "I guess he's inside me. He's in here somewhere." He pulled his hair with both hands in frustration. "Why can't I find him? I don't know what else to do, Andy. You know what happened in town today?"

"You mean with Mrs. Fitzsimmons? Don't pay any attention to her, Jacob."

"I was so rude to her. I didn't mean to make a scene. But people look at me like I'm a freak. Or … I know some people think I'm pretending so I won't have to go back to Vietnam. God. Why would anybody pretend to lose their memory? It sucks big time. It's awful." Jake rested his face in his hands again, and Andrew put a comforting hand on his shoulder and bent close to him.

"You know what Dr. Forrester told us? He said no matter what, you're still Jake. He said he thinks there's something special about each of us, and no matter what happens to us, that part of us … he said essence, or maybe it's our soul … never changes. And that's what I see in you. *You're still Jake*. I believe that."

Jake seemed calmer. "You really mean that, don't you?"

"You bet I do. We'll figure this out together. I know it has to be hard. Try not to let it get you down too much." He thought for a minute. "You know what? I'm going to pick up a Walkman for you so you can listen to tapes at night when you can't sleep. And I'll get some tapes, too. How about Puccini's *Madama Butterfly*? I know you love that; and I'll get my favorite piece of music, the Brahms *Requiem*."

Jake sighed and finished his milk. "That would be great. Thanks, Andy."

"Listen, promise me if you need to talk, or if you can't sleep, come and get me. Just tap on the door. I'm not a very sound sleeper."

"I don't like taking you away from your wife." Jake gave a small smile.

"She'll understand." He looked directly into Jake's face. "You're not alone. Don't ever forget that. I'm always here for you."

Andrew was rewarded with a grin. "I won't forget. It really means a lot." Jake yawned. "I think I can sleep now."

***

Isabel was their guest at dinner the following night. This time she breezed into the house, grandly presented Toni with a bottle of wine, and her opening greeting, *"Salut tout le monde, ça va!?"* made Jake laugh with delight. They were seated together at dinner, and Isabel flirted openly with Jake, who was obviously enchanted. At one point Andrew noticed Isabel lean close to Jake and he saw his brother's startled expression.

What on earth is she doing under the table? he thought, smiling to himself. After dinner, Isabel talked to Jake about Andrew's paintings and what made them unique.

"Jacob, I would like to show you some of my paintings. So you can see how Andrew's work is similar to mine, but different. Perhaps you would come to my place for dinner one night soon?" They were speaking French, and Jake replied he would like that very much.

When she left Jake asked Andrew to come to his room.

"She's wonderful. *Si belle*. And she seems to like me. She … she was pressing her leg against mine under the table."

"I wondered what you were looking surprised about," Andrew said, grinning.

"So what should I do? I can't remember ever …" he stopped. "I feel like she's coming on to me. Am I wrong?"

"No. My French is limited, but didn't she just invite you to come to her apartment for dinner?" Jake nodded. "She really likes you, Jake. Go for it."

"I'm not sure … I don't know if I can …"

"Oh, you can. Trust me on this one."

Three nights later a nervous Jake was collected by Isabel for their tête-à-tête. The family waited and wondered until the phone rang. Toni picked it up and spoke briefly, laughing as she hung up. "Jake's staying at Issy's tonight."

Susan Moore Jordan

Andrew gave a thumbs up. "Good for Issy. Good for Jake. He's asked me some things about … well, you know."

"So you had the birds and bees talk with him?" Mary laughed and shook her head.

"I told him it was like riding a bicycle. Or driving a car. You just do it. You don't have to think about it."

"So that's what's been going on between us all these years."

"Of course not. What's between us is a lot more than sex. But with a guy, well, he doesn't really have to … I mean, the way a man's body responds is …"

Max interrupted him. "Quit while you're ahead, son. You're just digging the hole wider and deeper."

CHAPTER 18

Jake was very quiet on the ride to Walter Reed. It was mid-June, and they were headed back for his re-evaluation appointment with Dr. Forrester. He would also be given a physical examination while he was there.

He passed the physical with flying colors and sat through the tests with Dr. Forrester and another doctor, Captain Louise Harman, whom they were told was a psychiatrist. The family went to lunch, which was also somewhat subdued, and returned to the hospital mid-afternoon for a meeting with Dr. Forrester in his office.

"Jake, it's great that you've had some recall of childhood memories. And even better that at least one was very detailed and apparently quite vivid."

Jake studied his doctor and tried to smile. "I hear a big 'but' there, Dr. Forrester."

"The time period you've recalled is very limited. It seems nearly every memory is from the time before you moved to Pennsylvania, so during your childhood and elementary school years."

"And that's a problem, isn't it? At least, as far as me returning to active duty."

"I would have liked for you to have had some memory of your time in the service, even if it was vague. Even some memories from high school, before you entered the service."

Jake sighed and looked down at his hands. "So that's it, then."

"I didn't say that. I'm not ready to make any decisions just yet. You're still a valuable member of the United States Army and we don't want to lose you. Let's try something. Dr. Harman knows a good neuropsychologist in Philadelphia who would be willing to work with you. There are some techniques that have been developed which might help with memory recall. There are definitely no guarantees, but I think it's worth a try, since you have had partial recall of your early life just from being home with your family."

Jake looked up and gave Dr. Forrester a slight smile. "That sounds ... interesting."

"It may not work. But we won't know unless you give it a shot." He turned to Max. "Unfortunately, since she is not on the staff of a military facility, this would be an expense you would have to cover."

"No, Dad," Jake said abruptly. "I don't want you to do that."

"Jake, do you think for one minute I would hesitate to do everything in my power to help you recover? Of course we'll take care of it."

Dr. Forrester nodded. "I'm going to hold off on the active duty decision for six months." He paused and glanced around the room. "I know that doesn't seem like much time, but I have to be fair to everybody about this. Let's see what happens during that period of time and then I can make a better decision. You'll need to make weekly appointments with this professional, Dr. Penelope Abramson." He handed Jake a slip of paper with Dr. Abramson's contact information.

"That's not a problem at all," said Toni quickly. "Would it be best if he had a family member with him? To verify anything he might remember?"

"Yes, definitely. I'm going to write this up and see you back here next January. That's a year from the time you were admitted."

***

The car was even quieter on the drive home. It was apparent Jake was disheartened by what had happened. He finally said, "I'm sorry I'm such a downer, folks."

"No, Jake, don't say that. I thought it was very positive," Toni commented.

"Mom, he was being super nice to me, but I think the truth is this is what's called 'grasping at straws.' Sure, maybe someday I'll remember more stuff. But it could be years from now. I think I have to face that. And what the hell is a 'neuropsychologist' anyway? Something none of us ever heard of until this morning, I'm sure."

"But you'll go and see this woman Dr. Harman suggested, won't you? We can set up the appointments for weekends so I could go with you. Or I could plan to take an afternoon off and get a substitute." Andrew was determined for Jake to make the effort.

"Yes, Andy, I'll try it. But what could she do that being with my family can't? You know me; you know everything that ever happened to me. But this woman hasn't a clue. What does she do, look into a crystal ball? Read Tarot cards? Wave bat wings over a clove of garlic? Hell, I could make up all kinds of wild stories and how would she know? If I feel like it's bullshit, I'll stop going."

No one said anything for several minutes.

Max broke the silence. "We don't know what happened to you in Vietnam. Not after you went back. You couldn't really tell us anything when you wrote home." Jake knew that; he had read the letters he sent them. They had nothing of substance in them about his missions.

Andrew was driving and Mary was in the front seat with him, and she reached over and turned on the radio and quickly found a classical music station.

"Oh, Jake, this will make you feel better," she exclaimed. "It's the Verdi *Requiem*. It's just starting. It begins quietly, but you'll soon hear one of the most thrilling moments in all music."

Andrew wasn't familiar with this composition. Soft strings opened the piece, and he found the quiet, simple opening chorus soothing. The chorus sang a more powerful statement, voices weaving into another softer moment. Then orchestra and chorus repeated the entire opening.

Glancing in the rear view mirror, Andrew could see that Jake was paying close attention to the music. The chorus swelled again, followed by a descending scale in the low strings as a brilliant solo tenor voice soared upward.

Jake's eyes were shining as the other soloists joined, and then the chorus and the soloists sang intricate, beautiful patterns above full orchestra. Andrew had to remind himself to watch the road. Mary was right; how could you not be moved by this beautiful, emotional music? The first movement of the piece drew to a quiet close, and Mary said, "Shall I leave it on?"

Three voices responded: "Please!" "Don't you dare turn it off!" "My God, Mary, that's just incredible!" Andy smiled at her. *My angel Mary. It's almost as if she planned this.*

When the brass started what he later learned was the "Tuba mirum" section, Andrew had to pull off the road to listen. A single trumpet, joined by another and another and another, layering sound with increasing intensity until the chorus and full orchestra burst in with almost overwhelming power. He was scarcely aware of Max tapping on the window to take over the driving duties. "Sit with your brother," he said. Andrew slid into the back seat and saw that Jake's eyes were streaming. He put an arm around his brother's shoulders as he wiped away his own tears.

Wave after wave of Verdi's magnificent music carried them home. The double chorus "Sanctus" and the tenor's solo "Ingemisco" Andrew found especially beautiful. But the work as a whole was an experience none of them would ever forget. Andrew heard it as a powerful affirmation of the life of the spirit, in which he believed so strongly, rather than the finality of death. He promised himself to buy the recording as soon as possible and he knew they would listen to it often, hearing more and more layers of beauty as they did.

When the last quiet notes of the brilliant final section were performed, Jake leaned forward and said to his sister-in-law, "You were right, Mary. How can you be depressed when there's music like that in the world?"

Mary covered his hand with hers. "It is glorious, isn't it? And what a beautiful recording."

"One good thing that came from my head injury. It sure opened my ears."

They drove to Longwood Gardens and took their time over dinner. When they reached the house, Jake immediately went to the phone and called Isabel. When he hung up and turned around, Andrew was standing behind him, car keys in hand. His brother accepted them gratefully and smiled; a real smile that went into his eyes.

"I won't be back tonight."

"God, I hope not. Stay as long as you need to."

Jake laughed, and Andrew felt the knot in his stomach begin to untie itself.

"You mean it?"

"Sure. We've got two other cars here."

Jake took the keys but kept his hand in Andrew's and their eyes met. "Thanks for everything, Andy." In that moment, they truly felt like brothers again.

***

The following months were an emotional rollercoaster for all the Camerons. When he first returned home Jake had glanced through his high school yearbooks as well as scrapbooks which Toni had kept. But Andrew thought more of an effort should be made to use them to help Jake recover his memories. He sat on the living room sofa with his brother as they went through a scrapbook page by page.

Pictures and mementos of Jake's graduation were featured in one section, and Andrew liked looking at them. "I was in Vietnam when you graduated. So I missed all this," he said wistfully.

"Mary's in this picture," Jake said.

"Yes, we were a couple when I left. We'd already started talking about marriage."

"Who is this lovely creature?"

"Tara Lake. You had a thing with her. You actually went steady for a couple of years."

"She's hot. Is she still around?"

"She's married."

Jake didn't comment, and Andrew flipped back to pictures of a surprise party the family gave Jake for his sixteenth birthday.

"You have to remember this. You said it was the best time you'd ever had in your life." Toni and Max had gone all out, hiring a deejay, having a catered buffet. The entire football team had been included. "Remember Mike Davenport? He was your favorite receiver. The two of you worked out some plays on your own and won a couple of games with them." He laughed. "You drove your coaches crazy, Jacob, but you were one hell of a quarterback."

Jake flushed and slammed the scrapbook closed. "Goddammit, Andy, I don't remember. Don't you get it? *I can't remember.*"

He stood and stalked into the kitchen, and Andrew, stunned, put the scrapbook aside and followed him. Jake was drinking a glass of water and turned to his brother. "I'm sorry I yelled at you, Andy. I know you're trying to help."

"No, I'm sorry, Jake. I'm sorry I pushed you so hard. I promised myself I wouldn't do that. I won't do it again." He put his arms around his brother, who returned the embrace. "Let's go listen to some music. Mom bought a new recording of Brahms' piano music and I haven't heard it yet."

Jake nodded. "I haven't either. I haven't heard much Brahms except for the tape you gave me, and I love that."

Andrew promised himself to ease up, and to quit saying things like "you have to remember this." But it was difficult. He wanted so much for Jake to remember, to be his brother again.

At first the sessions with Jake's neuropsychologist, Dr. Penelope Abramson, were benign. Andrew sat anxiously in the waiting room, hoping to be called into her office to confirm a memory Jake had recovered, but that didn't happen. As the months passed the sessions became confusing and frustrating to the patient and he left them feeling depressed.

"Lately she's really been pushing me to remember my time in Vietnam. I understand that's what Dr. Forrester had hoped would happen when he suggested I see her, but, shit, Andy, I can't recall a goddam thing about that entire part of my life."

"What's she doing, Jake?"

"Word association. Eye movements … eye movement exercises, she says they may help the two hemispheres of my frontal lobe connect better. Whatever the hell that means. The last couple of sessions we've listened to sounds, like gunfire and bombs and helicopters. I don't think she appreciated it when I asked her if she had any Puccini in her record collection." They both laughed.

"She shows me tons of pictures of Vietnam. They are really awful. I can't believe I was actually involved in that mess." He sighed and looked out of the car window; it was now late fall and the leaves were almost gone from the trees.

"This is just pointless. She wants to try to hypnotize me and I won't allow that. I *will not* be hypnotized. I'm pretty much fed up. Recently, every time I come here I get depressed and it affects everybody. I told her I'm not coming next week. I may not go back at all."

Andrew bit his lip to keep from telling Jake he thought that would be a mistake, and Jake continued: "But you know what? I dream about carrying a football down the field for a touchdown. Now, am I remembering that, or is it just because I've seen so many pictures of me in a football uniform and heard so often what a great quarterback I was?"

The two were silent for the rest of the drive back to West Chester.

***

178

Being with Isabel was the best medicine for Jake after a session with Dr. Penny. Music and Mary were also helpful; she would play for him, or they would listen to a recording together and discuss the music. Jake would begin to relax after a couple of days. Andrew was unable to do that. He was desperate for Jake to regain his memory, but he saw the ill effects of the "treatment" his brother was receiving.

"Maybe he's right," Andrew said to his parents as they sat at the kitchen table drinking coffee. "This isn't helping at all, as far as I can see. Jake gets so stressed out when he sees her. He dreads going back for his next appointment."

Toni commented, "He's getting restless. He wants to try to find a job somewhere, to think past his discharge from the service. He's sure that's what will happen in January."

"Where's he going to work? He doesn't even like to walk through town, and I don't blame him. I see the looks he gets. Half the people in this town think he's crazy, and most of the rest think he's faking so he doesn't have to go back to Vietnam." Andrew had begun to pull at his cuticles and bite his nails, something he hadn't done since he was in sixth grade.

Toni put her hands over her son's, hoping to help him stop. "I wish I knew what the answer was. Perhaps he *should* discontinue his sessions with Dr. Abramson. He'll have to contact Walter Reed and let Dr. Forrester know, though, if that's his decision."

"Isabel and Mary are the most help to him. I just seem to make things worse. I wish there was some way I could trade places with him." Andrew rubbed a hand over his face.

Max responded, "Well, you can't. Sadly, this is Jake's journey, and none of us can take it for him. Is that what you're trying to do? You once asked us to let you know if we thought you were pressuring him too much. I'm afraid you *are* doing that, son.

He's sick of looking at photos and newspaper write-ups from his high school days and going through his yearbooks. It would help if you'd just try to relax and accept that he may never regain much more of his memory."

Andrew took a deep breath and tried to ignore the nearly permanent pain he had in his stomach these days. "I know I've put too much pressure on him. I've apologized to Jake. I'm trying, Dad."

The extra time between appointments was helpful to Jake, and he and Mary continued to listen to and discuss the Verdi *Requiem*. Andrew was sketching the two of them as they sat together at the piano. Jake was smiling and laughing; that was wonderful to see, he did it so seldom these days. Andrew was still amazed at Jake's new-found love of classical music, which Mary was nurturing.

She put her hand on Jake's arm. "After we finish this, we need to listen to the Brahms *Requiem*. It's a piece Andy and I love."

Jake nodded eagerly. "I have a tape Andy gave me. I'd like to learn more about it."

Andrew froze. *How could she suggest that? That's our music.* He looked again at them; the glint in Jake's eye, the admiration on Mary's face. *Just like high school. Jake moving in on a girl I think I might like. Only this time it's my wife he's hitting on.*

He stood abruptly, slamming the sketch pad onto the sofa, and walked to the piano, standing behind Mary.

"It's getting late. I'm sure Mom and Dad are already asleep." He put his hands firmly on her shoulders and glared at Jake, who looked startled.

"Coming to bed, Mary?"

"In a minute," she replied, placing a loving hand on top of one of his. "I'll just check to see if anything needs to be done in the kitchen."

"Yes, it's late. I guess I'll turn in," Jake said. He shot Andrew a questioning look and went upstairs to his room.

Andrew turned abruptly and went into their room, pacing until Mary joined him. She appeared a little stunned when she saw his face.

"What the hell are you doing?" He struggled to keep his voice down; he wanted to shout at her.

"What on earth are you talking about?"

Andrew moved closer, confronting her. "I swear to God, Mary, if there's something going on between you and Jake ..." he didn't finish the sentence; he was stopped by the shock of a powerful slap that snapped his head to one side and left him stunned.

"How dare you," she almost hissed at him. "How *dare* you say that. Jake is my brother, and he's hurting. Anything I can do to help him deal with his sadness and confusion, I will. But I would never ... how could you even *think* that?"

She stared him down. "Don't you remember how terrified you were when you thought he had died, and how relieved you were to learn he was alive? We knew he had a head injury. You were very much aware he might be impaired, and you said it didn't matter, he was alive.

"I don't even know you any more, Andy. Have you *once* tried to put yourself in Jake's shoes? Tried to imagine how bewildered and confused he is? No matter what I've said to you, what Toni and Max have said to you, you continue to make this about *you*. It's not about you. We're all trying to help Jake. I don't know what *you're* doing."

Andrew's knees turned to water and he sank down on the bed, covering his face with his hands. He choked out, "I just want my brother back."

Mary knelt in front of him, her anger melting away, a gentle hand on his shoulder. "I know you do. But don't you think the person who wants that more than anyone is Jake? Do you know how much he hates that he feels he keeps failing you? And I know you try not to, but you pressure him. Sometimes not by what you say, but just by the way you look at him."

Andrew began to sob, and Mary sat next to him and held him, rocking him gently. "Let it out. I know you're hurting, my love."

He pressed his face against her breast, partly to muffle the awful sobs, partly to feel her warmth, and eventually he cried himself out.

She put a cool hand on his face and tipped it up. "I'm sorry I slapped you."

He almost smiled. "I'm not. You knocked some sense into my thick head." He put a hand to his chin, moving it gingerly back and forth. "I don't think I realized how strong you are, though."

Mary stroked his face and gave him a slight smile. "Well, anger can do that, I guess. I didn't mean to hit you so hard. Or maybe I did. I love you with all my heart, Andrew. You know that." She paused and swallowed hard. "You've hardly touched me in weeks."

They sat quietly for a moment. "What should I do, Mary?"

"Apologize to your brother. And tell him about Allan Martin and the murders." She put a finger to his lips. "It's part of who he is, Andy. He needs that information. It might help him. It might be a trigger, and you've been doing him a disservice by withholding it."

He sighed. "You're right. I'll tell him the whole story tomorrow."

"I know it won't be easy, but it's the right thing."

Andrew looked at his wife. Her eyes were red; she'd obviously been crying with him. She looked tired and drained because of the weeks and months of stress which he had contributed to and the scene they'd just been through. In that moment he loved her more than ever. *She's my better self,* he thought. *She makes me a better person, even when I don't want to be.*

He kissed her, what was intended as a tender, loving kiss, but both of them were overcome with intense desire and they made love like two wild creatures, not bothering to remove their clothing at first because they were in such a hurry to be part of each other as they had not for weeks. Then they tenderly undressed each other and came together again … and again.

And finally, wrapped in each other's arms, they slept.

Sketch #3
MARY

I lay beside Andrew, gently stroking his face and head as he gazed at me, his eyes closing and fluttering open to look at me again, as though he were a child fighting sleep. He gradually drifted off, and it hurt my heart to see there was still a faint red spot on his cheek where I had struck him. My beautiful, gentle Andy, the boy who won my heart the first time I saw him.

He caused quite a stir, this stranger from Tennessee who walked through the doors of the junior high school as an eighth grader. Straight dark hair, almost black. Dark eyes, framed with impossibly long lashes. A beautiful boy. A boy with an aura. The girls weren't sure what to make of him; he was pleasant, but he wouldn't flirt. "Maybe he's shy," said one. "I think he's stuck up," said another.

I knew better. He was thoughtful. He studied all of us carefully, though few realized it. Andy and I smiled and nodded when we saw each other, and that eventually became "Hi, Andy." "Hi, Mary." In ninth grade we had English and Social Studies together and sometimes discussed assignments.

"Mary, have you read this Edgar Allan Poe story? I'm not sure I understand some of it. Can we talk about it?"

"Sure, Andy. I think we have the same lunch period. Maybe we could do it then."

In tenth grade he joined the high school chorus and entered my world. Music was my life and had been for as long as I could remember. Piano lessons from the age of four. Philadelphia Orchestra concerts, Philadelphia Opera performances, even trips to New York to the Metropolitan Opera and to hear the New York Philharmonic. Listening to the Met Opera broadcasts every Saturday and enjoying my family's extensive record collection. Music filled my soul, filled my heart, made me who I was.

Now Andy had stepped into the world of music, and I loved watching him during sectional rehearsals, his face alight as he sang. He was just beginning to discover what I had always known: music could move you, heal you, bring you joy. When we were juniors I first saw his artwork and I understood that art was his life.

Jake was … well, what was Jake? More than a brother. I saw how Jake moved in on the girls Andy seemed interested in and took over. What surprised me was that Andy let him. But that was fine with me. *One of these days you'll look at me and really see me, and know what I know. You and I are meant for each other.*

I watched Andy sitting in the stands with his parents during football games, cheering for Jake. Jake the star. Andy was proud of him. Andy was protective of him, somehow. They seemed to have a bond that was unusually strong, even for brothers.

When we were seniors, Andy and I became friends, good friends. "Let's go to The Pig for a soda" friends. During our first semester in college we became more. Finally, he saw me. "I've been right here, Andy," I told him one night. I played Chopin for him and he took me in his arms, kissed me, and said he loved me. It was my dream come true, with the promise of happily ever after.

From that moment he seemed to know what I had always known: we would always belong to each other. "Mary, one of these days I'm going to ask you to marry me. Be ready." His eyes sparkled every time he said it.

"Andy, when you do, I'll say yes. *You* be ready." He would laugh and kiss me. The kisses became more, though we chose to wait.

But Vietnam exploded, and Andy decided to enlist in the Marine Corps. That was when he told me what had happened to him and Jake when they were very young. And I began to understand the bond between them. And to realize there were dark places in Andrew's soul that needed to be healed.

When Andrew was ready to leave for Vietnam, I couldn't wait any longer. What if he never came back? What if I had never known – in every way – this beautiful young man I so loved? Never explored his body, never felt ecstasy with him? What if he died never having experienced the overwhelming love I felt for him?

But he did come back, and we married a year later. We shared our love of beauty; Andy painted my portrait. I played piano for him. We sang together in the college choir. We almost had it all.

But Vietnam had changed him. He tried to put it away, but how can you do that? My gentle, thoughtful Andrew shot and killed people in Vietnam. He had to. It's part of war. He would never speak of it. *What happened to you in Vietnam, my love?*

Then Jake came home with no memory of his past life, and Andy didn't just lose his brother. He lost part of himself. His carefully planned, orderly life began to sift through his fingers like sand, and he started to fall apart. He didn't even realize what he was doing, how hard he was trying to hold onto something that simply wasn't there anymore.

As hard as Jake tried, he couldn't be the Jake he was *then*. And as hard as Andy tried, he couldn't accept the Jake he was *now*. And I couldn't seem to help Andy, no matter how I tried to reach out to him.

We had been so happy. All I wanted was to help Andrew get back to that golden place we had begun to make for ourselves, where he felt safe, and it didn't seem I could. Not until he stopped holding part of himself away from me. I couldn't help him with the demons that haunted him if he would not let me see them.

I couldn't believe I had struck Andy, but what he suggested about Jake and me was such a shock, such a betrayal of everything Andy and I had always been to each other, it awakened in me the instinct to fight with every atom of my being to protect what we have.

Now I gently touched his face and softly kissed the wound I had given him. I ached to make his life right again. Banish the darkness and bring him into the light. *I wonder if I ever can. But I'll never stop trying.*

"I'm right here, my love. I'll always be right here." I whispered.

CHAPTER 19

Mary watched Andrew as he examined the slight bruise on his left cheek in the bathroom mirror.

"I'm so sorry, Andy." She put her arms around his waist and leaned her head against the back of his shoulder.

"I'm the one who's sorry, angel. I can't believe what I said to you. I just haven't been thinking straight lately." He turned and embraced her and chuckled, "Never underestimate the power of a woman in love. Especially one with a mean left hook."

"So you understand why I smacked you."

"Of course I do. And you were right about everything."

It was Saturday, and Andrew sat down with Jake after breakfast and told him the entire story of their life with Allan Martin. He didn't leave anything out and finished by telling him about Martin being sentenced to prison in 1956. They sat in silence for a long moment.

"Is he still there?" Jake poured himself another cup of coffee.

"He was due to be released in 1968. Can you believe that ... just twelve years for murdering three people?"

"So nobody's heard anything from him, I take it."

Andrew was surprised that Jake seemed so detached. "No, though our relatives in Tennessee did confirm he was released. They seem to think he may have gone back to South Carolina and crawled into Tawndee Swamp, where his family had that cabin."

Jake sighed. "Sorry, Andy. I can tell this wasn't easy for you to talk about; it's an awful story. I'm sure you told me because you thought it might jar some memories loose, but I'm not getting anything. It's like it's a story about people I don't even know."

"No, Jake, in a way I'm glad you don't remember. I wish to hell I could forget him. But Mom and Mary were right, it's part of who you are … were … and you needed to know about it. We've told you everything else."

Jake looked thoughtfully into his cup. "You really hate him, don't you?"

"I try not to think about him."

"But it's more than hate. You … *dread* him."

Andrew was gripping his cup so tightly he realized it might shatter. "I hope to God I never lay eyes on him again as long as I live. And that's the last thing I want to say about it."

***

Andrew and Mary had busy schedules at school right up until the Christmas holidays began. They had agreed to have a Christmas Arts Celebration at Kennett High School, with a juried art exhibit accompanying the chorus concert. Andrew's students had been working on projects to submit since the beginning of the year, and Isabel had agreed to be one of three judges for the event.

Andrew was feeling less stressed about Jake and better about himself. He told Toni and Mary about the night Jake had shared with him what his memory recall of Clingman's Dome was like. "I know it can't be forced. Either he's going to remember or he's not. I guess there's a fine line between encouraging him and pushing him, and I have to be careful not to cross it again."

A few days later Andrew walked into the kitchen to find Jake holding the phone and looking annoyed.

"What's up?"

"Dr. Penny has me on hold. She wants to send me copies of my sessions and she wants her assistant to check our mailing address with me, so that's what I'm waiting for. She really wanted me to come over and get them in person Saturday, but I'm seeing Issy."

"I need to run to Philly Saturday to pick up a few things for some of my kids' projects. I can stop by and pick up the paperwork if she's okay with that. I'd like to thank her for working with you, anyhow."

"You sure you don't mind?"

"Not at all." Andrew welcomed the chance to meet with the somewhat unorthodox Dr. Penny, since he'd never had a chance to speak with her alone. He had some vague questions in mind he had thought he might ask if he ever had the chance. He drove to Philadelphia the following Saturday.

Dr. Abramson invited him into her office and he sat down on the sofa as she sat in a chair nearby. *She'd be pretty if she'd do something with herself,* Andrew thought. Brown hair with a red tint to it hung to her shoulders, straight and a little unkempt, as if she were trying to ignore the curls that wanted to happen. She wore "no-nonsense" clothing under her white lab coat; today, a tan plaid skirt and a yellow long-sleeved shirt. No makeup and rather severe wire-rimmed eyeglasses.

"You know Jacob called me to let me know he's not coming back."

"He just didn't think it was helping, Dr. Abramson. He was very discouraged … in fact, he was depressed after every session he had with you recently. He also called Dr. Forrester after he talked with you. He knows he'll be discharged from the Army."

"None of this surprises me, Andrew. At times your brother wasn't a very cooperative patient. That is simply an observation. Actually, I like Jake. I regret I wasn't able to be of more help to him."

"He resisted the whole idea from the beginning. I nagged him to come. I've been putting way too much pressure on him. I realize I shouldn't have done that."

"You want him to be the old Jake, the boy you knew growing up. That's understandable. I imagine you were his champion all his life."

"I always felt responsible for him. Except when he went into the service."

Dr. Abramson gave Andrew a skeptical look. "Really? Are you so sure that's true? You were in Vietnam. You knew what was going on there."

Andrew was surprised at his reaction to this comment. He felt a chill run up his spine, and he started to perspire lightly. "What could I have done? He was half a world away."

"Indeed. Are you telling me you never worried about him while he was in Vietnam?"

Can't fool this lady, thought Andrew. "No, you're right. I worried about him constantly, Dr. Abramson. I tried to pretend I didn't."

"Ah. I thought as much." She took her glasses off and cleaned them on the tail of her lab coat. "Did Jacob tell you I had been encouraging him to allow me to hypnotize him?"

"Yes. I think that's one reason he decided not to come back. He seemed to hate the idea."

She tipped her head to one side as if she were deciding whether to say something to him. "Andrew, I believe I should tell you something I suspect about Jake's condition."

"You mean his amnesia?"

"Yes. I'm not sure it's entirely neurological. I mean I don't know that it can be completely attributed to his head injury."

Andrew wiped his forehead. He had been perspiring more than he realized. He felt as if he were somewhere in a swamp and he didn't like it.

"This is a guess, because I was unable to confirm it, which I might have done with hypnosis." She leaned forward. "I believe it's possible something traumatized Jake on that last mission. Traumatized him so badly that he never wants to remember it."

The hair on the back of Andrew's neck stood up. *I don't want to hear this*, he thought. He tried to say it but his throat had closed up.

"I'm telling you because I think someone should be aware of my hypothesis. It's possible he may have spontaneous recall sometime in the future. You, or someone in your family, should be aware this could happen." She stood and extended a hand, and gave Andrew a firm handshake and a smile. He'd never seen her smile; it almost seemed out of character. She looked younger and more vulnerable. She handed him a file folder to give to Jake.

"I appreciate your stopping by to pick this up. Jacob is fortunate to have you in his life."

Andrew shook her hand and mumbled, "Thank you." He didn't know what else to say to her, so he turned and almost stumbled out of her office. He had completely forgotten about the questions he meant to ask.

Even though he was shivering when he reached his car, he rolled down the window and took deep breaths. He still felt the oppressive air of the swamp he'd begun to imagine himself in.

On the drive home he turned on the radio, found a top forties station and sang at the top of his voice: "Leavin' on a Jet Plane"; "Green, Green Grass of Home"; "Purple Haze"; and finally, "We Gotta Get Out of This Place" … all songs he'd heard in Vietnam, and hadn't paid much attention to. He knew every word of every one of them.

***

Andrew stopped at Isabel's to pick Jake up. They didn't talk until they were back in the car when Jake asked, "So what did she say?"

"She thanked me for stopping by the office to pick up your stuff."

"Was she pissed?"

"No, she was fine. She said she had figured she wouldn't see you again after that last session."

"I wasn't a very good patient."

"No, you weren't, but she said she liked you."

"Thanks for giving me a hand with this," Jake said.

Andrew grinned. "She said you were lucky to have me as a big brother."

"She's got that right."

Thanksgiving was good. Isabel joined them and she always livened up any event, and Andrew relaxed. He had decided not to tell anyone about Dr. Penny's "hypothesis." It had thrown him right back into Vietnam. *Better to just forget it. I don't know what the hell she meant by that, anyway, or why she said it.*

194

After Thanksgiving, preparations at the high school kicked into high gear. A number of faculty members offered Andrew their assistance with hanging the art show, and he had several students who showed true leadership qualities. It reminded him why he had wanted to teach art; he loved working with these kids. The stress of those last weeks of preparation caused him to be short with some of them, and he personally apologized to the few with whom he had spoken sharply. They seemed surprised by the apology, as if they didn't even realize it had happened.

The concert and art show were on December 18 and the winter break began the following Wednesday. Preparations for Christmas at the Cameron house had begun earlier that week, with Jake helping pick out the tree … for the first time in his new life … and helping Toni with baking and decorating.

Andrew was proud to show his family the fine work his students had done. While it was not a requirement, he had suggested they try to find a seasonal subject for their paintings, and some were outstanding. Isabel and the two other judges, artists from Philadelphia she had contacted, spent some time earlier that day carefully perusing the twenty-two paintings which Andrew had selected to be in the competition. The doors to the lobby, where the art was on display, were opened to the public at 6:30, and Mary's concert began at 7:30.

Andrew stood against a wall feeling a great sense of pride and accomplishment as he watched the audience stroll around the lobby. The theater department at the high school had decorated it beautifully: it was a veritable winter wonderland, with draped twinkling white lights artfully interlaced with tree branches sprayed silver. An evergreen tree, decorated with twinkling lights and large silver bows, stood in the center of the lobby. Nervous student artists huddled in groups watching the crowd study their paintings, occasionally walking over to Andrew for reassurance.

"You've already won. Your work is up there and people are admiring and appreciating it," he told them. "Don't forget, art is always subjective, at least to a point. That's the way life works. But I see twenty-two blue ribbon winners standing in this lobby right now. You've won because you've been willing to put yourselves out there."

Jake and Isabel walked over to him. Jake's eyes were shining. "Andy, you're a terrific teacher. These kids are doing amazing stuff. Isabel tells me it wasn't easy to select the winners."

Toni and Max joined him as Jake and Issy moved to another painting. "Jake seems to be really enjoying himself," said Max. "I don't think I've seen him so relaxed in a crowd since he got home."

"We haven't seen him in a crowd at all. Just around people in town. You know why he's more relaxed, don't you?" Toni looked at both of them. "We're not in West Chester. These people don't know him. It's much easier for him to not be on guard about someone running up to him, expecting Jake to embrace them with open arms and start reminiscing."

Andrew watched Jake for a moment, talking and laughing with Kennett Square residents, very much at ease. It was the old Jake, displaying his natural charm. "Yes, I guess you're right. It's good to see him this way."

An announcement was made that the concert was to begin in ten minutes, and the crowd filed into the auditorium. Before the chorus entered, the winning artwork was announced: third prize to a senior girl for a watercolor of the graceful neck, head and antlers of a deer; second prize to a junior girl, a snowscape at night, also a watercolor, a standout for the use of patterns of light from church windows on the snow.

First prize was awarded to a senior boy Andrew privately considered his star pupil, an acrylic painting of the northern lights, softened to an impressionistic glow against a starlit sky, seeming almost alive. Andrew had thought these would be the standouts, and he was proud of all his kids as he watched them heartily congratulate the winners. *They know it was fair*, he thought. *That's important.*

Andrew was thrilled with Mary's concert. He had heard her students rehearsing a time or two, and he was impressed with everything she had done. Some of the music was difficult, especially the selections from Benjamin Britten's "Ceremony of Carols," and he saw Mary's command of both the music and her singers through their professional, skilled performance. He wasn't surprised to see how connected the choir and conductor were; that was part of Mary's gift. Some of the pieces were those he and Mary had sung with the College Choir and they brought back happy memories. He glanced at Jake, who was listening attentively, immersed in the music.

Back at the house after the close of a highly successful evening for young Mr. and Mrs. Cameron, Max and Toni prepared coffee and Christmas cookies as Mary and Jake sat at the piano, discussing some of the music from the concert. Andrew, watching them, realized it was exactly the same scenario that had created such a negative response in him only a few weeks earlier, and he was amazed and dismayed by how he had reacted. *Mary sharing her music with a brother she loves. How could I have so misread that?*

"Jake seemed to have had a good time tonight," he remarked to Isabel, seated near him.

197

"*Oui, vachement.* And you realize why, do you not? No one in that crowd had any expectations of him."

"Yes, Mom commented on that."

"Being in his home town is not easy for him, Andrew. Everyone here knows him. He knows no one."

Andrew sighed. "Let's not talk about that tonight, Issy. I just want to enjoy Christmas with him."

***

Dr. Abramson's cryptic comments about Jake's amnesia stayed with Andrew, as much as he tried to put them in the back of his mind. In order to avoid mentioning Vietnam to Jake, Andrew instead focused on good memories: family vacations, trips to Tennessee, other Christmases they had celebrated.

Jake enjoyed hearing those stories, and one day after Christmas break Andrew was at work on a painting when Jake came into the room carrying a photo album.

"Have we looked at this?" he asked Andrew. It was the album of his and Mary's wedding.

"I'm sure we did, but do you want to go through it again?" Andrew wiped his brushes and his hands, and put down his palette.

"Yes, I'd like that." They went into the living room and sat on the sofa, enjoying the warmth from the fire.

Together they admired pictures of the bride, of the bride and her attendants, of the family. Andrew reminded Jake who the Tennessee family members were: Alice, her husband Ben, the four daughters and Grace's fiancé Sam, now her husband.

"Isabel was there?" Jake pointed to a picture of her talking with Alice and Ben at the reception.

"Yes, she helped Mom with the rehearsal dinner and the reception."

"So I must have met her."

"Yes."

There was a photo of the Cameron brothers: Andrew, serious in his Marine dress blues; Jake, every inch the proud, confident soldier in Army dress greens.

Jake gazed at the photo for a long time, touching it. There was anguish in his eyes as he said to his brother, "That's the Jake you want back, isn't it?"

He didn't wait for an answer, but stood abruptly and went upstairs to his room. Andrew followed him up and tapped on the door. "Let me in, Jake."

"I need to be alone right now, Andy." His voice sounded broken.

"I need to talk to you. Just for a minute."

Jake opened the door, his eyes red.

Andrew stepped inside and put his arms around his brother, giving him a rough, fierce embrace. "I love you, Jake. I mean that."

"I know you're trying to, Andy. It's okay. I understand."

Andrew didn't know what else to say. He stood with this man, this stranger, his brother but not his brother. There was a chasm between them that Andrew didn't know how to cross.

CHAPTER 20

In early March Jake asked for a family conference and they gathered in the living room. He seemed nervous as he started to speak. "You know, I wish I could remember more. I really do. And I have an idea. I hope you'll understand and be okay with this."

He took a deep breath. "I've been doing a lot of thinking over the past few months. It doesn't seem likely that I'm going to remember much more about who I was. I really haven't had any kind of recall since last summer. It seems kind of odd to me that I still haven't remembered anything at all about the years we've lived here. None of my school friends, even when I've seen them, even the people who tell me we were football or baseball teammates."

Andrew started to speak but thought better of it. *Where's he going with this?*

"One thing I've decided. I can't spend every waking moment trying to find this person I can't remember. Somehow I've got to find a way to move on." He looked at each of them, and they nodded.

"What can we do to help, Jake?" asked Mary.

"I don't think you can. I think I have to do this on my own. And it's going to be easier if I am someplace else besides West Chester. Every person in this town has memories of Jake Cameron. Except me. If one more person corners me and asks me how I could forget that game where I won the league title, I think I may slit my throat." He laughed, but no one joined him.

"So what are you thinking, son?" Max leaned forward.

"I want to go away. I'm not sure for how long, but I want to drive south. I want to go to Tennessee and … and South Carolina. Being places where I grew up might trigger something."

Andrew said eagerly, "I think that's a great idea. We could leave as soon as school lets out."

Jake hesitated and seemed to choose his words carefully as he replied, "I need to do this by myself, Andy. I may be gone for a while. I have a lot to figure out. I may spend a few months someplace, if I like it. Find a job, meet new people. Maybe move on and do that all over again. One way or another, I need to find out who this Jake Cameron is."

Andrew tried not to let his face reflect the disappointment he felt. *Back off, Andrew. Let Jake do this his way.*

No one spoke until Toni said, "Why not get a job here? Or someplace nearby? Maybe in Kennett Square?"

"I suppose I could do that, but it's just not easy for me to be here."

"I think I understand, Jake," Mary said. "You have to be aware, though, that all of us would rather you stay here, or at least someplace nearby."

"What, wrapped in cotton and kept in a box? That's no way to live, Mary. All of you try to protect me. I know why, you love me and you don't want to see me hurt." He looked around at each of them. "I love all of you more than I can ever say. But I can't stay here. Not right now. Maybe I need to get out and get some bumps and bruises. It will be an adventure. Please try to understand. Isabel does."

Andrew felt as if a bolt of electricity had just shot through his gut. *Isabel.* She had suggested this, he was sure. He looked down and bit his lip hard. He had a roaring in his ears and heard bits and pieces of the conversation around him: "When are you thinking of leaving?" "Later this month, if the weather holds." "Are you sure about this?" "You'll let us know if you need anything?" "I'll stay in touch."

He was aware they were getting up and going into the kitchen. "How about some ice cream, Andy?" Max bent over and squeezed his shoulder. He looked up and saw the concern in Max's eyes.

"No ... I ... I have to run to the school. I forgot something."

He drove straight to Isabel's and knocked heavily, pushing his way in as soon as she started to open the door.

"Andrew?"

"What the hell have you done?" He was shaking with anger.

"Ah. Jacob has talked with you, I see." She folded her arms and leaned against the wall.

"It's a terrible plan, Isabel. He can't do it."

"He needs to do it, Andrew. He needs to find his way into the world again. He needs to realize he's strong, and smart, and capable of doing anything he wants to do, and being anyone he wants to be."

He began to pace around her apartment. "He doesn't even know who he is."

"You saw how different he was at your Christmas event at Kennett High School. He was truly enjoying himself, laughing and talking with people he had never met. Perhaps that is who he is — who he's meant to be."

She stood in front of Andrew and put her hands on his shoulders to stop his pacing. "He has to have the freedom to find out who he is. As long as he is with his family, he continues to try

202

to recapture a person who does not seem to be here any longer. At some point he would come to resent that."

"If anything bad happens to him ..." he had an index finger in her face.

"What could happen to him that would be worse than what he already has to deal with?"

"It could ... what if ... people might ..." His mind was churning, seeing all kinds of horrible scenes. Jake dead by the side of a road. Jake drowned at the bottom of a lake. Jake in jail. Only that Jake looked more like Allan Martin.

"Do you think he has forgotten all the skills he learned in Special Forces? He has not. He remembered French; it was part of his training. His skills in survival, I am sure, are intact. I would think with the skills he has Jacob could take care of himself in any situation."

"You're a cold-hearted bitch. Throwing him to the wolves."

"*C'est pas vrai*, I care for him. Very much. More than I have ever let him know."

Andrew felt the tears gathering in his throat, and he sank down into a chair.

"I can't let him do this, Issy. What if he doesn't come back?"

"That could happen. He could find someplace where he can thrive. Where he feels he has found the new Jake Cameron, and is able to build a life for himself."

Andrew was silent and Issy knelt beside him. "Do you love your brother, Andrew?"

"You know I do."

She put a gentle hand on his arm. "Then love him more. Let him go."

***

By the time the Camerons saw Jake drive his "new" used car out of sight, Andrew had reconciled himself to his brother's leaving. The family had helped Jake with some planning: the first thing they did was contact Toni's sister Alice and her husband Ben Rogers, who invited Jake to come and stay with them for as long as he wanted.

It was a generous offer and Jake accepted. Alice and Ben had moved into the house on Norris Lake after Ben's parents moved to Florida to enjoy their golden years. Grace and Leslie were now both married and living in nearby Knoxville, and Grace and Sam had a baby girl. Louise and Stephanie were still at home and were busy teenagers. Ben now owned a chain of sporting goods stores in the Knoxville area, and he suggested Jake might like to come to work for him.

Jake had spent time at the WCSC fieldhouse running and using the workout room, thanks to Max's connections with the athletic coaches, and he was in great shape physically. His natural ability as an athlete was intact, and he usually ran circles around the people with whom he played pickup basketball games.

While he had insisted on contributing to the Cameron household expenses, as Mary and Andrew did, Jake had saved much of his military pay and used that to buy a used car in good condition. He had withdrawn most of the balance and converted some into traveler's checks and kept some as cash, which worried Toni a little. "I don't know how I feel about you driving around the country with over a thousand dollars in cash in the trunk of your car, Jake."

"It's well hidden, Mom. It's my emergency fund. I'll keep it with me at Alice's and Ben's and trust me, nobody will ever know I have it. But I don't want to mooch off of them for long. I'm going to look for a place of my own after a couple of weeks. Maybe near the store where I'll be working." Jake liked the idea of working in a sporting goods store, especially since Ben's Knoxville and Clinton stores stocked guns: handguns as well as rifles and shotguns.

There was another reason Andrew began to feel better about Jake leaving. They would all be together in late July, when Toni's and Alice's sister Melanie would bring her family from California to the Norris Lake house for a family reunion. It would be the first time the Stewart sisters would all be together in many years. So even though Jake was not at home, Andrew knew he would see him again in a few months. And maybe being around the Rogers family and visiting locations in Pine Glen where he had grown up would awaken more memories for him.

"Well, I met your Aunt Alice and her family at our wedding four years ago, and I'm looking forward to seeing all of them again. But I'm really excited about meeting Melanie and her family. Your Aunt Melanie ... she's kind of a legend in this family," Mary laughed.

"She is. Star of stage, screen, and television. Although most of her performances were on stage in the Los Angeles area, and the screen performances were walk-ons or small roles, one or two lines. She did have a recurring role in a soap opera for a couple of years," said Toni.

"Don't forget the commercials. She's still receiving residuals for some of those," added Max.

"The most important thing is that she's happily married to a really good man now and has two lovely daughters," Toni commented. Melanie's girls were now eight and six, and Andrew realized with a start those were the exact ages he and Jake had been when Allan Martin had shot and killed his grandparents.

205

Alicia, the older, was a lovely little girl with golden curls and blue eyes, and Victoria, whom they called Tori, had dark hair and brown eyes but the same fair skin as her sister. Yearly Christmas cards showed that Melanie was as lovely as ever, and it was obvious her husband David adored the beautiful ladies in his life.

Jake kept his promise about staying in touch, phoning every couple of weeks after he got to Tennessee and talking to whomever was at home. His second phone call came after he had been in Tennessee for about a month, and he talked at length to Andrew.

"Alice gave me the addresses of the places we lived in Pine Glen, and the last time I had a day off I drove over there and found two of them. Plus the house she lived in after she married Ben."

Andrew didn't comment and Jake went on, "It's a really nice town, Andy. First I went to the house we lived in across from Cedar Hill School. It's on a dead-end street, did you remember that? And there are these great woods at the end of the road. Mom had told me you and I used to climb trees there. But did we ever … did we find branches that had fallen and carry those up into the trees and build tree forts? Or am I just imagining we did that?"

"We did exactly that, Jake. When I think about it, it's really pretty amazing neither one of us fell out of those forts. We had no clue what we were doing." They both laughed.

"Yeah, we had fun, for sure. That playground … did you come down a slide hands first so fast that you were airborne for about three feet and landed on the ground, and there was a sharp rock sticking up and you cut your hand?"

Andrew had to sit down. "That happened, Jake. I had a nasty cut and it hurt like crazy. I still have a scar."

"We had to take you to the emergency room. I remember the smells. And you had better not be sitting there crying right now. You did enough of that when you cut your hand."

Andrew laughed through the tears that he couldn't hold back.

"I did not. I was very brave," he said. "Where else did you go?"

"To the house we lived in with Aunt Alice and Aunt Melanie and the two little girls, Gracie and Leslie. It didn't bring anything back, but I was surprised at how tiny it was .We had seven people crammed into that little house?"

"Not for long. Mom and Alice bought the house on Cedar Hill Lane not long after Uncle Steve died."

"Yes, and then she ... I mean Alice ... and Ben were married not too long after that, right? I went by the house they lived in on Connecticut Avenue. It was close to the one we stayed in after Alice and the girls left."

"Yes, we could walk there in about ten minutes." He hesitated. "Did you go to our grandparents' house?"

"No, ran out of time. I'll stop by there sometime soon."

After he hung up Andrew thought, *Ran out of time, or are you avoiding it?*

207

CHAPTER 21

In late July, the Camerons made the ten-hour drive from West Chester to the Rogers' home in East Tennessee, crossing Pennsylvania and driving through scenic and sometimes rugged parts of West Virginia and Kentucky. With four adults handling the driving and nice weather, it was a pleasant trip and seemed shorter to Andrew than the trip he recalled from their high school days.

Jake had phoned again a couple of times before they left, speaking with Toni each time. She reported that he liked his job in Ben's store and had also qualified as an instructor at a shooting range outside of Knoxville. He'd found an apartment in the town of Clinton where he was working. Andrew's plan was to encourage Jake to stay put, to remain in the Knoxville area. He couldn't see any reason for Jake to look for Allan Martin, and he intended to tell him so when he saw him.

The Stewart sisters' reunion was in full swing at the Rogers' house on Norris Lake, and a buffet supper was followed by dessert. The party spilled through the sliding glass doors from the living room onto the patio, and Andrew was enjoying himself. Melanie had hardly aged at all; she and Mary were at the Rogers' piano, looking through albums of musical theater songs and playing and singing through them occasionally as Melanie's daughters watched and sometimes joined in.

On the patio, Toni was playing with Grace's seven-month-old daughter, Andrea, named after Andrew; he had been touched and told her he was honored. Sam and Grace were sitting with her as they laughed at Andi playing peek-a-boo. Alice, Max, and David Winters, Mel's husband, were chatting; the newlyweds, Leslie and her new husband, Calvin Grayson, were drifting in their own lovely little universe as they sipped wine. Ben and his daughters, Louise and Stephanie, were in the kitchen loading the dishwasher.

Jake leaned against the door to the patio, nursing a beer as he observed the chatting, relaxed family members. But Andrew saw a restlessness — a *disconnect* in Jake that concerned him. He watched as Jake looked searchingly at each of them. It seemed he was trying to find something that would help him feel he was part of this family.

He's a guest here, thought Andrew. *He doesn't really know these people.* Jake smiled at Melanie as she glanced over at him and started to sing "If I Loved You." He seemed more at ease with her than anyone else, and he had told Andrew his earlier memories of her singing to him as a child had become more vivid since he had actually met her.

Ben brought out more beer, and Andrew picked up two bottles and said to his brother, "Why don't we go sit out by the water? It's quieter and we can talk."

They grabbed folding lounge chairs and put them on the dock, relaxing into them. "Talk to me, Jake."

"This is nice. More nice people in this family. I think us males are outnumbered, though." He laughed briefly.

"Yes, well. You have something you want to talk about, I think."

Jake sipped his beer. "I went by the Stewart house last week, Andy."

209

"And?"

"I sat outside and looked at it for a long time. You told me we lived there for several months before Allan Martin kicked in the door and shot our grandparents and Steve Jackson. I was trying to remember what it looked like inside."

"Nothing?"

"I went to the door and was completely honest with the man who answered. Well, to a point. I didn't tell him about the murders, but I did tell him about my memory loss, and I asked if he'd be willing to let me come inside and look around."

Andrew raised his eyebrows and took a gulp of beer. "And he let you come in?"

"Yes. And I remembered some things. At least, I think I did."

"Go on."

"That night …you and I were on the steps leading from the living room to the second floor. Grace and Leslie were with us. We were playing with something. Cars, maybe."

"Yes. We were playing with cars."

Jake leaned forward. "I remember we started to go upstairs only I tripped or something, and you caught me."

"That happened."

"I got a fuzzy picture of a dark-haired man near the front door. I couldn't really see his face."

Andrew was very still. "So you saw him."

"Not really. It just flashed by. But I think that's why I tripped … I was looking down at him."

"Nothing else?"

"No. Only that. Except …" he hesitated. "Fear. You put your arms around me. Was I scared?"

"I sure as hell was. I'm not sure about you."

"You were shaking, but you wanted to protect me. I remember that, Andy."

"I never wanted him to hurt you."

Jake looked off into the distance. Andrew again saw the strain on his face and the shadows in his eyes. *Haunted by things he can't remember*, he thought. *My beloved brother, I would give just about anything if I could help you.*

Jake said slowly, "Not knowing who you are … it's scary as hell. You read stuff about people wandering around in some town, not knowing who they are, and I can't even imagine what a nightmare that would be. I've been lucky to have my family."

He gazed out across the water for a moment. "That insomnia I had. Before I talked to you about it I'd try to … I'd lie in bed and think, 'My name is Jacob Cameron. I have a brother named Andy. A mother named Antonia, but people call her Toni. A dad named Max.'" He gave Andrew a wistful smile. "I always thought of you first. Then my heart would stop pounding, and I'd be okay."

Andrew sighed. "I wish I'd known sooner. I should have been more help to you."

"No, it's fine. The longer I was home, the more I began to make new memories with all of you, the better I felt. Music was a huge help. And Mary. And Isabel." He smiled wryly. "Isabel. She's in Europe, I guess."

"Yes, she left at the end of May. She should be back sometime next month."

"I was really nervous about leaving home. You didn't know that, did you?"

"No. I thought you were eager to leave."

"Well, I was and I wasn't. But coming here was a good thing. Ben and Alice have been kind and generous to me, and I'll never forget that. I've learned a lot about myself. I'm good at my job. I get along with most people. I'm responsible. I'm organized." He grinned. "Things I learned in the military, maybe?"

Andrew laughed. "The organized part, definitely. The rest of it is … who you've always been."

"I'm a good instructor, too. I'm patient, most of the time. Although there was this one asshole … I almost ripped his head off. I was sure he was going to shoot somebody because he was so goddam careless." He laughed. "My boss had a discussion with me, and we agreed if it happened again I'd talk to him before I tore a customer a new one."

They laughed together, and after a moment Andrew said, "Why not just stay here, Jake? You've got a job you enjoy, a place of your own, and you're near family. Couldn't you make a life here?"

"I need to go to South Carolina, Andy. I need to try to find Allan Martin. I want to look into his face and ask him why he did what he did, why he hurt the people I love." He paused. "He's been out of prison for over four years. Ben told me he was released in 1968. Obviously he didn't come back here. He has to be out there somewhere."

"I wish you wouldn't, Jake. Just let it go."

"I can't do that. If I see him, it might be a way to remember. Maybe even remember everything."

Andrew felt flutters in his gut again. "This is my fault. I pushed you too hard. It doesn't matter, really. Please don't do it."

"I can't stop trying to remember. I thought if I got away from … well, from West Chester, it would be better. It's really not. And it wasn't you. It was me. It was always me who wanted to remember my life before the injury."

He put down the beer bottle and turned to face his brother.

212

"Those sessions with Dr. Penny — I didn't just sit and stare at the walls. We talked about what I was trying to do, recover my memory. She said we're connected to the people we love through our shared memories, both good and bad, and she talked about how people in her field are trying different techniques to help people with amnesia regain those memories."

"She mentioned to me that she wanted to hypnotize you."

"I never told anybody this, but that idea scared the shit out of me. What if I couldn't be brought out of the trance? Where the hell would I be then?"

"Hypnosis is considered completely safe, Jake. I don't believe I've ever heard of anything like that happening."

"Easy for you to say. You have a normal brain. Mine is anything but normal, you know? And even if I had been brought out of the trance … would I have lost even more, maybe lost all my new memories?"

Jake shook his head. "I couldn't do it. But she talked about how memory might be stored not only in the mind. She talked about 'sense memories' — things might be recalled through taste, or smell, or touch. How mothers and children, especially, are connected in that way. I didn't really get it, but since I've been around Grace and her baby it's beginning to make sense."

He lay back with an arm behind his head and looked up at the clear night sky. "All those nice people … our family … you can see those connections. Especially the Stewart sisters. I guess what they went through made their bond stronger than most." He sat up and gazed intently at his brother.

"Do you know who Mom is to me? She's a nice lady I met at Walter Reed Hospital. She's been so kind to me. She'll be talking and reach over and touch my hand or my arm. She fixes foods she says were my favorites, and when she puts the plate down in front of me she'll kiss my forehead. I just don't know how to react to any of this. I know that has to hurt her. She's tried to help fill in some of the blanks, and I've certainly grown to care about her. Especially when she was nursing me through those awful migraines, I had a sense of what Dr. Penny had talked about. So I can accept that she's my mother.

"But I hate this part. She'll be so hopeful about something she tells me or does for me, and when it doesn't work — when I don't react the way I used to, it just kills me to see how sad she looks. She tries not to, but I see it in her eyes.

"And then I see her say something to you, or do something with you, and it just clicks and you share a laugh, or a smile ... it's just *there*. Do you know what I mean?"

Andrew nodded. *God, how hard this is for Jake. I never realized. Mary tried to tell me, but I just didn't get it.*

"Dr. Penny explained her hypothesis about this. About you and Mom. She thinks you might have an 'emotional history' that is so dense and intricate you don't actively remember but a small part of it. It's the thousands and thousands of times she touched you as an infant and young child. Bathing you, rubbing baby powder on your body. Kissing you all over, the way mothers do, smelling your toes, pulling you up to a sitting position, walking you around before you actually learned to walk ... all that stuff. It's the times she kissed away your 'boo-boos,' wiped away your tears, put a hand on your head to see if you had a fever.

"Then later, teaching you to talk, reading to you, teaching you to read, helping you learn to draw and color and cut things out. I mean, you *know* she did all of those things, even if you don't recall when they happened.

"So you and Mom have a connection so deep and intense that you don't even think about it. It's just part of who you are. But it's all there when you call her 'Mom.'"

He grew very quiet and they both became aware of the sound of water lapping gently against the dock.

"That's what I've lost, and I don't know that I'll ever have that with her again. Or with you, or with Dad."

He stood and said forcefully, "But I sure as hell want to try."

Sketch #4
TONI

I'll never forget the look on Andy's face when Jake announced he was leaving. He looked as if he were ill. And then he didn't join us for the celebratory ice cream, something we did whenever Jake recovered a memory. This was different, though. We were trying to give him support and encouragement, but Andy couldn't do it. Max told me he mumbled something about needing to go back to Kennett High School.

I learned later where he had gone. Issy eventually told me that he had gone to her apartment, hoping she would convince Jake to stay with us. That didn't surprise me. It was obvious Andy wanted Jake to stay at home or at least to stay nearby – so he could make sure Jake was safe.

Jake and I had a long talk the following day. I was reading, and he sat next to me on the sofa. "Good book?" He stretched his legs out and laced his fingers behind his head.

"Yes." I put the bookmark in it, closed it and smiled at him. "You'd like to talk."

He sat up and turned toward me. "I hope you understand why I'm doing this," he began. "I know Andy doesn't, and I know I've upset him."

I had noticed that when Jake gave us his news, he never looked directly at his brother. I'm sure he anticipated the effect his announcement would have on Andrew.

"I truly believe I understand, Jake."

He smiled, and it gave me a twinge in my heart. Physically, he hadn't changed at all. But he was different, and I realized he always would be. I loved him. More importantly, I liked him. He had tried hard to recover his memories, to understand what he had been to us. He was respectful and sometimes affectionate. I remember what Dr. Forrester had said to us about people with amnesia having the same soul even if they never recovered the mind's memories.

"I know I've disappointed Andy. He wants so much for me to be the old Jake. Were we so much alike?"

I laughed in surprise. "Good heavens, no. You could have hardly been more different," I told him. "Andrew likes order in his life, to have a plan and try to make it happen. He's always had that trait. You, on the other hand, were always something of a free spirit. Andrew worked hard for good grades so he could get a scholarship and go to West Chester State. You worked just hard enough for grades that ensured you wouldn't be thrown off the sports teams. Actually, you did better than that, and Max and I thought you could get into college. But I don't believe college was a goal for you. And that was okay; I was sure you'd land on your feet no matter what you did."

217

"Did Andy and I always get along?"

"When you were little you were very close, but as you grew older that changed. No pictures of Andy in a football or baseball uniform. And that habit you had of taking girls away from him once you got to high school — that led to some interesting discussions."

"Andy's so cautious about everything. You can't be a cautious football player, you'll get your bell rung," he settled back comfortably. "From what you've all told me, I was anything but cautious. I'm told I surprised my football coaches and invented some of my own plays."

"You won more than one game that way. I cheered louder than anybody."

"So I was something of a daredevil, I guess. And no, I've sure never seen that in Andy. Were you surprised when he enlisted in the Marine Corps?"

"Not after Max talked to me, and then both of us discussed it with him. Andrew made it fit into his plans. It seemed like the smart thing to do, and he agreed."

He leaned forward, his elbows on his knees. "I think I was very lucky that you were my mother."

I noticed his choice of verb tense. "I was lucky that you were my son. I saw something of myself in you. I left home as soon as I got married, unlike my sister Alice." I hesitated and added, "And

218

something of your father. The things about him that I fell in love with."

"Please tell me about him. All I've heard has been from Andy. I think he hated Allan – our father."

"I'd like to tell you about the handsome, charming man I fell in love with when I was twenty," I said. "He wasn't always a monster, Jake. He treated me like a princess. He gave me everything I ever wanted." I stopped and smiled at him. "Most of all, he gave me two wonderful, beautiful sons."

"What changed him?"

"I wish I knew. He had a volatile relationship with his father, whom I've come to realize was probably a narcissist. A person who thought only of himself, and apparently always had. Allan became very controlling. I left him once and he seemed to come to his senses, and things were good again for a while. Sadly, I was too naïve to recognize that he had serious problems. I finally realized I had to get you and your brother away from him for good. I wasn't sure what he might do."

"You think he might have hurt us?"

"I really didn't know. I saw how terrified your brother was. For some reason, you didn't seem to be. Though spending that night in the hunting cabin traumatized you."

He hesitated, and I thought I knew what was coming next. "May I ask you a question?"

"Of course. Ask me anything you want."

"That must have been so hard for you, what he did. I know it was a long time ago, but how did you manage to get past it?"

"It was a terrible shock. I never dreamed he was capable of murder." I hadn't thought of this in a while, and it wasn't easy to go back to that time, but he deserved my best answer.

"At first, we were so busy just dealing with decisions about what we would do next, there was hardly time to think about it. I did feel responsible, especially about Steve – your Aunt Alice's husband. My sisters were great. Oh, there was definitely tension, but we managed to work through it. We loved each other, and that never changed. It was a help that I was able to see a pastoral counselor. I blamed myself."

"It wasn't your fault. How could you know he'd do what he did?"

I smiled at him. "You and your brother were a big help to me, too. That's almost exactly what Andy said when I told you both I was so sorry."

I turned my head to one side and wiped the tears from the corners of my eyes, and Jake put his arms around me and hugged me.

"Thank you for telling me, Mom. I'm sorry I made you cry."

He was so sweet. "No, you needed to know about it. My life has been full and happy, thanks to your dad – Max – and you boys. And now Mary.

She's the daughter I never had." I couldn't resist. "I'd like another one."

He laughed. "What is it with moms, that they want their sons to get married?"

We laughed together, and he became thoughtful again.

"Am I so much different now than I was before I was injured?"

"In some ways. But I think you would have been restless and left home eventually. I think that's one reason you joined the Army. It was a glorious adventure. So the choice you're making now to strike out on your own is really no surprise."

"So you do understand." He smiled again, and for a moment I felt the connection we had before he became the new Jake.

"One thing Andy has enjoyed is your new-found love of classical music. You used to tease him about singing, until I put a stop to it."

He laughed, and then grew pensive. "Whatever happens, I want you to know how much I have appreciated your kindness. All of you. I know Andy will be angry with me for a while – maybe for a long time. But staying here in West Chester ..." his voice trailed off and he sighed.

"I have no idea what will happen in the future. I just know I have to move on, to stop trying to be the Jake Cameron who lived here for what must have been a lot of happy years." He leaned forward

221

and gave me another warm hug. "In case I forget to say it, thank you for everything. Most of all, for understanding."

"That's what moms are for." I tried to keep it light but could feel the tears very close to the surface.

We didn't have another opportunity to talk. And thinking back, Jake may have preferred it that way.

He had told me goodbye.

CHAPTER 22

Isabel raised an eyebrow as she examined the painting Andrew was working on. "Where are these coming from?"

A perfectly executed crystal suspension bridge spanned a red-violet river across hills of teal. The bare limbs of lavender trees, highlighted in white, lifted to a cloudy twilight sky. Another painting, not quite finished, showed a steep hill, three figures climbing toward a far-off platform which left the hill and spiraled into a cloudy blue sky. The path was dark against a green forest, but the spiral was a purplish swirl which rose from the hill directly into the sky.

"Dreamscapes," Andrew grinned. "Who the hell knows? It seems I have weird stuff in my head, Issy."

"Violet seems to be your new favorite color, Andrew. *Pourquoi?*"

He grinned again. "I guess I'm dreaming in violet these days, Issy."

He had begun to paint again when they returned from Tennessee. He moved his easel into the dining room; the family seldom used it since Jake had left. Andrew was determined to stop worrying about his brother. *He has to figure this out on his own,* he thought. *What's meant to be is what will be.* Taking Mary in his arms every night helped him as well, and it thrilled him that she matched his passion.

They talked about looking for a house; they had saved enough for a decent down payment at this point, and the plan had always been to begin their family once they had their own home. The thought of Mary carrying his child excited Andrew in a way he had never expected, and their lovemaking was intense and prolonged. Andrew was surprised at his stamina, and Mary stoked the flames every way she could.

"Violet. Some call it the color of passion, Andrew. Things are good with you and Mary these days, *je vois*."

"What makes you think so, Isabel?"

She laughed. "It's good to see you so relaxed, *mon ami*. Does that mean you are no longer angry with me?"

He leaned against the back of a chair. "I was never angry with you, Isabel. I was scared for Jake. But you were right. We had a great talk the night before we left to come home, and I understand better what he's going through. Jake needs to find a way to make a life for himself, since it seems less and less likely he'll remember who he was before he was injured."

"*Bien*. This has been very difficult for all of you, I'm sure. He is still in Tennessee?"

"For the moment. He's helping Ben to find a replacement and train him. He wants to go to the Smoky Mountains and spend some time there, then maybe drive down to South Carolina."

It surprised Andrew that Isabel had been able to let Jake go as she had. There hadn't seemed to be any thought of continuing their relationship once he decided to leave, and she had apparently let him go without hesitation. It made Andrew wonder exactly what their relationship had been. She had been important to Jake and vital in helping him move forward.

"May I ask you a very personal question, Issy?"

"Of course you may ask, but I will not promise to answer." She tipped her head to one side and gave him a sideways glance.

"Did Jake know you had been lovers before?"

"Why do you ask that, Andrew?"

"Well … was he different? Did the memory loss affect his ability to …" he began to regret he had asked the question, and felt himself blush.

He joined in her laugh. "Forget I asked, Issy. That was completely inappropriate."

"*Non*, I will answer you. What you want to know is whether Jacob is a good lover. He is. And he is the same as he was then. The mind may forget, but it would seem the body does not."

"You did what you asked me to do … you let him go. Yet you told me you care for him."

"I will always care for him. He needed to move on." She cocked her head toward the stereo, closing her eyes for a moment, listening to the angelic strains of music.

"Gabriel Fauré, is it not? Lovely … *c'est charmant*."

The sounds of singers and orchestra flowed and floated through the room, producing a restless, dreamy, ethereal beauty, briefly bursting into moments of brilliance. It evoked Andrew's "dreamscapes" perfectly.

"Yes, the *Requiem*. French impressionism. My new love. Maybe this is where the violet is coming from."

"It is my favorite color, Andrew. I have heard it said it indicates one has a free spirit. I never thought that of you, you always craved order in your life. Perhaps this is who Andrew is now trying to become?"

Andrew wiped his brushes on a cloth, and then rubbed linseed oil into them. "I'm trying to do as you suggested, Issy, and let Jake go. Time for me to move on as well. I've been putting my life on hold for months, and that's not fair to anyone. Especially not to Mary."

Andrew's remaining concern was Jake looking for Allan Martin. He tried telling himself if that happened, it might mean Jake would remember more about his childhood. Andrew didn't think it would go beyond that; he believed what he had just said to Issy, that Jake would most likely never completely regain his memory.

And if Jake wanted to settle down somewhere else after he had done some traveling — which seemed to be what he was considering — Andrew thought he could accept that. He realized that more than anything, he wanted Jake to be happy again. *Whatever it takes.*

In early October Jake called; he talked to each of them and let them know he'd be leaving Clinton before the end of the month. "I'm going to Gatlinburg first, and hang around there for a few days, anyway. I want to climb Clingman's Dome again. And just drive around the mountains for a bit, and maybe do some hiking. I'll probably go over the mountain to Cherokee. I know *Unto These Hills* isn't performing now, but I can visit the amphitheater and poke around the town. I don't know how long I'll stay."

"It snows early in the mountains, son. Be sure you have some warm clothes with you," said Toni.

"Will do, Mom. Thanks." Jake replied. They were crowded around the phone, all trying to listen to him. Andrew thought he sounded good — strong and confident.

"I'll stay in touch. I'm not sure what I'll do next, or where I'll go. I do want to go to South Carolina at some point. There's no rush. But I'd like to see the ocean. I don't remember living there at all." There was silence for a moment, and Jake said,

"Well, have a great Thanksgiving, folks. I'll be thinking about you."

They said their goodbyes and Toni and Max went into the living room. Andrew and Mary were doing kitchen detail and finished putting dishes away.

"I don't think he's planning on coming back here for a while," Andrew said. "And I'm okay with that, Mary. I really am."

She smiled. "I know you are. What did Issy say about your dreamscapes?"

"She wanted to know where all the violet — the purple — came from," he said, returning her smile. She took him in her arms.

"Purple is for passion. I could have told her that," she breathed against his neck.

He kissed her and murmured, his lips still close to hers, "Time for bed, my angel."

She returned the kiss and said, "It's only seven-thirty. Is it unseemly for us to keep these 'early to bed' hours?"

"You don't really think Mom and Dad care, do you? They've never cramped our style."

They both laughed and went into the living room, and were surprised to see Toni and Max had apparently gone upstairs.

Andrew laughed and took his wife in his arms. "Looks like the coast is clear."

***

Two weeks later they received a postcard from Gatlinburg, a photo of Clingman's Dome.

This time I climbed this sucker all by myself. Aren't you guys proud of me? — Jake

227

It made all of them laugh. He called again after Thanksgiving. He was in Cherokee and had some news. "I was having coffee and this guy walked up to me and called me by name," he told them. "He looked Indian ... Native American and was wearing jeans and a fatigue jacket. He said we served together in Special Forces. He talked about some of the stuff we had done, but I didn't remember any of it. I didn't get any pictures in my head. It was pretty interesting to find out about that stuff, though; there was some crazy shit that went on over there."

"Did you have Thanksgiving dinner anywhere, Jake?" Toni asked.

"Mom, I'm in an Indian settlement here. Native Americans don't get too excited about Thanksgiving, as you might understand."

"Oh, Jacob, I'm sorry, I just didn't think. How do you like the people there?"

"They are really great — thoughtful and generous and very kind to me. They call me 'man with no yesterdays.' In Cherokee it's 'asgaya átla sáhi.' Kind of cool. Oh, and I've been talking to some folks about what their beliefs are. What they have to say makes a lot of sense to me, you know?"

"How do you mean?" Toni asked.

"Well, I'm still learning. But they believe everybody is connected to the universe and that we're all connected to each other. And if you want to find peace, first you have to find your connection to what's at the center, what they call 'The Great Spirit.' I guess we kind of believe that part. But they talk about 'the Spirit World,' too; how that's the real world and what we see here is a shadow of that world." He laughed. "Like I said, I'm still trying to understand it, but it's pretty interesting."

Max commented, "I've done some reading on Native American philosophy, Jake. It's intriguing, and it sounds as if you may have stumbled onto something meaningful for you."

"Could be," said Jake.

Andrew said, "Tell us more about your new friend ... well, your old Army buddy ... well, you know who I mean."

"Yeah. Choctaw."

"What?"

"That's what everybody here calls him. His name is George Smallwood, but he's not Cherokee. He's from Oklahoma and he's a member of the Choctaw tribe. He's great. I'm helping him build a cabin back in the woods."

Toni couldn't keep herself from asking. "Do you think you might come home for Christmas?"

A pause, and Jake said gently, "I don't think I am. I'm in a different place now, Mom."

"It's fine, Jake," Andrew said quickly. "We understand you're working through a lot. But you have to know we miss you and any time you want to swing through West Chester, we'll be happy to see you."

"I do know that. I love you guys. Have a great Christmas."

They were quiet after they hung up the phone, and Andrew hugged his mother. "He's okay, Mom. He's doing what he needs to do."

"I know, Andy. I'm trying to accept that, and you're setting me a good example."

They received a package from Jake just before Christmas: gifts for each of them, purchased in Cherokee. Soft moccasins for Toni. Wallets worked in leather for Andrew and Max, and a leather portfolio for Mary, embossed with clef signs and music notes. No doubt Jake had it made to order for her. They had no address for

229

him, but they sent a package care of General Delivery in Cherokee: new sweaters and gloves and a warm scarf.

Just after the first of the year they received another postcard, this one a photo of the amphitheater where *Unto These Hills* was performed.

> *Thanks for the Christmas gifts, family. Just got back from a couple of days at Fontana Lake. I'm going south for a bit. More later.*

No signature this time, but it wasn't necessary. As much as Andrew tried not to react, he felt his stomach lurch. *He's going to look for Allan Martin. I wish he wouldn't. Let sleeping dogs lie, Jake, and that man is a filthy cur.*

***

Andrew's calm that had seemed so unshakable through the fall began to show weak spots. He had trouble sleeping. He stopped painting. Mary continued to be his solace, his refuge, providing unfailing love and support.

"I'll be okay once we hear from Jake again," Andrew told her. "Anything could happen. I hope the man is dead and Jake never finds him. I'd give just about anything if he hadn't been so determined to find him."

"What frightens you so, Andy? Allan Martin is sixty years old now. It doesn't seem as though he ever tried to find you. We've never had any indication of that."

"That's true. Maybe he just crawled into the swamp like the slime he is."

Near the end of January an envelope arrived addressed to Andrew, postmarked from Cherokee but with no return address. He stared at it for long moments before opening it, feeling a cold dread creep through his body.

With shaking hands he removed a folded piece of paper with a newspaper clipping in it.

REMAINS OF FORMER MYRTLE BEACH RESIDENT FOUND IN HUNTING CABIN — January 12, 1973

Human remains that authorities believe are those of Allan Martin, formerly of Myrtle Beach, were discovered by a duck hunting party in the Tawndee Swamp on January 10. The cabin he had apparently been living in had burned and the remains were decomposed and partially destroyed by fire.

In 1956 Martin, 60, was convicted of manslaughter in the shooting deaths of Louis and Mona Stewart and Stephen Jackson, all of Pine Glen, Tennessee. He was released from prison in 1968 and it is believed he returned to South Carolina at that time.

The Stewarts were the parents of Martin's former wife Antonia, whereabouts unknown, with whom he had two children.

The Sheriff's Department of Orangeburg County is conducting an investigation into Martin's death.

Andrew suddenly couldn't see. Bile rose in his throat and he swallowed repeatedly. A wave of dizziness caused him to lose his balance and he sat down abruptly. He forced himself to take deep

231

breaths as he put his head between his knees. Gradually he regained control of himself. His vision cleared and he read the clipping again.

What did you do, Jake?

CHAPTER 23

"Do you think Jake killed him?" Max and Andrew were in the garage on the pretext of checking Andrew's car.

"I don't know what to think," Andrew said. He hadn't shared his mail with Mary or his mother yet; he had no idea how or even if to tell either of them what he had just learned.

"We have to tell them, son. Hard as it is, we can't keep this from your mother." He paused for a moment. "Jake never gave us a contact person in Cherokee, did he? There's no one we can call to try to reach him."

Andrew shook his head. "No. And I don't think it's a good idea to just phone the local police department — if there is one — or the Swain County sheriff's office, for obvious reasons."

He felt sick. "How do I tell Mom and Mary, Dad? I don't know if Jake … I think he must have known about it, and maybe he was there. I've been trying to think through every possible scenario. The guy he met in Cherokee, the Smallwood guy. Maybe the two of them went to South Carolina together and …" He shivered. "Maybe I should go down there to see what I can find out."

"Bad idea, Andy. If Jake was involved somehow, that might just tip off the authorities. The article says the death is under investigation. And look at the date … this article is from over two weeks ago. Maybe Jacob will send more information."

"What the hell do we do?"

"Just let your mother and your wife know that apparently Jake learned about Allan Martin's death while he was in South Carolina and wanted us to know. Leave it at that, let them read the article, and let's just sit tight for now. I'll drive over to Philly from time to time and pick up current issues of the Myrtle Beach paper to see if there's anything more recent about the case."

"If I say something now, they may wonder why I only told you first."

"I don't think they will. It's logical you would confide in me before you told your mother. If you want to say something more to Mary, do it when you're alone."

Andrew was grateful to Max for being the one to break the news to Toni. "Andrew had a piece of mail from Jacob today, and he asked me to share it with you. Jake has learned that Allan Martin apparently died in a fire in the hunting cabin he owned."

Just that simple, thought Andrew. The article didn't really say there was suspicion of foul play. *I guess when someone dies alone like that, it would be investigated. Maybe I'm making way too big a deal of this.*

Toni's eyes widened. "When did this happen?"

Andrew responded, "His body was found by hunters on January 10. I guess they're trying to find out more details. Dad said he'd drive over to Philly tomorrow and pick up copies of Myrtle Beach newspapers to see if they've learned anything else."

Max put an arm around Toni. "Are you okay, honey? This has to be a shock."

"I'm more relieved than you can ever know. It may sound cold-hearted, but I'm glad the bastard is dead. Burning seems a good way for him to leave this earth."

Mary took Andrew in her arms later than night. "There's more to the news you received today. Something you didn't tell Toni."

"Dad and I wondered if Jake was there. Don't say anything to Mom."

"He went to Myrtle Beach, didn't he?"

"He said that was what he planned to do. The envelope was postmarked Cherokee, so if he did go to South Carolina, I guess he's back in North Carolina."

She leaned up on one elbow. "Do you really think Jake may have had something to do with this?"

"I honestly don't know. I guess anything is possible. I'd think he would have had to be in Myrtle Beach, or near there, to find that article. Let's just hold off and see if Jake writes or calls to let us know more."

***

In early March they found a follow up item in the Myrtle Beach paper:

> INVESTIGATION INTO DEATH OF ALLAN MARTIN, FORMERLY OF MYRTLE BEACH, CONTINUES — March 5. 1973
>
> Human remains that authorities have determined are those of Allan Martin, formerly of Myrtle Beach, were discovered by a duck hunting party in the Tawndee Swamp on January 10. The cabin he had apparently been living in had burned and the remains were partially destroyed by fire.
>
> Martin, 60, was convicted of manslaughter in the 1954 shooting deaths of Louis and Mona Stewart and Stephen Jackson, all of Pine Glen,

> Tennessee. He was released from prison in 1968. Residents of the village of Tawndee confirmed that Martin had been living alone in the hunting cabin for the past few years.
>
> An autopsy revealed that Martin was in the advanced stages of lung cancer. It appeared his death was caused by asphyxiation or smoke inhalation. The investigation into the fire is incomplete. The Sheriff's Department of Orangeburg County is in charge of the case.

While this was reassuring, the family was concerned that they had received no further communication of any kind from Jake. Eventually Andrew confided in Isabel and asked if she had heard from him.

"No, not a word," she said, reading the two newspaper articles. "It is surprising that you have not heard from him for this long a period of time."

While Andrew believed Jake had been in some way involved with Allan Martin's death, he didn't want to voice this to his mother. Instead, Andrew made excuses; Jake and his new friend "Choctaw" had probably gone off on a trek into the mountains. Toni accepted it; she wanted to believe it. Andrew almost convinced himself that was the case.

By mid-April, the family began to fear something might have happened to Jake. They had heard nothing from him for almost four months.

They sat around the kitchen table and discussed their best course of action. "Should we file a missing person's report?" said Toni. Andrew was worried about her, but he was impressed by her strength and her calm. It helped him to stay on an even keel.

"If we do that, it should probably be filed in Cherokee. That's the last place we heard from him. Maybe somebody in that village knows where Jake and his buddy might be. If they're up in the mountains, there wouldn't be phones or a post office," Max commented.

"I'm going crazy, just sitting here waiting to hear something. I want to go down there and talk to people," Andrew said. Mary put a hand over his. He wasn't sleeping well and he had stopped painting. He and Mary often sat together and listened to music; resting in her arms and losing himself in the Brahms *Requiem* brought him some sense of peace.

"He's a Vietnam veteran, a former member of Special Forces, young, strong, and healthy," Mary commented. "It's quite possible he's simply taking some time away to … to think about what he wants to do next."

Toni smiled gratefully at Mary. "Yes, that makes sense. Andrew, you said the last time you talked to him … at Alice's … he was struggling with … well, with everything."

Max leaned forward. "Something else you should all know. I talked to my friend in the Pentagon. I didn't tell him much, but I learned that there are Vietnam vets living in wilderness areas all over this country. Mainly in Washington State, but it's been rumored some are in Colorado, Wyoming, even the Florida swamps. And who knows where else. These men haven't been able to reintegrate into civilian life, so they seem to just be dropping out. Dozens of them, apparently. Maybe hundreds. There's really no way to tell how many."

Mary asked, "So they may not even know Nixon has agreed to end the war?"

"It's possible. And the worst is that for some of these men, the war may never end." Max sighed.

237

Andrew said abruptly, "Vietnam changed every person who was there. But I just don't see Jake doing that. I really think I should go to Cherokee to see if anyone knows anything."

"School will be out in a few weeks. Why don't you and I drive down then? If we don't get satisfactory answers we could talk to the authorities about filing a missing person's report," Mary said.

"The hell of it is these vets who go into the wilderness don't want to be found. We don't really know what's going on with Jake at this point." Max took Toni's hand. "I don't want to upset you, sweetheart, but it's a possibility and I think we should accept it."

"I just want to know he's all right," Toni said. "If he wants to live in the woods I don't care, as long as he's okay."

Max took Andrew aside. "You do realize if you start an active search for him by law enforcement, you may learn something you don't really want to know."

"I don't think he killed Allan Martin. I think he might have been involved in some way, maybe with the fire. That last newspaper item said Martin had advanced stage lung cancer. He may have been dead when Jake found him."

"Are you saying you think Jake might have started the fire? That would be a hell of a thing."

"Arson is difficult to prove, from what I've read. And honestly, I have no idea what happened. I hate how he's letting Mom worry like this. Before you say it, yes, I know, he can take care of himself. And Dad? I think he's okay. I believe I'd know if he weren't."

***

Andrew had in his head he and Mary would arrive in Cherokee, find out where Choctaw's cabin was, drive to it and give Jake hell for not being in touch with them for months, and he'd have some excuse, and everything would be okay.

They left at the end of the first week of June, following a different route than the one they had taken the previous summer. They drove west to Harrisburg and headed south on Interstate 81 through Virginia, leaving the main highway below Blacksburg and going first to Asheville and then continuing to Cherokee. It was a long drive, and they broke it up by treating themselves to a stop at a resort between Roanoke and Blacksburg.

It was a good decision, giving them a brief respite from the concerns they were dealing with, and Andrew relaxed and lost himself in Mary's arms for a night. He liked being away with her again; they had so much enjoyed their time in Canada. But that trip had been a carefree holiday for them. This wasn't really a vacation, and Andrew at times found himself feeling uneasy and anxious.

When they arrived in Cherokee they stopped at a small restaurant and talked to the proprietor, who told them he hadn't seen either Jake or Choctaw for several weeks. Maybe even a couple of months. Andrew's apprehension grew as he asked how to get to the cabin.

He was very quiet as they drove out of town, Mary giving him careful directions. Andrew gripped the wheel, almost dreading what they would find. They pulled up to the cabin and walked around the outside. Andrew called Jake's name and when there was no answer, he kicked the door open. They found empty rooms that showed no sign of anyone having been there for weeks.

"Wonder where they went?" Mary said, trying not to panic.

"I didn't expect this. I was sure he'd be here."

"The restaurant owner said maybe they had gone into the mountains."

"Maybe. But Jake's car isn't here. I think they've left the area."

He hesitated, "I know I never specifically told you, but Max and I both thought Jake might have somehow been involved with Allan Martin's death. If we follow through on this, file a missing person's report, it might lead to a lot of questions in South Carolina. We suspect he went there, but we don't know that."

"So what do you want to do?" Mary walked through the cabin again, thinking they might have missed something. She opened and closed the few drawers and cabinets in the kitchen. "They did a nice job of building this cabin." She stopped suddenly. "Andy."

She was holding Jake's dog tags.

"Why would he leave them here?"

Andrew took them from her. "He knew I'd try to find him." He gazed at them for a long moment. "I can only think he left them behind because he wanted to drop off the radar."

"You mean he doesn't want us to look for him."

Both of them went through the cabin again, opening cabinets, turning drawers upside down, getting down on their hands and knees to peer under chairs and tables. There was nothing else there.

Finally Andrew said, "You know what I think? I think he's protecting us. If we have no idea where he is, we would never have to lie."

This time he said it aloud. "My God, Jake. What did you do?"

CHAPTER 24

"The Great Smoky Mountains National Park was once the homeland of the Cherokee Nation, an indigenous tribe driven across the Mississippi River by the United States government as part of its push to claim new territory for its immigrant settlers from Europe." Mary was reading from a brochure she had picked up in Cherokee as they drove back to Gatlinburg.

"It says most of the Cherokees had to leave their homes and were taken overland to Oklahoma Territory along something called the 'Trail of Tears.'"

"Yes, that's what the play is about. I mean *Unto These Hills*. Some managed to stay behind. They hid in the mountains, and eventually came to an understanding with the government and were able to buy some of their land back. Most of the people we saw today are their descendants, though some Cherokee returned from Oklahoma. They longed for their home."

Mary had continued to read and commented, "A lot of people died on that march, that's why it was called 'The Trail of Tears.' That's awful. And Oklahoma? It says in the brochure it was 'quite different from their ancestral mountains.' I would think so."

During the hour drive through the park, Andrew and Mary saw what the Cherokee had always venerated about their land. Mary had never been here, and she commented on the rich abundance of trees of every kind, the glimpses of wild life she saw, the stunning vistas and soaring majesty of the hillsides as the road wound its way through the popular park. Even Andrew, distracted as he was, appreciated anew the beauty of this place he had visited as a child.

"You grew up here," Mary said in awe.

"Well, not *right* here, but close enough to visit often. Mom and Max loved these mountains."

He recalled the feeling he had experienced as a child — the serenity of the mountains. *It's peaceful here,* he thought. *No wonder Mary loves it; she has this kind of serenity.*

He made a promise to himself to come back some day with paints in hand. *I need to paint this.* Driving through the park helped him to step back from the emotional precipice he sensed and focus on the problem at hand. They had checked into the Gatlinburg Inn the day before and on returning walked through town to find a place for dinner, deciding instead to take food back to their room so they could talk privately.

"We've all agreed that Jake has to find his own way, and when I think back, ever since he left for Tennessee we've really not heard a lot from him. Oh, I mean he's been in touch, but it seems like it was less and less often," Andrew said.

"Yes, but he *had* stayed in touch with us. He'd called or sent a postcard every few weeks. He still thinks of us as family. I'm concerned, Andy. Families stand by each other when there's trouble. He must know that about the Camerons."

Andrew walked to the window and looked at the darkening sky. "One thing we have to remember. None of us can really understand Jake. When we talked last summer, he tried to give me some sense of what it's like to have completely lost your memory of the people who are part of your past. He's grown to care for us, I don't think there's any question of that. But he's remembered so little."

"Maybe he's remembered more than we realize. I think we should file a missing person's report. I don't know how hard the authorities will look for him, though. He's an adult and a Vietnam veteran. But he is suffering from retrograde amnesia and he may not be thinking straight at all." She paused and added softly, "Think of your mother, Andy. If Jake were my son, I'd want to try to find him."

That convinced Andrew, and they agreed to call Max in the morning and let him know about finding the dog tags and their decision to file the report. They also agreed to make no mention of South Carolina to the authorities unless they were asked, and Andrew thought it unlikely that would happen.

"They'll want his physical description, his age, and it's important to let them know about his amnesia. Allan Martin's name never has to be mentioned," Andrew cautioned his wife.

"Oh, I agree. Why borrow trouble? It seems he came back here after he was down there. It may be nobody is even aware of that trip. And it seems George Smallwood — Choctaw — may have been with him. These men were both Special Forces, Andy. I'm sure they knew how to cover their tracks."

"They weren't in the jungle."

"No. But they were in a swamp. Close enough."

"We don't know a thing about this Smallwood guy. I'm not so sure I feel okay about Jake joining up with him and taking off for God knows where."

When Max and Andy talked the next morning, Max agreed with Mary. "File the report. I agree, I want to locate Jake. But as far as we know, there's no proof they were in South Carolina. I don't know that I'd tell the authorities about finding Jake's dog tags, either."

"Well, I'd like to find Jake without getting him in a mess."

"Andy, I'm not sure how hard they'll look for him after what we've learned about some of the Vietnam vets. It seems a lot of them don't want to be found."

"I have to try, Dad."

Max sighed. "I know you do, son. And your mother will appreciate it. I think she'll feel better knowing we're trying to find him. I'll need to tell her everything, I think."

"Yes, I think you should. Well, Mary and I will drive back over to Cherokee. I don't even know where to start. The village is on Indian land, but it's a relatively small area in Swain County. I know the village has its own government, and I guess the county sheriff would work with the Indians on something like this."

What they learned was that the village was not under the jurisdiction of the Swain County Sheriff. The Cherokee had their own police department, and access to the regional office of the Bureau of Indian Affairs in Nashville, which would need to be brought in on this case. Learning that made Andrew nervous; getting involved with federal law enforcement might lead to a connection between Jake's disappearance and Allan Martin's death.

"We play dumb," he warned Mary. "All we know is that Jake was here, he'd suffered memory loss from a head injury in Vietnam and had come to the mountains to try to recapture some childhood memories. And when we hadn't heard from him for several months we became concerned and came down here to try to find him."

They had to wait until the next day for the BIA officials to arrive, so they spent the day walking around the village. They went into the restaurant they had stopped at the day before, and the owner spoke with them about Jake. "Man with no yesterdays … with no memory. Your brother. You have his face."

244

"Can you tell me anything about him? What he did while he was here?"

"He's a good man. He was kind to the Choctaw. They said they served together in Vietnam, but your brother didn't remember what they did. He helped build the cabin."

"Yes, we saw it. But it's been empty for weeks. Did they ever talk about going somewhere else?"

"No, they kept to themselves. I think they made one or two trips. Once to Fontana Village. The other time I don't know where they went. Then we didn't see them for a long time and thought they had gone into the hills."

"It seems they went further than that. My brother's car is gone. Did they ever talk about maybe visiting the Choctaw's family? Jake said he was from Oklahoma."

"George Smallwood came to us two years ago. He brought one of our sons home. He was welcome here and came back after he left the Army."

Andrew understood; Smallwood had been appointed to accompany the body of a soldier who had been killed in action. It was considered an honor, and the Native Americans may have made the military escort an honorary member of the dead soldier's tribe.

Once the BIA people came in from Nashville they filed the report. Andy held his breath but no question was asked about where Jake was born. They wanted his physical description, where he had been and what he had been doing when he went missing, his age. They asked if the Camerons could send a photo to both Cherokee and Nashville.

"Any medical problems?" asked one of the agents.

"My brother had a severe head injury while he was serving in Vietnam. That was in January of 1971. He suffered retrograde

245

amnesia and has been struggling with his identity ever since. He came to Cherokee because one of the few memories he had was of being here when we were little boys to see *Unto These Hills.* He had also remembered a few other things about childhood trips to the Smokies. But not remembering his past was frustrating for him."

The other BIA agent was taking notes and asked, "Had he been in West Chester until recently?"

"No, he left home last March … over a year ago. He came to Tennessee to visit an aunt and uncle who live on Norris Lake, and he stayed with them for a while. He got a job and found an apartment in Clinton. Then last fall he came to Cherokee. He liked being here."

Mary smiled at the Cherokee police chief. "He said the people here were kind and understanding. It seemed to us he was thinking about staying here."

"And this was the last place he was seen, in the cabin he and George Smallwood built?" asked the BIA official. Andrew had thought they might be "suits," FBI types, but both were dressed comfortably in jeans and jackets; one suede, one leather. Both men were obviously of Native heritage.

The agent slapped his notebook closed. "That's where we'll start, at that cabin. You say you went there yesterday?"

"Yes. I had to break the lock to get inside, so that's the vandalism you'll find. We looked around pretty thoroughly and found absolutely nothing. Oh, and my brother's car is gone."

There were glances around the room. "So they could have left some time ago and could be pretty much anywhere in North America at this point."

Andrew replied. "Jake had been pulling away from us. Living in West Chester was difficult for him. It's a small town and the people there remembered him, but he couldn't remember them. When we didn't hear from him after the end of January, we thought he and Smallwood might have gone into the mountains for a while. We've heard about Vietnam vets who are doing that."

"You found no signs of foul play in the cabin?" the sheriff asked.

"No, nothing. It was slightly dusty but clean. And I'm afraid we walked around inside for quite a while, looking to see if Jake had left anything behind." *I'm sure they are probably pissed that we did that*, Andrew thought, and he added, "I'm sorry. We were so sure we'd find him when we drove down here. It was a shock to realize he was gone."

"We'll need information about the car. Make, model, color, VIN number if you can get it, and license plate number." The BIA man was scribbling in his notebook again.

"I'll send you those along with pictures once we get back to Pennsylvania."

"We'll put this report out there. You must realize finding him at this point is a long shot."

"Jake was a Green Beret, so if he's in the woods somewhere he's probably okay. Funny thing about the kind of amnesia he has. He's kept all his skills. What he lost was his personal history. He didn't remember any of us."

After the report had been filed it seemed pointless to stay in the mountains. Mary and Andrew agreed to drive to Norris Lake and spend a couple of days with Alice and Ben. Being on the lake with family was pleasant, and Andrew was able to relax and not think too much about Jake.

Sitting on the dock after dinner, they watched the sun sink behind the hills as Alice talked about her family. Grace was pregnant again, and little Andi, Andrew's namesake, was almost a

247

year and a half old and was walking everywhere and starting to talk.

"How's your mother?" asked Alice.

"She's amazing. She's a strong lady. We're all hoping Jake will contact us soon. I'm sure he's okay." Andrew looked out over the water, remembering his talk with Jake the previous summer.

Maybe I shouldn't try to find him. Maybe he's decided he'll never again be part of our family. But I don't like this. This isn't the way, Jake.

CHAPTER 25

Summer seemed to crawl by and Andrew felt as if he were treading water. He stood in front of his easel with his palette in his hands and played with paint, mixing colors. He listened to music he loved which usually inspired him, but he felt as if he were in a vacuum and the paint brushes were carefully cleaned and put away while the canvas remained empty. Mary continued to be his refuge and he lost himself in her sweetness often.

They contacted the sheriff in Swain County, an affable man named Matt Benson, every week or so, but there was no news. Surprisingly, Toni was the strongest person in the family. She gardened and baked and canned, and faithfully went twice a week to her volunteer job in the library's children's room. She was cheerful and positive.

She sat down with Andrew after breakfast and talked to him. "You said you're sure Jake is all right. He's doing something he has to do, and it may take a while. I've accepted that, Andy. You and Mary should go on with your plans. When was the last time you looked at a house?"

He stared at her blankly. What little sleep he was getting was troubled by dreams. Dreams of being in a swamp with his little brother and a vile man he feared and hated. Dreams of flying over a jungle. Dreams of frantically searching for Jake, who sometimes morphed into Allan Martin.

"Last November?" he said dully.

"Ridiculous. You and Mary need your own home. I want a grandchild, and you need a child. We can't put our lives on hold. We simply can't. We don't know when Jake will show up. He wouldn't want you to just stop living. I know you aren't painting, I see you standing in front of your easel staring at a blank canvas that doesn't have one speck of paint on it. This has to stop."

Andrew felt his lips twitch. He didn't know whether he needed to laugh or cry, but his mother was right. He had to find a way to get past this awful numbness that gripped him.

"You're right, Mom. School starts in three weeks. Mary and I need to see if we can't find a house before that." He gave her a bear hug. "Do you have any idea how much I love you?"

Andrew felt a little less tense once school started and he was able to immerse himself in teaching. Once again he and Mary decided to combine the school's Christmas concert with a holiday juried art show. They spent almost every weekend looking at houses.

There had been no inquiries from South Carolina concerning Allan Martin's death, though Max said he was sure sooner or later the authorities would track Toni down and officially notify her that her ex-husband was no longer among the living. "Just be sure to act surprised if somebody shows up in person. I doubt that will happen. I think it's more likely you'll get a letter from some minor government official, since your marriage ended decades ago."

"Official notification? Do I respond?"

"I don't know that you need to. You could thank them for the information, just to confirm that you received it."

In the middle of October Andrew's dreams returned, more vivid than ever. He tried taking sleeping pills but they made him groggy and irritable. He tried again to paint, and started a couple of half-hearted landscapes which were meant to be of the Smoky

Mountains but instead were uncomfortably close to his memories of Vietnam. From the Myrtle Beach newspapers they learned that the fire at Allan Martin's cabin was still under investigation, which meant if Jake's name somehow surfaced there could be trouble.

I can't deal with this. There has to be some way to track Jake down. We have to find him. Andrew went to the library, searching through books about missing persons cases and what people had done to try to find someone who disappeared. Frustrated because they had agreed to keep contact with authorities to a minimum, he decided to try another path.

At Halloween Andrew made an announcement at dinner. "I've contacted two psychics." They all stared at him. "I need some kind of resolution. I've barely been able to paint for nearly a year. Somebody has to be able to help us find Jake."

Toni said, alarmed, "You think something bad has happened to him."

"No, I don't think that. I would know if it had. It's just … I can't believe he's doing this to us. He has to be aware it's … how difficult it is for us."

Max said, "Actually, I don't know if that's true. You know yourself he doesn't feel the connection to us that we feel to him. His history with us was pretty brief, when you think about it. None of us can really understand what Jake's been going through."

Mary said to her husband later, "You took money from our savings account to pay the psychics, didn't you?" They were in their room, getting ready for bed.

"I should have asked you before I did that."

"Yes, you should have, and I would have been fine with it. Do you think I don't realize how stressed you are? You worry me, Andrew. Recently you've been eating antacids like candy. I wish you'd see a doctor if your stomach is bothering you as much as it seems to be."

"I'll be okay once we find Jake. And will I ever ream him out for doing this to us. For doing this to Mom. How much weight has she lost?"

"Your mother is fine, and you're the one who's lost weight. Andrew, please go to the doctor."

"That's enough, Mary," he snapped at her. "I don't want to hear any more about it. If I get sick, I'll see a doctor." He abruptly turned away from her and switched off the light.

He wasn't about to tell her how much his stomach burned sometimes. *It's just stress, and she's making it worse.*

***

In mid-November they kept Andrew's appointment with one of the psychics in Philadelphia. She wanted an article of clothing, something Jake had handled. They took his dog tags and his green beret.

For over two hours she rambled, guessed, told them she saw Jake in a place where there were Native Americans in native dress. She also said she saw him in a swamp. While they hadn't given her the information, she knew about Toni's parents being deceased and claimed they had conversed with her spirit guides. She said they were looking over Jake. She assured them that he was still alive, but it seemed he had lost all knowledge of who he was. For this she collected five thousand dollars from them.

The other psychic they communicated with through the mail, and he said his spirit guides advised him Jacob had joined those who had gone before and was now in the spirit world, where he was living happily with some of his fellow soldiers. He also mentioned that Jake's grandparents, whom he identified as L and M, were there as well; and that was correct ... Louis and Mona. For this information they sent him a check for a thousand dollars.

Mary never reproached him about the outcome of these efforts. *She has every right to be angry. Dammit, why doesn't she ream me out? I'm an asshole.* When she moved close to him in bed he feigned fatigue. He sensed her hurt but he couldn't bring himself to respond to her. *What the hell is the matter with me?*

Andrew's stomach was in a constant state of turmoil. A nightly routine was dissolving antacid tablets in water before bed, then again at about one a.m. He blamed Mary. He blamed Jake. *Isabel. This is her fault.* Not long after the visit to the psychic in Philadelphia he finally went to see Isabel, with whom he hadn't spoken in months.

Furious, he pounded heavily at her door until she opened it. He pushed his way inside.

"This is all your doing," he raged at her. "You sent him off, and God knows what's happened to him. I'll never forgive you for this, Isabel."

"Andrew, you cannot believe I would have encouraged Jake to strike out on his own if I'd had any inkling it would lead to this. I did what I thought best at the time; I encouraged him to follow his instincts." She sighed deeply. "Sadly, one cannot foresee the future."

"*Oui. Vachement,*" he almost spat at her. "Something you might consider before you offer advice again." Andrew turned and strode from her apartment, slamming the door behind him.

The art show at Christmas was almost more than Andrew could handle, but he managed to get through it, and it was a distraction for a short time. The season seemed sad to all of them as they recalled their celebration of two years earlier. Despite all Mary's entreaties, Andrew adamantly refused to see a doctor.

On January tenth Max picked up the phone, and they heard him say, "Yes, Sheriff Benson."

Everyone froze. Max listened at length, only saying, "Yes, I see."… "I understand."

Finally he ended the conversation. "Thank you for letting us know. Do you have any idea when you'll know something more?"

Another pause, then he said. "Very well. Thank you again."

He turned to them, struggling to remain calm. "He called to let us know that human remains have been found in Swain County which he suspects might be Jake. Right age, right general build. But they're decomposed. The Department of Defense has been contacted with a request for Jake's medical records. His dental records will give them the information they need to confirm whether or not it's Jake."

He took a deep breath. "Let's not panic. It may not be Jake. We probably won't know for at least a couple of weeks, so let's not assume the worst."

Andrew's fragile universe exploded. A magenta sun fell from a blue-violet sky and crashed into a fiery Earth as he fell to his knees and vomited blood.

CHAPTER 26

He was in a darkened, quiet room. He felt something on the back of his hand that was uncomfortable; and when he looked to his left he saw the IV bag above his shoulder and the tube leading down into the needle. He felt tired and weak, and it seemed he was thinking in slow motion. He turned his head to his right and there was Mary; curled up in a chair, wrapped in a blanket, her face pressed against a pillow.

His eyes stung with tears. She was so beautiful, but she looked tired and tense, and he knew it was because of him. *Dear God, what have I done to her? My Mary. My angel.* He frowned, trying to think, slowly remembering what had happened. His mouth felt sandpaper dry, and when he tried to speak her name nothing came out. He closed his eyes, tried hard to focus, and managed to croak out, "Mary."

She opened her eyes immediately, gave him a beautiful smile, and stood and moved to sit beside him on the bed. "Welcome back, stranger," she said, her voice shaking slightly. She picked up a plastic cup from the rolling tray and brought a straw to his lips, and he sucked in a gulp of water and nearly choked on it.

Mary moved the straw away. "Just sips, Andy." He nodded and took three careful sips.

That was better. His mouth no longer felt like the Sahara. "How long have I been here?"

"A week. Well, nearly eight days. You've been … asleep … most of the time." She put a warm hand on his face. "Andy, it wasn't Jake. The dental records proved that it wasn't Jake."

He nodded. "I think part of me knew that. I'm sorry I scared all of you." He glanced around the room. "I've been here a week? Asleep?"

"Well, maybe not exactly asleep. Do you remember what day it was wc had that phone call from Sheriff Benson?" Mary eased the pillow she had been using behind his head and neck, and he was more comfortable.

"Of course I do. It was January tenth." He tried to sit up. "I have to get out of here. What's going on with my art classes?"

She gently pressed him back against the pillows. "Easy, tiger. The school has hired a long-term sub. She's actually quite good, and the kids seem to like her."

"Have you been here every day?"

"Of course I have. I've been doing half days at the school recently. I took a little time off when you were first admitted and we weren't sure what had happened."

He tried to relax. "What exactly did happen? How did I lose a whole week of my life?"

"Don't be alarmed, Andy. Your doctors believe you had what's called a psychotic break. You simply withdrew from us for a while. Apparently you needed that. And I'm happy you're talking to me now; it's what we hoped for. Your mind has begun to heal, just as your body has."

"I vomited blood."

"Yes, you did. That was scary. But it was an ulcer, and it's healing. The human body is amazing, you know?"

"God, Mary, I'm so sorry. I've been such a ... my head is messed up." What he had just said awakened an echo in him. *I just heard somebody say that,* he thought.

"That's kind of what the doctors here decided, my love. When you're stronger, everyone agrees you need to spend some time in therapy."

"So am I crazy? Is that what a ... what did you call it ... 'psychotic break' means?"

"You lost touch with reality for a while, Andy. You've been under so much stress, you just snapped. It was a way for your mind to cope. You needed to rest."

"You said they want me to spend time in therapy. Having my head shrunk, you mean."

She laughed softly. "I'm so pleased you're not arguing about it. You aren't going to argue about it, are you?"

"No, I'm not. I know I need help." He tugged at her gently. "Please lie down with me."

She sighed and lay beside him, resting her head on his shoulder and putting a knee over his leg. "Oh, I've missed you so much."

"This is Chester County Hospital, right?" He stroked her hair, savoring the soft texture, inhaling her sweet scent. *Carnations and something else.* He had never been able to identify the something else, but it was perfect. It was Mary.

"It is. Right now you're still in the ICU. I think in a day or two they will want to transfer you to psychiatric care. You understand why, don't you?"

"Yes." He was surprised he was so calm about this. "Am I on some kind of medication? I feel kind of groggy. But peaceful."

"Yes. You've been receiving something to help you relax and sleep better."

"Why did I need that? Was I acting wild when they first brought me in?"

"You were obviously disoriented. You weren't yourself."

"Whatever that means."

"You were talking, but you weren't making any sense at all."

He thought for a moment. "Will you do something for me?"

She leaned up on an elbow so she could look into his face. "If I can."

"Can you see about having me transferred to the Institute of Pennsylvania Hospital? If I'm going to be ... uh ... *shrinked*, I want Penny Abramson to be the shrinker."

Mary sat up. "Andy, I can't believe you're being so cooperative about this, but it's wonderful. Of course I'll get you over there. I'll do that right away. I have to meet this amazing lady my husband wants to do his shrinking."

She blew him a kiss as she left the room, passing a doctor who smiled at her and then at Andrew. "Good to see you back, Andrew. I'm Dr. Donovan."

After checking Andrew's vital signs and making notes on the chart which hung on the end of the bed, Dr. Donovan explained to Andrew what he and his team of physicians had done and the course of treatment they were suggesting. A psychiatrist and a surgeon completed the medical personnel who had been in charge of his care to this point.

"I'm encouraged by your progress, Andy," he ended. "Are you hungry?"

"Yes, I am. Food sounds good."

"I'll send someone in to take your breakfast order. You're on a soft diet for the present."

Toni and Max came into the room after Dr. Donovan left, and Toni sat beside her son and smiled at him. "You already look better," she said. "How does your stomach feel?"

"Actually, Dr. Donovan said I can have breakfast. He said I'm on soft foods for now … so I guess something yummy like cream of wheat? What I'd like is a four-egg Western omelet and about six strips of bacon."

Toni and Max laughed, and Max said, "Let me see if I can hurry that cream of wheat along for you," as he left the room.

Toni was holding the now folded blanket Mary had been using. "Would you like to have another blanket? It's cold outside this morning, and it even seems cool in here."

"Yes, that would be nice. It does seem chilly."

She unfolded the blanket carefully and tucked it around him. Their eyes met and held for a moment. "Thank you, Mom."

She sat beside him again. "Mary's on her way to Philadelphia after she showers and changes," Toni told Andrew. "She tells us you want to be transferred to the Institute and have Dr. Abramson as your therapist."

"I'm so sorry, Mom. I never meant to worry all of you this way." He sighed. "I've been a little crazy, I guess. I haven't been thinking of anyone except myself. I know I need help, and I trust Dr. Abramson. And she knows … knew … Jake. I know he stopped his sessions with her, but he liked her. I think she was a help to him in understanding his amnesia."

Toni took Andrew's hand. "I know how much you wanted to help Jake. How much you wanted him to be the Jake you knew growing up."

"Didn't we all want that? Didn't you?"

Toni smiled wistfully at her oldest son. "Andy, when I saw Jake at Walter Reed I think I realized he'd never be the same. I

259

tried to accept that we'd have to find a different way to be his family. I think the few memories he recovered were memories he shared with you." She sighed. "I believe that's why you tried so hard, and why this has been harder on you than anyone else."

He lay back against the pillows. "Mary said I lost touch with reality for a while. I understand I was babbling."

"Yes, you were. It was distressing, son. Then the medicine you were on made you sleep quite a bit. We helped you eat … well, drink, mostly. Lots of dairy products. Milk and cream."

"I don't remember any of that. I guess I was crazy for a while. I'm so sorry, Mom," he said again.

"Just get well, Andrew. Don't worry about anything. You worry far too much; you always have. My serious little boy." She leaned forward and kissed his cheek.

He seemed to hear her words as an echo: *You worry far too much.* He shivered and Toni pulled the blanket up to his shoulders.

***

Andrew had to wait until Dr. Donovan was convinced his ulcer was healing and it was safe for him to leave West Chester County Hospital before he could be transferred to the Institute, nearly a week later. Penny Abramson came into his private room the afternoon he was admitted.

"Well, Andrew," she said. "We meet again. You have an impressive wife. She was very persuasive when she came to see me. Fortunately, we had space opening up, but even if we hadn't I think I would have found some way for us to accept you."

"Thank you, Dr. Abramson. I'm grateful you agreed to take me on as a patient."

"Why so formal? Mary calls me 'Dr. Penny.' She says that's how you refer to me."

Andrew felt himself flush. "I don't want to seem disrespectful. That's what Jake always called you when he spoke of you. I didn't know if that was how he actually addressed you."

"He didn't always remember the 'Dr.' part. I do prefer you use that. It's just a reminder this is a professional relationship, but I don't want it to be a stuffy one."

Andrew had to smile. She was exactly as he remembered her; straightforward, no-nonsense; her direct gaze seemed to see inside his head. He recognized her skirt, a tan plaid, but she was wearing a white shirt. Today she had her hair pulled back and clipped at the neck, but a few tendrils of curls escaped around her face. *What does she have against curls? Too cute, I guess.* The same glasses. He was intrigued by her. *I think we could be friends.*

"Why do you want me to treat you, Andrew?"

"You knew Jake. It appears this is all about my … the trouble I'm having dealing with Jake's disappearance. How much did Mary tell you?"

"You haven't seen Jake since July of 1972, and haven't heard from him for nearly a year. You filed a missing person's report in June of 1973 in Cherokee, North Carolina, because that was the last place he had been seen. You had word about two weeks ago that a decomposed body had been found near there and it was thought it might be Jake."

She pushed her glasses up on her nose almost unconsciously. "When you heard that, you collapsed and vomited blood. You were then transported by ambulance to Chester County Hospital. It was apparent to the admitting staff that you were having some kind of psychotic episode: you were …" she glanced at the chart she had in her hand … "'agitated and incoherent,' so you were given

261

antipsychotic medication and kept in the ER overnight where you received a transfusion because of the blood loss. When it was apparent there would be no further bleeding you were transferred to the ICU where treatment continued."

"Well, I guess I know everything now about what happened to me, except what medication I received. Was I acting totally out of my mind? I'm still trying to wrap my head around being crazy. I feel perfectly normal."

"'Agitated and incoherent.' Yes, that qualifies as crazy."

He laughed with surprise at her comment, and she gave him an indulgent smile.

"You had to be sedated so your bleeding ulcer could be treated." She glanced again at the chart in her hand. "So you were given Haldol on admission. It was replaced with low doses of Thorazine, and medication was discontinued when it was determined the psychosis, as suspected, had been temporary."

"So now I'm a nut case," Andrew said, almost to himself.

"No, now you're my patient," she said, with a wry smile. "You just arrived, I believe. I'll need to remind you to remove your belt if you have one on under the sweater. I'm afraid you'll have to get used to baggy pants for a while. If you didn't bring loafers you can wear hospital slippers; no shoelaces allowed. And I trust you brought an electric razor."

"Yes, Mary and I read the rules. Razor blades not allowed here."

She nodded and smiled at him again. "Tomorrow morning you will come to my office and we'll get to work. There are TVs in the common room, magazines … I see you have a cassette tape player. What's your music?"

"Classical. Mostly choral music."

She smiled more warmly. "Do you know the Brahms *Requiem*? My favorite piece."

Surprised, Andrew smiled and nodded. "Yes, I do. I've even had a chance to sing it."

She turned to leave, and he added, "I think I'm in the right place, Dr. Penny."

CHAPTER 27

Dr. Penelope Abramson's office in the Institute struck Andrew as comfortable and safe. Pale green walls, an oriental area rug with a soft forest green the predominant color, two large chairs upholstered in a striped pattern of ivory and pale green. The antique desk and chair surprised him; they appeared to be authentic Colonial pieces. An occasional table between the chairs, with a box of tissues and coasters. In a corner of the room, utilitarian filing cabinets; on top of one, a pitcher of water and a stack of plastic cups.

He liked her choice of paintings: two watercolors, one a landscape and one a seascape; and one simple abstract in oil. She was leaning against the desk when he came in, and gestured for him to take a seat. Another surprise: rather than sitting behind the desk, she settled comfortably into the other chair. He noticed that a file folder was on her desk along with a legal pad.

"You don't take notes while we talk?"

"I may make a few notes after we finish our session. You're not a case, Andrew. You're my patient."

"So I just start talking? About what, my earliest memories?"

She took off her glasses and held them folded in one hand. "When you and I first talked, it was apparent to me that something very disturbing happened to you in Vietnam. Why don't we start there?"

"I don't like to even think about Vietnam."

"I'm aware of that. You were in the Marine Corps. Infantry?"

"No, I was on a helicopter crew. My tour of duty was comparatively easy."

"Were you a crew chief?"

"Aviation metalsmith and door gunner. I enjoyed the 'metalsmith' part. I had special training for that at the NATTC — Naval Air Technical Training Center. Mostly sheet metal work and I was good at it. I was trained as a door gunner by my unit, HMM-460, when I arrived in Vietnam — we were at Marble Mountain near Da Nang, on the South China Sea. I slept indoors on a bunk every night and ate hot food. I think all of us sometimes felt a little guilty, when we were so much aware of where the grunts were and how they were living." He sighed. "And dying."

"Why did you request that? You enlisted, I believe."

He hesitated. "Anything I tell you is in strictest confidence, right?" She nodded.

He shifted in the chair, gripping the arms and taking a deep breath. "I didn't want to kill people. Especially because…because when I was eight years old I saw a man named Allan Martin shoot my grandparents to death and mortally wound my uncle."

Penny's eyebrows went up. "Did you know this man?"

"Yes, I did. He was my birth father. That was the last time I ever laid eyes on him."

"Max Cameron is your adoptive father?"

"Yes. He was a gift from God. Max is my father. Allan Martin was …" he looked down as his voice trailed off.

"Go on. What was Allan Martin?"

"Unpredictable. Moody. Once Max came into our lives and I learned what a real father was, I understood how unhappy I'd been as a young child."

"Did Jake feel the same way about your biological father?"

265

"Jake didn't let him get under his skin the way I did, but we agreed he wasn't ... I never doubted that my mother loved us. I wasn't so sure about him. Sometimes I thought he didn't even like us very much."

"Did he beat you and Jake?"

"No. Never. But he was one scary son-of-a-bitch. From what Mom has told me, at first they had a good marriage. And even after Jake and I came along. She said there were some odd things she saw with his family, but she was young and in love, and he was good to her."

"When did that change?"

"She left him the first time when I was five or six. I don't really remember much about that. She took Jake and me to our grandparents' home in Tennessee — from where we lived in South Carolina, on the coast — and after a few months he came and took us all back with him. I remember he cried when he saw us. And after that, he was okay for a year or so. Then he started to get really weird."

"How so?"

"We could be having a good time together, and the next minute it was like a storm had blown up. The scariest thing was he would get very quiet but the tone of his voice gave me chills. He started carrying a handgun all the time, and he'd make Jake and me stand close to him while he did what he called 'target practice' — shooting cans and bottles off rocks and tree stumps in our back yard. The least little thing could set him off, and we'd have to sit in a corner for at least an hour. One time he locked us in a closet for about that long."

Dr. Penny wiped her glasses on the tail of her skirt, almost absent-mindedly. The gesture broke the tension and made Andrew smile; he recalled her doing that with the lab coat she'd been wearing the first time they talked.

"How did your mother react to this behavior?"

"She tried to talk to him. But I think she was afraid of him, so she tried not to upset him."

"And eventually she left him again?" He nodded. "What prompted that?"

Andrew shifted in his chair again, feeling a knot twisting in his stomach. "He took Jake and me away for a day and told her we'd be back in time for dinner. Instead, he took us to a hunting cabin in Tawndee Swamp and left us alone there all night."

She didn't comment, so he continued, "Mom and his sister, my Aunt Connie, found us the next morning. We threw as much stuff as we could in our car and took off for my grandparents' again, and she told us this time we weren't going back. That was in the fall, and in January he showed up at my grandparents' house and murdered three people."

"And that's why you didn't want to fight in the infantry in Vietnam. Understandable. But you were a door gunner; you had to shoot at the enemy."

"That was different. I wasn't on the ground. They were figures in the distance, and I was sending out a spray of bullets to protect the Marines that we were inserting into combat or extracting from a landing zone. I remember when I was in training one of the men in my outfit asked the Sergeant how accurate we had to be when we were shooting. He said it didn't matter if we hit anybody or not, because the purpose was to make the enemy keep their distance. He said machine guns are pretty persuasive when you're being shot at by one."

"So for the most part you were fighting the war in the way you wanted to fight it." She thought for a moment. "You were at

Marble Mountain Air Facility the entire time you were in Vietnam?"

"Yes. The base was attacked only a couple of days after I arrived." He ran a hand through his hair. "I sure had a baptism by fire. It was a shock to be awakened in the middle of the night to this enormous blast and realize there was a fireball above our heads from the fuel tanks having been blown up. I spent hours eating dirt and firing at things ... people ... I couldn't see. If you put your head up too far it would get blown off. God, what an experience. I was scared shitless. We didn't lose many men, but a lot were wounded. And we lost aircraft as well ... some were destroyed and a lot more were damaged."

He stopped. "Is it okay if I get some water?"

She stood, walked to the cabinet and poured water into one of the plastic cups and handed it to him. He took it gratefully, gulped it down and placed the cup on a coaster.

"That must have been difficult. You'd just arrived, and you saw men wounded and killed."

"Yes. Welcome to Vietnam." Andrew twisted uncomfortably in his chair and said slowly, "There were ... a lot of VC were killed and a few were captured."

He pressed his hands on his knees. *God, this was awful.* "One of my first jobs. Collecting the enemy dead and piling them up. And adding body parts to the pile. I'd been warned about how ugly this war was. After that there wasn't much I saw that shocked me."

"How did you handle it?"

He sighed. "All the time I was there, I tried to compartmentalize myself. I wasn't really there. At least, that's what I tried to convince myself." He ran a hand through his hair again.

"Don't get me wrong. I did my job, and I did it well. I was a Marine. But that was one thing that helped me deal — trying to detach myself. And no matter how difficult the mission, no matter what awful things I saw, eventually we'd get off the ground. We'd be above the jungle and I could breathe again."

"Were you ever in a helicopter crash?"

"Not a bad one. Once we had to set down unexpectedly because the hydraulic system failed. Mike, our pilot, was a genius. I couldn't believe the things he could do. We were inbound and had to pull out of the group. The chopper behind us came back and picked us up and took us back to the base. I don't know how, but I was never wounded. Oh, some nicks … sometimes from the casings from the machine gun. Those things are hot as blazes, and if one pops into your collar it hurts like hell. But I usually didn't even notice until we were headed back."

"So you managed to stay calm through most of the action you saw."

"Mostly I was on autopilot. It was happening. I had to do my best. No matter what. I kind of was a loner. I wasn't a big drinker, and I didn't like grass. I did try it. I wasn't a hell raiser. Some of the guys called me Lone, as in 'Lone Ranger.'" He smiled. "They trusted me. They knew I would always have their back." He leaned forward, elbows on knees.

"And there was this. When we'd get back, I'd make sketches of what I'd seen, of what had happened. Putting it on paper … that gave me a way to control it. I made hundreds of sketches, and I brought them home with me. I haven't looked at them since I got back."

He looked at his hands and then at Penny. "You know, I want to paint some of them. I think I always knew I would, someday."

"Your wife told me you are an artist."

269

"Yes, but nothing like that ... mostly landscapes, and a few portraits of Mary."

He walked to the filing cabinet and poured himself a glass of water. "Mary's letters were my lifeline. She wrote me at least once a day. They connected me to her ... to home. I read them and re-read them. I dreamed about her. About making love with her. About hearing her play piano. Listening to music with her. Talking to her. Mary and I never seemed to run out of things to say to each other ... until recently, when all I've been able to think about is Jake.

"I guess everyone deals with war in their own way. Some guys were super gung-ho. They loved being in battle. Mom always said I was a cautious child. You can't be cautious and survive a firefight, but because I kind of turned myself off I don't remember a lot about the battles. I don't know how I managed to do that, but it saved my sanity."

Andrew took a deep breath and clutched the arms of the chair. "It didn't always work. We got shot up pretty good on one mission and the co-pilot was killed. Bullet penetrated his helmet and he died instantly. He was maybe a year older than me. We'd been pretty friendly. He had a wife and they were expecting their first child." He stood and paced the room.

"On one mission the Huey in front of us exploded in mid-air. It had been hit by two RPGs ... rocket propelled grenades ... and it went down hard, and we couldn't do anything except watch it burn. I prayed that the crew of that aircraft were killed in the explosion. The burn victims ... those were the worst. When we picked up wounded and some were badly burned ... God." He dropped into his chair and closed his eyes.

Penny gave him a moment, and then said, "Something you said that surprised me the first time we met ... you said you didn't worry about Jake when he was there."

"And you called me on that. Of course I worried about him. Even though I hadn't been on patrol or combat in the jungle, I saw what happened to the guys who were out there. Once I knew Jake was in country I hardly slept at night, real bed or not. And whenever we flew a mission, I'd look down and wonder if my brother might be down there somewhere."

"I'd have been very surprised if you hadn't reacted that way."

"Those helicopter pilots ... they're heroes. What those guys have been doing over there is magnificent."

"I've heard it said all members of the helicopter crews are heroes."

"I never felt like a hero. A lot of pilots and crew died, sometimes horribly. But being in the air ... it was different. I almost felt invulnerable. Even though one of our co-pilots was killed on one mission. And we'd get back to base and see holes in the chopper, and rips in our uniforms. They *were* shooting at us."

"But you made it home. And Jake made it home."

"Did he? Then why isn't he here now?"

"I think we need to talk more about this, Andrew. But I understand how difficult this was for you. We can pick up tomorrow, unless you want to continue."

Andrew felt a wave of relief. "So you know why I don't even like to think about Vietnam."

"Yes, I do." She was thoughtful for a moment and then said, "Where do you think Jake is now? You say you believe there's a good chance he's alive."

"I *know* he's alive. If Jake were dead I would know. I have no idea where he might be. Well, no, that's not true. He had a friend

271

he discovered in North Carolina; a man who had served with him in Special Forces. Jake didn't remember any of that, but apparently the two hit it off. They may be together somewhere. Maybe they went into the wilderness, maybe in Washington State. I'm told a lot of vets are living there. And other places as well."

Penny stood and walked to the door with him. "Why don't you try to relax? Have you been in the pool yet?"

He shook his head. "I think I want to try to paint. Your art therapy room is beautiful. It looks like they have a lot of supplies available."

"They do. That's excellent. You're free to go in there whenever you want."

***

Andrew felt raw inside. He had allowed himself to expose a nerve to Dr. Penny, a nerve he had carefully guarded since he came back from Vietnam. He decided to skip lunch; his stomach felt queasy after the session he'd just had.

The art room was spacious and well supplied, not only with easels and tables for art, but with a number of different craft stations. Several patients were occupied at different stations, some very focused on what they were doing, others enjoying the opportunity to socialize.

The director, a pleasant woman named Francine, welcomed him and asked what he'd like to do. She provided him with a 24 by 36 inch canvas and showed him brushes, oils, palettes, palette knives, everything he would need. He studied the paints, then selected titanium white, yellow ochre, chromium green oxide, burnt sienna, ultramarine blue and phthalo blue, cadmium red and alizarin crimson. He studied the brushes and decided to use a palette knife.

Night missions were the hardest. You felt what was below, but couldn't really see it. Fires and smoke in the distance indicated where the action was taking place. The countryside was often covered with clouds so moonlit nights were rare; stars were seldom visible. He toned the canvas with a medium gray, then began to add the jungle. Green and dark gray. Dense, thick, foreboding. Fires were next; one off in the distance, one almost beneath him. The body of the chopper next, in the foreground and obviously above the jungle, then the edges of the rotors, bleeding off the canvas. Directly below the helicopter, faint figures. He mixed ultramarine blue, burnt sienna and white for his grays: lighter gray for clouds, another shade of gray for smoke. Tracer bullets, streaks of red-orange and yellow-green. Some darker patches of sky showing through the cloud cover.

Andrew fell into a rhythm. It felt good. He felt good. He hadn't painted with such focus in months. This was what he had to do: paint Vietnam. He was surprised when Francine came up to him and reminded him it was dinnertime. "You can come back after dinner if you want," she said conversationally, then stopped, her eyes widening as she looked at the painting.

"My God. You're a professional."

"I teach art at Kennett High School."

"I think I'll see about enrolling. This is wonderful. Powerful. It's Vietnam, of course. Are you a veteran?"

"Yes. It … it stays with you."

"So I've been told. Andrew, isn't it? May I call you Andy?"

"Sure."

"We have another veteran here. Have you met him yet? Jim Thornton. He was a Marine and was wounded; went back for

273

another tour and suffered another wound." She thought for a minute. "I don't think he'd mind my telling you this; that second wound wasn't physical."

Andrew nodded. "I guess we have that in common. Being Marines. And ... that other thing."

***

When Mary came he showed her around the building. The common room, which they called the living room. Another room with a grand piano. The dining room. The swimming pool, a real luxury. The art studio. "This is lovely. I had no idea."

"Yes, it's unusual. It's also expensive. I didn't even think about that when I asked you to get me in here. I'm afraid our insurance won't cover everything."

"We have money put away. I can tell already that you feel good about being here. And you were painting, that's so great."

"For hours. It was kind of a breakthrough, I guess. And I feel very comfortable with Dr. Penny. I know she's going to help me get past this." He put his arms around her. "But that money you're talking about, that's for our house. I don't like using it."

"Get well, Andy. The house will wait. Once you're better we can start saving again. We really have quite a bit in that account. We'll make it work."

"I don't feel right about this at all." She felt so good in his arms. How long had it been since they'd made love? Weeks, at least.

She put her hands on his shoulders and looked into his face. "For once in your life, let me do the worrying. I know, I *know*, if our positions were reversed you would do the same for me. Just this once, let me take care of you." She kissed him tenderly. "You're my life, Andy. Just get well. I need you well and whole."

He looked down, his eyes swimming with tears. "I love you so much, Mary. I don't deserve you."

She put a hand under his chin and gently lifted his face. "Those vows we took … 'in sickness and in health' … I meant that when I said it. Promise me you'll just concentrate on getting well."

"I promise."

"Mean it."

He laughed. "I mean it. You humble me, Mary. I may not deserve you, but I'm sure going to try. And I will get well. I hope to be out of here before long."

"Well, with that attitude, it could happen. What do you need? What can I bring you?"

He didn't hesitate. "In the bottom of my duffel bag. Sketches I made in Vietnam. I used whatever paper I could find. Don't look at them."

She nodded. *I have to let her in*, he thought. *I need to let her help me live with this.*

"No, look at them. I want you to see them, because some of them are … I want to paint them. They're not pretty, most of them. But they're what I saw. What I have to live with. We can talk more when I get home."

Mary had tears in her eyes. "Thank you, Andy."

"And I need Isabel to bring me supplies. Large canvasses, 24 by 36 inches, maybe even 36 by 48. More paint. I don't want to use up the supplies they have here. I need to see her, anyway. I owe her an apology."

Mary gave him a smile that turned him inside out. "I'll see if she can come tomorrow."

CHAPTER 28

"You've caused quite a stir with your artwork, Andrew."

"Yes, it would seem I have. Maybe I shouldn't continue to paint." Andrew had spent the morning completing one painting and beginning a second, and a surprising number of patients and staff had come in to see what he was doing. Not many had spoken to him directly, but Francine had told him quietly that he'd excited a lot of conversation because it was apparent his paintings were of the war in Vietnam.

"Don't even consider that. It's given some of our patients something to think about besides their own problems, and the staff thinks you're great." Once again, Dr. Abramson was seated beside him rather than behind her desk. He liked that, it made him feel they were friends. *Well, as much as you can feel that way about your psychotherapist.*

"More importantly, apparently we made a breakthrough yesterday. Mary told me you haven't been able to paint for nearly a year. Keep painting."

"I can't even tell you how good it feels. I told Francine that I'll be replacing all the paint I've been using. Hopefully, my art prof from my college days is coming to see me this evening and bringing me supplies." Andrew relaxed into the chair. "And I asked Mary to bring me the sketches I made while I was in Vietnam. She's been waiting a long time for me to talk to her about what happened there."

"The first time you and I talked briefly about this … when you came to see me after Jake had discontinued his sessions … it was apparent something happened there which had a strong impact on you. Something you didn't talk about yesterday."

He sat up straighter. "I guess … yes, something … I've had a recurring nightmare."

"This is important, Andrew. I know this isn't easy, but you're making excellent progress. You opened up quite a bit yesterday."

"I know I did. And it helped me start painting again." He stood and started to pace. "I don't want to go there, Dr. Penny. I'm not sure I can."

"Sit down, Andrew. Let me see if we can go there together."

Reluctantly, he sat, not sure what she meant.

"That first battle you were in must have been pretty horrific, yet you said you didn't see what you were shooting at. How did you manage that? It had to have been close combat."

"Well … we were in a bunker. The guys on either side of me knew I'd just arrived, and they kept yelling at me to keep my head down. So I mainly just pointed my rifle and fired." He shuddered involuntarily. "But once the shooting stopped and we were able to get a look … the carnage was …"

"But you didn't know if you had actually shot anyone."

"Somebody sure as hell had. There were a lot of dead VC. But, no, I didn't know if any of them were dead because of one of my bullets."

"Was there another time you had to engage in close combat?"

He looked at her. *Don't make me do this. Please don't make me do this.*

She seemed to know what he was thinking because she said gently, "It's important, Andrew. And it will be worth it." She asked him again, "Was there another time you had to engage in close combat?"

"Yes." He started to perspire, and he felt himself just above the jungle, the smells and sounds assaulting him again. He gripped the arms of the chair, forcing himself to relate this. "We'd been extracting men from a hot LZ ... landing zone, Marines who were surrounded by North Vietnamese Army troops. We had only a small area to touch down, and it was ringed by trees. There were several choppers and we were going in one at a time, taking them out as fast as we could, but it was getting dark and the enemy was so close to our Huey ... helicopter ... that the gunships that were trying to cover the extraction weren't able to fire."

Andrew pulled several tissues from the box and wiped his face and the back of his neck.

"Our helicopter went in for the last few men, and as we came down those men were in a circle with their backs to the aircraft and were shooting to cover our landing. As soon as we set down they turned and ran to get on, and the other gunner — the crew chief — and I kept firing while they pulled themselves in. One had to be dragged in and we found out later he had died. We both yelled to the pilot that we were loaded and clear." His voice started to crack open and he had to stop for a minute.

"It felt like everything was happening in slow motion ... it was taking forever for us to get the hell out of there. I kept firing, and they just kept coming. I couldn't believe it when some of the crazy bastards started running toward the chopper. They were so close I could see their faces in the light of the flashes. I cut one down, then two. The third one wasn't more than fifteen yards from the aircraft when I fired directly into his face and watched his head explode."

The room grew very quiet. Andrew began to shiver uncontrollably. Dr. Penny went to a closet and came back with a blanket which she handed to him. He wrapped himself in it.

Without asking, she poured a glass of water and handed it to him.

"Thank you." He pressed his fingers hard against his forehead. "That's the kind of shit that gives you nightmares."

"There's more, I think."

"No … I … *oh my God*." He was shaking so hard his teeth were chattering.

She waited for him to continue.

"Oh, God. I just realized … when I looked in that enemy's face I didn't see an enemy soldier; I saw Allan Martin. *Oh, God.*" He was suddenly very still; a wave of light surged through his consciousness followed by a sharp intake of breath. He stared at her.

"Something else?"

"I know why I saw his face. I wanted to kill the bastard. I've wanted to kill him since I was eight years old."

"When he killed your grandparents?"

"No. Before that. The night he took me and Jake to that hunting cabin. *Oh God!*"

***

Their father slammed their supplies down on the table: a box of cereal and a box of crackers, then he filled a bucket with water and set an empty bucket beside it.

"Be sure you drink out of the bucket you didn't piss in," said Allan, laughing uproariously. Then he went to Jake and bent down, putting a hand on the back of his neck.

Andrew froze. His father had done that to him twice, and each time it had frightened and confused him. Allan stroked Jake's neck now and talked softly to him. "You aren't scared, are you? My brave Jakey-boy. You look just like your pretty mommy, you know that?"

Andrew wanted to scream at him, "Don't do that to Jake! If you have to touch somebody like that, do it to me!" *Jake is so scared*, he thought.

Before he could say a word, his father turned to him. "Take care of your little brother, Andy. Don't let any bears or alligators get him." He laughed again and left.

Jake started to cry and Andrew ran to him and put his arms around him. "Why did he do that, Andy?"

Andrew rocked him and tried hard to stay calm. "It's okay, Jakey. You know how Daddy can just be weird sometimes. Forget about it."

Jake was almost hysterical. "Can an alligator get inside here? Are there bears in the swamp?"

"I won't let anything bad happen to you. You know that. Look, you just lie down here on this cot and I'll find a knife. I don't think anything can get into the cabin, but maybe you'll feel better if you know I have a weapon."

Fighting down the rising fear he felt, Andrew rummaged through the cabinet drawers and found two knives; a hunting knife that seemed fairly sharp, and a knife used for boning and scaling fish. "See, Jake? I have two knives. I promise I'll take care of you. Don't be scared."

Jake continued to sob and Andrew lay down beside him, pulled him close, and soothed the little boy as best he could. "Do you want me to sing to you, Jakey? Tell you a story?"

"No, that's okay. Just don't leave me alone."

"Why would I leave you alone? I'm right here. Can you try to go to sleep?"

Jake grew calmer. "There's a lot of weird noises in a swamp, aren't there, Andy?"

"It's almost like music. Listen and hear the music, and let it put you to sleep." He patted Jake's shoulders, then gently rubbed them.

Frightened and exhausted, Jake allowed himself to be soothed, and eventually he slept.

Andrew didn't sleep. He held Jake and sat watching the door, trying to still his pounding heart and listening carefully to every sound he heard. Finally, light began to come through the windows. Andrew heard two car doors slam and his mother's voice: "Andy? Jake?"

***

Andrew pulled the blanket tighter, trying to keep his teeth from chattering.

"When Mom and Aunt Connie found us the next morning, Jake was … he didn't speak for two days. He hardly moved. When he finally talked he said to Mom, 'Daddy left us all alone, Mommy. He told Andy to not let the alligators and bears get me.'

"She told him I'd taken good care of him and he was safe now. He was … he stuck really close to Mom. Our Aunt Melanie sang to him a lot and told him stories. That seemed to be what helped him the most. He never mentioned how Allan Martin had touched him just before he left us. I don't think he even remembered that. I was relieved that he didn't remember. I wanted to forget it. Later I did forget ... until now."

Dr. Penny asked softly, "Did he abuse you, Andy?"

"I think he would have if Mom hadn't left him when she did. And you know what I was most scared of, that whole long night? Not wild animals. I was terrified that my father would come back. I was terrified of what he might do to Jake. And knife or not, I doubt I could have stopped him. But I sure as hell would have tried. I wanted to kill him for the way he terrified my brother." He stopped and stared at Penny, struggling to breathe.

"That's why I did what I did in Vietnam. I could have shot that enemy soldier the way I did the other two, just raked him with machine gun rounds. But I didn't do that, because at that moment he was Allan Martin. I didn't hesitate to shoot him in the face. I wanted to blow his head apart."

"You never told your mother about what your father had threatened."

He shook his head. "No, I didn't. I was only eight, too young to understand exactly what he was threatening. I just knew that it terrified me and made me sick to my stomach to think about it. But Jake was okay. I think my telling him our father was just being his usual weird, unpredictable self, made it okay. He didn't question it, he accepted it. He was more scared of alligators and bears."

Penny was silent for a moment. "What you did was remarkable. You were a noble child."

Andrew felt tears gathering in his throat and tried to choke them back. He couldn't speak.

"Let it go, Andy. You've earned this. Let it out."

And he did, sobbing so hard his body shook. Crying for the two little boys in that cabin with a predatory adult male who came very close to destroying their lives. Crying for Jake, who had lost the person he had been when his memory was obliterated. Crying for himself, because he missed Jake so terribly.

CHAPTER 29

Dr. Penny sat quietly and let the storm pass.

Andrew mopped his face with several tissues and drew a long, shuddering breath, accepting gratefully the water she poured for him.

"What he did ... I mean *him*, you know, Allan Martin ... when I think about it ... I'm glad I never told Mom. What end would it have served? He went to prison for murdering my grandparents and my Uncle Steve. My mother felt guilty enough without me adding to her burden. Do you think when I saw him shoot my grandparents to death it wiped that other thing out of my mind?"

"It could have helped you bury it. Both events were traumatic, but you managed to diffuse the threat of sexual abuse for Jake. So you were Jake's parent as well as his brother. That's a lot for a child to assume."

"I never thought of it that way. Once Max came into our lives, it made a big difference. Max was everything Allan Martin wasn't. He taught me what it means to be a father."

"It's difficult for parents to let a child go, Andrew. As a parent, you try to make them self-reliant, to be able to deal with life. And at some point, you have to send them off into the world, and it's something not every parent deals with well."

"You think that's what's going on with me? There was something about feeling so responsible for Jake when I was a kid that makes me want to hang onto him?"

"What do you think?"

"My head hurts, Dr. Penny. I'm not thinking very clearly right now."

She looked directly at him. "Do you really need aspirin or are you stalling?"

He gave her a lopsided grin. "Stalling. But I do have a headache. I hardly ever cry. It's not much fun."

He sighed and leaned against the back of the chair, ran his hands through his hair and laced his fingers behind his head. "Okay. Why do I miss Jake so much that it's ripping me to pieces? In one way, I love him more than any other person on this earth. I have a connection … well, I *had* a connection with him like I have with nobody else. It's a different kind of love than the love I feel for my parents, or for Mary."

He sat up and leaned forward, elbows on knees. "What I feel for Mary … she's my life. She's my refuge. I don't think I could live without her. It kills me how I've been neglecting her because of this … obsession I have about needing to find Jake. It's not fair to her. It's not fair to *us*. I know that." He covered his face with his hands and leaned back again.

"I need to know where the people I love are. I need to know they're okay. It terrifies me to realize I may never know that again about Jake. It's not fair."

"You know life is never fair, Andrew. We have almost no control over our lives, no matter how much we'd like to think we do. That's not easy for anyone to accept; especially for someone like you, who craves order in his life."

He nodded. "When I saw Jake at Walter Reed, it seemed like he recognized me. But Dr. Forrester tried to warn me … he said for Jake, seeing me was almost like looking in a mirror. That was something he could latch onto. I convinced myself it was more. I was so sure that in a few weeks or months Jake would be back, and the earth would start rotating in the right direction again."

He sighed. "I know that's one of the reasons he left. I tried hard not to, but I constantly pressured him to be Jake. You know … the Jake I remembered. I just couldn't understand why that wasn't happening. The last time I saw him, he tried hard to explain to me what he was dealing with. I thought I was beginning to understand, but I don't think I was, not really."

He looked into the distance. "My head understands I may never see Jake again. Everything else in me refuses to accept that."

"So you're fighting a battle, Andrew. Reconciliation of the mind and the emotions. It's never easy, and for you I think it's an epic struggle."

"That's why I'm here, isn't it? For me to find some way to accept something I find unacceptable."

He saw that Dr. Penny was studying him.

"Are you comfortable with stopping for today? I think you need some time to rest. Sleep if you can. But I want to be sure you're in a safe place before we end this session."

"No, we can stop. You're right, I'm exhausted. I think I can catch a nap before dinner." He stood and folded the blanket, then handed it to Penny.

"You said Mary's coming back tonight with your art professor. Do you want me to call and suggest she wait until tomorrow?"

"No, I want to see her, and I need to apologize to Issy. She and Jake had a relationship, and she encouraged him to leave. I know she was just trying to help him, but the last time I saw her I was pretty awful."

"Very well. If you're tired, though, let them know I suggested they make it a short visit."

She walked him to the door.

"I don't have you scheduled for another session until Friday, but if you need me, be sure to have one of the staff let me know and we'll find a time."

He nodded. "I will. I think I can use a couple of days. Digging like that … it's not easy."

She smiled at him and he felt a rush of love for her as she replied, "No, it isn't. But it's worth it."

***

He slept heavily for two hours, waking when a staff member tapped at his door to remind him dinner was being served. He went to the common bathroom on the floor and pressed a cold washcloth against his swollen eyes, then splashed cold water on his splotchy face, patting it dry.

No session for two days. I can paint.

He was still on a modified diet because of the ulcer, but tonight he had steak, mashed potatoes, and green beans, with apple pie for dessert, and he ate every bite. He would have loved a steaming cup of coffee along with the pie, but his caffeine intake was severely restricted; he had to be satisfied with a tall glass of milk. The food restored some of his energy and he felt better.

Mary and Isabel arrived just as he was walking out of the dining room, each pushing a hospital cart loaded with art supplies and the canvasses, Issy with a bag slung over her shoulder. "Give me a minute with Issy, will you, Mary?" She nodded and went into the art room.

Isabel embraced him and Andrew held her close. "I'm so sorry for the harsh things I said to you, Issy. Please forgive me."

She stepped back and smiled. *"Bien sûr*, Andrew. I knew you did not mean those words."

"You're kinder than I deserve."

"I am happy to see you. I want to see what you are painting."

He let her precede him into the therapy room and she went immediately to the easel where he had been working all morning. He watched her eyes widen.

Andrew's new painting was the helicopter crash he had told Dr. Penny about; it was daylight in the jungle. Once again his perspective was from above. He had painted these two works completely from memory, but they were seared into his mind. Two choppers hovered above the burning craft, flames shooting upward, smoke billowing above the triple canopy of the jungle. A serene blue sky above; Andrew recalled how crazy it had been to look up and see that sky when he knew what horror was going on in the aircraft. His memories of Vietnam, in vivid colors and with the bold strokes of his palette knife.

"Are there more?"

"One more." The first painting he had done was leaning against a wall, and he set it on an empty easel.

"Such intensity; quite a departure from your lovely impressionistic paintings of the past. More emotional than representational. The juxtaposition…that is the word, yes? … of the colors is remarkable. I would call these your own version of abstract expressionism."

She studied both paintings, walking from one to the other, moving closer and further away, looking at them from different angles.

"*Mon Dieu*, Andrew. You can sell these paintings."

He smiled. "Maybe."

"*Mais non*, trust me. I mean these will bring excellent prices. I'm thinking five figures."

Now he laughed. "You're kidding."

"I would not kid about something like this." She sounded excited. "May I bring Evelyn to see these? She will confirm what I am thinking, I am sure." Evelyn Wenders, proprietor of Wenders Gallery, was the art dealer who had sold some of Isabel's and Andrew's paintings over the past few years.

"Do you really think someone would pay ten thousand dollars for one of these?"

"Possibly more."

Mary looked from Isabel to Andrew, her mouth open. "An unknown artist wouldn't be able to ask that kind of price, Isabel. Would he?"

"Let us see what Evelyn thinks," Isabel replied.

Mary had a large envelope which she handed to her husband. Glancing inside to confirm it held his sketches, he kissed her tenderly by way of thanking her.

Isabel, still admiring Andrew's work, asked: "Do you have more of these in you?"

"Oh, yes. Many more. And I need to get them out."

The three of them walked over to an area where they could sit down. Other patients and staff members wandered in and were looking at Andrew's work.

Andrew whispered to the two women, "They seem to appeal to the folks in here. Wonder what that means."

One man, who looked about forty or so, came in and examined them closely. He walked up to Andrew. "Are you the artist? Andrew Cameron?"

Andrew stood. "Yes, I am."

"Jim Thornton." He extended his hand, and Andrew took it. "Semper fi, Marine."

"Semper fi, Jim. I heard there was a brother enjoying the hospitality here."

Jim smiled. "Are you planning on selling these?"

"I might." Andrew was surprised. He hadn't had any thought of selling these paintings, and now Issy had suggested they might be of interest to collectors. And Jim seemed on the verge of making him an offer.

Isabel stood and extended her hand. "Isabel Jeanseau. Andrew's agent."

Mary almost choked as she turned her startled laugh into a cough. She and Andrew watched Isabel go into agent mode.

Issy continued, "We work through Wenders Gallery."

"I'm not surprised. This is quality art."

"You are a collector?"

"My family is. Please allow me to make an offer before you sell to someone else."

"Andrew promises me there will be more. And Evelyn will be in tomorrow to appraise these."

"Fair enough. Please just keep in mind that I want one of these two. In fact, I want this one. The night mission. I lived that."

"Agreed. *Merci.*"

Jim turned to Andrew and said, "I'd like to talk to you. I looked in this morning but you were hard at work and I hated to interrupt."

"Please interrupt me. I get very engrossed, but I'll be happy to stop and talk."

Jim smiled at all of them, looked one more time at the painting he had named "Night Mission" without realizing it, and left the room.

Isabel picked up the bag she had brought in and handed it to Andrew. "Would you go through these supplies and see if you need anything else? I will let you and Mary have some time while you do that. May I wander around?"

"I don't see why not. Thanks," Andrew replied. Mary sat close to him and handed him each item. Issy had thoughtfully included a list of the paints and other supplies she had packed. He leaned the large canvasses against a wall, three 24 by 36 inches and two 36 by 48 inches, noticing that Issy had tagged each of them with his initials.

Mary touched his face and kissed each eye softly. "Rough session today?"

"God, was it ever." He sighed. "You look so beautiful, my Mary. My angel." He smiled at her, caressing her hair back from her face. He heard her sharp intake of breath as he touched her.

"This weekend … come and stay over," he said softly.

"You mean like a conjugal visit? Is that allowed?"

"Get a hotel room. I'm not locked in here, I admitted myself. I can spend the day out in the world with my desirable wife."

"Are you sure?"

"Oh, yes."

He kissed her, a lingering kiss full of promise, and she sighed and leaned her head against his shoulder for a moment. "We probably shouldn't be making out in here."

He tipped her face up. "Thanks so much for bringing Isabel with you. It's so good to see her."

She looked at him for a long moment. "I really have you back, don't I?"

He kissed her again.

CHAPTER 30

The time Andrew spent painting over the next two days was therapeutic; he felt the release of emotions as he transferred long-denied feelings to the canvasses. He worked more on the first two paintings — putting the finishing touches on the helicopter crash, tears streaming unchecked down his face as he allowed himself to feel the sorrow he had denied when he had watched this take place.

He had known all of the men on the crew and one he had considered a friend. He mourned them now, all these years later. A gentle hand on his shoulder: Francine.

"You okay, Andy?"

"Yeah, I am. You know what, Francine? It feels good to cry for them. They were heroes."

Two additional paintings, one of two Hueys flying side by side, the jungle beneath them, a gathering storm ahead of them. *Symbolic, this one,* he thought. Another night mission, inside the triple canopy this time but above the ground, vague figures in motion coming to be extracted from a hot LZ.

The mission that had seared his soul. It had been his final mission: their colonel had been made aware of how rattled he was and gave Andrew base duties for his final three weeks in country. A good man, a great officer.

Thursday night Mary, Isabel and Evelyn Wenders came to see him; Evelyn thoughtfully studied each painting, making notes to herself. A petite, attractive brunette, impeccably groomed, Evelyn was a woman in her forties who had begun as a struggling art student and was now a highly successful entrepreneur.

"Andrew, these paintings are amazing. I've always admired your work, especially since your training and experience have been so limited compared to the other artists who exhibit at my gallery. That's a credit to Isabel, who recognized your talent and nurtured it so beautifully. But these paintings represent a real breakthrough, with an emotional impact that equals your skill.

"I can find buyers for these, Andy, I'm sure of it. I think the selling price will be between ten and thirteen thousand." He had never dreamed he'd be able to sell his art for those sums. Even after Evelyn's commission, if the pieces sold he and Mary would recover the money he was spending as a patient. Jim Thornton had stopped in twice to talk, and Andrew told him he would let Evelyn know Jim wanted to buy "Night Mission."

When they left Mary whispered to him where she had made her reservation for the weekend visit to the city. When he sat down in Dr. Penny's office on Friday morning, the first thing out of his mouth was, "Mary's coming to stay in Philly for the weekend. She wants to know if I can do a sleepover on Saturday night?"

Dr. Abramson smiled indulgently. "Oh, I think that can be arranged. I'll give you a weekend pass, but you will need to be back Sunday evening. Don't go AWOL on me."

He laughed. "Cross my heart. Why would I do that? I know I need more time with you. There's a lot of work we haven't done yet."

"Yes, there is. Can you tell me about the rest of that mission, the one where you had a flashback to your childhood trauma?"

"My flashback …is that what that was?" *Childhood trauma. Yes, I guess that describes it, but it's pretty clinical for something*

292

that was so awful I hid it from myself for years. He shivered. *Shit. The man still gets to me, even now.*

Dr. Penny waited patiently. "I know this is not easy for you to talk about. But it's important for you to face it so you can deal with it."

Andrew nodded. "Yes, I understand what you're saying. And I guess what happened next ... might be what you'd expect. I flipped out. I kept firing even after we were well off the ground. Now I think I know why, but then it just seemed crazy. Mike ... our pilot ... had to get rough with me, I think he knew I had just lost it."

"He got rough with you? How?"

"Yes, he ... the pilots had radios they were using for air to ground and air to air communication and we had an intercom in the aircraft for the crew. Mike flipped on his mike to the intercom and yelled at me to cease firing. I finally heard him and stopped, but it was a while before I stopped shaking."

He sighed heavily. "That time it didn't work ... getting above the jungle, I mean. I think I left something of myself in Vietnam on that mission. And when we got back to the base I didn't even speak to anybody, just did the inspection and clean-up of our Huey and guns without even thinking. I was numb."

"Was there anyone you could talk to about what had happened?"

"No, not really. Mike tried to talk to me and I just walked away. But the next day he told me since I was short ... meaning I only had three weeks left in country ... they weren't going to include me on any more missions. He had to clear that with the commanding officer, and I really appreciated what he did. When I left to come back to the world ... that's what we called coming home ... he told me I'd been a great door gunner and a real asset to

293

the squadron. I was feeling a little more normal by then and I was determined to put all of that out of my mind. And I thought I had succeeded."

She nodded. "Time to let go of all of it, Andrew. Easier said than done, I know."

"I'll work on it." He poured himself a cup of water and drained it.

"I'd like to hear more about Allan Martin."

He told her what he could remember about his birth father's erratic behavior. "Two things I thought about. Neither Jake nor I ever told Mom we witnessed the murder. We talked it over, and we both just kind of felt she didn't need to know that. She never asked us because her back was turned to us and she thought we'd already gone upstairs." He paused.

"But he knew we saw him. And now I understand why I always had this awful feeling of dread about him looking for us once he got out of jail. That eased over the years, but it took a long time."

"Where is he now?"

He hesitated. "This is another one of those 'strict confidence' things, Dr. Penny. Allan Martin is dead. Jake sent me a newspaper clipping last year about this time. Martin had been found dead in that hunting cabin and it had burned. Good riddance to both of them."

Dr. Penny's eyebrows went up. "What did Jake tell you?"

"Nothing. That was the last communication we had from him, just the clipping in an envelope. He wanted us to know the bastard was dead, and for all I know, Jake may have had something to do with it. We couldn't contact the authorities in South Carolina for fear they might start looking for Jake."

"Do you think Jake remembered what happened and killed him?"

"Anything's possible. I think Jake found him. We saw another article later that said the autopsy indicated Martin was terminally ill from lung cancer. Jake may have burned the cabin."

"Was the fire suspicious?"

"So far as we know, the case is still open. And another part of the puzzle: Mary found Jake's dog tags in a cabin Jake helped his old Army buddy, George Smallwood, build near Cherokee, North Carolina. I thought it might be a signal that he didn't want us to look for him. We filed a missing person's report which eventually resulted in that phone call about ..."

"... a body being found, which resulted in your extreme reaction. Ah."

She put the tips of her fingers together. "You said at our last session you were sure Jake is still alive. What makes you think that?"

Andrew brought the water pitcher and a cup to the table and poured water for himself. He drained the cup and refilled it before he continued. *None of this is easy to talk about*, he thought. Recounting all of this made him re-live it.

"When Jake was injured, I had a nightmare. The worst nightmare of my life. I knew he was either dead or had been badly wounded. We figured out later, from what we learned about when his accident happened, my nightmare took place at pretty much the exact same time."

"And you've had nothing comparable since?"

"No. In fact ..." he hesitated, but knew he had to continue. "When I had that psychotic episode, I think I had a dream about Jake. I don't really remember it, but it was ... I remember hearing his voice." He leaned forward.

"In a way, it was … so vivid, but I don't remember any of the details. Not like the memory of the nightmare. And it's odd. Sometimes people have said something to me since then and it's like an echo. Like I've heard it before." He smiled. "Now you *will* think I'm crazy."

"Not at all. You could very well have been hallucinating. Or it might have been exactly what you believe it was; a vivid dream."

"When I finally came out of that, I felt … almost peaceful. I woke up knowing I needed to get my head straightened out. I had this feeling. Wherever Jake is, he's okay."

"The last time we talked, you said you were here to find some way to accept something you find unacceptable. What do you think it will take for you to do that?"

He sighed deeply. "This one is for you, Dr. Penny. What will it take?"

"You don't believe he's dead, and it seems there's a case for that. So he's staying away from his family deliberately. Why might he do that?"

"If he was involved in Allan Martin's death he may want to stay out of touch with us, so if for some reason the police start hunting for him, we can honestly say we don't know where he is. But I'd feel so much better if I knew. If I at least knew he's okay."

She stood and walked to her desk and leaned against it, crossing her arms over her chest. "Can we play 'Let's Pretend' here? Let's think about where Jake might be."

Andrew settled back to listen, and Dr. Penny continued, "The last time he was seen he was with George Smallwood. Has anyone been able to track Smallwood down?"

"My dad wrote the Choctaw nation in Oklahoma. No one there has seen or heard from Smallwood in over two years. So they might still be together, but somewhere else."

"Both men were in Special Forces, so they have excellent survival skills. They may be with or near some other Vietnam vets who are living in a wilderness area. I'm not sure that's living, it seems more like surviving; but I wasn't in Vietnam. For those vets, it may be the life they need."

"If that's the case they could be anywhere. If Jake considers himself a fugitive, that would be a safe place for him. Brothers protect each other, and I would think that's a strong brotherhood."

"So that's one thought. If they did choose to disappear into the wilderness, from what I understand there's a good chance they might be in the Northwest someplace. I think you mentioned that. And they might prefer to stay there until they decide to emerge. You could go out there to look for him. But for how long? Months? Years?"

"And if he doesn't want to be found … I think that could have a bad ending. I've hounded Jake enough."

"Could you accept that and move on with your life?"

"If I had to, I could try."

"Here's another hypothesis. Jake has assumed a new identity. An identity that fits who he is now. It seems difficult, but people have done exactly that. He could be living anywhere. He may even be married. He's not Jake Cameron any more. But he's not just surviving … he's living. By allowing himself to leave his old life, he's found a new life. And it could be a happy one."

Andrew thought about that, and he felt something inside him unlock and open up. "People have done that before? Why would anyone do that?"

She raised an eyebrow and he laughed. "I have to stop thinking like Andrew and try to put myself in Jacob's head here. Why not make that choice?"

"I think we're getting somewhere now. So let's say he makes that choice … finds a job … marries, has a family … maybe even starts a business. He doesn't forget Jake Cameron. He puts that person away, at least for the present." She paused for a moment. "Or maybe for good."

"If I can believe that, I can be okay with it. But I don't have any way to prove that's what happened."

"No, you don't. It's part of life's unpredictability, and we have to live with that every day. Every hour. Every minute. Who knows which of us might go to sleep tonight and never wake up again? But we don't obsess over that. We focus on living." She looked into his eyes and repeated it. *"We focus on living."*

"And that's what I have to do, right? Accept that there may be this new Jake out there somewhere. Don't ever stop loving him and wishing him well. But get back to my life, focus on Mary. And Mom and Dad … put my energy into the people who are still here. Cherish them. They are all such magnificent people."

"And?"

"Keep painting." He grinned. "Evelyn — my agent — is excited about this new stuff. I can't believe the price tags she's putting on these paintings. Oh, and maybe most important of all … have a baby. Well, Mary can actually have it, but … I've put that on the back burner for far too long."

"Can you really do this, Andrew? Let Jake go and rejoin the living?"

"I have to, Dr. Penny," he said. "I have to do this. If I don't, I'll go crazy."

***

Andrew was as nervous as a teenager as he walked down the hall to Mary's hotel room. She had breathed in his ear, "Be sure to identify yourself when you knock. Since I don't expect to be wearing anything, I wouldn't want to open the door to the wrong man."

He almost laughed as he stood outside the door with sweaty palms, breathing unevenly. "Mary? It's Andy."

She opened the door and pulled him inside, reaching for his belt buckle. She was a flame in his arms, and all he wanted to do was bury himself inside her forever. He pressed her against the back of the door as they melted into each other, and his mind fragmented.

Afterward, they both laughed and moved to the bed, where she removed his clothing as if she were unwrapping the most wonderful gift she had ever received, and they discovered each other all over again. Finally he said, "I just came to invite you to lunch."

They moved closer together, continuing to laugh. Andrew didn't know when he had been so happy. They ordered room service, ate, showered, and fell back into bed again.

Later, lying quietly in her arms, he said, "I want to tell you, but I'm nervous about this. You won't like what you hear."

"Nothing you could say to me would ever make me feel differently about you. You must know that."

So he talked as she listened. Telling her about Vietnam. About what he and Penny had uncovered about his dread of his birth father. And this time when he wept … and he wept copiously … Mary wept with him, comforting him as only she could. Loving everything he was with everything she had to give him.

They slept in each other's arms through the night, ordered room service again, and spent the morning in bed, sometimes talking, sometimes losing themselves in each other. She had to check out by three, so they dressed reluctantly and went for a late lunch before she drove him back to the Institute on her way to West Chester.

"I don't think I'll need to be here too long. Maybe another three or four weeks. But I feel safe here, and I think I should stay until Penny … Dr. Penny and I agree I'm ready to leave."

"Stay as long as you need to, my dearest love. I'll be back next weekend. Do you want me to run over during the week?"

He gazed at her, appreciating her anew. At twenty-eight, she was almost achingly beautiful, especially with the weekend they had just spent and the glow it had produced. "I'm always happy to see you. I know you have a Wednesday night chorale rehearsal, though, and it's not always easy to find a parking place. We've just had the most … *incredible* … two days together."

She caressed his face with her gloved hand. "I don't think I've ever felt so loved, my darling." She leaned against him and ran her lips down his jaw.

He put a hand to the back of her head, gently pressing it against him. "Don't start."

She pulled away and smiled. "I know. About coming over this week … I'll probably see you Tuesday after school. I'll have a hard time keeping my hands off you, though."

"Safe travels. Call me when you get home."

They kissed one last time, and he got out of the car, turning back and waving before he walked inside. *Drive safely, my angel.*

Something I need to talk to Dr. Penny about. Bad things happen when you least expect them, but I can't spend my life anticipating they'll happen. Mary will be fine.

He turned on his tape player and put on the Brahms *Requiem*. Mary called to say she was safely home during "How Lovely Is

Your Dwelling Place," the peaceful, hopeful music that always calmed him.

> *How lovely is Your dwelling place,*
> *O Lord of Hosts.*
> *My soul longs for the courts of the Lord.*

He was relieved when she called.

CHAPTER 31

Andrew and Dr. Penny agreed to take his treatment a week at a time; he would see her Tuesdays and Fridays for therapy. He painted constantly. Isabel brought more canvasses and Evelyn stopped in on Fridays to pick up the paintings he reluctantly parted with. He always looked at them critically and commented they could use more work, and Evelyn always told him nonsense, they were perfect.

He spent time with Jim Thornton, who was suffering from what he was told was stress response syndrome. Andrew had thought Jim to be in his early forties, and was stunned to learn he was only twenty-six — two years younger than Andrew. This was the third time Jim's family had persuaded him to seek help; and he confided in Andrew that he had twice attempted suicide.

"My God, Jim. What happened?"

"You know what happened at My Lai? The massacre of Vietnamese women and children? Well, that wasn't the first time. And I saw the aftermath. And I never ratted out my" … his lip curled … "fellow soldiers." He released a sigh that came from the depths of his soul. "Not everybody over there was a hero, Andy."

"Calley claimed he was given direct orders at My Lai, and if that's true … it's nearly impossible to ignore a direct order. You weren't there when it happened, I take it."

"The only thing that's keeping me from completely losing my sanity is that I didn't participate. What a world of shit we live in."

Andrew wasn't sure what to say to him. "It was Marines who did that?"

"Thankfully, it was pretty clear it wasn't. I was with a detail that passed by a village after a massacre happened. We called for assistance for the survivors. One of the women spoke enough English to try to tell us it had been soldiers, though I'm not sure how she knew that. We kept asking her 'Like us?' and she said 'No Marine. Soldiers.'"

It couldn't have been U.S. Army, thought Andrew. *It must have been South Vietnamese army troops. Or maybe even VC masquerading as ARVN. Who the hell knows? Jim is really confused about this.*

"So other men were with you?"

"We agreed it wasn't our business so we all kept our mouths shut even though we were pretty sure we knew who it was. I'll regret that until the day I die. I am beginning to feel like I may be able to live with myself, though. This is a good place. It's the first time I've begun to feel a glimmer of hope in four years."

"That's good to hear."

Jim sighed. "This will probably sound really crazy to you, especially given what I've just told you. But you know, Andy … a part of me misses being there. I miss the camaraderie I experienced. Those men were the best friends I ever had … no, they were more than that. They were my brothers. What is it about being in a war … it's terrible and wonderful at the same time. I guess that's why I went back. Every day I wish I had never done that."

Andrew couldn't relate; he had been relieved to have survived his one tour. He did appreciate what Jim said about the men he had served with, how close they felt to each other.

303

He had been in the Institute for five weeks and was anxious to get back to his life, and Dr. Penny agreed, saying if he ever needed her he should contact her immediately and they would find a way to get together. At his final inpatient session, he told Dr. Penny about his conversation with Jim, which had disturbed him.

"Jim didn't really know exactly what happened, what caused those deaths and injuries. But he couldn't deal with how guilty it made him feel ... and how guilty he feels about even feeling guilty. As if it's a betrayal of his fellow soldiers. It's a nightmare."

Dr. Penny nodded, and Andrew continued, "You know, I had heard other Marines say something similar about being in a war ... it changed them completely. It was hard for some of them to let go of it. And apparently, some simply couldn't adjust to being back in the world; that must be why so many are living in wilderness areas.

"Vietnam ... sometimes I was able to look around and see the beauty. We didn't have much down time. Marines always have to scramble. But there were a couple of days early in my tour, when our helicopter was being serviced, we had some free time. Mike — our pilot — and I climbed to the top of the mountain ... Marble Mountain." He paused for a moment, remembering.

"There were actually five tall hills, and each one had its own name. The one we climbed was the Mountain of Water and there were stone steps that led to the top, and the view from up there was magnificent. It was peaceful. There were Buddhist monks, Buddhist sanctuaries there. Pagodas that had been there for who knows how long. Inside the mountain a cave with a Buddha."

"A different culture. Did you ever go back?"

"Yes, we managed to climb all of them eventually. But the Mountain of Water was our favorite. Mike finally said something on one of these climbs that I had been thinking, maybe a couple of months before my tour ended. He said, 'Have you ever wondered about this land and these people … what was it like before the French attempted to establish a colony here?' And I had wondered that, and wondered what the hell we were even doing there."

"What year was that?"

"1967. So it was before the 1968 Tet Offensive."

Dr. Penny commented, "In the past few years a lot of people are asking that … why were we there? With so much starting to come to light … My Lai, the Pentagon Papers, the hearings on the Phoenix Program … all indications that the American people were lied to by our government. The soldiers who reported what happened at My Lai … how regrettable that at first there was apparently a cover-up. And very few paid any price for what they did."

"It was a slap in the face to the brave young men who served honorably and gave their lives. What a horrific waste. As proud as I was to serve with my fellow Marines, I believe we should never have been there. It's surprising there are still Americans in Saigon. I have a bad feeling about that. Everybody should be out by now."

"From what I understand, a lot of veterans are as conflicted as you are, Andrew."

He sighed. "In a way, I envy Jake, that he's lost the memory of his time in Vietnam."

"You think of him often."

"Yes, but I try to think of him as you and I talked about. Leading a happy and productive life somewhere. And I think about all the great times we had together. What is it I've heard — 'Don't be sad it's over. Be glad it happened.' Mary told me that. I'm so happy to be going home to her, Dr. Penny."

"Have you talked about when you might start your family?"

"No, I want to get home first, and get settled into a routine. I'm not ready to go back to teaching yet. I want to paint more pieces for the art show Evelyn's planning. I want to go home and paint … and I want to paint more than just the war. I want to paint the beauty I saw in Vietnam. That may be the end of my fifteen minutes of fame, though." He laughed.

"Then again, it may not be. If this show is successful, you may have a full-time career."

"One day at a time, Dr. Abramson. A wise lady I know helped me understand that."

She smiled and nodded, acknowledging the compliment. "It's easier to say than to practice. But you're well-armed to deal with your anxiety … you have art and music. And your Mary."

"And a call to my therapist if I really have trouble dealing. I don't want to be medicated, though."

"I know you would prefer not to, but being on something short term isn't a bad thing. Much better than going through again what you went through in January."

"I'll keep it in mind."

She stood, and he knew this time with her was over, at least for the present. He walked toward the door, reluctant to leave without telling her what was in his heart.

"I don't know how to thank you. You've brought me back to life."

"You've done that, Andrew. I just gave you some suggestions. You did all the work."

He still hesitated, wanting to express his gratitude. "I really want to hug you. Would that be okay? I love you, Dr. Penny." Her eyebrows went up and she started to speak, and he added hastily, "Oh, I don't mean I'm in love with you. But I can understand how that sometimes happens. When you allow somebody to help you crack your soul open, you develop a connection unlike any other."

"You've been pretty much an ideal patient, Andrew. I appreciate how willingly you accepted my suggestions."

"I guess that means you kind of like me?" He grinned at her and opened his arms. She allowed herself to embrace him briefly, then stepped away and pushed her glasses up on her nose.

"Stay in touch. I'd love to hear how you and Mary are doing. I know I've said it before, but you two have a strong marriage."

***

Andrew's gallery show was planned for mid-April, and he decided not to return to teaching until fall so he wouldn't feel pressured to hurry the completion of the paintings he wanted to do. He and Mary also resumed house-hunting. If he sold several of his paintings they would easily have a sizable down payment. They wanted a house which could include a studio as well as rooms for the two children they talked about.

The first weekend of April they found the house, not far from Tony and Max's home. Slightly larger, newer, dove gray vinyl siding, a dormer window on the second floor, a fireplace in the living room. A spacious sun room that could be converted into an art studio, situated in an extension of the first floor. A nice large yard for their children to play in. Andrew loved it. Even though Mary had needed to withdraw some money from their savings account to pay for his time at the Institute, they still had nearly enough for a down payment ... and when Jim Thornton brought Evelyn a check for "Night Mission," they made up their shortfall with a little left over. So the closing on the house took place two days before Andrew's formal debut into the art world, and they planned to move in on the first of May.

Andrew had thought he'd be nervous about the show, but he enjoyed it immensely. It was nice to see the "sold" sign on "Night Mission" and Evelyn said it was good to have one or two pieces with that display of confidence included among the art other patrons and potential buyers would see. She had found a buyer for another painting, so two "sold" signs in the dozen paintings reinforced that Andrew Cameron was an emerging, hot new artist.

Isabel, Toni and Max were on hand, and Andrew admired his wife as he watched Evelyn introduce Mary to the art patrons. She had bought a new dress for the occasion, a soft ivory silk which flowed as she walked. She wore her ash blonde hair to her shoulders; a natural wave made it fall softly with a slight flip on the end. She seemed more a Botticelli angel than ever. It was evident she loved being the artist's wife, and she didn't hesitate to speak to people who were gazing at one painting or another and to encourage their questions and comments.

Isabel, standing next to Andrew, remarked, "She is an asset to you as a rising star in the art world, Andrew. She loves your work and is proud to let a potential buyer know how much of your soul has gone into it."

"This isn't real, is it, Issy? I'm going to wake up in five minutes and realize it was all just a nice dream."

Isabel laughed, and Andrew heard the tinkle of bells as he always had. "*Mais non, mon ami,* this is very real. And what I always hoped for you. I sensed you could do this."

Jim Thornton arrived with his parents, Warren and Cecile, whom Andrew had met while he and Jim were patients at the Institute. Jim and his father spoke to Andrew briefly but Cecile lingered after the Thornton men walked away to view the paintings.

"You need to know how much Jim values your friendship, Andy," she said. "He's doing much better, and at least part of that is because of you. I hope you'll stay in touch with him. He never made friends easily."

"Of course I will, Cecile. Jim was as much a help to me as I was to him, and he's one of the few people I can talk to about Vietnam who understands."

"Thank you, Andy." She embraced him and kissed his cheek. "That means a lot."

As Cecile moved away to join her men, more people entered the gallery, and Andrew did a double-take when he realized one of them was his neuropsychologist. But it was a Dr. Penny Abramson he had never seen. Her hair, gathered into an elegant French twist, shone red in the artificial light. She was wearing a draped black dress with sequins around the stylishly cut neckline, with a skirt short enough to show off a pair of great legs. He'd had no idea what a beautiful woman she was. Mary was standing with him and touched his arm. "Your mouth is hanging open, Andy," she teased.

She hugged Dr. Abramson warmly and said, "Thanks for coming, Penny."

His doctor turned to him and he saw the artfully applied makeup, just the right touch to enhance her natural beauty. "Congratulations, Andy. This is quite an event." He hadn't recovered enough to be able to answer her, and she chuckled. "Yes, it's actually me. The me who exists out of the office. And call me Penny."

He swallowed. *No wonder she had acted startled when I told her I loved her. She had probably had a lot of patients actually hit on her until she developed the camouflage.*

"Thank you … uh … Penny. I'm happy to see you here."

At the end of the evening, "sold" stickers were on an additional seven of Andrew's paintings. Including the two he had already sold, even after Evelyn's commission he would realize $56,000 from this one show. That was something of a shock for an art teacher making $12,000 a year.

It was a perfect evening. The only thing missing was Jake; thinking of him gave Andrew a brief stab of pain. Mary saw it in his face, and she put her arms around him and said, "He would have been so proud of you. Someday you may be able to tell him about this."

He sighed, and rested his cheek against hers for a moment. "I'm fine. I really am. Yes, of course I wish he could have been here. But you're here, and Mom and Dad. Let's go somewhere and celebrate, why don't we?"

***

The young Camerons were nearly settled in their new home by the end of May. School was nearing its end and Mary was looking forward to the summer. Andrew had actively been involved in decorating the house and getting everything moved in. Mary insisted the first and most important room was his studio. He was thrilled with it. It had been one big selling point: the former sun room was spacious, airy, and provided wonderful light from the north, perfect for an artist. She urged him to make time to paint; she and Toni could do the final touches on the rest of the house.

He went to Longwood Gardens and made sketches; then using the new techniques he had developed, bold strokes and vivid, saturated colors, he began to paint the gardens and landscapes of the state he loved. He wanted them to travel during the summer to see more of Pennsylvania. He was also painting something Mary hadn't seen yet; he wanted to show it to her once school ended.

One particularly lovely evening in early June, Andrew took Mary to dinner at Longwood Gardens. They found the spot where he had told her about enlisting in the Marine Corps, and they sat together on the same bench with their arms around each other, thinking back on the years that had passed.

They watched the moon rise, and then Andrew pulled her to her feet and said, "Let's go home, my Mary. Doesn't that sound wonderful? Home."

When they went inside he asked her to come into the studio with him. She sat in an easy chair he had put in the room. A chair especially for her, a place she could sit if she wanted to talk to him or watch him paint, or just be near him.

He led her to the chair, went to the corner and took a cloth cover from a small 16 by 20 inch canvas. He put the painting behind his back and walked to her.

"I've been working on this painting, and I want you to see it. It's not quite finished."

He knelt in front of her as he turned the canvas around and put it into her hands. It was a portrait of her in soft, muted colors, so lovely and delicate it made her gasp. "This isn't me."

"It is you," he said, and his voice shook. "But I need you to help me finish this painting, my Mary."

Mary had tears in her eyes as she saw the blank space, waiting to hold the image of a child. She whispered, "Oh, Andy."

Andrew put the painting gently to one side as he took his wife in his arms.

CHAPTER 32

Lindsey Antonia Cameron was born on May 14, 1975, and the first time Andrew held her he was flooded with love. She was Mary all over again; she was perfect, she was theirs. His heart nearly burst with what he felt for her. He began painting her almost immediately. Little Miss Lindsey's platinum curls, big blue eyes, and angelic smile appeared on many canvasses.

Toni and Max were thrilled to have a grandchild. Toni loved dressing her, and spent far too much money on little girl clothes, especially because she grew so quickly some outfits weren't worn but a few times before they no longer fit. Mary planned to take the school year off and wasn't sure when she would go back to teaching. The high school hired a long-term substitute for the coming year, and Mary felt she should let them know after the first of the year if she intended to return.

Isabel came often to their new home to see what Andrew was painting and to spend time with Mary and especially Lindsey, on whom she doted. Issy had been part of their lives for so long they were stunned when she announced to them she was returning to France in August.

"I have been invited to join the faculty at the École des Beaux-Arts. It is a great honor, and I believe I should accept. It is an offer that will not be extended again."

"You can't leave. I need your guidance," Andrew told her.

"You're part of our family, Issy," said Mary. "We all love you."

"That is a lovely compliment, Mary. Andrew, you are a mature artist. You do not need a mentor any longer. But I thank you for the incredible gift you have given me."

"I have no idea what you mean."

"It is partly because of your success that I have received this offer. Your fame is spreading, Andrew. My dream as a teacher was to have a student who achieved recognition. You have done that, and your success will continue to grow. Every teacher wishes for this. It seldom happens, and it is often only once in a lifetime."

Andrew replied, "I don't know what to say. We'll all miss you, Isabel."

"Come visit me, Andrew. You need to see the Louvre. Perhaps one of your paintings will one day find a place there." She laughed her bell-like trill. "Besides, I have felt for a while that it is time for me to return home. I have enjoyed my time here, but *mon pays est Paris* ... my country is Paris."

Isabel recommended that Andrew take her position at West Chester State College, and he jumped at the chance. The lighter schedule would give him more time to paint, and the salary was definitely an increase. His art continued to sell and he was now receiving sometimes fifteen thousand dollars for a piece of art: he was painting mostly landscapes with his new style, sometimes using even larger canvasses.

Between his income at the college and what he was taking in as an artist, there was no need for Mary to continue to work. However, when the music department at WCSC offered her a position teaching accompanying, she accepted. It would only mean three half days a week, and accompanying had been her first love.

It meant she would be home with Lindsey more, and she loved being a mother and spending time with her little girl.

Toni was happy to take care of Lindsey when her parents were both busy. Watching his mother with her first grandchild, Andrew realized this sweet little girl was helping to ease her grandmother's heartache as much as she was easing his own.

***

The following spring, Mary and Andrew went into Philadelphia to the Academy of Music to hear a recital of vocal music by the renowned Metropolitan Opera tenor, Jamie Logan. They had some of his recordings and Andrew was excited to hear him in person. He had told Mary about meeting Jamie when he had played opposite his Aunt Melanie more than twenty years earlier in that Pine Glen High School production of *Carousel*.

Mary was obviously enthralled by the recital. Jamie Logan's reputation was well-deserved; she thought he sounded even better in person than he did on his recordings. She also didn't think his pictures did him justice. "Was he this good-looking when he was in high school?" she whispered to her husband.

Andrew tried not to laugh out loud. "I was a kid. I didn't really notice," he whispered back.

Andrew glanced at her from time to time and saw how attentively she was watching the pianist, Eli Levin. After the recital she told Andrew that Levin was undoubtedly the finest accompanist she had ever heard. "Do you think we might meet him backstage? I'd like to know if he ever gives workshops or clinics. I know I could convince the music faculty at the college to invite him. I'd love to have a chance to learn from him."

They waited near the end of the line to speak to Logan, and Eli Levin, a slender man with curly dark hair and dark eyes behind thick glasses, was with him and seemed pleasant and cordial. Finally, they were able to speak with the two men.

"Mr. Logan, I'm sure you don't remember me, but I'm Melanie Stewart's nephew. I met you a long time ago when I heard you perform in *Carousel* with my aunt."

Jamie shook his hand warmly. "Of course I remember you. Are you Andrew or Jacob?"

Andrew was impressed. "Andrew Cameron," he responded.

"I put you on a carousel horse, if I remember correctly."

"I'm amazed you remember that. I'll never forget it. It was a very kind thing for you to do."

Logan spoke to a small woman who was standing near Eli Levin. From the way the pianist was gazing at her, it was apparent she was his wife. "Krissy, come and say hello to Melanie Stewart's nephew, Andrew."

As soon as she turned and smiled at him, Andrew remembered her. She hardly seemed changed at all: soft brown eyes, light brown hair, and a sweet smile. "You were Krissy Porter. You used to go to the playground with us on Saturdays. And you played harp in the orchestra for *Carousel*," he said to her.

"Yes, I did. How nice of you to remember. And now you're living in Philadelphia?"

"West Chester. It's a town just west of Philadelphia. I'm teaching art at the college there. This is my wife, Mary, who is also on the faculty; she teaches accompanying."

The two women exchanged greetings, and Krissy said to her husband, "Eli, meet a young man from my past, Andrew Cameron, and his wife, Mary. She's a fellow accompanist."

315

Levin joined them and soon he and Mary were deep in conversation. Jamie Logan had turned to other audience members waiting to shake his hand and ask for autographs, and Krissy Levin said to Andrew, "How is your brother?"

Andrew tensed. He had known there would be a time when someone would ask this, and he and Mary had talked about how best to answer. "The last time I saw him, he was well."

"He doesn't live here in Pennsylvania?"

"No, he's traveling. We're not sure when we'll see him again."

Mary had heard this exchange, and she put a hand on Andrew's back, but Krissy followed with, "What do you hear from Melanie?" and Andrew relaxed.

On the way back to West Chester, Mary sat close to Andrew, a hand on his knee, her head resting against his shoulder. "Thank you for bringing me to this wonderful concert. Eli Levin gave me contact information for his personal manager and I am hopeful we might have him come for a workshop. He is really nice, and his wife seems lovely."

"She and Melanie were very close friends. But it seems they don't hear much from each other these days. Krissy was always very sweet to Jake and me."

Mary squeezed his knee. "Are you okay?"

He sighed. "Yes. Right at this moment I really miss Jake, though. Sometimes it's hard."

"It has to be."

When they arrived home he went to Lindsey's room. Toni and Max had stayed with her, as they often did when Mary and Andrew went out. Andrew stood by her bed; seeing the dark lashes against the pink and white cheek, whorls of fair hair framing her face, the rosebud of her tiny mouth. He wanted to pick her up and hold her tight, but she was sleeping so peacefully he decided against it.

Penny Abramson's voice echoed in his head: "Don't have a child in the hope of replacing your brother." He didn't think he had done that; he and Mary had always wanted children. But when he longed to see Jake, having Lindsey to pick up and hug eased the ache he felt.

Where are you, Jake? If only he would call. Or send a note, or a postcard. *Do you remember sitting on those carousel horses backstage? Would you have remembered Jamie Logan if you'd been there tonight?*

Stop it, Andrew. You'll just make yourself crazy again. He had to accept the empty space in his heart and trust that Jake was alive and well … and happy.

***

The Levins came to West Chester that fall; Eli conducted a clinic in collaborative piano at the college, attended by pianists from all over Pennsylvania. Mary had made all the arrangements and Andrew knew how thrilled she was to see it come to fruition. Mary and Andrew invited Krissy and Eli to be their house guests, and they accepted with pleasure.

They arrived the Friday evening before the Saturday clinic and the Camerons took them to Longwood Gardens for dinner, while Toni and Max took care of Lindsey. When they returned to the house, Lindsey had yet another pair of adults to pay homage to her, and she basked happily in the attention until she was put to bed.

Krissy and Eli had learned of Andrew's accomplishments and admired the work in his studio. Portraits, landscapes, paintings of the air war in Vietnam. Krissy was enchanted with the portraits of Mary, who showed her the one she loved most … the one Andrew had asked her to help him finish. It now included Lindsey's angelic little face.

Andrew expected Krissy at any minute to ask again about Jake, and he had decided to be honest with her. She remarked on the photo of Andrew and Jake in uniform which sat on the fireplace mantel.

"Was this at your wedding?"

"Yes. Jake was home on leave. He went back and began his training for Special Forces at the end of that time," Mary replied.

Andrew invited Krissy to sit down with him. "The fact is, Krissy … we don't know where Jake is. He …" He had to stop. He thought he had this all worked out, but his voice failed him.

Krissy waited quietly, and finally Andrew managed to say, "We haven't seen him or heard from him for almost three years."

The Levins heard the entire story, listening without comment. Andrew ended, "Sometimes it's so hard. If I just knew he was okay, it would help. I think he is. But I don't know that."

"How do you bear it?" Krissy asked. Andrew noticed she had one of her hands in Eli's and their fingers were laced together. *What are they dealing with?* He wondered with a start.

"I have a therapist I still see on occasion. Talking with her helps. I couldn't manage without Mary and Lindsey. And my parents. And my work."

Eli nodded. "Art in your case. Music in mine. And the people we love, especially our wives."

"What do you mean, Eli?" Andrew asked.

A look passed between the Levins, and Krissy began, "Not knowing about Jake, wondering if he's alive, that's very difficult. But there are other …" she stopped, unable to continue.

Eli put an arm around his wife and drew her close. "We don't say much about this, but maybe it would be helpful for you to hear it. I was born with a severe congenital heart condition. I've been living on borrowed time for years. And this amazing woman has elected to share my time on earth with me." He smiled at his wife, and she kissed him.

And now Andrew asked Krissy and Eli, "How do you do it?"

Krissy answered, "I had great advice from a cardiologist friend before I married Eli. He told me to make every minute we have together the best minute of our lives. And that's how we've chosen to live."

Mary said, "Make every minute you have together ..."

" ... the best minute of your lives." Krissy finished.

Andrew said, "I'm trying to learn to live one day at a time. It's not easy."

"Sometimes an hour at a time. A minute at a time. Eli and I have learned to try to live in the moment," Krissy said softly.

Eli slapped his hands on his knees, jumped up and went to the piano. "Okay, enough with the gloom and doom. Right now, in *this* moment, we're here and we're alive. How about some Chopin? Rachmaninoff? What's your pleasure? If I play really loud, will it wake Lindsey up so I can play with her again?"

He made them all laugh. "Lindsey will sleep through anything," Mary said. "Are you really going to play for us?"

"What shall I play, Krissy?"

"Play Ravel. Play Debussy. You can start with 'Dr. Gradus ad Parnassum.'"

And for the next hour, Mary's piano responded to the touch of one of the finest pianists on the planet. Andrew made several sketches of Eli as he played, one of which he signed and gave to

319

Krissy, who was thrilled. Andrew knew he would never forget that evening and the indomitable spirit he witnessed.

They drove the Levins to Philadelphia to take a train back to Manhattan after the workshop the next day, and Andrew had a moment to speak with Eli.

"You have no idea how much you helped me. I can't thank you enough for letting me see what courage looks like."

"I'm not courageous, Andy. I love life. I love Krissy. I love music. I plan to enjoy all of them for as long as I can, and I try to focus on that."

***

Eli Levin's imperfect heart stopped beating two years later, in October of 1978. He was forty-one years old, and a light went out in the music world.

Andrew painted him playing at Mary's piano, a man full of life, love and music; and sent the painting to Krissy.

She responded with a note:

How can I ever thank you for the painting? It's beautiful, Andy. Eli's still alive, you know. He's in my heart and he always will be. I am so grateful for the years we had together ... for all those wonderful moments, one of which you captured so perfectly. Keep thinking good thoughts about Jake. He'll feel them, wherever he is.

CHAPTER 33

Maxwell Jacob joined the Cameron family in September of 1977. As much as Lindsey continued to resemble Mary, Andrew and Mary's son bore a strong resemblance to both his father and his uncle: dark eyes that shone with curiosity, a chubby face with rosy cheeks, fair hair, not as light as Lindsey's — Toni said it would darken as he grew older. She thought him a combination of both of her sons. Andrew was reminded of Jake every time he looked at his son's face; at first with a mixture of sadness and joy, but then increasingly only with joy.

Andrew had thought of calling him Max, but his grandfather insisted he should be Jake. Toni suggested, "What about calling him M.J.?"

And M.J. he became. Andrew watched Max, who was holding the baby when this momentous decision was made, and saw the intense love his father felt for his son. It grew daily, and Andrew realized what M.J. meant to Max … this was what he had missed with him and Jake, the joy of watching a baby boy's developing awareness of the world.

Lindsey had christened her grandparents "Grandy" and "Grammy" — her version of "granddaddy" and "grandmommy," and Toni and Max delighted in the names, in their new roles, and in both their grandchildren.

Even as a very young child, Lindsey displayed a love of music. She listened attentively to the recordings which were heard in her home, and by the time she was three wanted her mother to let her try to play piano. M.J. seemed to like music as well, and they were curious to see if he would display an interest in sports.

Once M.J. started walking he was in constant motion, seemingly tireless. Mary joked that her son had two speeds, "high" and "off." He was a good-natured toddler with a ready smile and a generous nature. Lindsey had Mary's sweetness, but she was also a very determined little girl. Toni claimed responsibility for that.

Andrew continued to teach because he loved doing it; he had a burgeoning career, a loving family, and now a son as well as a daughter. He left to go to his college classes somewhat reluctantly; he loved being at home with his family. Painting was a joy — partly because his studio was in his home. Blankets were spread across the floor in the studio when the children were babies, and it wasn't unusual to see them sleeping peacefully there, carefully covered with a blanket by their father.

Eventually, small tables with art and craft supplies were set up for Lindsey and M.J. in the studio. Either Mary or Toni was always on hand to supervise the children or remove the toddlers if they became too rambunctious. Andrew would make time to help them color or paint or work with clay. He played with them, fed them, watched them sleep, read to them.

There were many paintings of the Cameron children. He painted each of them alone numerous times; painted the two of them together; painted them with their mother, separately and collectively. He liked using watercolors when the children were small; the delicacy of their features lent themselves to the transparency of the medium.

***

In 1981 Andrew watched with interest when Maya Lin's controversial design for the Vietnam War Memorial was revealed. He read her premise: a memorial to America's fallen, a granite V-shaped wall engraved with their names. He admired her ideas, and was sorry to see how controversial the choice became. Max stopped by the house to talk to Andrew, who was at work on a commissioned painting of the war.

"You've seen the selection for the Vietnam War Memorial?"

"Yes, I have. I like it," Andrew replied. He was listening to music as he worked, the Brahms *Requiem*. His family had been mystified the first time they saw him painting the war to this music, but he explained that it was the only way he could make sense of Vietnam. It helped him hold onto hope — unlike other requiems, Brahms' theme moved from anguish to comfort.

"Well, a lot of veterans' groups aren't happy," Max said, indicating the newspaper he had in his hand.

"It was a completely anonymous competition." Andrew continued to work. "It couldn't have possibly been more fair. Nobody knew the identity of any of the entrants. So what if she's young and her parents emigrated from China? She's a brilliant designer."

"It's not just that. There's some objection to the concept. People like tradition, and this is anything but a traditional war memorial."

"I don't believe Vietnam could possibly have a memorial that could be described as 'traditional.' We lost the war, and this country is still suffering from the aftereffects. There weren't any victory parades, that's for damn sure. This memorial *has* to be different."

"Will you go to see it, once it's completed?"

Andrew took a break, putting his palette knife aside and wiping his face with the towel lying on a table near his easel. When he worked on a painting of the war he used a large canvas, sometimes almost slashing on the paint. In his mind he was right back in country, feeling the heat, moving vigorously as he painted, almost with a sense of holding a machine gun and standing in the door of his helicopter.

He pulled two beers from the mini-fridge in the studio, opened them, handed one to Max and then sank into an easy chair.

"I'm sure I will. Ever since I read about the memorial I've been thinking about guys I served with who never made it home."

Max examined his beer. "Yes, you told me about some of them ... one in particular, a helicopter pilot. Didn't you reach out to his wife after you were in therapy?"

"Mary and I both stay in touch with her. He never saw his little girl; she was born after he was killed." He shook his head. "That happened so much over there. Most of those guys ... Dad, they were so *young*."

"You were only nineteen when you enlisted. I wonder sometimes if I did the right thing when I encouraged you to do that. I didn't sleep much while you were in country."

Andrew smiled. "I made it home. And you did the right thing; I've told you that."

"All I know is I'm sure glad I'm sitting here talking to you." He looked around the room at the toys and coloring books that had become part of the décor. "And I like having your kids in my life." The men grinned at each other and clinked beer bottles.

"Another thing ...you know I get together with Jim Thornton every few months. I think it would be good for him to go to D.C. once the memorial is completed. He seems to be better, but he's still seeing a therapist and he's still fighting that damn war."

"And you're not?"

Andrew smiled. "Not really." He waved a hand toward the painting. "I'm lucky. I've been able to exorcise most of my demons."

Three years later, the adults in the Cameron family and Jim Thornton and his parents, Warren and Cecile, made the pilgrimage together to see the Memorial. By then, the Wall had been joined by a more traditional monument of three military men in combat gear which stood near the Wall but was not part of it, as some people had suggested. Andrew admired the designer; young as she was, and the victim of prejudice because of her Asian heritage, she stood her ground and hadn't allowed her concept to be compromised.

As he began to walk with Jim down the path and watch the Wall rise beside them, Andrew felt a pain stab his heart. *God, all these names. All these young men.* Jim wept openly as he searched for names of two of the men he had served with who had been killed in action on the same date. Andrew had to wipe his own eyes to help Jim look for his comrades, and as they found each name, Jim's mother did a rubbing for him to take home.

Max and Warren Thornton consulted the registry to help Andrew find the names of two of his fallen brothers in arms, remembering each of them as they were in life. Mary had brought flowers, and placed those at the base of the wall for each of Jim's and Andrew's comrades, joining the thousands of other flowers, keepsakes and messages left by other mourners. Without planning it, their group stopped and held each other as they silently saluted these warriors, cut down before they had lived.

Andrew was struck by the reflections in the black granite, the sense that he was seeing beyond this world ... just as Maya Lin had planned. *What inspired her? So young, and yet such amazing*

325

choices. He ran a finger over some of the names, grateful Jake's wasn't among them. *But in a way, Jake did die in Vietnam.* He had to lean against the wall for a moment, overcome with emotion. Andrew felt Max's strong arm supporting him, and he wiped his face and stepped back.

They lingered for a long time, and Jim's face showed how much this trip had meant to him. He looked younger, more hopeful; the lines of grief and despair smoothed out. "Thanks for coming with me, Andy. Visiting this place has definitely made a difference for me … it seems to bring a kind of closure to what I've been feeling."

"I hope so, Jim. I know one thing, when my kids are old enough to understand, I'm bringing them here. After I tell them everything about the war and my part in it. We just can't let this happen again."

"Amen to that," said Jim. "Semper fi, Andy."

"Semper fi, Jim," Andrew responded as the men saluted each other and then embraced.

***

All through their school years, "Dad's studio" was Lindsey's and M.J.'s favorite place to be, whether to read, to study, or simply to listen to the music which played nearly non-stop. Andrew would paint as he talked with them. Lindsey told him once: "Dad, I think I'm the luckiest girl in the world to have a father who's an artist, and who works at home. I've grown up in this room, surrounded by beauty." Andrew was surprised to hear her say that, and his heart swelled with love.

Lindsey loved to sing and as she grew it became obvious that along with her innate musical ability she had a beautiful voice; her dream was to be an opera singer someday. Piano lessons from her mother became part of her life from the time she was four, and she developed into a fine pianist as well. Trips to the Philadelphia Academy of Music became a regular part of the family's life. Those that meant seeing an opera performance filled Lindsey with joy. She was also first chair flute in the high school marching and concert bands, and her senior year she was president of both band and chorus.

M.J., while an athlete, was also a thoughtful boy who loved to read. He was a talker from an early age and eventually used that ability to express himself on the debate team. He was liked and respected by his peers and was elected president of his ninth grade class. His sport was basketball; he was a forward and captain of the junior high team. He read avidly — fiction, non-fiction — history and philosophy mostly. "You know what, Dad?" M.J. asked him. "I really love to sit in here and read. It makes me feel like I'm in a special place, like nowhere else I've ever been."

Andrew often heard his son and his father having intense discussions about a myriad of topics. M.J. wanted to be a teacher, he said, like his Grandy. Along with the portraits of his children, Andrew painted portraits of both of his parents and of Mary, and he finally felt he had captured Mary's inner beauty.

Andrew painted the war only for occasional commissioned works. He focused on landscapes, but he continued to use the whole-hearted emotional involvement, the same bold strokes, the same explosion of saturated colors, that he had first used in his war paintings. The Camerons made another trip to Niagara Falls and he painted them in his abstract expressionistic style.

Evelyn sold three of his paintings of the Falls for twenty-five thousand each. Andrew was stunned when he looked at his bank account. He could stop teaching if he wanted; it seemed he was now considered something of a star in the world of art.

And in all this time, no word from Jake. As the years passed, Andrew's thoughts of his brother began to change; the feeling of loss became less sharply painful. He realized that at some point he had stopped searching the face of every dark-haired stranger he saw, looking for Jake. Sometimes he even wondered if he had only dreamed his brother; maybe Jake was just another side of who he, Andrew, was — a manifestation of some daring, more reckless, unpredictable Andrew Cameron.

The old photo albums couldn't be denied, though: a picture of Toni with Jake on her lap and Andrew at their side. Andrew and Jake on a Christmas morning, smiling happily beside a huge pile of gifts. The two of them paused while riding their bikes, an impish grin on Jake's face while Andrew looked very serious. Jake leaping to sink a basket as Andrew stood ready to catch the basketball. And the one he loved the most: the picture taken of him with his brother on the day he and Mary exchanged their wedding vows.

Andrew sometimes re-read his favorite letter from Jake, when he talked about believing he was called to be a warrior, and why he wanted to be a member of Special Forces:

> *Each member of this force is a unit unto himself and will face situations that require an emotional and mental preparedness that's difficult to explain and more difficult to understand. It requires a commitment far beyond anything I've ever done. But I believe I am ready for this.*

On a bookcase in his studio were Jake's green beret and his dog tags ... two items Toni had given him years before, when she donated Jake's clothing to charity. "He'd want you to have these," she had said, and Andrew held her as she wept. From time to time he would try to sketch Jake, but his mind always took him back to the day in Walter Reed Hospital when Jake had met his family and seen them as strangers.

What if he had awakened and known us? And his memory had been intact? He would no doubt have returned to Vietnam, and his name might now be on that Wall in Washington.

The sketches were never finished. Perhaps that was best.

Sitting in his studio listening to the Verdi *Requiem* Andrew thought, *If he is alive, who is Jake now? Does anything at all remain of the warrior he had wanted to be?* Andrew still wondered whether his brother might have stayed away from them because he felt a need to keep them safe. Or perhaps he had opted to build a new life for himself, and was staying away because it would be too painful and too complicated to reconnect with the family of the man he no longer was.

Sighing, Andrew reminded himself these were questions with no answers. He turned his attention to the music, recalling the first time he had heard it, sitting in the car with Jake as they drove home from Walter Reed Hospital. The beautiful "Sanctus" was playing now, and he allowed himself to become immersed in it. When the double chorus reached the section *"Pleni sunt coeli et terra maiestatis tuae* – heaven and earth are filled with Your glory," the choirs were singing a dialogue with each other over a quiet orchestration, a transcendent moment in the piece. He and Jake had both reacted strongly to that section, turning to each other in delight. Andrew remembered the connection he had felt to Jake.

A connection he could still feel.

329

CHAPTER 34

In the spring of 1991 all the Camerons, including Toni and Max, spent a long weekend in New York City for a gallery show of Andrew's latest paintings. They stayed at the Waldorf-Astoria, a luxury they permitted themselves mainly for the teenagers; and since on earlier visits they had seen the tourist attractions this became an arts weekend. Visits to art museums. A performance at the Met, courtesy of the generosity of Jamie Logan; a performance at the City Opera Company, thanks to Krissy Levin, who had for many years been personal assistant to the general director and was still a part of that organization.

Jamie and his accomplished and charming wife Meredith invited them to dinner at their home in Montclair, New Jersey, where Lindsey sang for Jamie. He listened thoughtfully to her perform three arias: "Deh vieni, non tardar" from Mozart's *Le Nozze di Figaro*; "Willow Song" from American composer Douglas Moore's *The Ballad of Baby Doe*. Her third choice was the difficult and dazzling "Bell Song" from Leo Delibes' *Lakmé*.

Andrew watched Jamie closely as Lindsey sang, and he was aware of how attentive he was during the opening *a cappella* section of her final choice. He knew she sang it impeccably, and was pleased to see Jamie smile and nod encouragement to the young coloratura soprano. These arias were three she was considering for her audition at the Cincinnati Conservatory.

When she finished she was applauded, then Jamie took her hand and drew her to a sofa, where he sat next to her. "Lindsey, you truly have a gift. You're musical to your fingertips, and you've had a fine voice teacher who is allowing that beautiful voice to grow naturally. What you hope to do isn't easy, but I'm sure your parents have told you that."

Lindsey laughed. "They have, and I'm aware singing opera successfully isn't always about how good you are. There's a lot of luck involved." Andrew saw her tip her chin up … a sign of how determined his daughter could be. "Despite all that, I have to do this. If I don't try, I think I would die."

Jamie smiled broadly. "That's exactly what I wanted to hear. You have the passion you need." He grew serious. "Always remember this. Sing because you love to sing. Sing because you've been provided all this amazing music by great composers. Sing to share the love of music you have in your soul. If you do that, no matter what happens with your career, you will be a happy and successful singer."

Lindsey impulsively threw her arms around him and the onlookers applauded. Andrew looked at his wife, who was smiling somewhat ruefully, knowing that nothing anyone said after that could possibly deter their daughter from her chosen path.

"Oh, and sing the Douglas Moore piece for your audition. A perfect choice for you," Jamie added.

Another guest that evening was Krissy Levin, who had invited the same contingent to her Upper West Side apartment for brunch the following day. As they entered the apartment Andrew saw his painting of Eli hanging above the great pianist's Bösendorfer grand piano. Both Mary and Lindsey were invited to play.

They rounded out their trip with a Broadway musical, a revival of *Man of La Mancha* starring an actor Max admired, Raul

Julia. It was M.J.'s and Max's favorite part of the trip ... Cervantes' whimsical and brilliant character Don Quixote brought to life on the stage.

Sometime during this whirlwind of activity Krissy found a quiet moment to speak with Andrew and ask how he was doing with taking life a day at a time.

"Better. My life is filled with painting, my fantastic wife, and my remarkable kids," he smiled.

"They are remarkable indeed. It's such a joy to see how Lindsey has grown. She has a shot at a career, Andrew. Jamie gave her some great advice. And it's been a real treat to have a chance to talk with M.J. It's hard to believe he's only fifteen; what a brilliant mind your son has. Almost scary. What do you think he might do with that?"

"Well, it's hard to say, because he *is* only fifteen, after all. He's thinking of following in his grandfather's footsteps and becoming a college professor in history or philosophy. That's on some days. Other days he talks about medicine."

On their return home their lives were busy with end of the year school activities, for Mary as well as the children, and Andrew was painting in preparation for a show the following year in Montreal. His first Canadian show, and he was thrilled to have received the invitation.

Over the summer, fifteen-year-old M.J. attended both a basketball camp and a leadership camp at Penn State University; Lindsey spent her second summer at Brevard Music Camp in North Carolina after a successful audition had landed her a spot. She was planning to apply at the Cincinnati Conservatory of Music as a vocal performance major, and Mary had struggled a little with this. As much as she wanted to see her daughter succeed, she was very much aware what a daunting road Lindsey had ahead of her.

***

On a late October afternoon, just as Andrew and Mary were preparing dinner, the phone rang. Andrew was closest so he picked it up.

"Andrew Cameron, please."

"This is Andrew Cameron."

"Mr. Cameron, this is Ed Doherty. I'm the Sheriff of Swain County, North Carolina, where you filed a missing person's report back in 1973, is that correct?"

Andrew felt a chill run up his spine, and he leaned against the kitchen counter for support.

"Yes. My brother had disappeared." He was surprised his voice wasn't shaking, since his hand was. In fact, he realized he was shaking all over, and he clenched his jaw to keep his teeth from chattering. Mary turned off the stove and put her arms around him.

"We haven't closed that file. It's been eighteen years since we last contacted you; has there been a resolution to the case that we're not aware of?"

"No. He's ... we've never heard from him, or heard anything about him."

"I don't want to alarm you, sir, but human remains were uncovered today during an excavation for a new home, and we're following up on all open missing persons cases in an attempt to identify them. We still have Jacob Cameron's medical files, and I'm calling to ask if you have any objection to our using them."

"No. What do you know about ..." he wasn't sure what to call them.

"The bones had apparently been there for a very long time. We're looking at it as a suspicious death, since they appear to have been deliberately buried."

"When will you know if … if it's Jake or not?"

"We'll do this as quickly as possible. I'll try to get back to you within the week. Thank you for your cooperation, sir."

Andrew wordlessly hung up the phone and pressed Mary close. He didn't have to tell her, she'd heard enough of the conversation to understand.

"How long before they know?"

"He said a few days. Within the week."

He took a deep breath and relaxed slightly. "I don't believe it's Jake. I still believe I'd know if he were dead. But this was an awful shock."

"I'm sure. Why don't you call Penny? I'm sure talking to her would help."

"Yes." He continued to hold her close. "Hang onto me, Mary. I need you." All those years ago he had shut her out of the dark places in his life. He would never do that again.

"He said bones. So they've been there a long time. If it is Jake, he could have been dead all these years."

"You need to talk about all this with Penny. Call her now."

***

He called Penny and they agreed to meet the next morning. She suggested a mild sedative to get him through the night, and said she would phone it in to his pharmacy. Andrew agreed; he had been shaken to his core. Mary picked up the medication for him so he could sleep.

Dinner that evening was subdued. Lindsey and M.J. were aware of what had happened, and both of them hugged their father extra tight when they said goodnight to him.

Rather than going to Penny's office, Andrew went to her apartment in downtown Philadelphia. Over the years she had become a friend, coming to West Chester from time to time for dinner, meeting Mary and Andrew for dinner and a concert or an art show in the city. Out of curiosity she had given M.J. an IQ test when he was a youngster and told Mary and Andrew he was brilliant.

She met him at the door, casually dressed in a sweater and slacks. She had office hours in the afternoon and hadn't yet donned what he thought of as the "Dr. Penny camouflage outfit."

"What if it's Jake, and all these years I've been fooling myself with the thought that he's alive?"

"If that's the case, was the way you've been coping really a bad thing? And if you believe in a life beyond this one … and I suspect you do … don't you think it's a place of peace and happiness?"

He was silent for a moment. "Yes, I do. Especially after talking to Krissy Levin. She believes Eli is alive somewhere … and she says she's aware of his presence sometimes. And she seems completely sane to me."

"If it is Jake's remains that have been found, what's the next step?"

"We bring him home and bury him in West Chester, and grieve for him. So I guess it's … I guess that would be closure. We'd know for sure. Except the sheriff said it was a suspicious death, so it starts all over again. Who killed him and why?"

He groaned and pressed his head with both hands. "I hate this. I was doing okay. I haven't said anything to my parents; what's the point? If it is Jake I'll tell them. If not, why put them through what I'm going through right now?"

"This will be a difficult week for you. I can give you medication which will ease the anxiety, if you want."

He thought about that. "No, let's hold off on that. My family is a huge help. Mary and I talked about this last night. The kids know, and they are so sweet. God, I love my children. The best thing I ever did. My greatest accomplishment."

"So you've said. They are exceptional people."

"Did I ever tell you this ... when we first explained about Jake to M.J., I mean exactly what had happened, he spent a day in the library researching retrograde amnesia. M.J. was *eleven*. He talked about it for weeks, wondering why the psychiatric community couldn't do more to help people with not just that, but all mental problems." He smiled. "Who knows? Maybe he'll be a medical researcher someday."

"There's a need for people with vision in the profession. I'd welcome him as a colleague."

"He told me last night if I need to talk, he's there for me." Now Andrew had to laugh. "I'm not sure why I'm even here, when I have a budding psychologist living under my own roof."

Penny laughed with him. "A major rule in our profession: never treat a family member."

"I'll pass that on, but I may talk to him. He's bright, but he's also sensitive. There's so much love in my son."

Penny smiled. "He's emulating his father. And you realize what you're doing, don't you? The exact thing you said you would do when you were my patient at the Institute. Focusing on your family and not obsessing about Jake."

"I am, aren't I? Well, these next days won't be easy. But I'll be okay. Thanks for helping remind me of that, Penny." He grinned at her, appreciating what an attractive woman she was. "Just out of curiosity … how many marriage proposals have you had from male patients over the years?"

"You know that's confidential information. But, yes, I've certainly received them; not just proposals, but propositions as well. And not just from male patients."

He laughed heartily, and she smiled in approval.

"I don't think you're going to fall apart, Andrew. 'Perspective' — that's the key word."

***

Three days later the sheriff called again, with the news that the bones were not Jake's.

CHAPTER 35

I'm in the clouds, climbing the ramp to the observation tower at Clingman's Dome. Only I'm not walking up it, I'm floating. Something at the top is drawing me up, and I think I know what it is.

I reach the top and sure enough, there he is, relaxing comfortably against the wall, grinning at me. "Hi, Andy."

"Hi, Jake. Are you dead?"

He throws back his head and laughs; the infectious Jake-laugh, full of joy, that we heard when something truly delighted him. I have to laugh with him.

"Okay, not dead, so this isn't a visitation," I say. "Then I must be dreaming."

"Maybe. Or maybe we're both dreaming, and we ran into each other in the spirit world."

"Where are you, Jake?"

"I'm safe. I'm with some terrific people. You worry way too much, Andy. The Cherokee would call you 'asgaya-something-something-something' — 'man who worries too much.'"

I'm aware of music. It's been there all the time, swirling around us with the clouds, sounds unlike any I've ever heard before.

The clouds are getting thicker and I try to wave them away. "I can hardly see you, Jake. What's happening?"

"Who the hell knows? Be happy, Andy. Keep painting great pictures. Love your family. Have good thoughts about me; I'm fine, really "

"Jake? Are you still there?" I can only see a faint outline now.

He sounds far away. "By the way, speaking of great pictures, how come you've never painted one of me?"

***

Andrew woke with the dream still resonating in his mind. He recalled it vividly; he could still hear Jake's voice, still see his face. It hadn't been the young Jake. He had seen a man his own age. *Jake is alive. And he's well and happy.*

It was early; the first light of dawn was just creeping through the bedroom window, washing the room with a misty blue through the sheer curtains. He saw it as Mary's bedroom: they had decorated it with pale blue and ivory. A four-poster bed, French provincial furniture. He liked it; it always made him feel as if she were welcoming him into her space, into her arms. The room embraced him as if he were one of Dumas' *Three Musketeers* having a secret liaison with a member of royalty.

He gazed at her now, drowsing and warm next to him. He touched her face, stroked her shoulders and she opened her eyes and put her arms around him. He kissed her tenderly.

"Go back to sleep. I'll fix breakfast and bring us a tray after I feed the kids."

She smiled and nodded, hugging her pillow and drifting back to sleep.

Lindsey was already in the kitchen when he went downstairs; she had coffee brewing and was standing in the center of the room, fully dressed, trying to decide what to fix for breakfast. She smiled at him. "Feeling better, Dad?"

"Much, sweetheart. You're up early."

"We have an away game this morning. The band has to be at the school by eight."

"What's your pleasure? I volunteered for chef duty this morning." She was such a lovely young woman, so much like Mary, yet her own person.

"Banana pancakes," she said. That was Lindsey: no dithering, make a decision.

M.J. joined them, rubbing his eyes and yawning, as they were putting the pancakes and bacon on plates. "How are you, Dad?"

"I'm great, M.J. Thanks for asking."

"Shall we call Mom?" Lindsey asked.

"No, I'll fix a tray for her. I let her sleep in this morning."

As he prepared a tray for Mary and himself, Lindsey appeared at his elbow with an aster from the arrangement of fall flowers in the living room — a present from Toni's garden — and added it to the tray. "Thanks, honey. Nice touch." She smiled at him and he added, "Do you need a ride to the school?"

"Wendy's picking me up. But thanks. I should be home by four." She kissed his cheek. "Have a good day, Dad."

"I'm outta here soon, Pop. Basketball with the guys. I'll be home in time for lunch."

Andrew grinned at his son. He remembered being fifteen and constantly hungry. "Take some fruit with you, why don't you?"

"Good idea," M.J. clapped his father on the shoulder.

Mary sat up as Andrew opened the door. He had brought plates for both of them, and he put the footed tray on the bed and they poured maple syrup on the pancakes. "Lindsey's off to the school, away football game. She'll be back mid-afternoon. M.J.'s meeting friends for basketball and says he'll be home for lunch."

An ordinary Saturday, thought Andrew. *Yet it isn't. It's far from that.*

"I dreamed about Jake last night. Only it seemed to be much more than a dream. I saw him and talked to him."

Mary's eyes widened and she put her fork down. "How do you mean, 'more than a dream'?"

"He was Jake as he would be today. My age. A mature man. Same old Jake, though — giving me a hard time about being such a worrier."

"More than a dream. It sounds as if he ... this is a little hard to wrap my mind around, Andy. What do you think?"

"I think he somehow reached out to me and let me know he's fine. I have no earthly idea how that could happen. But it wasn't earthly in any way. It was ... other-worldly."

"You sound like Krissy Levin. She's convinced Eli is around sometimes. But that's different."

"'There are more things in heaven and earth, Horatio, than are dreamt of in your philosophy,'" Andrew quoted. "Maybe Shakespeare knew things we don't."

"This is giving me chills," Mary said. "Maybe you're right." She looked closely at her husband. "Whatever it was, it's given you more peace than I think you've ever had."

"Yes, it has." He paused for a moment. "I'll be in my studio all day, Mary. There's something I have to do."

***

The clouds lift me up, high above the mountains. I drift for a while, filled with a sense of peace, warmed by memories of Jake. Jake as a little boy, teasing me to put down my paints and come outside so we can throw a ball around. Jake climbing up in the trees higher than he should. Jake eating watermelon as fast as he can.

Jake crying when our Aunt Melanie has to leave him to go to rehearsal for <u>Carousel</u>; snuggling up to her as she sings to him the next day. Jake raising his arms in triumph when he reaches the top of Clingman's Dome on Max's back. Jake as a teenager —watching him play baseball and football, while I burst with pride for him. Seeing him grin with delight when he spots us in the stands, giving us a big thumbs up. Jake the warrior in his dress greens, looking proud and assured, steadying me at my wedding.

Most of all, I remember the hundreds of times he let me know how much he loved me without saying the words.

Jake, my brother, you gave me so much more than I ever understood.

***

He showered, dressed, and went into his studio, taking a cup of coffee with him. What he needed was to paint Jake's portrait. He knew why he'd never done this: he'd been waiting for Jake to come home and sit for him. Hoping that would happen someday.

He thought about the size for the portrait. He wanted it to be Jake, head and shoulders. *No, I'd like more of him in the painting. I can use 24 by 36 inches ... that's large for a portrait, but I can have him down to the elbows if I do that.*

In uniform? No, that's in his past. This will be Jake as he is today. So a suit? A sports coat? No, more casual. A sweater with a turtleneck. I can see him wearing that.

He knew Jake's face as well as he knew his own. A face almost the same, yet different. A stronger jawline. The lips less full. Slightly different hairline. A rakish grin, a twinkle in his eye.

He was planning to work fast. A realistic portrait; he would use brushes and acrylics, layers of soft glazes to make the skin luminous.

He knew he was painting age progression. He had the photo from the wedding; he'd refer to that and then give Jake the twenty-plus years to bring him into the present. But he also had the image in his mind from the dream, or whatever it was he had experienced.

A soft background in a neutral color, beiges and pale green. Jake in an ivory turtleneck with a forest green, cable-knit crewneck pullover. His head tipped slightly to one side, shoulders tilted as if he were leaning against something. Andrew smiled as he painted.

Music. Jake had loved the Verdi *Requiem* and Andrew put the CD on; Jamie Logan's beautiful tenor soon filled the room as he sang the opening notes of the "Kyrie," his voice soaring above the descending low strings.

Andrew painted all morning, his love for Jake in every brush stroke. Mary tapped on the door once and said, "Do you want some lunch?"

"Yes, I'll be out in a minute. Thanks."

They ate in the kitchen, not talking much. Mary asked, "Are you trying to finish this today?"

"I want to. Well, you know me. I'll probably go back and work on it a few times, but I think I can have it ready for viewing by sometime this evening."

He was sure she knew what he was painting even though they hadn't discussed it.

M.J. came into the house while they were finishing lunch and made himself a sandwich. Andrew felt a nostalgic tug at his chest: *Just like Jake used to do.*

"What are you painting, Dad?"

"It's a surprise, M.J. But I'm sure you'll like it."

He went back into the studio, and this time it was Brahms that he wanted to listen to. The *German Requiem*; his favorite piece of music, the music that soothed him and lifted his spirit as it had so many times.

Worthy are You, Lord, of honor and glory,
For You have created heaven and earth,
And for Your good pleasure all things have their being.

He was tired. His neck muscles ached, his arm felt heavy, but he was so close. He almost had his subject. He heard Lindsey come in, a quiet family conversation in the living room. He smelled tomato sauce. Mary and Lindsey were fixing some kind of pasta for dinner.

One final touch: the tiniest of white highlights to bring Jake's eyes to life.

And there he was.

Andrew smiled at his brother and opened the door. "Come and see this, family."

Mary gasped and put her arms around Andrew, and Lindsey and M.J. both stared. Lindsey said, in awe, "He looks so real."

M.J. commented, "I guess I never thought about how much he looks like you, Dad."

Mary hugged Andrew hard as she said softly,

"Welcome home, Jake."

EPILOGUE (1992)

April flowed into May, and before Lindsey's graduation Andrew and Mary made a quick trip to Montreal. His gallery show was scheduled for June, and he wanted to visit the space to be sure what he planned to include would work well.

It was their second time in Montreal, and once again they were enchanted with this taste of Europe. They often thought of Isabel as they heard French spoken frequently, especially when they were having a meal. Andrew was looking forward to returning in a few weeks with his entire family.

Their last evening in the city they were strolling through Old Montreal and came upon a restaurant that intrigued them. It was fairly small and Andrew wondered aloud if they could be seated without a reservation.

"We won't know unless we ask. All I care about is, can I get poutine?"

Andrew laughed. "You had poutine last night."

"I know. I need to learn how to make it. I still can't believe anything that looks so much like fries and gravy can be so incredible. I never liked fries and gravy. Maybe it's what they put in the gravy. Or it's the cheese curds."

"Or both."

They were lucky; a party had just cancelled their dinner reservation, so there was a booth available if they didn't mind being seated there instead of a table.

As they slipped into their seats Andrew noticed a family in the booth behind theirs chatting away in French. They glanced over the menu, ordered, and were waiting to be served when he heard a sound he couldn't believe.

The man in the booth next to theirs was talking to his children, and one of the children apparently said something extremely funny, because he laughed heartily.

It was Jake.

Andrew looked at Mary and she took his hand. "Andrew."

He said, struggling to control himself, "You heard it, too."

"Yes. But it can't be."

Andrew's heart was pounding; his mouth was dry as cotton. He took a long drink of water, trying to stay calm. The family continued to talk, and again, the man laughed.

A wave of emotion he couldn't even identify swept over Andrew. He took another drink of water, his hand shaking.

"It's Jake, Mary. I would know that laugh anywhere."

"Let me go to the ladies' room. I'll let you know what I see."

She left the booth, and Andrew sat for an eternity, feeling as if he had just been turned inside out, until she returned. He felt suspended, somehow, remembering the dream he'd had in the fall; floating over the earth, feeling connected to Jake. Maybe this was just a continuation of that dream and he had imagined hearing Jake laugh.

Mary returned and sat down, and he saw from the color in her cheeks that he was right. She nodded.

"He has a beard. But yes, I think it's Jake. I'm sure it is." Her voice was trembling with excitement.

Andrew took deep breaths. "He has children."

"Two girls, one boy. The little boy is about four. The girls are older, maybe six and eight. Lovely wife."

Andrew drained his water glass and took a gulp of wine.

"I need to speak to him." He wasn't sure whether he was on the verge of laughter or tears.

Mary put her hand over his. "Of course you do. What on earth will you say to him, though?"

Hands shaking, Andrew folded his napkin into as small a square as possible. "Maybe I shouldn't do this. After all, he hasn't made any effort to contact me ... us ... in almost two decades. He may want to keep it that way."

Mary said softly, "I don't think you mean that. If you don't let him know you're here, sitting just inches away from him, you'll never forgive yourself."

He frowned at the napkin as he unfolded it carefully. *She's right, of course. And what do I say to him? I have to give him the option of not talking to me, if that's what he wants. If he does that, though ... but remember the dream. I think he'll want to see me.*

"You're right. I do have to speak to him." He thought for a moment. "I can do this." He inhaled sharply. *It's Jake. He's right here. This is really happening.*

He wiped his sweaty palms with his napkin, took another drink of wine, took several deep breaths and stood and went to the next booth, unsure of whether he was walking or floating.

It was Jake; Jake looking very debonair, with a neatly trimmed mustache and goatee. He was wearing a well-tailored suit, a sign he was obviously doing well. Andrew saw the immediate recognition in his eyes, and the half smile Jake gave him.

With great presence of mind and more composure than he had ever dreamed he would be able to muster, Andrew said, "*Pardon, monsieur.* My wife believes we may have met at some time, at the home of a mutual friend. Perhaps not, but I hope you will forgive me for asking. Do you know Jacob Cameron?"

Jake smiled, and Andrew could imagine what he was thinking: *So you found me.* Aloud, his brother said, *"Oui, monsieur.* I do know Jacob Cameron. Perhaps we could talk in the bar? Noémi, *chérie*, please excuse me for a few moments."

Andrew realized the children were staring at him curiously and he smiled at them. The little boy looked so much like M.J. at that age, and the girls had the same lively dark eyes and curly dark hair as their beautiful mother. *Noémi. Happy to meet you, sister-in-law.*

Jake walked to the bar beside Andrew and put an arm around his shoulders, giving him an affectionate squeeze.

"Jake." Andrew's voice cracked.

"Hang on. I'll get us some brandy." Andrew realized his brother's voice wasn't working any better than his was. They found a secluded booth and Jake helped Andrew sit, then went to the bar and brought back snifters and a bottle of brandy. Andrew watched Jake pour the brandy with a slightly unsteady hand. *He's as nervous about this as I am. And maybe as happy.*

Andrew felt complete, unbridled joy. He didn't care why Jake had stayed away. The only thing that mattered was that he was looking at his brother right now. It was enough. It was everything.

"My God. It's really you." He laughed softly, fighting the urge to shout. "I can barely think straight … God, I am so, *so* happy to see you."

Jake's smile was at least as broad as Andrew's. "How did you find me?"

"I stopped trying to find you years ago. This is really a chance meeting." Andrew couldn't stop smiling. He gazed at Jake, drinking him in. "You look fantastic … uh …who are you, anyway?"

Jake laughed; an echo of the joy Andrew was experiencing. "Jean Couvreur."

Andrew repeated it. "Jean Couvreur. Nice name."

A pause, a sigh. Jake — *Jean* — took a sip of brandy. "You don't know how many times I almost called you." He grew serious. "But there was that Allan Martin thing." He looked directly at Andrew. "I was with the pathetic piece of shit when he died, but I didn't kill him. Easy to say, not so easy to prove. I thought it would be best for you to think I was dead."

Andrew put his hand on his brother's arm. "I never thought that. I always knew you were alive." He gripped Jake's arm harder, as though he were afraid he might vanish if he weren't holding onto him.

Jake smiled. "I'm not going anywhere, Andy."

They both laughed and Andrew loosened his grip. "Sorry. I guess I'm still trying to hang on, in a way." He sighed. "Well … eventually … I accepted that you'd never be Jake again. That I might never see you again."

"I had a lot to work through after what happened in South Carolina." Andrew saw a look of pain cross Jake's eyes.

"I don't doubt that. You did what you had to do. I'm just so glad to know you're here, and alive and well, with a beautiful family. I hoped that was what had happened."

He paused for a moment and examined his brandy snifter. "I was sure I'd have sensed it if anything … if you were …"

"Dead," Jake finished. "You're thinking about that dream you had when I was injured in Vietnam."

"Yes. I've always felt … I guess *connected* is the best word. Connected to you." *Jean. This is Jean I'm talking to now.*

"I should have called," Jean said again.

349

"No, it was probably better that you didn't. I might have continued to insist that you had to be Jake, because I had to take care of you."

"Perhaps. We'll never know."

"I was scared of losing control. I finally learned we don't really have control over much of anything."

"How's Mom?"

"She's well. I convinced her you were alive and you were okay. And now you're sitting here with me confirming all of that. May I tell her?"

"*Mais oui.* I would love to see her."

"You can, and soon. Our family is all coming here next month. I have a gallery show."

"Yes, I knew that. You're famous, Andy. I was trying to figure out how I could see it without running into you."

Andrew laughed. "Well, that's been resolved."

Jean sighed again. "I regret that I remembered so little about her — our mother. And about you."

"You had no control over that. Nor did I, though I tried like hell to make it happen."

"You did that," Jean said with a chuckle. He looked at Andrew with love. "You were just trying to be a good brother."

They smiled at each other, relaxing a little. Andrew took a sip of brandy.

"Your wife is lovely. Noémi, right? How old are your children?"

"I'm a lucky man, Andy. Noémi is a beautiful soul. We've been married twelve years. Toinette is eight. She's definitely your niece; she loves art and shows some talent. Marie is our little ballerina, she's six. And my son mainly spends his time bedeviling his sisters. André is four."

Andrew felt a thrill. "You named him after me."

Jean put a hand on Andrew's arm and squeezed it. "Of course I did. I recognized Mary when she walked past our booth. She looks fantastic. You have children, of course."

"Two. Lindsey is seventeen. She graduates from West Chester High later this month. She's a singer. I mean a serious singer. She wants opera."

Jean nodded. "Good for her. Do you have a boy?"

"M.J. — Maxwell Jacob." Andrew was rewarded with a broad smile, and a brandy snifter lifted in his direction in thanks. "He's fifteen. You'd like him. He plays basketball. He's probably going into medicine." He sipped the brandy. "What are you doing? I mean, what kind of work? I'd guess you're doing well."

"I'm director of Radio Two of CBC … Canadian Broadcasting Corporation-Montreal. We specialize in classical music. I started there in 1975 and worked my way up. I love what I'm doing, and yes, we have a comfortable life."

Andrew laughed with delight. "Classical music. I love it."

Jean smiled. "Noémi knows who I am. The children don't, not yet. But I had planned to tell them at some point, when they're older."

"Don't change your plans. This is complicated, and I don't want to turn your life upside down." Andrew smiled as once again he felt joy well up inside him. "I'm just so happy to have had this chance to meet you, Jean Couvreur. And to know you've taken good care of my brother Jacob."

Jean glanced away and covered his mouth briefly. He looked back, his eyes glistening with tears, and gave Andrew a wistful smile. "We'll talk more when you're here next month. I'll check with the gallery to find out where you're staying."

He finished his brandy and they sat quietly, savoring the moment.

"I should get back to my family. And I want to say hello to Mary."

"Is that a good idea? You'll see her next month."

"I'll keep it brief."

They stood, started to shake hands, but instead embraced and held each other for a long moment.

"I love you, Jake — Jean," Andrew said.

Jean cocked a finger at his brother. "I remembered a few more things," he said.

"Such as?"

"I love you, too, asshole." He laughed heartily, and Andrew joined in the laughter as the brothers embraced once more.

ACKNOWLEDGEMENTS

When I wrote *How I Grew Up* in 2013, I thought it would be a one-time happening, an event in my advanced youth that was the realization of a lifelong dream. It amazes me that instead, writing has become a passion that I find immensely fulfilling, and here I am nearly four years later finishing my fifth novel.

Memories of Jake returns to *How I Grew Up* and that family tragedy in 1954 when three people were shot and killed in the fictitious Stewart family. Two little boys ... the children of the shooter ... watched their father commit that horrific act, murdering their grandparents and their uncle. The boys were eight and six at that time, which meant they reached young manhood just as the Vietnam War was escalating.

Writing about subjects of which I had no firsthand knowledge meant research was vital, especially about the Vietnam War. Of the many books and articles I read, Philip Caputo's *A Rumor of War* had the greatest impact. Mr. Caputo took me right into the war and the country, and gave me a real sense of the experience. As always, equally important was the expertise provided by a number of generous people, and I wish to thank them for their assistance.

Ashleigh Evans, who has been my copy editor since my second novel, *Eli's Heart*, proved more valuable than ever since she is an accomplished fine artist and was able to provide me with an understanding of the tools and skill Andrew needed to produce his art. Ashleigh is much more than a copy editor. She keeps me from wandering into the thorny paths of repetitive writing and convoluted plot points, as well as reining me in on crossing the line from emotional to maudlin and many other pitfalls that lurk along the way. As always, she came to care about the characters, and in this book in particular shared insights more than once which helped me realize them more fully.

It was my great good fortune to be introduced through mutual friends to retired Army Lt. Col. Charles Vincent, Corps of Engineers, who served in Korea as a Marine Sergeant and served one of his tours in Vietnam with the Green Berets, and he was kind enough to read through the passages about the war and offer corrections and suggestions. He was immensely helpful, and if there are mistakes they are definitely mine and not his.

Special thanks to James C. Jordan, my brother-in-law, who served in Vietnam with pride as a member of the Marine Corps from 1965-67, roughly the same time as my character Andrew. Jim was a Sergeant with B Company, 1st Amtrac Battalion, 3rd Marine Division. I greatly appreciated his willingness to share some of his experiences with me.

The other Marine in my life, my son Sam, served in Desert Storm. His memories of boot camp at Parris Island provided some of the material for Chapter 6.

Additional assistance came from my friend and colleague Linda Schaller, who attended West Chester State College at the same time Andrew and Mary were there. Linda, who is an educator as well as a fine pianist and accompanist, shared her experiences both as a resident of West Chester and a student at the college and read and approved the passages about both the town and the school.

Donna Schneider, the daughter of another friend, is a writer, editor, and Human Resources Manager who is fluent in French. She was kind enough to take my basic college French (one year as a vocal performance major) and make Isabel the polished and sophisticated Parisian lady she needed to be.

Judy Lawler, a longtime friend and mental health care professional, spent many hours helping me work through both Jake's confusion and distress because of his memory loss and Andrew's emotional collapse and P.T.S.D. She also read through the manuscript with an eye to the therapy sessions and agreed with my conclusions about Jake's retrograde amnesia: while unusual, what happened to Jake is possible.

Michaele Benedict and Eric Mark have been invaluable in reading through my manuscripts from my very first effort, and again both provided me with excellent observations and suggestions. Ken Van Camp, Marti Lantz, and Nathaniel Taylor also provided positive input and suggestions which strengthened the story. Dr. Theodore Kowalyshyn and Mary Ann Kowalyshyn were kind enough to answer medical questions about Andrew's ulcer and possible treatment for Jake's head injury.

Tristan Flanagan, who continues to grow as an artist in multiple endeavors, once again provided the cover photograph and design. Theresa Lawrence provided the art work which appears in the cover photograph. The beautiful photo of Lake Wallenpaupack which graces the back cover was taken by my friend Michael Meilinger, and was the inspiration for one of Andrew's paintings.

As in all my novels, my characters find help in meeting the challenges in their lives through the power of creativity in the universe, in this book art as well as music. Some of the great choral compositions that have come down through the ages are the music that is most meaningful to both Andrew and Jake, in particular the magnificent Brahms *Requiem*. As Andrew does, I find it uplifting, healing, and inspiring — and an affirmation that life continues.

Susan Moore Jordan
Pocono Mountains, March, 2017

MAN WITH NO YESTERDAYS

Susan Moore Jordan

CHAPTER 1

I was born somewhere over the South China Sea or the Pacific Ocean, on a medical transport plane en route from Vietnam to Walter Reed Hospital by way of Japan. Or it might be more accurate to say I was re-born, because at the age of twenty-two those became my earliest memories for a long time.

The first thing I remember was hearing the hum. It sounded far away, but it grew louder, filling my ears and my head. *My head.* It felt strange; heavy and achy. I was lying on a bed or a cot of some kind. A sudden lurch, then a sharp drop. Then a leveling off. The humming grew louder again, then quieted. *A plane. I must be on a plane.*

My left leg was killing me. *Broken? Something's wrong with it.* I must have groaned, because somebody next to me said, "Captain? I think he's awake."

I forced my eyes open and there, hovering over me, a strange face staring into mine. My head was throbbing. I had trouble focusing; he looked blurry. "Glad to see you back with us, Sergeant."

"Unh."

"Don't try to move."

I groaned again.

"We're taking you home. Enjoy the ride."

None of this made the slightest bit of sense. The plane lurched again and my stomach went with it.

"Home?" I kind of croaked it out. My mouth felt like crap … cottony. Somebody put a spoonful of ice chips into it, and I shivered. But the cold wetness felt good.

"We're almost to Japan. We'll land briefly and some patients will be de-planed. Then we're flying to the U.S. To Walter Reed Hospital."

A military hospital? What the hell am I doing in a military transport plane?

The guy … I figured he must be a doctor … who had been talking to me gently opened my eyes and shone a light into them. My head ready to explode, I tried pushing his hands away, but other hands pulled mine back down.

"Sorry, Sergeant. I know this is uncomfortable. I need to check to see how your pupils are reacting to light. You've had a severe concussion and you probably feel confused right now."

You got that right, genius. He switched off the light. "Are you in pain, Sergeant?"

"My leg."

"It was broken in the crash. We're giving you pain medication. Try to rest easy for the remainder of the flight."

I felt a prickling on the back of my hand. Opened my eyes again. I was hooked up to an IV. Closed my eyes, they didn't feel right.

I was hurting and I was scared. I didn't know who I was. *Sergeant. Was that what they had called me?* I drifted off.

When I woke up again the plane was taking off. That huge, deafening roar hit me hard, and then I felt the plane lift. I made myself open my eyes again. There was a guy standing close. *What's that word again? Medic, I think. Yeah, medic.*

358

"Medic?"

He moved closer. "Yes, Sergeant? How ya doin'?"

"Do you have …," I tried to find the words, they were swimming around in my head somewhere. "That … those … ice chips?"

He gave me a stingy half spoonful. "Easy, Sergeant. Just a little at a time." He adjusted the IV. "Leg feeling any better?"

"Yes, it's … okay."

"Try to rest."

"The … the Captain? He said I was …" I had to stop. It hurt to think and I wasn't coming up with the words I needed. I tried again. "In … in an … in a … crash?"

I guess this must have been above his pay grade, because he said immediately, "I'll get Captain Turner."

I tried to focus. But my eyes still hurt and there was a heavy feeling in the back of my head.

The Captain reappeared and he looked the same. That was good. *One thing I can hold onto. Nothing else makes any sense.*

"What can I do for you, Sergeant?"

"What happened? I can't … remember … anything."

"There's time enough to discuss this later. You need to rest for now."

"No! Tell me."

The Captain chose his words carefully. "You were in an accident. You received a blow to your head when you were thrown from the helicopter you were in. We're transporting you to Walter Reed Hospital for treatment."

Most of this didn't make any sense at all, but I hung onto one thought. *My head was hit. Or I hit my head.* My leg was throbbing. "What about … my leg?"

"It's been put in a cast. You never had a broken limb before?"

Fear is strange. It wraps around your insides like icy tentacles and starts pulling all the blood out of you. Leaves you cold everywhere. I started to shake.

"I don't know. I can't remember."

I must have looked like shit, because he seemed concerned. "That's normal, Sergeant. When you get that bad a whack on the head, it makes it hard to think. Is your leg still hurting you?"

"Captain ... Turner, right?" He nodded. The fear thing inside me was growing bigger and bigger. "I don't remember ... anything. *Anything.*"

He placed a reassuring hand on my shoulder. "Easy, soldier. Do you know where you were before you woke up in this plane?"

"No. Wait — Vietnam? There's a war ..." I did know that. And the uniforms I could tell were Army. So I must be in the Army.

"Yes. You're Sergeant Jake Cameron, Special Forces."

The fear thing backed off a little. I had a name. That helped. Captain Turner must have figured I meant it when I said I didn't remember anything.

I could breathe a little better. "Thank you." I tried to focus, and came up with something. "Is it 1970?"

He grinned at me. "January, 1971. Good for you."

"And Richard Nixon is president, right?"

"See, Jake? You do remember some things."

"My eyes hurt. And my leg is ... is killing me."

Captain Turner reached up and did something to the IV.

"Go back to sleep, Sergeant. When you wake up we'll be back home."

***

When we landed I was loaded off the plane and taken by ambulance to what must have been a large complex of buildings; it was kind of a long drive. When we reached our destination I was brought into a private room, where an IV was hung above me with fluids dripping from the bag into the back of my hand — same as on the plane. A catheter was inserted; that was tons of fun.

My gut hurt, but I couldn't tell if the pain came from hunger or if there was something wrong with it. I went back into the peace and quiet of oblivion. I liked it there. The fear thing stayed huddled in a corner.

When I woke up there was a nurse changing the IV bag. I must have made some kind of sound because she smiled at me and touched my shoulder gently. "I see you're back with us, soldier."

"It's cold in here." My teeth were chattering. The fear thing began unwrapping itself.

"It's cold outside. A lot different from Vietnam." She tucked another blanket around me as she talked. I could see the concern on her face.

A doctor entered the room and identified himself as Major William Forrester. He spoke kindly to me. "Do you know where you are, soldier?"

I tried to stop shaking. "Truth is, sir, I don't even know who I am." *God, that is so cliché. I can't believe I said it.*

He smiled. "You had a very bad bump to your head. A severe concussion. It's not surprising that your brains are a little scrambled, Sergeant."

"I'm a sergeant? In the Army?" Now I remembered they'd called me Sergeant on the plane.

"Yes, son. Sergeant Jacob Cameron, Special Forces."

I clutched at my left leg; it had really been bothering me. "My leg hurts like a motherf ... oh, sorry, Major."

361

"It was broken when the helicopter crashed and you were thrown from the craft. Fortunately, a simple fracture, nice and clean. No need for surgery."

"How do we … um, unscramble … my brains, sir?" I was still shivering. *Cold. So goddam cold.*

"Let's give it some time. Your body needs to heal."

"Where am I right now?" The fear thing had uncoiled itself and was wrapped around my gut.

"This is Walter Reed Hospital, just outside Washington, D.C."

Oh, yeah. Somebody on the plane had told me that's where we were headed.

I was fighting to keep my eyes open, but at least I had stopped shaking. "Why am I so sleepy? And why does my gut feel … so tied in knots?"

"The drowsiness is mainly due to the concussion. We just gave you some pain medication; that should ease the muscles in your abdomen. Just try to relax and not stress."

He didn't have to tell me twice. I drifted off into blessed oblivion.

MAN WITH NO YESTERDAYS by Susan Moore Jordan.
To be released Fall, 2017
www.susanmoorejordan.com

The *Carousel* Trilogy

How I Grew Up
Eli's Heart
You Are My Song

by
Susan Moore Jordan

Melanie Stewart, Krissy Porter, Jamie Logan
Three high school friends connected
by one life-changing event. Each with a story to tell.

How I Grew Up is Melanie's story. On a February night in 1954, her estranged brother-in-law entered her home with a gun and started shooting. When he left, her mother lay dead, her father was mortally wounded, and another brother-in-law was critically injured. Less than two weeks later, Melanie auditions for her high school's musical production of Rodgers' and Hammerstein's *Carousel*. How she wins the leading role of Julie Jordan and performs it brilliantly while her involvement in the show helps her begin to heal is a testament to the power of creativity in our lives.

Eli's Heart is Krissy's story. Just a few months prior to that *Carousel* production, for which she played harp in the orchestra, Krissy had met Eli Levin, a boy her own age born with two burdens: a prodigious musical gift and a frightening congenital heart condition. What seemed to be a budding romance between the brilliant young pianist and the girl he fell in love with during that summer was ended by the interference of his family. But Krissy and Eli manage to find their way back to each other some three years later. They marry while still college students when they are both twenty. Their story is one of learning to live a full life despite the odds against them.

You Are My Song is the story of Melanie's leading man in *Carousel*. Jamie Logan had a voice of unusual beauty and seemed destined to become a singer, but his high school sweetheart didn't want him to sing. Their marriage ended after two years, shattering Jamie's self-confidence. Jamie comes to realize music is vital to his life and he returns to college to study opera. With the encouragement of his teachers and his new love, Jamie finds the inner strength to pursue a most difficult path, facing both professional and personal challenges along the way.

JAMIE'S CHILDREN

by
Susan Moore Jordan

"It's more than music: it's light. It's love. It's life."

Laura and Niall Logan, children of a brilliant musician, have gifts of their own. Laura, first-born, child prodigy violinist suffers from emotional problems that haunt her well into adulthood. Niall, talented singer-songwriter, is tormented by bouts of bipolar disorder. Supported by the people they love and the power of music, they seek to overcome these daunting challenges as they strive to claim their own place in the spotlight.

If you enjoyed *Memories of Jake*, please consider leaving a review on Amazon and Goodreads. Reviews are music to an author. A good review is a standing ovation!

Susan Moore Jordan's books are available in paperback on amazon.com, barnesandnoble.com, and other online bookstores. The e-books are available on Kindle. Learn more: www.susanmoorejordan.com

About the Author

When Susan Moore Jordan was a high school student in the mid nineteen-fifties in Oak Ridge, Tennessee, a close friend went through a shattering event just as she was preparing to audition for the high school's annual musical. Decades later Jordan used that experience of tragedy to triumph to write her first novel, *How I Grew Up*, in 2013. Two additional novels followed: *Eli's Heart* in 2014 and *You Are My Song* in 2015, completing "The *Carousel* Trilogy." A fourth novel, *Jamie's Children*, was released in July, 2016. All of her novels are drawn from her life experiences as a voice teacher and stage director and are inspired by real people she has encountered.

Jordan attended the College-Conservatory of Music in Cincinnati and moved to the Pocono Mountains in Pennsylvania in 1971 with her late husband and three young children, where she established a private voice studio in 1979. Her students have gone on to leading schools of music and opera or musical theater companies around the world.

Beginning in 1984, Jordan directed some eighty local community and high school musical theater productions. She retired from directing in 2015 after over thirty years and wrote about her adventures in *"More Fog, Please": Thirty-One Years Directing Community and High School Musicals,* released in November, 2015.

All of her books are available on Amazon in paperback, and the novels are also available as Kindle editions. Paperback copies of Jordan's books can be purchased locally at the Pocono Cinema and Community Center in East Stroudsburg whenever the theater is open.

Made in United States
Troutdale, OR
01/25/2024

17103919R00206